GWYN THOMAS was born into a large and boisterous family in Porth, in the Rhondda Valley, in 1913. After a scholarship to Porth County School he went to St Edmund Hall, Oxford, where he read Spanish. Mass unemployment and widespread poverty in South Wales deepened his radicalism. After working for the Workers' Educational Association he became a teacher, first in Cardigan and from 1942 in Barry. In 1962 he left teaching and concentrated on writing and broadcasting. His many published works of fiction include *The Dark Philosophers* (1946); *The Alone to the Alone* (1947); *All Things Betray Thee* (1949); *The World Cannot Hear You* (1951) and *Now Lead Us Home* (1952). He also wrote several collections of short stories, six stage plays and the autobiography *A Few Selected Exits* (1968). He died in 1981.

ALL THINGS BETRAY THEE

GWYN THOMAS

LIBRARY OF WALES

Parthian
The Old Surgery
Napier Street
Cardigan
SA43 1ED
www.parthianbooks.com

The Library of Wales is a Welsh Government initiative which
highlights and celebrates Wales' literary heritage in the English
language.

Published with the financial support of the Welsh Books
Council

The Library of Wales publishing project is based at Swansea
University
www.thelibraryofwales.com

Series Editor: Dai Smith

All Things Betray Thee was first published in 1949
© Gywn Thomas Library of Wales edition 2011
Foreword © Raymond Williams
All Rights Reserved
ISBN 978-1-90806-973-3

Cover design by www.theundercard.com
Cover Image: *Merthyr Riots*, Penry Williams, 1816, Oil, 383 x 830
With kind permission of the National Musuem of Wales
Typesetting: www.littlefishpress.com

Printed and bound by Gwasg Gomer, Llandysul, Wales

British Library Cataloguing in Publication Data
A cataloguing record for this book is available from the British
Library.

LIBRARY OF WALES

Foreword

All Things Betray Thee is so unusual a novel, and in many ways so unlike Gwyn Thomas's better known writing, that some words of introduction may be especially necessary. In a summary of its action it appears comparatively straight-forward. In the late summer of 1835 a travelling harpist, Alan Hugh Leigh, arrives in one of the new towns of the ironmasters looking for his friend the singer John Simon Adams. He has seen, on his travels, people driven from their old villages as the great estates enclosed their lands, and knows how they have moved in their many thousands to 'the new noisy centres where cloth, iron, coal were creating new patterns of effort, reward, unease'. But it has always been his own plan to move fast enough, at the edge of these changes, to stop the forces they have released laying their hands on him. He expects to find his friend in the same mood, but two years in the uproar of the iron town Moonlea have changed him. There is a recession in the iron trade and some of the furnaces will be closed down. There is unrest and much talk of agitators and of violence. Adams the singer is now a popular leader, and slowly, unwillingly, even accidentally, Leigh the harpist is drawn into what becomes a bloody conflict. There is fighting and a rising, which is suppressed by the yeomanry. The story ends with the harpist leaving Moonlea.

The action thus barely described is important in itself. In

its broadest outline it can be related to the extraordinary Merthyr Rising of the same period, and the anger of that remembered history is clearly an element in the novel. But in several significant ways Gwyn Thomas chose a kind of story-telling which removes it from the ordinary shape of a historical novel. Thus, taking first one small indicative point, the novel is flooded with unmistakably Welsh language and feeling, and the general landscape of those first turbulent iron towns is retained, yet there is an evidently deliberate excision of local Welsh references and names. Moreover the convention of one kind of historical novel is retained, in the use of an account by someone coming relatively strange to the events, but in its handling, as we shall see, is transformed. And then, most strikingly, for within a few pages of the beginning it demands recognition from the reader – a recognition which if withheld can be disabling – the events, though vividly described, are in effect themes for what is the real movement of the novel: a pattern, a composition, of voices, in which what is being said is both of and beyond its time.

It is a remarkable experiment, which needs to be set not only within Gwyn Thomas's development as a writer but within the broader course of Welsh writing from the 1930s. Many forces worked to make Welsh writers of this period adopt different perspectives from most contemporary English writers whose language they now both shared and used for themselves.

First, in an unusually large number of cases – and certainly by comparison with what was most publicly happening in England – these writers were by family or upbringing or direct participation exposed to the full social crisis of poverty, depression and the disintegration of communities: exposed also to the movements that responded to these events: the positive movements of self-organisation, protest and political militancy; and those other movements, of emigration for a chance of work or the different ground gained through the openings of higher education.

Secondly, in both their received tradition and their local contemporary stance, they were not persuaded by that dominant English pressure, now crude, now subtle, to leave the pain and anger and intricacy of this crisis to politicians, economists, sociologists, historians, keeping literature to what was said to be its true deep concern with private lives and private feelings. In every year since that stance was gained, Welsh writers emboldened by what their colleagues were doing have encountered the indifference or the anxious correction of the English literary establishment, and some of them, since a good harpist can play many tunes, have found ways of going round about and offering new, often consciously comic, alternatives. If the wisdom of attachment to a people was not acceptable, the wit of a lyrical semi-detachment might be, though the rhythms of other songs still hammered in the mind.

In different phases, different modulations of the central stance seemed able to connect. There could be the steady construction of these lives and times from inside: pity and hopelessness – the move for sympathy; or in struggle and optimism – the move for shared change. Very different from these, there could be the historical reconstruction: the sweeping colourful narrative of what was, in sober truth, an epic history: the transformation, at once the exaltation and the depression, of an active and eloquent people.

There is a sense in which *All Things Betray Thee* might be seen to belong to this second kind, but we do not have to read far into it to be disconcerted if that form is our expectation. For although the form of the epic history is there in outline, the substance is consciously different. Some readers might suppose the novel an attempt at that kind of historical reconstruction, which fails. But if we wait and listen to what it is actually doing we will find a story which is as much part of the crisis as the most dramatic events.

For in and through the action this is essentially a story of how to live with, live through, pity and anger: not by displacing them but by recognising them without the props of their projections. The occasions for pity and anger are explicit, but the problem, reaching deeply into the minds of writer and reader, is how to speak of them, how to write of them, in ways that do not rely only on the stimulus of external events. What is being distilled, that is to say, is the experience of absolute connection with a place, a people, a history, which in the terms of ordinary narrative are often disconnecting, disintegrating, removing and disrupting.

What is then being written is the inner experience of that historical movement which was always more than depression and protest: a movement which experienced defeat, confusion, the deepening of uncertainty, and within these the heartfelt problems of those who could move, near or far, from the core of the tragedy, who knew and could sometimes realise a common longing for quiet and settlement and a different music, but who also could never really be themselves except within the shapes of this more general and more demanding life.

All Things Betray Thee is a moment of transition in Gwyn Thomas's writing, but it is best now seen, in wider terms, as a moment of unusual achievement. As such, if the composition of its voices is heard, it is an irreplaceable instance of a deep underlying problem in thought and feeling but also specifically in writing. The point to grasp is that shift of convention from observer to participant – the underlying movement of the story itself – which makes the harpist's history of the history at once a recognition of what that history truly is and an intricate construction of the often unforeseen and unwanted but finally inevitable connections with it, in the depths of the mind.

This is why, in this tradition, Welsh writers cannot accept the English pressure towards a fiction of private lives: not because they do not know privacy, or fail to value the flow of life at those levels that are called individual, but because they know these individuals at what is always the real level: a matter of inevitable human involvement, often disconcerting, which is at once the mode and the release of the deepest humanity of the self. This is a lesson painfully administered by the history of their own people; a lesson not to be forgotten if the most explicit pressures are distanced or temporarily removed, or while the music calls to a kind of life which everyone would prefer.

The point is clear in the last words of the novel:

I turned, walking away from Moonlea, yet eternally towards Moonlea, full of a strong, ripening, unanswerable bitterness, feeling in my fingers the promise of a new, enormous music.

It is doubtful if foreseeably that music will be heard, but it is the impulse, the general creative direction, that is affirmed. It is a step on from that anonymous dedication which Longridge affirms:

Men like John Simon Adams and myself, we are not much more than leaves in the wind, bits of painful feeling that gripe the guts of the masses. From the cottages, the hovels, the drink shops and sweat mills, anger rises and we are moved. No choice, Mr Connor, save perhaps the last-minute privilege of adjusting the key of the scream we utter.

For it is possible to move beyond that honourable commitment, in which revolt is dependent on how events are moving, and when others can say, in retrospect: 'they should have waited. They were in too much of a hurry. Has death some special call that lures these lads its way?' The larger music is of a longer history, rising and falling but still available to be composed:

> We state the facts, now softly, now loudly. The next time it will be softly for our best voices have ceased to speak. The silence and the softness will ripen. The lost blood will be made again. The chorus will shuffle out of its filthy aching corners and return. The world is full of voices, practising for the great anthem but hardly ever heard. We've been privileged. We've had our ears full of the singing. Silence will never be absolute for us again.

This is said from the experience of defeat, but also from a pride in the struggle which was defeated. Beyond both, which fall and rise over the years, there is the certainty of composition: not only the remaking of lost blood, but the memory of voices which is also a finding of voices: the vast struggle out of silence into a chorus which is at once being practised and composed.

Many voices contribute to this steady composition. In the movement itself there are disputes, evasions, offered alternatives, and powerful voices still speak confidently over and above them. But what comes through in the end is a connection which is the true promise of that music. It is a connection to the past and to the future, but in the intricacy of its own movement it is always primarily of the present: that endlessly repeated present in which the issues and the choices are personally active. The immediate location is 1835 but the connection is beyond it: to 1986 if we can hear it.

> Today is always a muck of ails, shifts and tasks, a fearsome bit of time to stare at and tackle. A man always hates to make a hostile grab at the fabric of the existence he actually knows. But yesterday's beliefs are nice, smooth drumsticks, and they are often brought to tap out reassurance against fears to which we have no answer.

The connection with those moments of hesitation and false reassurance is necessary, as part of the final composition. It is the same when the harpist, believing that his mobility is freedom, rejects all those who have walked into the great social trap. He gets the hard answer:

> They walked into what you call traps because they find a lot more shelter and a bit more food in the trap than elsewhere, even though they might finish up in the trap with no room or chance to do anything but wait patiently to be pecked to hell.

It is a break-out from the traps that is celebrated, and such a celebration is not cancelled even by repeated defeats. For instead of the simple voluntarism of skipping round the traps, the harpist learns both necessity and the necessity, within those hard terms, of the struggle beyond it.

Thus the uncertainties, the despairs, even the hard cynicism or the soft evasion that accompany this apparently never-ending struggle, have lodged deep in this writer's mind: deep enough to settle for, as the dominant culture was recommending and organising; but also so deep that they can be shared, articulated, and finally transformed as they enter the whole composition of this novel. The beliefs are strong because they have been tested to near-destruction. The music can be felt in the fingers because the singing has been heard and silenced but also remembered; it is there to be practised and developed for the next time.

In this way the voices of the novel speak quite especially to our own period: voices full in their immediate and at first hearing (the reading is often best with hearing) strange rhythms – an eloquence and a rhetoric, a wit and a pathos. The composition is so unlike almost all other novels of its time that it might go on being set aside, for simpler or more obviously encouraging modes and tones. Yet I believe it will be seen, beyond its period, as a quite exceptionally authentic work: authentic in embodying that historical moment, which continues now to include us, in which what is being lived and felt through is the full experience of struggle: not only its causes and its courage, but its defeats and the slow music of its renewal.

Raymond Williams

ALL THINGS BETRAY THEE

1

Facing me was the last mountain I would have to cross before reaching the valley at the head of which was the township which I sought, Moonlea. It was my tenth day of walking and my legs still moved swiftly strong over the soft grassy path that led towards the wooded upper slopes. Arthur's Crown they called that mountain, for some brooding eye had seen a serene sad majesty in its rounded peak.

They called me The Harpist. For years I had roamed the land, a small harp attached to my shoulders with cutting thongs of leather when I was on the move. On that harp I played at evening to any group of people who wanted to listen. I had never in all my life been a good player. My senses had always been too passionately attracted to the things and people about me ever to have achieved even a hint of glory in the mechanical sweep of hand on strings. And when I played, my desire was only to drag the hearts of those who heard me out into the shadowed orbit of my own thoughtfulness, to tempt their voices into a dusk-softness of melancholy sound. Around my harp, in all the villages of all the hills and valleys where I had stayed for a brief night or day, had crystallised whole layers of expressed longings and regret. Then, after each session of playing and singing, I had felt the layers peel away under the aseptic brush of wind and sun, for there was that within me which set a fence around my pity and bade all other men and women let me be and pass.

Now my harp was gone. My shoulders, as I moved, were itchily light and alien. Two days before, I had landed at an inn near Lindum. The inn's front windows had looked out upon a lake whose calm loveliness had called my whole being to a total halt. Moonlea and the mountains ahead called to me, but the cool magic of that lake laid a kiss upon me that made my limbs and mind surrender all movement, all desire. I laid my harp aside and enjoyed the kind of high-grade death of a fed, fretless tranquillity. The scum of even my most inveterate griefs yielded to and was dissolved by a cleansing wisdom of acceptance. My dark hollows vanished and I gave not a damn whether my feet ever came to Moonlea or not. Then a drover arrived, a prosperous yeoman in charge of his own herd, and a giant. He stood at least two feet and a fortified stomach above average peasant-level. He was solid and broad as a hillock and as dense. I watched the food and drink go down him as down a pitshaft. He was on his way to a market centre in one of the border counties where the new industrial towns had created a legion of lean bodies begging for his stock. I drank my ale and watched this man, the sight of whom took up and spat upon the whole wonderland of quiet forgiveness into which I had been led by my hour at the lake shore. I spoke to him of the places I had been, of the far hamlets where singing, clustered groups had dipped their slab of squalid wants for a short forgetting into the liquid of my music. I told him of the ironmasters whose dark little towns I had glanced at and fled from in my wanderings, who laid their black fingers on the heads of the field-folk, tensing their neck muscles for the laying of a clumsy knife. I whispered to him as the ale-pool grew deeper and the crazy malice of my ruined mood spread wing and gained fast in fury and power, I whispered to him

2

all I knew of hunger on earth, its fruition and flow, for all the world as if hunger were my sister, a dearly familiar slut. Then a hurled pot came within an inch of taking off my ear and I saw that this drover to whom life was clearly good and widening its grin, was viewing me as he would a toad, a mad, purposeful toad. He rose from his chair, his head down and eager to butt, and if I had not had as much speed as lyric impulse and not run around the table of that inn so often the man became giddy and helpless, I would have left the broken remnants of my neck and all my teeth on the borders of that lovely lake. My prattle of unease among mankind had fished deep down into the great bulk of that drover, had brought up on the hook his last feeling nerve and had scoured hell out of the thing.

When he recovered from his giddiness he went into the corner where my harp stood and he kicked it, as deliberately as I will ever see anything done, into splinters. He turned around to stare at me, gasping and malevolent, seeming to ask what my next move would be. There was no next move. I and life were all full up and not a muscle of either moved. I had felt, in the quiescence of will that had marked my mood on arriving at that spot, that some profound transformative antic might be in course of execution, and I felt no strangeness as I witnessed my harp's death and my own wondering survival. My meekness impressed the drover. He paid me for the damage and I left at dawn the next morning. It was odd to be leaving my harp, which was so much to me, so perfect and simple and sounding a soul to me, mangled in the midst of that loveliness of lake and hill, mangled and dumb like earth. And all that day, as I walked, my body at the sight of some tree or stream, some shaft of sun or thought, would come to a violent pause as the bitter shudder

3

of the smashed strings came ripping between my mind and ears. But by the end of the day the shuddering echo was faint and nearly gone. I no longer cared. The harp's death left me free. My life of wandering was at an end, anyway, and I would need it no longer. At first its going would leave traces of desolation, a trembling need for its solace in heart and hands, but I had always been a great sampler of the desolate in folk and things and had learned to digest even its stoniest particles of anguish into my blood stream. My journey to Moonlea would mark the induction of a brand new type of tomorrow into my days, a tomorrow resting on a diligent security and assurance, purged of my ancient vagabondage and sorrowful bardry.

I took a track westward which skirted the mountain. Two or three miles along the plateau would bring me to the slope down into Moonlea. My stomach was empty, and now and then giddiness made me swerve off the narrow path. In my pocket I had a lump of bread, but it was harder than the thigh bone it rested on, and I made up my mind that I would have to swerve a lot more dramatically than I had done so far before I would bother my teeth with it. My hunger gave the smell of the ferns a deep relish. The sun was becoming fierce.

I made towards a dingle where trees and bushes grew thickly, and I knew that among them there would be a cold stream in which I could steep my legs. In the dingle's middle was a broad clearing, enclosed on one side by a curve of stream. I sang with joy at the sound of water and ran towards it. Then I stopped dead, for before me was such a sight as I had never before seen in this land. A woman, a young woman whose bright beauty matched the press of sun through the surrounding leaves, sat by the stream's side, before a small easel, painting. She wore a light blue cape whose hood hung away from her hair, long, gently tended hair, black as mine. The woman did not turn at my approach for my years in solitary places had made me quiet in my movements as a fox. I could see her canvas. It was neither good nor bad, a vivid bubble of greens and yellows that said everything and nothing. Her fingers were darkened with colours, as if her hands were inexpert in the handling of the brush. As I came nearer she turned her face to stare at an old willow that dragged a scurvy cripple of a branch across the surface of the stream and I could see that her skin and expression were not as those of the village girls and mountain women I had known who grow rough as files and fierce as fire through their toilsome lives. This woman had been bred at great cost and care; there was a pride and aloofness about her that disturbed, then angered me.

On the side of the clearing opposite the stream was an embankment soft with whin-bushes and lichen. I lay full stretch upon it. I pulled down my sheepskin coat so that my nape would be bared to the touch of the cool, tiny leaves. My breathing grew louder with contentment and my teeth ran noisily over the bread lump which I had drawn from my pocket, to be played with, aired and dented, if not eaten. It was then she became conscious of me. There was no shout, no gasp, no tremor. I could have been an odd mountain pony, a poor specimen of pony at a time when their value was low, for all the significance I seemed to have for this woman. Her calmness grated on me. I had been alone for many days, counting out the interlude with the conservative drover, and under the suggestion of my long inner dialogues the private cosmos of my meaning had swelled enormously. Before her, I felt no diffidence, only curiosity. She was emblematic of many things I knew little of. In my roamings

I had seen the increase of wealth and power in the hands of the great landowners as the large estates broke their fences and drove out the small field-tillers. I had seen the empty cottages and quiet fields that had contributed their drop to the stream that was now flowing into the new noisy centres where cloth, iron, coal were creating new patterns of effort, reward, unease. The personal forces, the men of gold, the mighty, whose brains and hands directed these changes, I had kept well outside my private acre and as long as I could keep my moving undisciplined hide free from their manipulative frenzies I had cared nothing about them. Strong and fast they might be, I would always be too swift for them. I would never be found squirming in the life-traps they were creating in the new centres of power. I had never thought to meet one of their number face to face. Yet there I was nibbling a bread crust within three yards of that pouting woman who had upon her the marks of knowing brands of thinking and feeling that would be as deadly to me as the plague if ever their strangeness allowed them to get as far as my palate. She had known not even the shadow of comradeship, I could see that. Her own impulse to create and mould had become the dominant motive of her universe. She would always want a neat, dumb pat of existence under her hands to be fingered into the shape that gave her senses most peace. It was probably the lack of food and the strain of too much walking that caused this twitter in my mind at the sight of her, but whatever the way of it was, I was sick and disturbed as I looked at her. She got a handful of my fibre, with one accurate movement of her spirit, pressed it, taught it to ache with a shrill, embarrassing plaintiveness. For a moment, I was tempted to edge my way out of the clearing and away from her presence. Then she saw me.

'What do you want?' she asked, and she was still as without ripples as the face of that lake on whose shore I had left my mutilated harp. There was a sharp, plucked quality in her voice that brought the harp to my mind.

'Nothing I need ask anybody for.'

'You're impertinent.'

I had nothing to say to that. I had not realised that people were instructed with great pains to pass statements as pointless as that on to other people. I had expected words and notions as straight and sensible as sunlight. So I sat up, shrugged, looked directly at her, then at her painting.

'No shape on that,' I said, letting my eyes wander around the clearing. 'Frankly, you don't get the pattern of this beauty. Ten to one you think it's a pretty dingy show compared with you.'

'Who are you?'

'My name is Alan Leigh, Alan Hugh Leigh.'

'Are you a vagrant?'

'At the moment I'm nothing at all; only tired.'

'Why does your hand shake?'

'I told you. Dog-tired. I've come from North to South on foot and fast as a whippet.'

'Does your hand shake because you're nervous of me?'

'Nervous of you? What kind of a menace do you represent?'

'It isn't every day you discover ladies in glades, painting.'

'So that's a novelty? I didn't know. Of life above the level of goats I'm very ignorant and likely to get more so. No, I'm not nervous of you. Your cloak's very lovely. I'd say it was one of the loveliest things I had ever seen. I saw a lake that colour once and I lingered too long by the side of it. But you, no, you wouldn't make me shake unless you hired somebody to stand behind me and start the movement off.'

'What's that horrible thing you have in your hand?'

'A bit of a loaf. I've been carrying it so long it's worked to my shape. I haven't the heart to eat it or throw it away.'

'Are you a harpist?'

'Used to be. How did you know?'

'The way your fingers bend from time to time. An expectant sort of curve as if they are already listening to the note. It's easy to see. And there's a stupid look in your eyes that I've seen in those of harpists too.'

'You've a cunning fancy.'

'I paint badly, but I watch well. One day I'll see something so clearly it'll tell my brush what to do.'

'I hope so. There's a lot of joy even in that messy splash you've done there.'

'Where are you going?'

'Moonlea.'

'You going to work in the foundries?'

'God, no.'

'What's wrong with them?'

'What's wrong with chaining a bear and paying him a few pence per hobble? That foundry work's a pen for the idiot and the life-sick. Some men put on a coat of dirt and servility too swiftly for my taste. When a man accepts a master's hand or a rented hovel he's fit for the boneyard.'

'You're a savage or a radical. You ought to say those things to my father. He'd have you sitting over a furnace learning elementary logic in less than a minute.'

'Who's he, when he's not roasting the backward?'

'Richard Penbury.'

'I've heard of him. He started Moonlea. The strongest and cleverest of all the ironmasters.'

'My grandfather founded the place. But my father would be glad to hear you say those things.'

'Not the way I'd say them. I don't like ironmasters in the main. Clean air, movement, music. I live for these. Withdraw them and I beckon the sexton.'

'Where's your harp?'

'Smashed. Two days ago. A man put his foot through it, left it shivered and useless.'

'Who was he?'

'His name I don't know. But I should say you would have applauded his views.'

'A man of gentility, no doubt.'

'An oaf, a brutal ham-handed oaf, a man whose mind makes his bullocks sniff.'

'If you have no harp and no love for the ovens, what do you plan to do in Moonlea? It has no place for drones.'

'I have a friend. He and I were very close. We wandered all the mountains of the North and the plains of the Middle Country together. We always said that when our feet grew tired we would find some sweet solitude just right for the joint root of us to rest in. He heard his father was at Moonlea, feeble, rickety and playing the fool around the puddling yards of Penbury, your father. He left me, came down here, watched his father off the earth and stayed. It puzzled me. That was two years ago. Now I'm going to fetch him.'

'How do you know your journey won't be wasted? He might not want to return to your wilderness. There may be more in towns and steady useful labour than meets your eye.'

'There's nothing in steady useful labour that hasn't met my eye. I've looked it up and down like a doctor and the way your father and his helpers dress it up it's a leper. He'll come back with me.'

'Perhaps he's married. And Moonlea is a place where children fall like rain.'

'He's all alone on the earth, like I am. No one, no woman anyway, would get near him. He's like me, quiet, sufficient and a bit too far away for the average run of heart to get close enough to fiddle with him.'

'Even without your harp you make quite a twang, don't you?'

'I rehearse.'

'Who's your friend?'

'John Simon Adams.'

From the girl's face I could see that she had heard of John Simon, and her expression affected me like a thrust icicle. It was strange to be sharing any common territory of knowledge with this woman.

'Why?' I asked. 'What about him?'

'That man is a deadly nuisance. Wherever he is there is no peace.'

'John Simon Adams was never a deadly nuisance in all his days, never.'

'When did you see him last?'

'Two years ago.'

'Since then he has been learning, harpist. He is now a graduate, Moonlea's leading thorn.'

'A thorn to whom?'

'My father and almost all others.'

'How? What makes him prickle? He was always soft as a petal. I was the harpist and he was the singer. Together we could make even stones weep. How is he a thorn?'

'Go down there and find out. He's an evil man.'

'Do you know him?'

'No. I don't need to.'

10

I threw my bread lump angrily into the stream.

'For God's sake, woman, what is the relation between you and humanity? Oh, that's a big wild question and I don't need an answer. But there's a cold selfishness in your eyes and your heart that's new to me, that makes me...' I rose quickly to my feet. She grew paler and I was glad to see that, although I meant her no harm. When I spoke to her again, it was softly, almost humbly, sorry that I had sent my voice into that flight of fuss. 'In all the being of John Simon Adams, and compared with that of you and your father, it is a great lighted dome of being, there is no shadow of evil. I don't know what you've done to him in that smoky sty of a place down there in the valley, but whatever it is it can be cleaned away and he can become what he was in the days when Moonlea was a name to him and no more. You see, lady, I've found the sweet solitude we dreamed of. My father's father heard me play the harp just once and he saddened into a storm of singing that was too much for his frame and it swept him through the door of death. In the north-west corner of the land he has left me two hills and a valley that are so lovely they make paradise pout.'

I turned away.

'I wish you luck,' she said, quietly and smiling.

I walked on, nine, ten yards. I did things within my mind to erase the impression that this woman, her words, the colour and sound of her, had made upon my thoughts. But I turned around to face her once again before the path twisted out of the clearing and beyond her view.

'After a bit, after the first strangeness wears away,' I said, 'you're all right. You're soft and kindly, like the moss.'

She had her eyes fixed on the canvas and did not look up. I continued on my way, my pace easy and swift, moving downward now. I wondered what I would feel, what would become of me when I entered into the dark pool of men and women in their bald, huddled cottages in the township below with its ravelling cap of smoke and its air of sullen detachment from the joyful beauty of the hills around.

2

Someone had thought about Moonlea before letting it be built. Other places of the kind that I had seen had their new dwellings straggling around a nucleus of ancient cottages, teeming, patternless. But Moonlea had a long main street with side streets leading off it at regular intervals. The man whose design it was could not have been vague about himself or the universe.

There were few people to be seen as I walked down the main street. I thought this strange, for I remembered from the brief stay that I had made in Moonlea when I had come down to the place two years before to bear John Simon company that the people were chronically sociable and liked nothing better than to sit on their sills, talk, stare at each other and their slice of existence. The afternoon sun was still full and warm, a day to encourage a gentle friendliness, but of all the men and women I saw there was not one who turned towards me or gave me greeting. Beyond on the far eastern side of the town were the foundries. The air above them was faintly shaded and my senses reached out and smelled the powerful acridity of their fumes well in advance. The cottages flanking the well-made road were tiny, uniform, attached one to the other as if to secure them more firmly to Moonlea. To my right, a hundred feet up the hillside was a large gracious house with broad windows and two bold milk-white columns on each side of the main door. Those columns spoke out from the dark green hillside and were the most confident things in all that valley. An avenue of larch and beech led up to the house. There, I guessed, would be the dwelling place of Richard Penbury and of that woman who wore the lake-blue cloak and sat upon her own private hillock.

I stopped and looked at a shop, newly built on a plot of ground alongside a big red brick building that had the appearance of being a council meeting place. The shop was newly painted, a gleaming red, and its windows were chockablock with merchandise that also had the mark of freshness on it. The pane of the right-hand window had been broken, the opening patched with a dark board. The name above the door, 'L. Stevens', said something to me. I stood still staring at the name, my head rocking slowly back and fore, a thing I often did when trying to remember. Then a man came and stood on the shop's doorstep, a short man with a biggish smiling face, his arms hanging readily at his sides as if eager to be at a task. The sight of him gave my mind a push and I realised that I had talked several times with this man while waiting vainly for John Simon to join me on the journey northward when I had last been in Moonlea. This Lemuel Stevens had then been a baker in a small way of business. I could still remember his dark tiny hole of a bakery and the vivid pallor of his face against the frame of it. He had had a thin hangdog look then, but now there was a fair ration of flesh upon him and a confidence in his air. I could see that he had prospered. He screwed his eyes up at the sight of me. I knew that within a matter of seconds he would remember who I was. During the days when John Simon had tried to persuade me to stay in the town I had gazed diligently at all its houses and shops and workplaces, fascinated by the sight of so much trouble gone

14

to by so many people to change the shape and pace of living.

'The harpist,' shouted Lemuel Stevens gladly, and he promptly seized my hand and dragged me into his shop. He put me to stand in the very middle of the small brown board floor of the room. I noticed the loaves and other foodstuffs stacked on the counter and on the other side of the shop a combined clothes and ironmongery department. My nose filled with a hybrid and disquieting smell. It was clear that a great wind of increase had found and filled the sails of Lemuel. He walked around me gaping and laughing and I could think of nothing I had done that should make the man so delighted to see me unless it was that the whole mutilating effort which made up so much of life in Moonlea was so notably absent from the look of me. My appearance has often given cheer to and brought a tribute of thanks from men fanatically intent on the competition for wealth and greatness. They sense from every movement of my hands, eyes, legs, that I do not even give the memory of a damn for the objects of their desire; they know that they would never find my leg meanly lodged in a position to trip them over. One could feel Lemuel straining his miniature muscles to edge ahead.

He took me with him into the back room of his shop. 'This is my wife,' he said in his sing-song voice, waving at a dark, timid pretty woman who curtseyed clumsily to me, her back to the fire. 'My wife, Isabella. Make food for the harpist, Isabella. It is a great day for Moonlea when a harpist like this one returns.'

I smiled at Isabella and found it hard, after years of hardly bothering to say anything to anyone, to dredge up from the darkening depression caused in me by the damp unwholesome smack of Lemuel's calculating earnestness some formula of courtesy that would put Mrs Stevens at her ease.

'You are both very kind,' I said, and took the plain scrubbed chair by the table that Lemuel pulled out for me.

'We'll have the bacon, Isabella, the special,' said Lemuel. He went to the fireplace and reached up to a ledge for a ham that had been lodged there. It was as encrusted with grime as one of the chimney stones and all my attention was in my ears as Isabella began slicing the rashers, curious to know whether it was really meat that Lemuel had got down for my pleasure.

Isabella worked swiftly and in hardly less time than it took me to tell Lemuel that I was nearly dropping off my chair with hunger, the food was before me. All thought of my hosts died from my mind as my head got down to its work. My mouth moved obstinately as a sheep's and the sides of my face ached fiercely before I was finished. Once in a while my eyes glanced up at my dumb attentive donors. Lemuel was gazing at me astonished as if he were wishing to say that even a harpist who lived on his own obscure margin of fecklessness could carry hunger too far. And in the raven-dark timid Isabella there seemed to be a smiling thankful-ness that all men were not as the cautious abstemious Lemuel, that mad appetites were still making last stands in this corner of the land and that.

The eating done, Lemuel stepped into the shop and returned with a jar of nettle beer and tobacco for my pipe. I smoked and drank, waiting for them to start the talking, but all Lemuel did was sit there looking glad and grateful and I knew that he would not have been looking glad if my only virtues in his eyes had been a gift for plucking strings and an indifference to the accumulation of coins.

'Thank you for this fine welcome to Moonlea, Lemuel,' I said. 'The bacon and the nettle beer were a great treat. But pardon me if I don't quite understand.'

'Oh, it makes me very happy that you are here.'

'Why, if I remember the last time I was at Moonlea you didn't think so much of my harping. Indeed, when I gave you a little tune in that little hole of a bakery which badly needed the blessing of beauty you gave me one overbaked crust and told me there was no time or place on earth for such idleness. That said, you dived back into the hot darkness like a hell-bred mole. I remembered it because ever since then your words and your look as you spoke them have kept coming back to my mind as being extraspecially quaint.'

'I have more time now, more room. The harp's a lovely thing.' And he laughed falsely, awkwardly, and even a man blinder than a bat could see that Lemuel was still as stone deaf and numb to the charms of harping as the very dead. 'There is a strange sadness come upon Moonlea,' he went on. 'You and your carefree laughter and music, harpist, will coax their shadows from them. It's what we've been needing for a long time. I hope you have your dance measures in prime fettle, for we would like dancing in the long summer nights.'

I held out my glass to Lemuel before telling him that my harp was as mangled and mute as the average mind. I wanted to finish off the nettle before Lemuel found out that I was now little more than a liability if he was looking on me as a source of gaiety.

'My harp's dead,' I said, 'kicked over Jordan by a lout.'

'Oh, that's a pity, Alan, that's a terrible pity. But there'll be other harps. I'll get you one. I've got good friends who'll do much for me.'

17

'I'm glad to hear that, Lemuel. Friends are fine things.' I supped my beer and waited for him to come to the point. 'You've come on.'

'I've done all right. The bakehouse is at the back of the house. A big beautiful oven I've got. I've been set up very well.'

'Lemuel has come on splendidly,' said Isabella leaning forward and letting her voice tremble in a way that made me wonder why she was worried about the future of splendour.

'What are you afraid of, Lemuel?' I asked.

He gasped with surprise at my question. Slow indirectness was a way of life for Lemuel, but I have seen so much of creatures who seemed to do very well without any words at all, I thought it good that now and then I should tear away the cackle which men like Lemuel wore for trimmings on their minds and tongues.

'Afraid?' he asked, glancing nervously at Isabella.

'Yes, we are,' she said. 'We're afraid, harpist. We're very happy here. Mr Penbury has been good to Lemuel. Mr Penbury said Moonlea would be served well by so steady and reliable a man as Lemuel in one of its main shops.' She dropped her voice. She had laid her hand on Lemuel's arm and was pressing it as if to give him some of her own resolution. 'But Mr Penbury has enemies. There's been trouble at the foundries. Tongues are sharpening against Lemuel. People who were our friends look bitterly at us and say that Lemuel is raising the price of his bread at the same time as Mr Penbury is raising the rent of his cottages so that they will be helpless with debt and will have to do what Mr Penbury says. It's lies, harpist, all lies.'

'Indeed it is,' said Lemuel, dragging his chair towards mine and making me hot with the urgency of his voice and gestures. 'Can I help it if the millers charge me more for their flour? Can I or they help it if there is a scarcity in the land? Can I help it if Mr Penbury wishes to punish the laggards who dawdle with their rent by raising it a copper or two? Can I help it if there is not as much work or wages at the foundries as there have been for years past?'

'You can't help anything, Lemuel,' I said, thinking this a good neutral answer to give to a man who had just stretched up the chimney to give me part of his special ham. 'To me you look as innocent as a goat. I don't understand much of what you say. Millers, scarcity, rent, wages, God knows what lies behind these antics. I don't. This place is a black crab, Lemuel, and judging by the way you sound, you've annoyed one of its leading pincers.'

'They're jealous of the way Lemuel has come on,' said Isabella. Her shyness had all gone now. She was full of anger as I was of food, and that nettle-preparation. 'These bad times will pass. Why can't they be grateful for the things Mr Penbury has done for them? He's our friend and their friend and patience is all that we need.'

I jerked my finger in what I thought was the direction of the house on the hillside.

'Is that Mr Penbury behind those columns?'

'That's it. He's a wonderful man.'

'If he lives up to his columns he must be.'

'They say,' said Lemuel, only inches away from me now and whispering, 'that I am a spy for Mr Penbury, that I keep my ear in the mouths of the people and carry back to him their every word. But it's lies, harpist. I only explain to them about the rent and the scarcity. I'm their friend. I want to keep what I have, that's all. We've worked very hard for what we have, Isabella, and I, and nobody's going to rob us, harpist, nobody.'

19

'Be clear, Lemuel. I'm fresh down from the mountain. I don't know what the hell all you people are up to living in these places wrapping life like a soft black dough around your sticks of iron. Most of what you say is an ache in my ear and the crazy, worried way you're looking at me, I don't know if it's because I'm too sleepy to get you properly in my vision or because you're off your head. Who wants to rob you, boy?'

'Last night they came to my shop, a large crowd of them. They spoke about the trouble they've had getting enough bread since the beginning of last winter when the bad times really started. As if I didn't know that, I who for months have been selling only half the loaves I used to. They said that soon, if they could not buy my bread they would come and take it, that if the prices do not come down my shop would. And they uttered other sayings as horrible. I pleaded with them and told them again about the scarcity and then someone I could not see put a stone through my window, my new window.'

'You shouldn't have told them about the scarcity. Perhaps they thought they already knew all about it. It seems to be camping in their field.'

'Then I told them that if I had any more of that I would be up to Mr Penbury's like a shot to ask for protection. They said to hell with Mr Penbury in a nasty savage way and I went cold all over, hearing such words as hell coming from the poor people who have always been my friends. Then that big man, Lewis Humphreys, who was their leader last night and who has a voice like a drum, said they were sick of sinking deeper into debt to Mr Penbury and me and that one day they might be setting alight to the Town Hall where Mr Jarvis the Clerk has had the records of their debts taken for safe keeping. Have you ever heard such talk as that, harpist?'

'No. I've never wanted to. Debts gasp hard just behind me, but they never come abreast. I wouldn't even accompany them on the harp. But don't worry,' I wanted to encourage Lemuel, for he was pale with panic now. 'You know what these boys are. Anything for a warm. That was a sort of jest, no doubt, that mention of burning the Town Hall, meant to dilute the bitter patter about the bread earlier on. Is he a leader of all this strife, this Humphreys?'

'Oh no,' Lemuel and Isabella came nearer to me in a way that made it clear we had now come to the chief point. I was glad for I was finding it hard to keep awake.

'Humphreys is nobody, a loud-voiced nobody and daft as a jimmy. Neither he nor anyone else would have dared to set himself up to threaten Mr Penbury or make demands of me if it hadn't been for John Simon Adams who has always been like a brother to you.'

'Explain to me about John Simon. Make it simple. Stick to John Simon and leave out rent and the millers. This is twice today I've heard about him and on each occasion he is made to sound even worse than that man with the gunpowder, Fawkes. Who has he been trying to blow up?'

'Nothing like that, harpist. He doesn't mean half the mischief he creates. He's not happy here. He's sick for the days of freedom he knew with you. The foundries put a shadow on him and he spreads his unhappiness to those around him. He'll only make trouble for Moonlea and himself. You can talk to him, harpist. Take him back to where he belongs, with you.'

'If he's so miserable, why hasn't he left the place?'

'He would have done, if it hadn't been for that Katherine Brier.'

'Who is she now?'

'A woman, a slut.'

'And one without shame,' put in Isabella, whose mind I could see was raw and beyond reason on the score of this Katherine.

'John Simon was never a great one for the women,' I said. 'She must be lovely to his eyes, this Katherine.'

'They say there is some kind of magic about her, but I was never able to see it, being shielded by decent thoughts. She's a married woman.'

'Where's the husband? Why doesn't he debate with John Simon?'

'Debate, poor lad. He's under the same roof with them, he and his mother, Elizabeth Brier, the blind forgiving fools that they are. He is simple in the wits. Katherine only married him when she had no place to call her home. And now she is openly the bitch of John Simon Adams. Mr Bowen says that even if John Simon had not been guilty of poisoning the hearts of the foundry hands and setting man against master, that what he has done to poor Davy Brier would have been enough to set the brand of Cain upon him.'

'Who's Mr Bowen?'

'The minister in the new chapel that Mr Penbury has given us. A man of golden talents, harpist, like yourself, and watchful for the feints of sin.'

'What's the brand of Cain?'

'He didn't clearly tell us. He was in such a temper when he was talking about it. But he made it plain enough that it's all over John Simon from tip to toe, that John Simon can foam and mutter defiances all he will, he's as doomed as if the devil had him nailed to the bed. Talk to him, harpist. Show him the folly of remaining in a place where no good can await him.'

22

'You've got a fine lot of performers here, Lemuel. Penbury with his iron-making stink-holes that make a curious blackness in men and in the sky; John Simon with his woman and the shadow in his heart; Bowen the golden one with his brands. And the daughter of Penbury, what's she called?'

'Helen. How do you know about her?'

'Met her on the mountain top. She was in a dingle, painting.'

Lemuel and his wife exchanged a glance and giggled.

'She's a bold strong girl. But every inch a lady, mind you, every inch a lady.'

'The few inches I saw were up to standard. So long, Lemuel. I don't think John Simon will be a nuisance to you much longer. He'll be going back to the North with me. Where does he live?'

'Go right through the town, past the furnaces. Climb the earth road up the hillside towards a group of four cottages placed like a square. In the first of those, on the left hand, you will find him. Many thanks to you, harpist, and may God grant that John Simon listen to your wisdom.'

'He never used to. But then, he never used to make iron with one hand and go in for adultery with the other. So he may be in the mood for new experiences, my wisdom among them. So long, Lemuel; the food was good.'

3

I climbed the earth road Lemuel had mentioned in his directions. It was fairly steep. In front of me were the cottages, thickset and solitary on the hillside. I felt a sudden distaste for dipping my curiosity into the queer relationships in which John Simon had involved himself, types of commitment from which I had kept myself fiercely detached. I would find them alien, trackless. I paused in my climb and looked back to the town. I could see the house of Penbury with its beautiful proportions and bewildering columns: the big new greystone chapel in which Mr Bowen kept hell on a gilt leash; the Town Hall, also a building less than ten years old in which rested the long tricky debt documents that kept a fair slice of Moonlea's working lives in a thoughtful state about the County Gaol. There was a deliberate, serious look about the whole community that made me feel I was being worsted in the battle of stares we were waging.

I pushed open the gate of the first cottage on the left. It was a slightly larger dwelling than the other, seeming to have been added to at intervals. The vegetable garden, back and front, was in good condition, and I noticed that there was a heavy proportion of cabbages among the produce. A young man, heavily set and notably light-haired, was bending over a fork at the bottom of the garden. The gate creaked as I pushed it open. The gardener looked up and hailed me in a voice that was light and childish. His face was friendly but vacant, the face, undoubtedly, of that Davy, the simple of wit, about whom Lemuel had told me. I hailed him with a smile and he came slowly up the garden path, shouldering his fork. He was stooped as he walked and the tips of his fingers swept the heads of his cabbages lovingly as he came towards me. Twice he dropped his eyes to stare at them and appeared surprised when he lifted them again and found me still there waiting to be stared at.

He waved his hand to take in the whole garden as he stood before me.

'Good?' he said.

'Oh fine.'

'Who's there?' asked a woman's voice, a troubled voice.

I could see the woman's face through a window. It was a strong, lined, handsome face, that of one in whom laughter and compassion had had to fight hard for the right to practise and had given too much ground.

'Man,' said Davy.

'There's a man outside, a stranger,' said the woman to someone inside.

The door opened and a younger woman, her hands and arms steaming and red with laundry water, came into view. Her hair was darkly golden, her eyebrows heavily marked, and for a moment forbidding; then one caught the full intelligent loveliness of the eyes and mouth. In the very centre of that woman spun a great tidal whirl of comradely warmth. If pearls are secreted in the diseased organs of unequal and restless societies, she was one. About the shape of her head there was a hint of the woman I had met upon the mountain, but need had buried all the gift for contempt in Katherine and there was an integrity of passionate kindliness in her that was wine for the heart.

25

'My name is Alan Leigh. I am a friend of John Simon Adams.'

'The harpist?' asked Katherine, her face lighted now like a lamp.

'Not an evening passes,' said Mrs Brier, taking me warmly by the arm, 'but that he has spoken of you and wished you and your harp at hand to put a blessing on his talk and his singing.'

They took me into the cottage where the fireplace was a brilliant glow of burnished metal. They set me down before a dish of broth which I had not the heart to refuse for the big, fair, vacant lad Davy was grinning delightedly at me, urging me with his eyes to eat deeply.

John Simon, they said, had gone away early that morning to one of the valleys of the South. He had taken the mountain road and would not be back until late in the evening. I was not sorry for the chance to be able to sit back and watch these people, undistracted. Most of the time Davy was sitting on a corner stool, making baskets of wicker. His hands were patient and skilled. Often he would call over to me to come and admire this detail of his craft or that. I went and watched him, patted his back and said I had never seen such beauty of pattern as the squares of different shades he contrived in the basket's surface, such subtle bending of the wicker as made one sense a kinship between the life in his fingers and the fibre of the reed. His whole body became excited by words and the friendly touch of my hand and I could sense that in the being of this Davy were large lakes of forlornness on which my admiration shone like a pioneer star.

Katherine and Mrs Brier stood at a table in a far corner of the room making oatmeal cakes. From time to time they both

26

turned as if moved by an identical impulse and looked at us thoughtfully. It struck me that there was much to justify the silent pensive fixity of their eyes for there was enough in the spectacle of me alone, landed without warning in that place and groping after the dark, wandering heart of John Simon Adams, to raise a fair wind of thought. I could not move a single inch in all that cottage without having all my feelings jangled by eerie variations on an urgent theme of frustration and unrest. These people, with more or less consciousness, were looking at each other around delicately laboured shields of defensive watchfulness and were not made glad by what they saw.

At seven, John Simon Adams returned. I could feel his happiness as he shook my hand, but his face was solemn and unmoved. It was as if he had expected my coming, detected some profound and acceptable rightness in my being there. He guessed these thoughts in my mind as he looked into my face.

'You have been a lot in my thoughts, Alan,' he said, as if in explanation. 'And you've stepped out of my head. It's just as if you had been created by my very wish to see you. I'm glad you came, Alan.'

We assembled around the table. There was a dish of meat, a portion of sheep, boiled to a wonderful softness and flavoured with herbs. Mrs Brier told Davy not to make such a noise as he ate. I had not observed him until Mrs Brier spoke her caution, but afterwards, with my ears attentive, I found that Davy was one of the noisiest men with food between his teeth that I had ever heard. He had his head thrust over the table and he gave himself altogether to the meal.

I found myself joining Katherine in an examination of John Simon, who did not speak as he ate. He was thirty-one at the time and dark as the coming of sleep and as soft, with his deep voice gentle to the ear. His eyes were merciful and brown and his forehead and shoulders broader than most. He had stepped, since I saw him last, into a twilight of chronic gravity, and I could make no estimate of the way he would take when his mood ripened into nightfall. When I told him about the harp he just nodded as if that fact too had entered into the serene enclosure of his prevision.

The meal ended with the nettle beer which appeared to be common as rain in the area. Davy wanted some, but his mother, in a voice as firm and compactly intelligible as a stone, told him he should not have any, and she explained to me that after a cup or two of that mixture a wild savage sadness came upon Davy which was hard to put up with. Davy took the refusal cheerfully and walked behind John Simon and myself as we made our way out of the cottage and up the hillside to a spot where, sitting between two rocks that shielded our bodies from the sweeping hill-breeze, one had a fine long view of the whole valley of Moonlea.

After we had been sitting there a few minutes we were joined by four men who came from two of the other cottages and who seemed to have been waiting for John Simon to make an appearance. The two first men to arrive had large slow bodies and friendly faces. They were brothers, Lewis and Leyshon Andrews, and as they sat down they said they were pleased to see me, since new faces had become so rare. Following them came two men, less tall, both with eyes that were bright and merry. They were called Wilfie Bannion and Mathew Price. Mathew walked with a slight limp, the fruit of an iron ingot that had landed across his legs down at the foundries. All had the dark, rough-thickened fingers of the iron workers. The hands of the brothers Andrews were huge

28

and I could barely keep my eyes off them. We set our pipes going, filled with leaves of a herb that Wilfie Bannion said he had prepared in his own garden. The others seemed to enjoy it, but it had me rocking after ten drags. In front of us Davy hummed an old cradle song and swayed to the time of the melody.

'What's boiling up about here, John Simon?' I asked.

'Bubbles, and they'll make a loud sound when they go off.'

'Who's doing the stoking?'

'Penbury and others.'

'What'll the end of it be?'

'Trouble and some kind of change.'

'Explain that. In the wilderness there are no foundries.'

'You know how things have been. For as far back as we can remember the big farmers and the landlords have been putting their own special brand of boot into the small field-folk, making them flow like rivers from the West lands into valley towns like Moonlea. Towns like this one here have grown up all in the space of about ten or fifteen years. Streets, churches, chapels, courts, taverns, all around and serving the foundries. At first it was fine. It stayed fine for as long as Penbury and his friends were riding their partic-ular tide and the world kept calling out for iron and more iron. It seemed then as if this iron was going to be the biggest feature on earth, the very nose on the face we turned up to the sun. There was money for the people, more than they had ever had from their ploughs and crops. Their bodies ached like hell with the strain of new labour and their lungs might have turned to rust in the heat and smoke, but they still thought that life had taken a turn for the better. Then some time back the world stopped calling for iron; its gullet seemed to be choked with it and hundreds of furnaces went cold. Since then we've worked in fits and starts. With work scarce, Penbury has tightened his grip and wages have shrunk. The cottages are his, and although most of them are no bigger or better than coffins he says the people must pay more because he is not now having his old golden return on his investment. There's hunger in Moonlea and not only here. Today I was in the valley to the South, and it's the same there, exactly the same. What do you say to it all, Alan?'

John Simon and his companions all looked at me as if what I was going to reply was really of some importance to them.

'That you are fools,' I said. 'You've all walked into the trap. The Penburys have stalked you and hung you up to fester for their delight as I would a pheasant. John Simon, there's only one way to spit in the eye of these ironmongering rogues and that's to turn your back on them and return to the hills and fields you came from.'

'That's daft talk,' said Wilfie Bannion. 'Listen, harpist. You are what they call a poet. You are fleet with your tongue and your legs. It would take a good hunter to noose you. There are not many like you, more's the pity. Most folk are leaden. They walk into what you call traps because they find a lot more shelter and a bit more food in the trap than elsewhere, even though they might finish up in the trap with no room or chance to do anything but wait patiently to be pecked to hell.'

'Time,' I said, 'must be bruised black and blue by the ways some of you people have of passing it on.'

'You think people make a choice. There is no choice. Your roof is stripped off; you've got to get out of the rain. Your food is torn away; you can't hire out your stomach. Look. Five years ago, my father and brothers and I had a hill farm, a good farm, and our will and muscles made the hard land soft and made wheat grow where people said it would not. The land was enclosed by a speech-making, soldierly leader of men called Lord Plimmon, who has made a name for himself with a few radical speeches in the Parliament about the crime of working kids to death in mines. But we were fair game for this genius. He aims to become one of the greatest landowners since Darius the Bloody Persian. He enclosed our farm with the blessing of his friends in Parliament, said we had not the means to make the land yield as much wealth as it might. We refused to budge. In his role of military commandant of the garrison at Tudbury he brought up a little platoon of mounted Yeomanry and chased the whole tribe of us around the hillside as if we were foxes. I believe he enjoyed it for there is bound to be something comical in the sight of men who are running hard without any real wish to. Even now when I think of him I ponder on the quality and price of my brush. They got us off at last but only after my father had made a leap at one of the Yeomen and got a sword thrust that helped him to die within three weeks. And now I'm in Moonlea. Lewis and Leyshon there will tell you similar things. I tell you, harpist, there is no choice. There is the innocent rear of the people as they nibble their fertilised meadow and there is the shod foot of the smart ones who kick them into a more meagre pasture. It seems as simple as that to me, but they may only be because I happen to belong to one of the better-kicked parts of the rear.'

'More fool the kicked,' I said. 'There are ways of stripping boots off feet, there are ways of tripping the most gifted

31

kicker on to his nose, there must be ways of making meadows eternally secure and contriving freedom for the body and sustenance for the guts. But here you are more helpless than ever.'

You're wrong, Alan,' said John Simon. 'Here in Moonlea and places like it the people for the first time are not quite helpless. They are close together and in great numbers. Their collective hand is big enough to point at what is black and damnable in the present, at what is to be wished in the future. Back there in the fields they were in a solitude. They could be picked off at the leisure of anyone who wanted to do his own bit of private mangling. Hunger could rage among them all it wished, and never were there more than five or six lean distracted clowns with pitchforks to say it nay.'

'There'll be no change in them. They will endure dumbly here as they did elsewhere, a kind of walking dung that doesn't even insist on the traditional privilege of being carried to the furrow.'

'The light gets stronger, Alan. The land isn't quite as uncharted any more. We're beginning to see a landmark here and there. When the gutted villages first spewed their people out into the iron towns, either they were numb with misery or excited by the jingle of the ironmaster's shillings and they had little chance to marvel at the anguish of their slashed root. Now the numbness has worn off; the excitement is wearing away. They are looking around. They know from the feel of their every day that they are well within the doorway of a changed world.'

'I'll remind you of that, John Simon, when Penbury has let you into his iron grave. What lies at the back of it all? When your nails have sunk deeply enough into the ironmasters'

32

flesh to make them stop behaving like monkeys what do you expect to get from all this stirring of brains and bodies?'

'I told you we are entering into a new age, a bleak and draughty chamber in time.'

'I can believe it. If Moonlea's a signpost it'll be the kind of chamber in time that space will be lucky to get out of alive.'

'We are the lesser mules in a long convoy. We will make our own assertion.'

I lay back, resting my head on the grass. I nibbled at a grass stalk and looked at John Simon whose eyes were fixed on the rocking squarish head of Davy. I thought of the long days he and I had spent on like hillsides in the North, but looking down on valleys that were empty and unsullied, passing the hours in talk about the heart of man with an uncle of John Simon, a sage old shepherd, sending the sheep to sleep with windy wisdom and me with them as often as not. But those hours of wonder had always ended with laughter and an agreement that as long as each night found us with the core of our own gladness still untouched there would be no chronic weeping over the stupefying cruelties of earth. But as I looked at John Simon now there was not even the remembrance of laughter. I wondered what muscle of misery it was that was causing him to bob like a cork on this stream of tormented dreaming.

'What's he like, this Penbury?'

'Neat looking. Tidily wrapped with no loose things hanging out. Probably winces at the thought of cruelty and would set Jarvis the law-clerk on the tail of your shirt if you said he was not the most benevolent man ever to live in the shadow of Arthur's Crown since Arthur. He's all right, if you just happen to take him as a bit of life and are strolling towards death without bothering to come to any conclusion about it all. But his eyes and notions are not like ours. I often feel like going up to him as he comes around the moulding yards and asking him how it is that two men so clearly on different planets should look so much as if they were living in the same town. We've not seen much of him lately. I heard the slowness in trade has worried him and made him ill. We are glad to see him so tender. If he gets used to the slowness there are lots of people down there who spend most of their time trying on new styles of anguish for fit who will be pleased to provide him with new reasons for fretting.'

'Lemuel thinks he's good. He nearly got down on his belly and whimpered at the mention of him. Penbury needs never to have dirty shoes with Lemuel's tongue within whistling distance.'

'Lemuel the baker? When did you see him?'

'On the way in. What kind of man has he become?'

'You saw his shop.'

'He's done well. The place was full of loaves and coats and God knows what not.'

'Penbury hoisted him out of that rat-hole where he baked his bread, about a year ago. The ironmaster made him, and now he's one of Penbury's lesser veins, a channel for some part of his master's blood and purpose. I think that Penbury aims to convert Lemuel's shop into some kind of truck-place where the slower-witted and more indebted can go and get in kind about a half of their real wages. There were two small shops doing a nice little trade near the spot where Lemuel had his new place built, but Penbury found means of closing them. With Jarvis the clerk even growing his hair long to look more like a poodle, Penbury finds no difficulty

34

in deciding which doors in Moonlea shall remain open or shut.'

'Lemuel told me the people regard him as a kind of a spy. True?'

'If you look hard at Lemuel's ear you will observe that the edge is scalloped. That comes from his not withdrawing it quickly enough when the person he is listening to decides to take a bite at something. He's Penbury's outer lobe. He's a mole and he's in the dark. His whole soul is tone deaf.'

I laughed. That was the John Simon I knew, his striped fancy coming out at you swiftly like a zebra.

'A dangerous mole,' said Lewis.

'Why dangerous?' I looked over at Lewis, thinking he was overdoing the sombre seriousness of his expression when he spoke of Lemuel. I still thought that the little baker had enough to be putting up with in the heat and dough of his trade and the scared panicky eyes of his wife Isabella without being burdened as well with charges of being a major menace to the peace of man. 'I don't see it. A mole, all right. We all have our different ways of keeping out the light. A maker of earth-lumps, all right. But who could ever be bitten deeply enough by Lemuel to draw even the look of blood?'

'You're a bit of a mole yourself, harpist, when it comes to knowing men and women,' said Lewis, his heavy voice palpable on the side of my face as he leaned over to do his bitter talking at closer range. 'The wind has got into your brain. A year ago Wilf Bannion's brother Sam made some trouble in the number three furnace when Penbury tried to lop a couple of coppers off the day's wage. That was when he started talking about the need to be pulling our belts in because the masters up in Scotland had better furnaces than we and were sending more and cheaper iron to the South. He warned Sam to shut up, but Sam had a lot of small kids and as often as not was without a belt to pull in. Then Lemuel took in a lodger, a broad, stony-faced performer with a finger and a half missing from his left hand. Nobody knew him. He came up from some town on the coast. Lemuel went about with him a lot, showing him over the place. Then Sam was found in a little ravine on the way up to Arthur's Crown. His head had been pushed in. It looked as though he might have fallen and landed up against a boulder. That is what Jarvis the clerk told the people to believe when inquiries were made and that is what the people believed because at that time there were only a few of us who had mastered the idea that Jarvis was not always to be believed. The man with the finger and a half short said he didn't fancy furnace-work much and made his way back down to the coast and Sam lay very quiet, in no way to argue with Penbury about wages or hunger.'

'You've got Penbury on the brain. You're building him into the likeness of a Satan to give a bit of dignity to the bloody nightmare you walked into when you set your buttocks down on this damp smoky hole. That's a daft tale you tell about Lemuel leading that man about Moonlea like an airedale pointing out this head and that and telling him to flatten it.'

'You've got a lot to learn, boy, a lot. There are clearly many shadows on earth that are strange and unbelievable to you and about which you could pluck your harp strings to an uncannier tune than they have played as yet. Oh yes, Penbury did a tidy job of Sam. He even had a woman called Flossie Bennett come forward to accuse him. She whose price, stripped, was never more than threepence, and who was always to be found outside the back door of that tavern, The Leaves After the Rain, aled to the roots of her hair and ready for action, claimed that she had been on the mountain plundering the early bluebells when Sam, his eyes red with lust, made a lunge at her. She side-stepped, said this nimble liar, and Sam went over into the ravine where his head smacked against a stone and put his desires to sleep. That woman never heard of early bluebells, and if she was ever on a mountain it was not after flowers that she went. As for Sam Bannion viewing her with love, a little compassion, perhaps a groan and a quick retreat is all she would have had from him. He loved his wife, as far as love can ever worm its way through the thickets of this place, and besides, he was up to his neck in kids. You are wrong about men being hard to change, harpist. You have seen too many men in the far hills who are just solitary clods, whose lives have little ferment save what prompts them to eat and die. Men can be changed. Sam was, quickly and without much fuss. We could do as much for others as was done for him, but for us there is no need to kill, for we have no such fears for ourselves as would make us seek safety in such terrible tomfoolery as that, nor, if we did kill, would we need to wrap the act in lies that hang like a shroud of sorrow in the memories of those who are left, like Sam's wife.'

'Most of the time now, she cries,' said Leyshon Andrews, 'they meant a lot to each other, Sam and his wife.'

'If it hadn't been for John Simon she and the children would have starved for certain.'

'I couldn't stand the look of those kids,' said John Simon. 'They and Sam's wife went to live with a neighbour in one of the older cottages. In the thick wall of that cottage a hole has been made. That's where Sam's wife and the children lived, in the hole. Hunger gave them a shiny sort of look as if the skin glowed with being stretched. It was a bad thing to see, hurtful.'

I looked at him again impatiently. His face had lost the moment's liveliness that had returned to it when he was speaking before. I sensed the slipping down upon him once more of some great crass torment. It maddened me to feel his real blithe unearnest self falling from between my hands and crawling into that grotesque stable of menace and calamity. But I had no wish to argue further, to do any more walking in the face of the darkness of the tunnel that these men seemed to have dug for themselves.

'You're a bright lot of sods,' I said. I saw in their eyes the sardonically patient look one often finds in the eyes of the highly skilled as they guide the fingers of the utterly ignorant and inept. 'Try to catch me putting even one toe into this bog.'

Wilf Bannion had fallen asleep. From Davy came the same insistent crooning of some old sleep-song. Our voices fitted in layers around his and in a moment the whole hillside was full of our lulling music.

4

John Simon and I made our way to the inn, The Leaves After the Rain. Like most of the rest of Moonlea, save the clump of cottages around the original furnace, the inn's building was new. It stood back from the road, the road leading west out of Moonlea, and it was framed in a crescent of oaks. Behind it the hill rose sharply; before was a cobbled area with tethering poles and drinking troughs on either side. Its windows were plain, small and without curtain or ornament. The paint of the woodwork was already thinned and streaked by the heavy mountain rains. It was late evening as John Simon and I approached its front door. The lights of the tavern were already on, although there was still a full flood of daylight in the sky. A wave of talking voices reached us while we were still on the road.

John Simon opened the front door. The latch was new and stubborn, the woodwork swollen, and he gave the base of the door a slight kick before it swung open. We found ourselves in a large room with twenty to thirty men standing around. The bulk of the men knew John Simon, and as he came into view there was a nodding of many heads and a lowering of drinks from mouths to give him greeting. In the right-hand corner was a small, roughly made serving counter placed in front of the door that led to the barrel room. To the left of that was another door, of light oak and unpainted, which gave on to a backyard. Halfway down the left-hand wall a huge fire was burning in a deep recess bricked and lined with benches on which two groups of men older than the others sat supping, spitting and quietly talking. In the centre of the room the air was quite cool despite the fire. I had never before been in so large a drinking house, and I asked John Simon what course the main stream of talk cut out for itself in such a place.

'They are mostly ironworkers here, but they talk little of it. Religion and the lives they lived before they came to Moonlea, God and remembered fields, are the two big topics you'll find on the lips of these men.'

'Why that? I'd have thought they'd be gabbing of iron the livelong day. Neatly snared, the whole damned lot,' I said and walked from group to group, listening intently. What John Simon said was true. I listened in astonishment to the talk of the younger men who, more than the old, seemed to be passionately off on a theological bent. They spoke of the conscience and the soul as if these were prominent vital limbs of the body, liable to active infection, decay, lopping off, healing. In the quick sweep of their sentences was a hard surface of bitterness against the established Church, which they identified with the expanding landowners and charged with ranging itself more and more overtly against the jagged splinters of Nonconformist opinion. From the talk, what little I made sense of, I got at first an impression of mental nakedness which made me creep, a feeling that men who made such a fuss about stitching and thrusting before each other's eyes the banners of their endless soul-doctrines had created a good deal of their own unease, like people coughing so hard in the dark to hide the sense of their own disquietude they land up with no throat to cough with.

'This is a joke,' I said quietly to John Simon. 'These boys

have taken the full weight of the boot. The boot went so far up there is the hint of a leathery look in the lost bewildered stare that comes from their eyes when the word-storm dies down for a moment and lets the full horror of knowing themselves slip back into the old position. The whole boot, and even as they whirl they swarm like ants to find the most honeyed and least hurtful notion of what the hell they might be doing on this earth. Every time the tissue of their clean ancient dignity shrinks an inch they dart off like whippets and come panting back with the bone of some conception of an ultimate heaven between their teeth. It's a joke, John Simon, and I feel like going around this room giving these boys a chuckle apiece.'

'There never was any dignity, clean or ancient, not for these. A lot of them can hardly walk, let alone dart. Many of them have no teeth. Few of them give a damn about heaven. They travel in the wake of other men and are maddened by the sting of other men's contrivances and wishes that swing back like pulled branches into their advancing faces.'

John Simon, as we walked about the room, kept stopping at one or other of the groups. He nodded his head in appreciation of the points raised. I watched him puzzled and remained silent when I found him looking very solemn as a stooped, grey-haired man explained to him some observation that had been made by Mr Bowen, the minister, about the relative value of pedal and total baptism. John Simon stared, friendly, into the old man's face and pouted his lips outwards as he took the exact philosophic weight of the old man's every word. I tapped him on the shoulder as we turned away.

'Who snipped the wick that once made you glow, boy?

Three years ago, you, John Simon, were pagan as a loon, a goat, leaping from day to day and showing nothing more respectful than your rear to the myths of prayerful toil. Yet here I find you pausing to get a headful of these closet matters of personal salvation, looking serious in the face of arguments that would have had you, in the old days, in a dead mental faint at the thought of such terrible panic among men.'

'Look, Alan, this matter of faith is a strip of territory where even a zanie could keep a sure foothold. It's the practice ground where we flex our muscles for the real business of changing the moulds into which we are forced. Today is always a muck of ails, shifts and tasks, a fearsome bit of time to stare at and tackle. A man always hates to make a hostile grab at the fabric of the existence he actually knows because he himself might turn out to be the first pulled thread. But yesterday's beliefs are nice, smooth drumsticks, and they are often brought to tap out reassurance against fears to which we have no answer at all. These people, brought here from a dozen counties, have no common understanding, no common language. They are still frozen and made dumb by the strangeness of their different yesterdays. Men are always shy to say clearly how the dream of freedom really strikes them.'

'So they talk of their souls and temples and sects and at the end of it all you will find a multitude of clear-eyed and clear-minded rebels to do war with the rule of wealth and squalor?'

'War?' He smiled and shook his head from side to side. 'Even to see, wonder and protest, that's a victory.'

'What do we drink here, boy? I'm beginning to feel the heat of that fire.'

42

We approached the serving counter. The door of the barrel room was open. On a stool, on the further side of a great tub, sat a man of forty or more, broad in the body and kindly in his expression. The room had an abundance of shelves on which were placed or hung hams, cheeses, loaves. The man was reading a book, a small brown-covered book. His head and shoulders were hunched over it and John Simon had to knock twice before he got the landlord's attention.

'Sorry, John Simon,' he said as he came towards us, 'the words of that book had me all coiled up. It's a book about the nature of human society and that is a subject that grips the inside of me.'

'This is my friend, Alan Leigh. Alan, this is Abel Jefferies, a thoughtful and reliable man.'

Abel shook me by the hand and went to draw two pots of ale for us. There was something admirably cool and cautious about his movements, and I complimented him on having the will and the stamina to read a book on any such topic as the nature of human society, surrounded as he was by barrels, hams, cheeses and drink-loaded men.

'All is not gross even in this trade,' he said. 'Often, in the long evenings of winter John Simon and the Bannion and Andrews boys used to gather around the fire and talk about the world and our lives on it.'

I leaned my back against the counter and watched, fascinated, the play of flame on the worn wrinkled faces of the old men who sat in the fire recess.

'Must have been very cosy there too,' I said. 'But I remember the day when John Simon Adams would have had all his delight in the swift movement of his body and the sound of my harp. Now he seems to be scratching like a mouse behind a wainscoting of sad private reflections. In those earlier days he was happier, and he can't deny it.'

'He won't want to,' said Abel wiping the counter. 'In some men the winds of joy drop quickly and in their silence all the grieving of earth seems to find an echo. Such a man, I think, is John Simon.'

'One should live to destroy that silence, that pity. The world's sorrow is an awful slut. Give it just one kind look and you'll find it at your door every whipstitch waiting for its sugar or a long caress.'

From outside the front door came a sudden fierce tumult. The door opened and a man wearing a rabbit-skin cap and a yellow kerchief around his neck came shooting in out of the twilight as if he had been kicked. After him came a woman who looked as if it was she who had done the kicking. She would have been about thirty-five and wearing clothes that had seen their best when she was about twenty-five. Her face was the finest lump of tumbledown loveliness I had ever seen. She stood by the door with her arms on her hips and her head flung back, her nostrils dilated almost to breaking and breathing so loud and hard I could hear all the tiny details of its passage even from where I stood. Abel the landlord slipped from behind his counter and made for her.

'Outside, Floss Bennett. I've warned you about coming here before. Where you are, there trouble is, and if it's trouble I want, I'll make my own.'

'Put the bung in, Jefferies,' shouted Floss, and lowered her head, her dull eyes fixed on Abel as he advanced towards her. She looked for a moment as if she were going to charge him. Then she grunted feebly, turned on her heel and slammed the door behind her. Abel came back to join us. As he passed the little man with the rabbit-skin cap who had taken his seat at a table and was mopping his face with his kerchief and taking sips at a friend's tankard, Abel said:

'And you, Oliver, for God's sake stop playing the goat. The next time you come in here bring only the draught. Leave that Floss behind. She's an outhouse of sin itself, that woman, and if you don't give up dickering with her you'll be landing up with the year's largest catch of French Evil and that kerchief will be the only thing holding you together. Why don't the pious join hands in a real snorting decree about that woman and banish her to the very deep darkness under one of the furnaces.'

'What about sitting out the back?' asked John Simon.

'A good idea. It'll be lovely out there at this time.'

Abel called through the barrel room to Mrs Jefferies to come and look after the trade. A sad desultory singing had broken out among one of the groups near the fire.

John Simon led the way through the door that led into the inn's backyard. I was bewitched from the moment I saw it. The yard itself, well-paved and clean, was not large. It ended with the sheer hillside that rose with its rocks formed into cool moist grottoes. On the right a fierce stream cut through and found a channel on the level ground that lay beyond the inn's western wall. Water oozed from each of the little caverns in the hillside barrier. We sat down on two flattish stones. As I drank, my hand trailed in a small puddle that had formed from the ceaseless water-drip from the rocks above. In the sky were massive combs of red and pink.

'That woman,' I said, 'the one who burst in here a minute ago, she looked a mutilated queen. What is her aim in life?'

'That's Floss Bennett. She's as steady an industry in Moonlea as iron, but she works at a slightly lower heat and a bit nearer the floor.'

45

'The heat wouldn't be much lower. She looked ready to erupt.'

'That's it. She's fierce.'

'Didn't I hear one of your friends up on the hillside speak of her?'

'You did. She was mixed up with the death of Sammy Bannion. She gave evidence. Wilfie, Sam's brother, didn't believe a word of what she said. A couple of days after Sam's funeral, she was down at The Leaves drunk. Wilfie went at her like a fiend. He would have beaten her to a pulp if we hadn't stepped in. He tried to make her own up to perjury, to having betrayed Sam. If you could keep your eyes off Wilf and the way anger and sorrow were making the tears stream down his face it was comical to see the way Floss lurched about, her eyes blinking and dafter than usual, wondering what the hell Wilf meant by all this talk of betrayal. Floss is one solid block of interlocking betrayals, and if she decided by a miracle to retract any one of them, her fingers wouldn't know what spot to make for. She's stamped on herself thoroughly.'

Mrs Jefferies, whose eyes were as happy and transparently clear as the water my hand rested in, brought us some more ale and told Abel that a quarrel was starting among the singers who could not agree about the words of the second verse of the song they were trying to sing.

'So they don't know the words of the second verse,' said Abel as he rose to leave us. 'When I get in there there'll be just one word for those quarrellers. Amen and then good night. This is strong ale and some of those boys have a sense of grievance that snoozes cosily through the day and starts to roar at about this time in the evening. I'll be back.' He pointed to the hand I had trailing in the water of the little pool. 'That water from the grottoes is colder than charity, harpist. Take care, if you don't want numb and useless fingers.'

John Simon and I sat for a few moments quietly watching the sky's deepening colours.

'Why?' I asked. 'Why, John Simon?'

'Why what?'

'Why am I so full of questions to ask you that I can hardly bring myself to ask them? Why do you hang around such a place as this, making iron and power for Penbury and misery for yourself. You have the expression of an undertaker at a cheaper funeral. You are up to the brow in shadow. Why did you stay here?'

'Keep your eyes and your mind open, Alan, and you'll soon find the reason. My father took a long time dying when I came down here to bear him company through the last stretch of the road. Most of the time he talked about iron and the wonder of all molten and malleable things. He told me all the secrets of his craft. The only thing in all his life since the day he walked away from my mother up in the North to run into the shape he wanted was that liquid iron. He was mad for it. When he died you were no longer here to take my mind off it. So I found the moulding yards dragging me like a magnet. Deep down I probably had something of the old man's elaborate misery, and it might have been calling for the same cure. So I didn't resist. Penbury liked the skill of my hands, and I liked the job. My father was right. Under the dirt there's a lot of beauty.'

'I bet you missed me.'

'Oh yes, I missed you a lot. Whenever I heard any of the songs you used to play I wondered what curse it was that chained my feet to this place.'

'What was the curse, John Simon? What shackled you, boy, when all the voices of your heart and mind must have been shouting at you to follow the path I had taken. The curse wasn't all your old man, talking iron as he waited to die. Nor was the curse altogether that evangelical notion to make a painless paradise out of Moonlea and sweeten lives made too bitter by this alien hole. What was it, John Simon?'

He leaned his head against the rockface and looked at me gravely.

'You remember you used to say we should keep other people's lives at arm's length?'

'I remember. Now I insist on two arms' lengths. They are full of terrible swamps, other people.'

'That's it. Sucking swamps.'

'Who sucks? Who pulls you? Who are those people up in the cottage? How do you fit into that picture?'

'You never paused long enough to love a woman, Alan. You wouldn't understand.'

'Anything involving you, I'd understand. My feelings about you, John Simon, are subtle and peculiar. Lemuel said you were carrying on with Katherine, that she was a bitch because the lad Davy is her husband. I don't follow this. You don't think simply any more. You've taken to copying the idiot grimaces of the people around you. This Davy is not full weight. He's a nice boy, but childish long after childhood. What does Katherine owe to him? What is there he can do for Katherine? Does she love you?'

'As much as I love her.'

'And that's a lot?'

'It couldn't be more.'

'All right, then. Get away, the two of you. It chimes beautifully with what I came down here to tell you. In the North

48

I've been left a lush little nook in a valley where the sun and the stream sing to each other all the day. I thought of it as a kingdom for two philosophers and poets such as we were meant to be. But I'm willing for any sacrifice to get you out of this eclipse of the moon. You can bring Katherine. Settled?'

'Nothing is ever settled, Alan. Not things like this.'

'I suppose you're thinking of the mother, the sad-looking woman. You don't want to hurt her. You are waiting for this Davy to die. Look, boy, I don't want to say things that are harsh, but I'm blown by a gale of wanting to see you free of this. That Davy'll wear you out. He wasn't picked to ride sorrow and pity like a dragon and that's the thing that kills. He's fitted into the rhythm of the earth, he's a brother to his own cabbage and he'll go his way with ease to be a hundred, and he'll drop you both by the roadside mumbling a short apology because you'll be getting so little after the long wait. Don't think about it. Tell Katherine tonight and we'll thumb our noses at Moonlea from the top of Arthur's Crown in the morning.'

'Nothing is ever settled like that.' He had left his seat on the rock. He was walking about in front of me. 'From outside it's simple. But inside, there's the swamp, the sucking swamp, of other people's helplessness, one's own compassion. Katherine is no bitch. That is one of the many errors that cheese-dweller Lemuel will make in this life. If she were, Moonlea would have seen the back of us before now and not all the childish wondering hurt in the eyes of Davy or the weeping of his mother would have drawn us back. Leave me to it, Alan, and get back to your patch. If it gets unbearable, you'll be seeing me. And about that painless paradise, it's nothing as highblown as that that we want.

We've seen too many lives in Moonlea dyed jet black and soaked with tears to the bone without need. People get skill in suffering and we want to break them of the habit. Six months ago things had reached a head. Penbury seemed to have hardened to the top of his bent and to have the materials for a drastic answer ready to hand, and we were tensed and ready to make the best answer we could. There was some talk of closing down the furnaces until we came to heel and scooping out the less obedient and putting them in gaol or other areas. Penbury came down to the furnaces one morning and we gathered around thinking this was to be the ultimatum. But all he did was stand there looking ill, shaking a bit and saying with something like a sob in his voice how serene things had been in his father's time. Then he fell quiet and since then he has come nowhere near the furnaces. Things have gone on from day to day getting worse in a polite and gradual way. Evictions for rent have eased off. What work there is has been shared around more evenly. But no blow has fallen. It makes me curious and unsettled. I had prophesied doom, a rush of events that would sweep us all to a climax and a solution. This isn't doom. This is a shabby little side street in hell where you might even get to like the sameness and quiet.'

'What's there to wonder at? It means Penbury isn't altogether evil. To be evil from tip to toe takes a lot of practice, and he may have got tired. He may have got as sick of trying to uproot and silence you as you have got making the same old points to him about wages and rent. Men need a change. He wants you all to hold your breath until the gripe-pains or you pass away. There are too many people in this place; when the less patient have had enough of food they can't find, kids they can't feed and rent they can't pay,

50

they'll crawl off and leave Penbury with his kingdom as obedient as before. He knows that, and so should you. He can wait. He doesn't have to stand outside Lemuel's for his bread, throwing a stone in every now and then to hurry the job of civilising Lemuel. His daughter doesn't look as if she will ever keep him awake at night with the hunger-whimpers. He's taller than Arthur's Crown. He's only got to look at the world and it comes to his shape.'

'He might have been banking on the summer.'

'What do you mean, on the summer.'

'He might have been hoping that those who led the protest had had a sickener after last winter and decided to leave Moonlea. He might have thought that most of the people here had got used to the idea of being booted on to the next waterhole. It's useful to have the same lot of people to do all the crawling. They and their kids get into the way of it and that saves a lot of time and training. But hardly anyone left in the course of the summer. This isn't a bad irontown as irontowns go. They left the fields for the furnaces and when the furnaces go cold, what then? The summer's ending and winter will bring all thought of a truce to an end.'

'God above, how can you live in this air, planning and looking forward to conflict as if it were a harvest to be garnered.'

I heard a gentle rapping on the small back window of the inn. John Simon was embedded in his thoughts and heard nothing. I went to the window from which the tapping came and saw, framed in the smoke of the large room, the face of Lemuel the baker. He was going through a broad syllabus of grimaces and gestures and there was a look of anxious urgency hanging from his face as thick and plain as a curtain. I could see he wished me to come inside for a few

51

words with him. John Simon noticed that I had left his side.

'Talking about these things to you makes my tongue feel odd and unsure. Get out of this place.' He raised his voice and looked wonderingly as he saw me stooped down and staring at Lemuel through the window. 'You in Moonlea are like a moth on a treadmill. When I got here some star spat malice and my feet stuck to a clod of resentment and desire. I stay. You'll never understand the key in which these melodies are pitched.'

I walked back slowly to where he sat.

'I wouldn't want to smell the rust on you,' he said.

'I'll take my time. On the other side of that window our little friend Lemuel is gesturing like a madman. He wants to say something to me and by the look of him it's something important.'

'It'll be something ill-flavoured and ominous if I know him. Gesture back to him that he may go to the devil.'

'He's there, boy. Between Moonlea and the shape of his mind, he's finished the course. He's horned and hard as fire-clay. I'll go and see what he has to say. I'll never rest easy if I leave this place with any part of the mystery that has whittled you down to your present stump still unknown. It may help me to fish you out of this lagoon.'

I picked up my pot and went back inside the inn, leaving John Simon still seated on the flat cold rock. The hubbub of voices had been raised by what seemed an octave, and my tender, silence-soaked ears ached at the bay of it. Lemuel stood in a corner, in a shallow recess, looking better informed and more cunning than a man ever should. He lifted his finger to his lips and went sh-sh for several seconds for all the world as if I were the cause of all the racket that was going on in the room.

'Good news, harpist,' he said, putting his mouth to the side of my head, and his speech was organised into short hard gasps that I found unpleasant against my flesh.

'News? The world has given iron notice to quit,' I said, hoping that this pale splinter of a jest would serve to make Lemuel less of a quiver, less full of drama.

'Mr Penbury has heard of you. He wants to see you, hear you.'

'Tomorrow?'

'Oh no. Catch Mr Penbury waiting as long as that. He gets an idea, then, bang, the idea lives. Tonight. Now.'

'What does he want with me?'

'What do you think anybody'd want with a harpist?'

'That's a searching question, boy, but my harp's gone. I told you about it.'

'Do you think,' asked Lemuel winking, 'that Mr Penbury will be worried by such a lack as that? He could buy all the harps in Britain. They tell me he's got a great love of the harp, although he never had the time or chance to practise the art himself.'

'Why all the mystery? The way you looked when you drew my attention was enough to put me off the drink. One would think you had come to ask me to play to a midnight meeting of witches. Why didn't you come out to the backyard and let me know in the normal way. It's lovely and cool out there. Have you seen those grottoes?'

'Never mind about grottoes. It's bad enough that I should come into such a place as this at all. I'll have to explain to Mr Bowen that I was only in here to deliver a message from the Hall. Grottoes, indeed. Besides, I saw you were with John Simon. He's very unreasonable about me. Those rodneys up on the hillside, Andrews and Bannion and those, have filled his mind with a lot of wickedness regarding me. I didn't want to have words with John Simon.'

'All right then. Somehow, I can't explain the ins and outs of it, I had an idea when I came down the side of Arthur's Crown this morning that I might be seeing Mr Penbury.'

'He's a wonderful man.'

'It's a bit late. By the time we walk through Moonlea and up through the big gates of that carriage drive it'll be pitch dark.'

'There's a short cut through the fields. And don't worry about the hour being late for Mr Penbury. There's always light on in the big house long after the rest of Moonlea is in darkness. I told you there was a terrible shortage of music in Moonlea. Doesn't this prove it, being sent for like this?'

'I suppose it does. Wait a minute.' I rejoined John Simon and told him of what Lemuel had said. He raised no objection, seemed, indeed, amused at the prospect of my expedition.

'The door of the cottage will be on the latch when you return. Sure you'll be able to find the way?'

'Like a pigeon. You know me. The only sure things on earth are my feet at night.'

With Lemuel just ahead of me, stared at uncordially by the groups of talking drinking men we left the inn. The shadows were moving down more swiftly now. It had been a long, wonderfully lighted day and I resented the darkness. I felt a tingle of the same resentment in the trees of the copse through which Lemuel led me. We took a path through fields that lay at the back of Moonlea's main, straight street. As we walked, Lemuel spoke to me of Isabella and what a good woman she was. There was a tremble in his voice and I did not have the heart to ask what the sly and winking terror

54

was that seemed to be camping in the lives of him and Isabella, why their nerves seemed to be picking their way along a taut, cutting wire. I halted in my swift walk and picked up a grass stem for suck and tasted the cold dew of it on my mouth, sweet.

The rough earth of the fields ended. We entered another thick clump of trees, silver birch, their faint gleam perceptible in the dark. Beyond the trees a downward roll of beautiful turf.

'Isn't it lovely?' asked Lemuel, stooping down and dragging his hand over the smooth close-cut surface. 'Isn't it like a mat?'

'It's fine. Somebody's handled this bit of mountain like a lover.'

I stopped. The house of the Penburys was about fifty yards in front of me, a cool, large house, built in light-coloured stone, shielded and curtained from the sight of most of Moonlea by another screen of trees to the south. It was a breathtaking house. To come upon it suddenly out of the trees was to be filled with the sensation of singing. The only sound I heard at that moment was the wind in the branches, the panting of Lemuel winded by keeping pace with me and half sobbing with wonder and praise as he kept his right arm outstretched towards the mansion. Then I turned my eyes to the right, to the group of cottages, at a fair distance now, in which John Simon had elected to live. In the cottage windows dim lights were coming into sight. I looked too at the higher hills from which the trees, sisters to those that Penbury now hugged to his chest like chain mail, had been torn and carted down to give heat to his furnaces.

'Come on,' I said, and we continued on our way across the fresh, smooth, noiseless lawn.

The side of the house which faced us was skirted by gardens in the middle of which stood a tall fountain. Between the gardens and the broad windows was an ornamented terrace. The window nearest us was brilliantly lit. A servant was drawing the curtains. She was having some difficulty and was pulling hard at the thick, heavy crimson fabric. The light rested on the curtain cloth with a greedy relish. At the door of the room, clear to my view and dressed in a white gown from which lace gushed, was the girl whom I had seen in the glen, the daughter of Penbury, Helen, the iced and remote person who had spoken without love of John Simon Adams.

Lemuel touched my arm and made a low frightened sound. I seemed to have strayed from the path he wished me to follow, for that lighted room and the lace-bound lady who still stood giving directions to the servant drew my eyes. We branched leftwards. Lemuel stopped at a small, green-painted door. The side of the house at which we now stood had none of the bulging majesty of the sides that faced north and south, especially of the southern wall with its snow-white pillars facing down into Moonlea. The door was opened by a man-servant dressed in some kind of blue uniform with white buttons which filled me with surprise but which, judging by the unceasing smile on his face, filled him with nothing but pleasure. I felt a need to ask this man what activity on earth could justify such a turn-out as he had levered his body into in this way. Lemuel whispered to the servant, filling the place with mystery, and I could see from the easy way in which Lemuel got on tiptoe and spoke directly into the inside of the uniformed man's head that nine-tenths of his life was carried on on a plane barely higher than a wink or a hiss.

When Lemuel had done explaining he turned to me and said: 'This is my friend, Jabez. He is the butler of Mr Penbury.'

I told Jabez that he was the first butler I had ever met and I quietly prayed, thinking of that little private solitude in the North where even the moles had a lot of carefree independence, that he would be the last. He was not a bad man and his smile would be a help on nights of desolation but he was purple in the face with the urge to be deferring to somebody, to be slipping his whole life into some smooth joint of subordination and that bit at me.

Jabez took me to the kitchen. He sat at a table at which a woman-servant, as gnawed and dour as Jabez was replete and expansive, was already making a meal. She gave us a nod and no more. Jabez ordered her to get three glasses of ale and she obeyed, walking with tiny strides and not moving her arms. Lemuel whispered to me that this woman, Agnes, modelled her walk on that of the late Mrs Penbury who, said Lemuel, had been full of grace. Agnes poured out our ale with a pout of unwillingness and returned to her meat.

'The night is drawing on, Jabez,' said Lemuel, 'and Mrs Stevens gets nervous of being left alone too long. When will Mr Penbury see the harpist?'

'In a moment. The Reverend Mr Purley and the Reverend Mr Bowen, together with their good ladies, of course, have been to dinner with us tonight. The master was in excellent mood over the wine, almost his old self.'

'What was he up to?' I asked, a stranger to these kinds of performance.

Jabez gave me a look that was full of reproof and I fell back among the goats. Lemuel gave me a little warning tap beneath the table telling me to keep my lips tight over my ale until I had groped my way into a surer knowledge of this medium. The woman Agnes was staring at me with disgust and I could feel that if she had had me on her plate, instead of all that baked meat, she would not have needed spices to push it down.

'The reverend gentlemen,' went on Jabez, 'were dismayed by the licence and freedom that are gaining ground in the county. They tried to persuade Mr Penbury that real danger might arise from the free preachers.'

'Who are they?' I asked, thinking that with these direct, fact-finding queries I was on safe ground.

'Men who go from town to town putting forth doctrines of bitterness and gall.'

'What are they bitter about?'

'Their own lack of worldly goods in the main, I should venture.'

'Too true,' said Lemuel admiringly. 'You've hit the nail right on the head there, Jabez.'

'Bitter about what?' I said again.

'Mostly about the churches and chapels when they do manage to get down to brass tacks, which is rare. They say that the churches and chapels are nothing more than a mouthpiece for Mammon. So they do their talking in solitary, out-of-the-way places and whenever a group collects to listen they cease to speak after the group has come to number five for they say that all men who can stand and listen to anyone at all in bigger groups than that must be fools and slaves.'

'There seems to be a fair ration of moony light in the notions of those boys,' I said, talking into my raised glass.

'Mr Bowen says the free preachers are not a whit better than the men who had their ears clipped for atheism and sedition in a more robust age.'

'What did Mr Penbury say to that? I bet he offered Mr Bowen the clippers.'

'He told the reverend gentlemen that as messengers of God, which is what they are, they should not shelter behind the skirts of the Church or even behind those who are benefactors of the faith, but to go out and do battle with the free preachers and confound them in their own rebellious language.' Jabez started laughing into his sleeve, laughing with force, his skin rapidly darkening and matching the colour of his coat. 'You should have seen them. You really should have seen them. They both sat there too amazed to drink their wine, pale and shaken to their very foundation. But it'll do them good. A few more broadsides like that from the master and something will surely be done to smoke such sullen foxes as that Eddie Parr and his friends from their holes.' Jabez's laughter died away as he thought of this Eddie Parr. Then he started to chuckle once again. 'Oh yes, Mr Stevens, the master had them properly shaken.'

Lemuel joined Jabez in his laughter, letting out a few dutiful guffaws that made the air of the small kitchen ugly and caused Agnes to look at us all as if we were a trio of maniacs. I looked out of the kitchen window and watched the hillside which was lightening under a fast rising moon. I was beginning to feel sorry that I had ever listened to Lemuel, ever left John Simon and that cool thoughtful rockface at the back of The Leaves After the Rain. The company of these people was affecting me like a pillow tied around the head.

'And are they still here, these ministers, being shaken?' I asked. 'I'm tired. I crossed a couple of mountains today, Jabez, and about a half of me is sleeping like a log already.'

A door opened in some other part of the house, not far from the kitchen. A bell rang not a yard away from me, frightening me with its cruel penetrating scream. Jabez jumped to his feet, pulling a handkerchief across his beer-flecked mouth and tugging his uniform smooth.

'That will be the ladies and gentlemen leaving,' he said, and made for the door.

'Don't be too long about it, Jabez,' I told him, 'or your master will be forgetting about me and nipping off to bed. I don't fancy a whole night in this kitchen with Agnes.'

'Don't worry about that,' said Jabez with a chuckle and a wink at Lemuel, 'we know the master's weaknesses, don't we, Lemuel?'

'Oh yes, we do,' said Lemuel.

'Of course we do,' said Jabez with a smile as thick as his face, as if this should reassure me utterly. He went through the door.

'Weaknesses?' I said, and leaned towards Lemuel. 'Look, Stevens, help me. He knows. You know. But I am one of today's recruits. What weakness? What is the matter with Penbury that makes him so careless about bed?'

Lemuel pushed his lips once again against my ear.

'He's a very poor sleeper. He's had a lot of worry. They tell me he sleeps hardly at all.'

'So he passes it on. If he doesn't hurry with whatever he wants to say to me he'll be getting his responses in snores. I'm all in.'

A carriage drove along the gravel drive in front of the house. I heard voices say 'Good night,' and whatever else it is that people who live with a sense of space and gracious-ness and high self-esteem say to each other on moonlit gravel drives. My own senses were dull with tiredness and perplexity, but from across the hallway I could hear the voice of the girl, Helen, clear, self-consciously incisive, as if she were putting the whole night in its shrinking obscure place. I hoped that when Jabez came for me and took me out of that room he would lead me to whatever place she was in. I wished to see her close with all that blown wind of lace about her shoulders, throwing her eyes into an even colder grey. And I wanted her too to see me, to find from her face if she saw anything different in me now that I had seen and talked to John Simon and the other folk whose shadowed being he wore upon himself like a cloak. And I wanted, even if only by a quick side-glance, to give her a clue to the prickly alienness I felt in being beneath her roof, and there-fore nearer to what passed for a heart in Moonlea, a heart of whose full nature my fingers which were the liveliest thing about me had a vivid and revolting premonition.

The noise of carriage wheels died away. There was a quick sound of footsteps on the wooden floor blocks outside. Jabez poked his head around the kitchen door and beckoned to me.

A short corridor, heavy with the smell of conserved meats and fruits from small rooms on either side, led into a broad hallway. It had a rich oaken glow and I was startled when the loud tread of my feet suddenly became quiet as death on a carpet that made my feet marvel. Jabez tittered at my surprise, and I told him with annoyance but softly that if he came with me to an open mountain I could show him a thing or two that would curdle his great smug guts. He sh-sh'd me. There was no one in the hallway. I had the feeling that there might be someone else whom I could not see, but I have that feeling often in enclosed places, and on second thought I saw no reason why the girl Helen or anybody else should

61

want to be peering at me through a spyhole. She, I was sure from what I had seen of her that morning, would have been the sort who, had she known I was there at all, would have come right out into the hallway, glad to be framed against its whole enchanting contrivance of gleaming beauty in glass, wood and colour, and she would have told me in tones so clear an idiot ten miles away could have followed them, how small a total of significance my bones and limbs, my desires and my music, made.

We stopped at a door at the end of the hallway. It was carefully bordered with green baize. Jabez knocked and I distinctly heard the voice which told us to come in. We entered. The room was in darkness and after the full light of the kitchen and hallway I wanted to protest against the cruel joke of this unexpected shadow into which Jabez was pushing me with a strong pressure of his hand.

The broadening moonlight was spilling over into the room from a big window whose curtains had been drawn back. Near the window, a man was sitting, in a short-backed chair, sitting upright and as if in a state of unusual tension. He pointed with his arm, saying nothing, and Jabez led me to a chair, a velvet, yielding thing, on which I sat myself. I resisted the chair's deep softness and arranged myself with prim stiffness on the lip of the seat, uneasy and prepared to move swiftly if this gloomy charade should become too much for me.

From where I sat I could now see the profile of the man who had summoned me. I soon found my eyes brushing aside the need for lamps. He wore a suit of black, shiny material that took the moonlight well. Under his chin bulged the folds of a large cravat which made me feel as I had felt when beholding Penbury's columns for the first time, that this man lived in a high noon of self-consciousness. I had expected his face to be long and severe, but it was broad, soft-lined, dark, the eyes deep and still. He put me oddly in mind of John Simon Adams, and when he spoke there was something of John Simon in his tones, although in the voice of this man one heard the undertone of vigilant sympathy often being brushed aside by a bristling impatience as if he had found too often a morbid slowness in time and men. His hands on the arms of the chair were not steady, giving a hint of depletion and terrible fatigue within his body.

'I am sorry to have made this call upon your time so late, harpist. It was not considerate of me.'

'I was idle, sipping ale; but talking to the mighty, in the quiet dark, that's new to me, but not unwelcome.'

'Are you a poet?'

'No. I have no acidy sickness in the heart from which the stuff could sprout. I eat and sleep as fixedly as a dog. Mostly I am blithe and daft in my ways, I am glad to say.'

'You harp well?'

'Not badly.'

'I've heard you wove some pretty spells in the villages of the North.'

'They did their own weaving. My harp only gave them the beat. In some of those villages life has a thin and itching skin and can do with a spell or two. I bring great ease to the sorrowful for I play directly to them, for them. Doing anything directly for the sorrowful brings them great ease for the poor sods are numb and solitary.'

'Could you bring great ease to the sleepless, harpist?'

'I've seen boys go out like logs after two tunes from me. But they'd mostly done a whole day of dragging heavy wood or ploughing heavy fields and their mood was on the watch for lullabies. I don't know how it would work with you. Have you a grief, Mr Penbury?'

'Not exactly. The inside of my head has been ravaged by too much thinking. The light has been on too long inside me. I'm full of whitewashed horrible cavities of awareness. That's why at the fall of night, I like sitting here in an unlighted room. Perhaps the darkness will lend me its recipe for stupor.'

'I bet there's a lot about Moonlea for thought to grow thick in, to chew great dells of sadness in the soft part of one's thinking.'

'Are you a free preacher, harpist?'

'I'm no sort of preacher. I'm a legate from the goats. I've come briefly over the mountains and I sit here full of wonder at the strange changes that can come over places and men.'

'Stick to the plucking of strings, harpist. When you talk of change, you dive into a tricky current.'

'For me there are no currents. The water of my being is smooth, even, and nowhere deep save at the rarer points of pity. It's you who are the tricky one. I never lured hungry fish from distant streams to gasp and shrivel in the black ponds of my designing.'

'You are lucky, harpist, lucky to lie between and safe from the torments of too little and too much knowing for they are mutually baleful and must for ever be molesting each other. You are lucky to have found a haven of dependable ecstasy, for mobility and cheap art are golden privileges in an age when man is sizing up the long dirty job of finishing his career as a starveling and a fool. I don't suppose you know much about the brain of man, harpist.'

'Not much. I told you. Eat and sleep like a dog.'

'It's a handsome, horrible thing.' He leaned over towards

me and I could tell by his voice that he was drawing the cork out of a long, anxious fermentation inside his head. I made no move to remind him of the harp. The prongs of my own curiosity held me still. 'It would like to be calm but it is shaken grey and sick by savage angers, for it plays fantastically with the idea of worrying all stupid and tolerated hungers from their lice-holes and outlawing them from the earth. There will be days in its journey of crazy leaps and crawls when it will seem inscrutable and ruthless, festooned with stunted lives and quaking bellies, for it can work freely to its end only when a great heat of change and movement has been wrought, when the stuff of living and feeling can be made to run into another mould. That's how it was at the beginning, the very beginning, you must have heard about that, harpist, with all things molten and awaiting shape. Then it sees the idiot grin of men and women willing the counter-coldness of obstinacy and death, clogging the stream of change and betterment for lifetimes on end. And this stupendous music of man's aim to make his unique genius the infallible sculptor of a controlled and kindlier universe sinks to a shabby moan while some feeble life-sickened loon makes an epic of pity about a few sores on the breast of Moonlea and cries for justice at the sight of a few ill-adjusted oafs who are equally incompetent to labour in field or foundry, who leak into life and are never less than half fluid. Not storm, nor pain nor death, but the plain filthy improvident helplessness of the world's unfit who seem to find some sense of distinction in being kicked or starved, that's the enemy. Man's brain will devise new weapons of power and authority against nature with her puking jests of flinty soil and useless minds. As the pattern of man's new power becomes plainer, harpist, men like you will be a

65

dwindling pack of pathetic and restless freaks. Man will acquire a wonderful serenity from fulfilled wisdom, from absolute power to dictate conditions to life. He must stop running in circles, sniffing his mind back into a noose of dead, irrecoverable loves and fears, shrieking when he finds his eyes staring into the anus of his mouldering brevity. It's to that kind of thinking the name of music should be given, harpist, not to the feeble roaming of your hands on strings.... A legate from the goats, is that what you said?'

'That's what I said. And they send you, through me, their apologies that they won't be making the whole of the trip to glory with you. Your visions are too sharp for the kidneys.'

He got slowly up from his chair, groaning in a restrained and private way. He stood with his back to me. His hands strummed against the leaded panes, and I did not blame him for doing that; you could almost hear sleep protesting and giving up the ghost inside his skull, before the onrush of his sharp-beaked dreams which swept its corridors clean of all the small friendly private torpors of which I had always been a partisan, which had given a tolerable numbness to most of my days. But some gigantic failure and breakdown was nosing about that man like a wolf, trying out his entrails for taste and softness before settling down for the last meal of the day. What it was in its details I did not know, but I could not have sensed its presence more acutely if the thing had been rubbing against my leg and asking me if I judged Penbury fit for the kill.

'In the meantime,' he said, 'my sleep is in tatters. One hour, two hours a night, no more. My head aches by day as if every thought were pinning an everlasting brooch. Doctors have looked at me, but the thing inside me upon which they normally rely to exchange reasons and words of encouragement is no longer present. Would you consent to play for me, harpist, at any time I requested?'

'I have no harp. I lost mine.'

'There's a harp in the corner. The moonlight's on it. Turn around and you will see it clearly. A finer one than ever you had. It's yours for the asking.'

'It's good. Its strings gleam.'

'Try it.'

I went and stood by the harp and ran my fingers over its strings. They answered my hands more swiftly and richly than any harp I had touched before.

'There are certain songs,' said Penbury, 'songs that have come with me from the beginning and are like the railing of the fence that marks my limits of feeling. Some you might know, others I could hum to you and you could learn. The sound of them at night might turn over a lot of old soil in my mind and the fresh morning smell of it might put a spell on the rigid awakened thing inside me that keeps me at full stretch.'

'You hum those tunes to me and my ear will catch them straightaway as in a net. And played on that harp, life will be mostly sleep.'

'There's one in particular, "When will sadness have an end"; do you know that? All the tranquillity of the days before my father passed the iron mania on to me is in that song. It goes like this.'

He began to hum in an urgent way and he walked towards me. It was like a hundred other songs I knew, a downright affair with a recurrent four-note phrase for which even the least subtle ear could foresee the harmonies. It would not have surprised me if Penbury had made up this particular item himself to dignify the crudeness of some common flat-footed regret. I yawned and moved away from the harp.

'Not tonight, please, Mr Penbury. When I'm dead I'll feel less active than I do now, but I'm not too sure about that. I'd like to go.'

'When I send for you, you'll come,' he said. All the near-hysterical sloppiness of tone with which he had talked to me about those songs had gone now. 'The payment will be adequate.'

I made no quick reply. I stood leaning hard against the chair, my head full of the soft stuff of half-sleep. The tone with which the man had just spoken to me had opened a beak of anger in me. The whole existence of this man was frighteningly opaque to me. He had made for himself, and his daughter too, a ridge of desolate and satisfying contempt. He had long reduced all the world that was not himself and his privately stamped longings to silence. He had never known, as I had, the great universe of significant sounds that can be heard in the quiet endurance of the oppressed and unassertive, I had a wish to tell him of the whole rustling undergrowth of sadness and compassion through which I had stooped my days and nights in company with the village folk. But to any such talk he would have been dead as a post. He would have said that I was lucky to have had the privilege of staring only at the simple rearside of life and he would not have followed my logic an inch if I had told him that it was precisely him and his contrivances that I saw when I did this staring. So, for those moments, I was silent. In a small field of me there was an urge to take that lovely harp which seemed to be smiling at the promise of new and less vagrant ways of life and drape it over his head in the hope that it would make a noise loud enough, bitterly false enough, to give him an idea of the crass discord

68

his thoughts had made when he poured them into my mind. I marvelled at the genius of effort that had laboured the ground of difference between Penbury and myself. I was glad the lamps in the room had not been lit. It would have been shocking to see the whole body of what was incommunicable between us cock its ears and scratch behind them.

'All right then,' I said, 'a couple of weeks won't kill me. I had meant to be here a day, no more. I wished to drag a friend of mine out of your smoke-pall. But he lies anchored to a solid rock of earnest toil, love and God knows what. The trip was worthwhile if only for the sake of feeling much less puzzled when I get back home.'

'You mean Adams?' He tried to make his voice sound as little concerned as possible.

'John Simon Adams. That's right. Stevens told you.'

'He did. And when he told me that your mission in Moonlea was to lead this stupid and short-sighted nuisance to the North I was glad. I would have been willing to pay you a bonus on every yard you managed to remove him from Moonlea. I was glad that away from here, in the sort of wilderness of which you appear to be the mayor, he might have found a greater composure than he has known here. John Simon Adams has intelligence without direction. His hands know iron and its ways as well as mine, but he whirls without cease on a curious windmill of mercy and revolt. Something is out of tune in the man and I would have been glad to see him at peace. I would like to see all men at peace. Then it struck me that the earth is all one to John Simon Adams. There is no part of it that would cause him to smart or smile more or less than another. Everywhere would be for him the rock on which he would wish to break his fists. If he wants me for his rock, he's welcome. Why in God's name

69

should he be like that?'

'I don't know. I find him a stranger to me after these years.'

'I wish I could keep the fellow out of my mind. This weariness gives a painful edge to my wonder. I'll be glad when you harp me into a long, fuzzy, emotional doze.'

'I'll make it a deep cosy one, Mr Penbury. I too like to see men at peace.'

'Thank you, harpist. And there was another suggestion that Mr Bowen made. Mr Bowen is a divine of the town, a man who might even promote a fast rapture in you. He says that too many of the people walk the streets of an evening in melancholy idleness, that their talk is intemperate and apt to make a mountain of gloom out of a molehill of grievance, simply because they lack a little sweetness in their recreation. So perhaps with you to give them the measure on your harp you might persuade them to sing and dance their way into a forgetful jollity.'

'That is a handy programme, Mr Penbury. I'm against gloom, and it is good of Mr Bowen to be finding these recipes for dissolving it. Between getting you drowsy and keeping the boys bright I should have time for one short nap a week. I don't mind though. Before I go back to the mountains I'd like to have a full meal of the games that power, hatred and hunger are playing with each other's skulls among these valleys. That'll be all the dose I'll need until I die.'

'Good night, harpist.'

In the hallway, Jabez wearing a black top coat was waiting for me with a lantern.

'I'll take you to the bottom of the drive,' he said. 'From there the road is easy.'

'No need,' I said, looking out into the moonlight. 'This light is as good as day. So long, Jabez.'

The door closed behind me. I started my walk down the avenue with its surface of small slipping stones which were strange and uncomfortable to my feet. When I was about fifty yards away from the house I heard the door through which I had left open again. I looked back. In the deeper shadow of the doorway was the girl Helen. The whiteness of her face and dress was vivid. She stood quite still. I waved my hand. A current of desire moved downward from my brain but gave up somewhere near the stomach, finding the journey bleak and arduous. I kept on walking.

Making my way up the hillside on which stood the cottage of John Simon, I made out the light in the rear portion of it. I was content to feel my body move slowly through the moonlight. My head was no longer bothered by thoughts of Penbury. The rhythm of my legs working against the gradient had coaxed the whole strange notion of the man out of me. I found John Simon waiting for me outside the cottage. He was smoking his pipe and I could tell by the way he looked at me that he was curious to know what had gone on between myself and the ironmaster. But I did not wish to stand there talking and he led me into the low-roofed annexe at the back of the cottage. A candle burned on the window ledge. In the annexe was a crudely made bed big enough for two people. On it were a thin mattress, a flannel blanket, and a black-and-red overlay so thick and rough to the touch it made all my nerves bend over and moan. A few times I cracked my head against the ceiling as I twisted clumsily over the job of undressing. The roof was feeble and seemed to yield at a touch. Two or three more tries and I knew my scalp would be out beneath the stars. I lay down at the side

71

of John Simon. He stretched his arm out to stifle the candle. I could hear the distinct notes of other people's breathing come from the main part of the building.

'What did he say?' asked John Simon.

'I couldn't be sure. His thoughts got thicker as my ears got narrower. This place is raving and no mistake. He talked about the brain of man. It seems as if he is a busy contributor to this brain and he and it are out to make a lot of changes. By the time he finishes there'll be no dirt or daftness. The state of Moonlea and the groans of such boys as you don't worry him at all. His vision is too broad to be held within so narrow a field. He sees ages beyond Moonlea and he tried so hard to drag me behind the telescope my eyes nearly fell out. He wants you people to stay molten so that he can pour you all into some kind of golden bucket where your sores will drop off and you will be clean enough to march up the aisle for a marriage of great bliss with Penbury and his brethren of the bulging dreams. But Moonlea and the fizzing of fussy wrath in the hearts of such men as you, John Simon, they could be flies on another planet for all he cares. To talk such stuff as that, a man has to be very sick and terrified. At what point did the life of this man go down the wrong lane?'

'I don't know. But he's lucky. That's heaven as I see it, never to have the thought of other people's lives drip blood upon your face, to be utterly content with what one has done, to be one's own infallible idol, to plough, harrow and harvest a mass of folk as if they were a field, to have willing hands make hard and straight a path for all your desires.'

'He says he's a rock and will you please stop breaking your fists against him. He wants all men to be at peace and is as little so as you. I'm to be his hired lullaby, and I'm to

72

keep the people reeling around the maypole until they get so giddy they won't give him any thought or Mr Bowen any lip. What kind of bloody loon drew the plans for this place?'

John Simon might have given a reply for as I glanced at him in lowering my head to its sleeping position I saw that his eyes were fixed on the window recess and that they were wide open and pensive. But I heard nothing for it was as if a trapdoor had opened beneath my senses and I slipped into a coma of excellent cut.

5

The next morning I awoke late. The tiny chamber in which I had slept was lit with a flood of sun. The place was quiet and still. The only sound I could hear was the deep crooning of Mrs Brier who was at some task in the kitchen and the beat of wet cloth on stone from Katherine who was washing in the stream that ran at the bottom of the garden.

Mrs Brier smiled as I came into the kitchen and said how much better I looked after my long sleep now that the wildness had gone from my eyes.

'Wildness? Did I look wild then?'

'It was the tiredness, no doubt, and the wandering from place to place.'

She gave me a heavy breakfast of pork and eggs and nettle beer.

'Where's your son?' I asked, 'and John Simon?'

'John Simon went early to the foundry. A new order has come in for the great railing that is being put around the park of Lord Plimmon. Davy has gone to the next valley where there is some work of timber-hauling on hand. It is the kind of work the lad understands and does with pleasure.'

'He doesn't like the furnaces?'

'He's tried. But always he's distracted and sad after an hour or so in the dirt and heat and home he comes. Mr Radcliffe, that is the manager for Mr Penbury, he told Davy to stay away. Now he does.'

I wanted to ask her more questions about Davy and John Simon, but I could tell from the slant of her body as she leaned over the table doing her repairs that there would be no delight for her in answering my questions.

I left the cottage and made my way down the valley. I was in a mood for snaring something, for being shrewd and purposeful. I also thought it would be good to contribute a gift of fresh fish and a few hares to the larder of Mrs Brier and Katherine from which I would be drawing during my stay. A mile away from Moonlea I met the little man, Oliver, whom I had seen wearing a yellow kerchief the night before at The Leaves After the Rain. I asked him if he could direct me to some stretch of water suitable for taking a trout or two. He pointed to a tributary valley which opened to the west a furlong away. 'There,' he said, 'the fish are closer than my fingers and fat as lard. And in the spinneys the sweetest hares God ever made for jugging.'

Then Oliver began to grin as if I had just been let into the best of jests. At first I thought that being so small a man he had been driven off his mental rail in the course of frolics with such great wantons as that woman Floss Bennett in whose company I had seen him when he entered the tavern. But the grin on his face continued long after I had fixed him with the grim stare I always used on those whose conduct I considered a bit out of plumb.

'What's funny about that, Oliver? Let your mind speak out, boy.'

'You'll find out; I'll wait here until you come out of the valley. You'll be a sight, honest to God.' He started to laugh, and I could see that a good half of Oliver's wit was off the string and in no mood to return even at its master's whistle.

'Don't stand there looking so foolish, Oliver. What's the secret?'

'The river in that cleft shimmers like silver and it is guarded like silver. That cleft is the heart of Lord Plimmon's kingdom.'

'Plimmon? What's he king of?'

'Many mountains, many fields. He's a great scourge for poachers.'

'Poachers?' It took me a whole minute to get the concept behind that word in full view. 'You mean he's got a kind of personal brand on all the creatures in his streams and woods?'

'Oh yes. And he wants it respected too. He and Penbury are Justices, and they see to it between them that the ironworkers get their food from iron alone. In the old days a man could live easy, but Plimmon and Penbury are cutting some mighty capers and they are growing taller than the hills. It's hard for a man to get out of sight of them, to fill his bag and draw his breath in the old easy way. There's many a lad in Tudbury Gaol or over the sea for forgetting that the old days are done for.'

'See you when I get back,' I said, and left Oliver to his mumbling. 'Ale and women have reduced your guts, friend. Your talk sounds moonstruck to me. Smoke and Penbury have you all bewitched.'

I made my way through a thinned belt of trees. I reached the entrance of the cleft. It was about a quarter mile deep. At its head a river gap had sliced the left-hand slope. On the right the hillside rose in three deep tiers and on the second of these stood the huge new dwelling of Lord Plimmon. It made Penbury's mansion seem a dingy warren by contrast, and it was clear to me that the men who had their hatchets

76

out among those hills and had their hearts sick with the need to possess were taking their presence on earth very earnestly. They were taking root like oaks. I walked alongside the brilliant stainless stream in which, according to Oliver, I would find my fish.

The sun mounted. I made my way to a spot where the river ran through a dense clump of elm. I lay down flat at the water's edge, my fingers searching delicately beneath the stones on the stream's bed for trout to be tickled and raised. I had two fish by my side, not big but eatable, when I heard two men speaking about ten yards behind me. A fringe of bushes stood between me and them, screening me. I did not stir, not altogether because I did not wish to be found by them, but because I was absorbed in the tranquillising job of dipping my arms with a cool clear purpose into the clear, cool water.

'You are sure you saw him come towards these trees?' asked one of the men.

'Why should I fancy it?' said the other, a rougher, deeper voice. 'Lord Plimmon won't have much left to call his own if all his keepers are as slow and soft as you. You must be blind as a bat not to have seen him. I bet he's emptying the stream under our very noses.'

'I don't want to hear talk like that from you, Bledgely. I don't exactly know what your business is here. You've been here two days and if the steward hadn't told me you were to be looked after I'd have sent you packing before now. I don't like your tone and I don't like your manner. And if you don't keep a respectful tongue in your head there'll be trouble.'

'All right, Mr Wedmore. No offence.' The voice's rasp had put on a wrapper of servility.

I felt curious about the men. I pulled down an arm of the

bush nearest me; I peeped through. The man with the lighter voice was of average height and powerful build. His companion, Bledgely, drew my eyes more strongly. He was a foot taller than Wedmore, as broad again, his hair was black and stiff in a way that made one think each bristle had been driven separately and without his feeling it into his head. His brow did not even make a struggle to appear. His face was as frankly cruel as a shark's. His right hand was mutilated; several of the fingers were missing, and the stumps, which I saw quite clearly as he edged nearer to the bush behind which I hid, looked harder than steel. Both men carried heavy sticks with which they beat the bushes. The dust dislodged settled on my face and I growled softly to ease the irritation at the back of my throat. The branches were torn apart and in a flash Bledgely's stick had crashed down on my shoulders making me scream with rage, shock and agony. I jumped to my feet, drawing my boot across his legs, then driving my head by instinct into his middle. He drew back with a gasp, showing his dark, spoiled teeth, bracing his arms for the blow that was to drive me inches into the ground. But Wedmore jumped to his side and pulled at his weapon arm.

'Enough of that,' he said. 'Get off, you. This is Lord Plimmon's estate. Off with you as fast as you can, and if I catch you at the same game again it'll be the stick and a trip up to the Hall for charges.'

I drew my hand across my aching shoulder. I kneeled down, taking a bit of time and pouring a handful of water over the spot where the stick had landed and which was feeling pulped. As I did, the man Bledgely stepped forward and made a sound that was exactly like the first part of a loud bark. My hatred of the man was already a mature and

78

confident thing, darkening in me like gangrene, horrible, irrepressible. I addressed myself to Wedmore who had a hint of cleanliness and humanity about him. 'I am a wanderer,' I said. 'I have no intention of letting your regulations snare my leg. I am new to this custom of standing guard like mad dogs over bits of metal and bits of earth. I can see you have no wish to stand there and argue about it. So this is Lord Plimmon's land. If he bought it, no part of the money was paid to me nor would I have willed the sale. If he fought for it I was not here to see the fighting. Count me out of the agreement. I'm glad to see you two standing there so quietly. I've had a lot of talking done to me since I arrived here, so I'm grateful for the chance to be making this statement. When I want to leave here, I'll go in my own time, and I won't need to be helped.'

There was no more debate. Wedmore made a gesture as if slipping Bledgely off the leash. They both came at me and after a short flurry on my part which had little significance and in which the face of Bledgely became portentously distinct, I lay down once again on the river bank but not this time to fish, for I was cold and inert as one of the catch. I thought as I fell that for me to be butchered by such a sample of barbarian as Bledgely would be a sore defeat for all the harpists of the world.

When I became conscious I was up on a hillside having my face bathed by John Simon's neighbour, the large slow-voiced Lewis Andrews. Below me was the beautiful floor of the cleft in which I had done my fishing and my falling, trees grouped as if in conscious design, the stream and, magnificent on its second tier, Plimmon's junior palace.

'Who tried to mince you, Alan?' asked Lewis.

'Two keepers. I tickled a couple of trout and they did as

79

much for me but with less art.'

'Do you remember the look of them?'

'Their look, their names and their cudgels, all bitten in here.' I tapped my head with what must have been an idiot expression for Lewis looked at me with real concern. 'There was a shortish man, Wedmore, of whom I expected better things. And a giant, Bledgely, who doesn't wait for full moons to be a werewolf.'

'Wedmore I've heard of, but Bledgely's a stranger.'

'I heard Wedmore say he was. All I know about him is that he enjoys beating people out of shape. Oh, and another thing, he didn't have all the fingers on his right hand.'

'The right hand?'

'That's it.' I moved my jaw gingerly. It felt as if it were a new one, just fitted on and still very strange to my face. 'That reminds me, Lewis: didn't Bannion say something about a great hound of a man with an incomplete hand who went about with Lemuel just before Sammy landed up dead on the mountain?'

'That's what he said. So Bledgely's the name, is it? At whom will Penbury point him this time?'

'You believe what Bannion said then?'

'Why not? Yesterday, at this time, harpist, would you have believed that for taking a couple of trout from a stream that two men speaking your own language would come upon you as if you had committed some crime against the Holy Ghost and leave you for dead?'

'Any sign of the fish? I'd like something for my pains.'

'Not a trace.'

'How did you come along?'

'Mrs Brier told me you had started out in this direction. Then I met Little Oliver and he told me you had come into the cleft. He thought that was a great joke.'

'He told me it had its funny side, but I'm only seeing it now.'

'Little Oliver is not plumb in the head. But I could have told you the sort of welcome you were to expect in this area. Plimmon has been spouting warnings against trespassers and thieves as a volcano does ash.'

'If Little Oliver is as you say, then he suits Moonlea. Wisdom would be a wasting disease here. Why the hell didn't I ask that drover to do as much for me as he did for my harp? Then I too could have stayed decently quiet and mutilated on the side of that lake.' I stood up slowly, groaning to mitigate the heavy press of anger and humiliation on my mind. My eyes travelled up and down the valley.

'It's quite a jewel this Lord Plimmon is cutting for himself here. I bet he would stand to see a lot of people made into manure to keep this garden fair.'

From down the valley came the sound of dogs barking and horses galloping.

'That's Bledgely,' I said. 'He barks like that but on a lower key.'

Along the narrow road that led up the cleft towards the Plimmon mansion came the hound pack followed by the horsemen and horsewomen in their coats of red and black, riding their horses at an easy gallop. Several of the leading hounds still full of the urge to be pleasing Plimmon by putting their teeth into something swerved off the path towards the point of the hillside where we were sitting. Lewis pulled me down out of sight in the ferns and a rider shouted the hounds back to their direct course. I resisted the pull of Lewis's hands on my coat. I did not like those people, or their ways or their dogs. After that meeting with Bledgely I would have

81

found an hour of bloody traffic with ordinary certified dogs pleasantly simple. But by the time I had got my bruised aching limbs upright again the hounds and the majority of the riders had passed on beyond the range of our scent or sight. Two riders followed at a distance of about a furlong. They rode slowly, close together, and seemed to be deep in some concentrated talk. The man had beautifully square and impressive shoulders and a long, notably white face.

'Plimmon,' said Lewis.

I was looking at the woman. Her head was unmistakable from any distance. It was Helen Penbury. The sight of her, riding with that massively elegant master of so much that I had always thought should be masterless, brought my anger to the ultimate bubble. I felt like rushing down and telling her in a ringing defiant style that I had seen enough of Moonlea, that I would be leaving there that day, that I wished her father a fine, long, agonising life. But I did no rushing down. It was all I could do to keep standing. Plimmon caught sight of me and waved his whip, shouting:

'What is your business there, fellows?'

'None at all,' said Lewis.

'Get out from there. Be off with you at once.'

'You go to the devil,' I said with slow relish, but my voice was weak and hardly carried to where he was. 'Come up here and shift us, you elegant bastard.'

He threw his head back in what I supposed he thought an imperious way and he spurred his horse towards us. It was clear that he meant to treat Lewis and myself to a quick course of whip and hoof. Lewis's arms hung in defensive expectancy at his side. Lewis was big and resolute, as strong as I would have wished to be, but I could not see either of us doing much against such a pair of stallions as Plimmon and his mount. Generations of owning and good feeding had made this man's spite a formidable obstacle. Then there was a call from the girl. He drew back and listened to what she had to tell him. He shouted again:

'I'm warning you. I'll give you a few minutes. Be off!'

Then they cantered side by side up the valley.

Lewis and I began our journey to the summit of the ridge that separated Plimmon's valley from Moonlea. As we reached the point of descent, I stopped to take my breath and said to Lewis:

'I've been thinking some more of Penbury and Plimmon. They're a real pair of wizards, the crazy sods. Plimmon is out to be a prince and a scourge to all unworthy yeomen who disgrace the countryside with their shabby fields and half-empty bellies. He does that by seeing that they have no countryside to disgrace and dumps them in handy packets of fertiliser in his own furrows or shackles them as furnace fodder to the knob of Penbury's door who himself is one of the greatest prophets since the bard Taliesin who saw and stated that this is the land of liberty and got off the list of bards for carrying vision and bardry too far for comfort. Penbury has been driven mad by the sight of impurities being roasted from ore and he plans to smelt the nonsense from the whole bloody species before he is retired. Between you and me, Lewis, if you give a much longer lease to such performers as these there will be such an ache in the life of man you'll need glasses with lenses as thick as my body to recognise the damned thing as the same article that used to be seen going around the planet stitching thick drawers of hope against the anguish of midwinter and reproving death as the greatest hindrance to joy.'

Lewis stopped and pointed to the right. He did not appear

to have been listening to a word I said.

'See that hollow there?'

I followed his finger. He was pointing to a trough in the hillside about twenty feet long, its bed strewn with large grey stones. 'That's where they found Sammy Bannion.'

I sat down on the trough's lip. The brisk walk downward, after my trouncing, had dizzied me. And Lewis's words had caused a wave of abnormally keen consciousness to rise in me. I saw Penbury's face, nervously unsure of what expression to assume, clear against the window panes of his darkened room. I could see Bledgely's face, ugly and at home with evil, closing in for the kill. I could see the face of John Simon Adams glancing with a thoughtful hopelessness at Katherine Brier. And in the background of these remembered things, a glimpse as real as if I beheld it, I saw the face of Sam Bannion, whom I had not known but whose name and whose career on earth had entered into my life like a distinct, strong fragrance, crushed and quiet against its appointed boulder.

6

Back in the cottage Mrs Brier fussed over me like a mother at the sight of my bruises. I had the impression that she was relieved at the sight of some wrong other and more specific than those which brooded permanently in her own mind. Davy was not yet back from his timber-hauling. John Simon was still at his work, and Katherine had gone down to the shop of Lemuel Stevens for a bag of flour. Lewis said he had some jobs waiting for him at home and I thanked him for what he had done for me.

Mrs Brier made me a basin of hot milk and bread and put me to sit in the largest fireside chair. I put on a tense, wan look to complete the paraphernalia of sickness. The deep bruise on my shoulder blade and the slighter one on the back of my neck had impressed her deeply. She looked rather weary herself and I persuaded her to stop her endless manoeuvring and fidgeting and settle down in the chair opposite mine. She did so at last, but uneasily, a cleaning rag in her right hand and her left playing with the grey hair that kept falling over eyes. Half her attention kept wandering from one side of the kitchen to the other as if tormented beyond bearing by the sight of tasks still left undone. I felt she liked dashing her thoughts to pieces on some bit of cleaning whenever they achieved a solid and disturbing bulk in her head.

'Are you comfortable now?'

'Oh yes. Thank you. This is a treat. If you promise to do as much as this for me every time I get cudgelled I'll get Plimmon to set aside two of his servants each day for the job.'

'Don't joke about it, harpist.'

'I've never been cared for like this. It's good.'

'When are you going back?'

'Want to see the last of me?'

'No, no indeed. But you'll find nothing in Moonlea to please you. Work, pain, danger, not much more.'

'A few days, then I'll be off. Surprising how many people have advised me to move my camp. What's so horrible about me in a state of stillness.' I scooped up the last spoonful of my pap and laid the porringer on the floor beneath the chair. Mrs Brier looked at it but seemed uncertain about groping beneath my legs for it.

'Will John Simon be going with you?' she asked, very quietly, but no one could have missed the eagerness in her voice.

'I have my section of road and I'll walk it. John Simon has his, and he'll be there at the end. Why he should choose Moonlea I don't know, because it strikes me as being a lump of plague. But he's part of its blood by now and he'll stay.' I pulled the shawl which hung from the chair's back to cause some movement that would serve to take her eyes away from my face. 'Don't you like him?'

'If he were my son I could not love him more.'

'I know. That was a foolish question I put to you. You'll have to forgive me, Mrs Brier, if some things that I say go into you like the prongs of a fork, but John Simon Adams is very dear to me. He and I for most of our lives have been very close, and there are things about his life here that I don't understand.'

'It would be better for John Simon if he would go.'

'You think he loves your son's wife, Katherine?'

'Of course he loves her. And it's only by fighting with all her heart and soul against it that she doesn't love him. It's a terrible thing for me to watch, harpist, a terrible thing, and the bitterness of it is something I may not be able to stand forever. That poor Davy would grieve away to his death if...'

'God, this sort of talk blisters me, Mrs Brier. I'm a great one for freedom. I play songs about it on the harp. Why truss yourselves like this, measuring yourselves like good little tailors for your suits of agony. Tell me all about this. I'm sick of half-light and guesses. I know I'd be happier if I heard no more, if I cleared back up to the North without hearing another word, leaving time to coax the poison out of your wounds or weave its moss over the parts that sting. But your face as you sit there, quietly flat with misery, would be around me like a wind and I'd always be curious. Did Katherine know John Simon when she married Davy?'

'No.'

'Why did Katherine marry your son?'

'I know what you're thinking, harpist. Katherine is a lovely girl and Davy is a fine lad, but not a proper man. I'll never make you understand what it is like to be the mother of one who is like Davy, who remains a child long after the years of manhood have come. Katherine was an orphan. Her father was a wild man in life and there were few in Moonlea who wished to take her in. I did. Davy would come to me day and night crying: "Get Katherine for me, mam, get Katherine for me." That was a hard thing to hear, harpist. It was the only thing he had ever asked for more than once, for he was always a patient and long-suffering lad. I couldn't stand it any longer and I asked Katherine. She said we had been very kind to her, Davy and I, and she took him.'

'Why did John Simon come to this cottage to live. Why did you let him? Have you no nose for calamity?'

'John Simon was a friend of the Andrews and Bannion boys. He started coming up to this hillside for an evening of talk and singing with them soon after he came to Moonlea. It was out there between the two rocks that Davy met him. John Simon had a way of talking to the lad that put him at his ease and made him happy. Davy has always worshipped John Simon. He would die for him. He would not dream of having John Simon anywhere but under this roof.'

'We hang each other with loving skill. Don't worry, Mrs Brier. I haven't had much chance to talk to John Simon yet. I don't think he understands yet that we have a place of our own up in the North, absolutely our own, to do with as we please. He's in a kind of mist with meditating about the woes of Moonlea. Not that they aren't a fine set of woes and in need of meditators, but there's room for something much better than mist in the skull of John Simon Adams. Katherine will forget him as he will forget Penbury and your Davy will stay happy.'

We heard Katherine coming in and laying down some packages on the wall seat of the porch. Mrs Brier smiled at me as if delighted by my assurance that I would bring some magic blade down upon the shadows that beset her and put them to flight. Her smile gave me a good opinion of myself and I set my head against the shawl to look as dramatically ill-treated as possible when Katherine came in.

She entered hurriedly, more disturbed than I had seen her before. 'Lewis Andrews told me you had been hurt. I was terrified. I ran back.'

'Nothing, nothing. A man and a guess at a man came at

me. Sorry about the fish though. They were beauties. They would have been good in the mouth.'

Mrs Brier left the kitchen, saying it was time to tend the pigs. Katherine came close to me to speak.

'Lewis Andrews told me that one of the men who attacked you was the man who was seen in Moonlea when Sam Bannion was killed.'

'Do you believe that story too?'

'There are some things we do not need to be told. One is that Sam Bannion did not fall into that hollow.'

'But this Bledgely isn't the only man with fingers off.'

'I know that. But Plimmon and Penbury are good friends. Odd that they should both select a tool with the same flaw. There's going to be danger.'

'You know about Bledgely now. You'll be forearmed.'

'It's more than just guarding this person or that from Bledgely. You know that Penbury's business is going from bad to worse as the orders for iron get thinner. Even Plimmon will stop fencing in his estates one day. The old people say that things have never been any good since the big war with France came to an end. And Penbury's sick of the grumbling at the furnaces. He says people ought to be as patient as he. So he talks now of closing the furnaces to teach the people a lesson.'

'With the furnaces closed, how are the people going to live? They've lost their fields and Plimmon has got his men marshalled to butcher the first person who tries to poach a little food off his table.'

'Most of the folk here are weak and stupid. Peace, war, plenty, hunger, it all seems to mean the same to them now. They'll take whatever crust Penbury is willing to give them. If trouble flares up he'll cut them down one by one and it will be as easy for him to do it as it is for Plimmon to get his foxes. And who do you think the first bit of game will be?'

'John Simon Adams.'

'Right. He can do no good here if it comes to an open fight between him and Penbury. The people are swayed like sheep. I know them better even than John Simon. I've lived here longer. They will veer for a moment towards John Simon when he fills them with shame at the thought of what they have lost, of what they endure. Then Bowen will speak and sing to them of heaven and they will spit John Simon out from their hearts as if he were the devil's son. They will crawl to the man with the loaves in his basket, not to the man with the great beauty of mercy in his dreams. John Simon does not see these things as I do, and he would risk any danger to oppose Penbury's claim to treat Moonlea as if it were part of his own body, to kiss it or kill it at will. But if I can help it, John Simon will not throw his life away. You've got to get him out of Moonlea, harpist.'

'I've told him that. Why did he ever strike even an inch of root in this place. Last night we had a talk. We're like brothers, as you know. We spoke of you. You love him, don't you?'

'If I didn't, I would be glad to see him die smashing his head against Penbury's throne. There's been too much silence in this place. There are too many people here walking quietly into the grave without speaking out clear of what they've seen and felt.'

'Why don't the two of you come away with me? Mrs Brier told me what happened. She gave you shelter when you were alone. That loneliness soured you a lot. I can hear that in the way you talk. You've made a handy little religion out of this Penbury too. You were grateful to be taken in out of the cold.

The sight of that poor Davy whimpering and blinking after you like a dog made your pity burn like dry hay. It was a fine thing you did to marry him. Fine but daft. Like hanging yourself on a cross of compassion on behalf of the poor dolts who trudge their lives out around the ovens, a large cross, with Penbury the nail maker charging you for the nails. Fine but daft.'

'I couldn't leave Davy now. He's like a child. But it's not so much him, it's his mother. I'm his happiness and she'll fight for it until she drops or I drop.'

'And if I take John Simon away? What then? What kind of solution is that? The way you feel for him, the way he feels for you, that has been laboured a long time in both your lives. It can't be tossed into the ditch simply because a pair of lost bewildered folk sink their freezing fingers into you and wish to hold you fast for ever, for their comfort.'

'The way you say it, harpist.... But it's not like that. Every day is like a field of growing things and there's a lot of life between me and Davy and his mother. Not the life that comes between man and woman. Davy's not a man. But John Simon could wait. Davy often falls sick and pines into a sadness. He might die. Something might happen, something.'

'We are the something that happens, Katherine. If we are still, the world's a desert. His mother said he'd die for John Simon.'

Her face twisted as if with a pain twinge.

'The solitude has made you very hard, harpist.'

'I'm untied. My eyes see further around than yours.'

'Oh, and there was another thing I was to tell you. Lemuel Stevens came on to me in the town and told me to be sure and remember to tell you that Mr Penbury wants you to be present at his house tomorrow evening. He is giving a dinner party, so Lemuel said, and wishes some music.'

'A dinner party? What is this programme? Is he going to sleep on the table?'

'Sleep?'

'Yes. I didn't tell you. Last night I had a long discussion with Penbury. He, like John Simon, is jammed tight with visions right up to the top of the skull. So he wishes me to console him and cure him of sleeplessness by giving him a round of old-fashioned airs about midnight.'

'Will you go?' There was a fierce contempt in Katherine's face as she asked the question that shivered my jocosity like a stone.

'It may teach me something.'

'Then I hope every tune sticks in his arrogant gizzard. It's a servile task you're taking on, harpist, fingering your strings for such a man.'

'In these matters, Katherine, I have no great feeling. There are those on earth whom I would wish to see unhurt, you and John Simon and myself for a start. I also hate iron, smoke and all conflicts that cannot simply and neatly be resolved, that are slow and corrupting in their action on the heart, that fall on lives gently and rustingly like rain.'

I stood up and looked out through the window. Up the hillside towards the cottage came Davy, his coat hanging open to show the great sweating chest, his face beaming with pride and fulfilment after his day of toilsome hauling, his eyes large, blue and thoughtless. I turned away from the window. Katherine was putting a kettle on the heaped fire, her brow pressed with an effort that I could feel in all its painful details against the scarred smoked wood of the mantel.

92

7

I stood once again in the kitchen of the Penbury home. Jabez and the maid Agnes were circulating with a fussy buzz of starched cloth around the enormous table loaded with the food that was shortly to be carried into the dining hall where Penbury and his friends would be eating. About me as I waited for my cue in this elaborate performance there were odd, unheard of marks of elegance. Lemuel had come to me earlier in the day, and I was told that the folk up in the mansion thought my appearance a disgrace and that if I had the idea of coming before them as a kind of minstrel I would need to look a lot less like the sheep whose skin had gone into making the coat I now wore. Lemuel said the lady of the mansion, Miss Helen, had sent some garments down to his shop where they were now waiting for me to try on. At first the man's message had made me fume and I told Lemuel that either Penbury would have to put up with the sheepskin or the folk at the dinner were going to have their first unspoiled view of a naked troubadour. The horrified look on Lemuel's face sobered me, and it struck me that against the general background of Penbury's conduct towards most of Moonlea's natives he really seemed, by the sending of these gifts, to be casting me for the role of darling and spoiled boy. I went down with Lemuel and found his parcel to consist of a black suit of a kind I had never seen before and a frigid looking shirt of a kind I had seen around the necks of the pious and sometimes too of mourners for the dead, and it came to my mind as I stared at this raiment that Penbury must have spent the day before looking for a preacher of just about my size to fell and strip so that I could be decently clad to keep time on the harp with his eating and brooding. I tried the clothes on. The jacket was tight and short for me. I walked about Lemuel's kitchen with the woman Isabella cooing praise and wonder in the manner of a pigeon, Lemuel hopping from left to right to get a better view and I advancing gingerly, for all the world like a man who is rationing his gestures until he gets back his own pair of arms. I had walked up the hillside to show this finery to John Simon and his friends. They had come to Mrs Brier's garden gate where I was on view. They stood around and told me how astonished or disgusted they were and they expressed these feelings in their different ways.

'Strikes me,' said Wilfie Bannion, 'that Penbury is entering on a cycle of high jesting. These impish manoeuvres with the harpist are the prelude to something very special. The climax might even find him winking at such ideas as justice and equality, willing at least to notice their presence on earth if not to hang them on the bedstead as mascots like we do.'

'He just doesn't want the smell of me in my native state upsetting his guests,' I said. 'There's no need for you boys to be so sardonic although I know your feelings about Penbury. As I was before I looked like the father of all goats even in sheepskin. That's all. You've got to admit that my original garments were rough and meet to set the teeth on edge.'

'They're up to something with you, Alan,' said Lewis Andrews. 'By the time Penbury finishes with you, if this suit is a sample of the course you're in for, you'll be carrying the incense around for the Reverend Purley who tends to be Romish in the way he conducts his services.'

'I plan in the next few days,' I said, 'to have such a bellyful of Moonlea that the only comment I'll need to make on the place is a long belch. This suit is part of the process. My belly is already beginning to creak.'

But they had all wished me good fortune in this new medium and asked me to keep my ears open for any news from Penbury and his friends that might give them and the other furnace workers a hint of what they were to expect as the autumn came on. At seven I had started on my way to the big house.

'When do I start playing?' I asked Jabez, making haste to help myself to a small jellied cake while Agnes was out of the room. I wanted no brush with Agnes although my appearance in the mourning suit and the lilywhite shirt with the frills had admitted me to the outer fringe of her approval.

'Not just yet. I'll tell you exactly what to do when the time comes. You'll be well rewarded for your time and labour.'

'The people in this house are very sure of their power to reward. With regard to the rest of us they seem to have the right kind of curve in their fingers.' I watched Jabez as he moved, the rapt intentness of his face, the passionate meticulousness of his fingers as he adjusted faults of detail on which my eye would not have lighted in a million years. I could see that his whole life had been spent in what he took to be full, rapturous flight with both wings pressed hard against the sides of his cage.

'You've had a happy life, haven't you, Jabez?'

'That's a silly question. Of course I have.'

'Never any longing for anything afar?'

'What is there better than this, near or afar?'

'Everything you wish is here.'

'I've never had a melancholy minute.'

'Holy God.'

'Watch your tongue, harpist.'

I chewed my cake and gave up any idea of discussing the mechanics of living with Jabez. He and I were being drawn through two different machines. To him the earth and all its miracles of splendour and filth was just a bread roll to be kept fresh and flavoured for Penbury.

The door from the courtyard opened and a young man in his very early twenties came in. He was dressed, like myself, in black, but his body was lean with a hint of disease and he had as much room in his raiment as I had not. His eyes were alight with fear or desire. His hands were trembling and gloved in some white cheap cotton articles, newly washed, sagging, seeming at points to drip from his fingers like drops of milky water. Under his arm he had a violin case.

'Sit down, Felix,' said Jabez. He turned to me: 'This is your colleague, harpist, Felix Jamieson. He will give out the melody clearly on his violin and you will accompany him vaguely on the harp. I heard Miss Helen tell Felix that this morning.'

'That's fair enough,' I said, and smiled, nodding at Felix to reduce his terror. Anything I did in the company of Felix I would wish to do vaguely; a zealous affirmation, even on the lowest plane, would tear the man to tatters. He gave me no smile back but wiped his face with his handkerchief and appeared to be quietly vibrating on the stool which Jabez had offered him.

'Give him some ale,' I said, 'he's pale as a ghost and looks as if he has a fresh faint ready for use in every pocket.'

Felix began to laugh in a hysterical, girlish way.

'What's the matter with him now?' I asked. 'There's no reason why he should laugh. That was no joke that I uttered about the fainting. That's how he looks. Pallid and begging death's door for a feel of the knob.'

'It's your crude savage way of talking, harpist,' said Jabez. 'That's what set him off. This Felix is one of the gentlest and godliest lads in Moonlea. He has been learning to play the violin for years. His father is one of the men at the foundries and wishful for Felix to fiddle his way out of the heavy labour that is sure to ruin his hands. This is the first time he has played before Mr Penbury. It was Mrs Bowen, the minister's wife, who really arranged it for Felix has always been a sweet singer and a prime reciter of the psalms for Mr Bowen and one of his favourites as a consequence. Mr Bowen was telling me only last Sunday that if Mr Penbury takes a fancy to Felix tonight he will have him sent to London which is a great city and offers fame to musicians. So, tonight, on top of being godly, he is nervous. On top of all this great strain you burst in upon him with your rough talk of ale and the knob on the door of death. It's too much, harpist, too much.'

'Sorry, Felix,' I said, 'if I had known something in advance of your desires and your plight I would have led off with something as gentle as a summer night, assuring as love. I have those things in my mind, too.'

'I'm sure he'll be a success,' added Jabez. 'Captain Wilson of the Yeomanry who will be here tonight has been known to weep, I heard Miss Helen say, at the sound of a violin if the melody is at all touched with sadness. And Felix on a sad tune is a marvel. He distils sorrow from every note. He makes a great sobbing in the brain.'

97

'I can believe that. He looks as if he might have been wrapped once around the very root of grief to keep the damned thing warm.'

Jabez gave us a glass of wine. It was a poor cloying sample, but it made me warmer. I leaned forward and studied the thin nerve-knotted face of Felix more closely. He grinned back but with a light foam of terror still floating on his senses. It was clear that my being, in terms of the strange soprano twitter that ran up and down his fibres, was novel to the point of painfulness. The meat of me, in the eyes of Felix, was raw, undressed, repellent. I was disappointed, for I felt very genteel in my new suit and I racked my brain for some topic innocently sweet enough to give his fears a ground of rest. But I was still searching twenty minutes after when Jabez came in to tell me that the guests were ready to be entertained.

We walked down the corridor towards the dining room, Jabez first, then Felix and I in the rear. It was hard work for me not to tell Felix as he watched his suit appearing to jiggle itself off his frame, and mine pressing so hard it made my head feel like a bubble, that we were the greatest pair of freaks ever to be unleashed under the banner of art in the halls of the gentry.

We entered the dining hall. Felix made a deep bow and I noted that it was a room of sufficient beauty to make eating feel important. A broad-faced man sitting at Penbury's left took a wine glass from his lips and stared frankly with laughter at the sight of us. He was hushed to silence by Penbury who lowered his head gravely and beckoned us to a far corner where stood two chairs and the gleaming harp which I had seen in the darkened room. Felix was overwhelmed and continued with his bowing, and I had to do a bit of steering to get him into the right corner or he would have been among the food in no time at all. The man who had laughed was still gasping with amusement. Helen Penbury sat at her father's right and kept her eyes fixed on a small grey-faced man with his thinning hair parted emphatically in the middle of his small skull who sat at the bottom of the table and appeared to be ill at ease. Next to him was a man of raven darkness and solemn, self-important expression in the dress of a divine whom I took to be Mr Bowen. Next to Helen Penbury sat a cavalry officer, in dress uniform, heavily moustached and attending quietly to his food. He did not give us a glance and him I assumed to be the Captain Wilson of the Yeomanry whom Jabez had mentioned.

As Felix was fumbling his instrument on to his shoulder and screwing his strings into pitch I observed a tiny room which opened to our right in which a small table full of food and drink had been laid. I guessed that these refreshments were for myself and Felix, and I felt there was some person in the house of Penbury who believed in decorating the blank wall of life with an occasional daub of thought and care. Penbury and Mr Bowen stared hard at me.

When our playing began, I listened attentively to Felix. I initiated nothing, thickening his melodies and bordering his climaxes with a periodical harmony. He played well, and as I grew to sense his moments of greatest stress and urgency in his progress through a tune, I made my support more overt, edging him on with a touch here and there into a passionate excitement over the considerable beauty we were making with our strings. After two pieces, the second being an ancient lament called 'How Sing the Winds in the Branches of My Heart?' that brought Felix to the verge of tears, had Mr Bowen groaning with admiring compassion and caused the Captain to lay aside his eating and listen, his face quite expressionless, Felix shed most of his dreads and smirked back at the praiseful smile of Mr Penbury.

'You're doing well,' I whispered to Felix. 'A few evenings of fiddling like this and you'll be clean away from Moonlea, in London winning fame like Jabez said, playing under the bed of the very king as far as I can see.'

We played for ten minutes, the playing of my companion becoming more assured and eloquent with every bar. There must have been great tracts of self-sickness in the past life of Felix prompting him to this effort. He was more on the stretch than any of his strings. The members of the little audience were appreciative and helpful. The music seemed to put some kind of a spell on the Captain, who glanced more frequently at Helen Penbury as we brought the emotions of most of those present to a pitch of pulpy softness. The red-faced man at Penbury's side was a dissenter. He was either deaf or drunk for he broke into a deep giggle from time to time when he glanced over at us and would, had it not been for the reproof he saw in Penbury's face, have been willing to let off a whole ripely bitter round of jests about Felix and myself. In a way I was sorry that he was hushed to silence. I would have been interested to hear what he had to say. The way that Felix and I looked, with our earnest faces and our funeral suits, would have made a smooth and easy stretch of road for any well-wheeled fancy.

When Felix finished his first cycle, Helen Penbury rose from her chair, walked into the t'ny room at the side and beckoned us to follow. We went in and sat down on the two chairs provided. She was dressed as she had been on the first evening of my stay in Moonlea. The lace effect broke in a wave at the base of her face and as she stood there by my side she loomed even larger in my eyes than the food. She told us that we would be looked after by Jabez as the night wore on, and that we were to be sure that we helped ourselves. She said that particularly to Felix, as if implying that his main difficulty would be nipping in and getting something before I did away with the lot. She seemed to catch the jest of the implication at the same moment as I did. Felix got up from his chair and went into a series of ragged bows. We smiled at each other over Felix's arched back.

'You look very different now, harpist,' she said quietly and with a suggestion of pride as if she had in some way put hobbles on me and threaded a ring through my nose. 'You could pass for a prospering tradesman in that garb, an undertaker for choice, although I would feel more sorrow than usual for the dead if they had to pass through hands as carelessly pagan as yours. You don't look nearly as Jacobinical as you did in that sheep's pelt you were wearing when you first came here.'

'Was it you who got this uniform for me?'

'I did. I thought you might have been grateful.'

'Oh, I am. I haven't been as pretty as this since my christening. Next time you get me a coat though, remind me to get my torso shrunken in advance. The first man to wear this article could have had little between his neck and his thighs except a taste for buttons. Like the music?'

'Lovely. You make a good shadow for Felix's light. My father likes it too. He says it's made him feel better than he's done for months. He's taken quite a fancy to you.'

'Why should he? I'm no obedient iron-toiler.'

'He thinks you're an oddity, an interesting primitive. He was amazed when you turned up here tonight. He didn't

101

think you would. He said you'd have taken counsel with the goats and decided to reject the invitation.'

'The goats are getting middle-aged and dozy. They said they didn't give a damn whether I harped for you or not. Were you amazed when I came?'

'A little. And pleased as well. You're quite a novelty for our guests. There's so little wild music left in the lives we lead at Moonlea. You're a new flavour.'

'Chew me well, madame. I shall be in and out of here at great speed.'

'When do you leave?'

'Tomorrow. Day after. I'm not sure.'

'What makes you unsure.'

'Nothing. Just struck me that when one's movements get slow and thoughtful all kinds of tendrils can come winding around your legs.'

'It will be a clever tendril to do for you. But don't hasten away. Wild music's rare, harpist.'

'Rare and horribly wearing for the player. There could be no peace for me here. It sets my teeth on edge.'

'And Adams, your friend?'

'He's all edge. God knows what kind of cellar he sits in.'

She left us. Felix had been following our conversation with hypnotised eyes and a lower lip that dangled stupefied to the bottom of his chin. I pressed a cake into his mouth as a sign that his face could now close up the gap and come to something nearer normal. His face was still pale from the effort he had put into his playing.

'You'll want to watch that, Felix. To keep humanity entertained you'll need the steadiness and stamina of a tree. If you're anything smaller or weaker than that they'll pluck you up like a buttercup.'

102

'I'll bear that in mind, harpist. You are a strange man, but wise.'

'What you need is ale to give you an appetite for meat, then the meat itself, on or off the animal you've singled out for the feast. When you have a gutful of it you'll find your fingers slower to lay a lining of passion around that bow, but you'll live longer and they say that's important. You've never had much food, have you, Felix?'

'My father is dead-set against gluttony. He says it's wickedness to give in to the body in any way at all. He says he's got his body on a strong leash.'

'What kind of a maniac is your old man?'

'He's no maniac. He gets headaches that nearly split his skull. He got those first when he was a kid, when he started working near the furnace mouths. He says a long fast is the only thing that holds his head together when the ache gets bad. Then there were times when he couldn't go to the foundries at all and then we had to fast, no option. At first he wasn't happy about the hunger at all. Then he heard Mr Bowen say that bit about the wickedness of giving in to the body and he made his leash and he's as happy as a lark about it.'

'I can see Bowen and your old man causing a great coolness to come over life between them. You hurry up and fiddle your way to fame and fortune, Felix, and blow a quick bubble at these austere pests who are out for a good look at your skeleton to give their own lean souls a bit of comfort. And when they prattle to you about wickedness stop up your ears and sing out this gospel – Two things only are wicked: to be helpless when you could be free, to be hungry when you could be fed. Eat up, lad. Make up for all your lost time. Make your stomach the ambassador of all those that have

103

ever sagged and known emptiness on earth. Try to fill up the gaps in yourself, Felix, for the sight of them makes me grieve. And if the novelty should prove too much for you and you look purple in the face and headed for the kind of seizure that'll play hell with your violin-playing I'll take you for a sharp run twice around the mansion. The sight of you working hard at having a mortal stroke would tickle the fancy of those jovial folk around the table out there. They would laugh it off easily as another unrehearsed jest called up out of the void by Penbury's imperial will.'

'I shouldn't listen to you, harpist.' He nibbled without appetite at a pasty.

'If you don't you won't be able to listen at all. Some bad jokes have got all their black teeth fixed in you, Felix. I'd like to see the finished pattern of bites in about twenty years' time. The ironmasters, the witchburners and the toiling fools, they are all out to cook you to a turn. I don't like the smell of roasting man.'

Jabez brought in a jug of ale. I gave a measure to Felix, hushing the rabid panic that came upon him as he thought of what Mr Bowen would say if he caught the whiff of malt upon his breath. I told him Bowen was stabled with the mighty and would not be able to spare the time from the job of making God available to the ironmasters to go sniffing at such humble articles as Felix and his laggard breath. The first gill relaxed him and his head came close to mine as his tongue tumbled forth a long story of how his father would come to his bedside at night, his eyes on fire with pain and weakness and desire, drag Felix to the violin, reading out a list of tunes which he had discovered were favourites of Mr Bowen, then make him play them for hours on end, forcing Felix to pledge that he would make the violin the instrument of their liberation, the sword that would cut through the filthy cord of all their deprivation.

'Your mother dead?' I asked, wishing to know more about the bedroom in Felix's cottage.

'No, she ran away,'

'That was a shrewd move. How did she ever come to be fit and fed and fast enough to run so well in the right direction?'

'She went when I was young. My father said she had too little faith.'

'Bad for the blood, that, too little faith.'

'Must be. It's good to hear you say that, harpist.'

'Tell me, Felix, who is the man with the crimson face, next to Penbury?'

'That's Mr Radcliffe, Mr Penbury's partner and manager. He's a big man down at the foundries.'

'He hasn't got much mercy. Did you hear the way he laughed when we came in?'

'Oh yes. It made me nervous.'

'He thinks we're a pair of clowns.'

'Clowns?' Felix said and giggled. He shook his head at me and I could see that some rising courage in the man was daring him to jest, 'Crimson face. Bloody man.'

'True, boy. He looks a bit like a furnace, that Radcliffe. With pity at the bottom of it done to a turn, like ash. I don't like the smell of roasted pity either, Felix.'

Felix looked grave and sniffed, as if he had the thing under his nose for judgement. But all he said was:

'I shouldn't listen to you, harpist.'

I hushed Felix to silence, for the talk from the table had become loud and clear. Radcliffe was talking. His voice was bold and authoritative.

'We should have done it two years back,' he said.

'What should have been done?' asked Mr Bowen, in a way that suggested he knew the answer quite well but was saying this in his quiet, pleasant way to quieten a certain turbulence that had crept into the atmosphere.

'Radcliffe was always impetuous,' said Penbury.

'Impetuous, indeed! You've been too soft and slow, Penbury. Through the whole of this year, you've been humming and hawing. You've brought yourself to the verge of ruin with your patience and kindliness. Let's have a little simple directness for a change and this will be a happier land for the experience. Just look around this table and you'll see the answer to all your anxieties and hesitations.'

'Explain, Radcliffe. You are in a high vein of exposition. The music has stimulated you in fine style.'

'You have a soldier, a minister, a lawyer. They symbolise the whole fabric of traditional guarantees against the folly of vindictive and presumptuous illiterates. If there is ever a hint of disturbance, it will be in Moonlea and Captain Wilson, with a dozen troopers, few more, will put an end to it with a wave of his sword. Agreed, Captain?'

'I am listening, sir.'

'Jarvis is the majesty of the law and you will never realise how fiendishly majestic the law can look when you are on the receiving end of it. Let Jarvis mumble a few words about a compromise with the most necessitous debtors and there will be as little talk of burning the legal records as of violating the Ark of the Covenant. Then again, these folk are as responsive to Mr Bowen as women's flesh to bruises. At the touch of his words, when the full hue and cry of the passionate God-search is upon them, the stoniest spirits among them will crumble to a ruin that will make a lovely mould for our every molten suggestion and flat. And if all else fails, set that fiddler and harpist to work their magic upon them. They curdle me, but from the look on your faces as they were playing, their efforts might enthral quite a few of the mutterers in the valley-bed.'

'You are quite a Napoleon in these matters,' said Helen Penbury, and her voice was amused. 'Quite a Lord Plimmon, to be a little more local.'

'Thank you, Helen. The second reference puts me in good company.'

'His ideas have the same strong persuasive sweep. Only yesterday he was quoting some French axiom, and very soldierly and rousing it was too, on the subject of poachers: *De l'audace*, you know the one.'

'There's no great reason for smiling, Helen. Genius, the whole of it, is the impudent assumption of power. Whether you exercise it in a closet or over a continent is of no great moment. It's getting the measure of your material that matters. The material is always so amazed to find that anyone has taken the trouble to measure it it can never answer back. Plimmon is a thousand times right. I've talked with him and some of his assertions could be written out as a gospel for this age. The poacher who goes out of Moonlea and pilfers part of the produce from the game preserves that Plimmon's care and knowledge have replenished is simply a recalcitrant trying to creep back into a paradise from which his own mortal unfitness has already expelled him. In any case, to poach is to find food and food is at the heart of our problem. Want, ghastly, unprovisional want, laid on as part of a programme, is the only parable with a full set of teeth in this context. There must be no trickle of stolen game or produce from the Plimmon estates or bread on credit from

107

Steven's store to fuel some persistent fragment of revolt in an odd stomach here and there. The wage we offer them for their simple thoughtless tasks of stoking and hauling is the best means of feeding themselves they have ever known. The exposition of that basic point must be meticulous and unforgettable.'

'Oh dear, dear, dear!' said Penbury, his voice a soft gurgle as if he were speaking into liquid, 'I'll never sleep tonight after all this. You are a plague, you know, Radcliffe. They tell me you had some little to do with verse when you were younger and less resolved to serve your epoch.'

'I did.'

'I too. An odd consummation. Iron and a pair of seats on our own dark, self-made volcano.'

'The sonnet was my particular fancy. Wrote some of the vilest sonnets on record. Beautifully shaped, all of them, but hard at the core. No love to make them really fluid, somebody told me.'

'A perfect form, the sonnet, a constant reproach to the squalid lurch of our progress from wish to fruition. But you'll find that dreams and the loves that breed them do not fall into any easy pattern of rhythm and rhyme. I wish they did. I do indeed wish they did. Now we'll have some more music. And this will be our domain of pleasure, Radcliffe, into which you will not obtrude with your Machiavellian foot. When the time is ripe you and we and they will all find our own noose of cunningly appointed mockery. Until then, I don't want to be savagely lucid about it.'

I listened to the flow of wine, staring at the face of Felix who was contentedly picking his teeth, his head on one side, his mind far beyond any interest in the conversation that had been taking place in the next room.

'And Mr Bowen?' I asked softly. 'What will have been washing about in his silence? Or has he mastered his echoes as they've mastered you, Felix?'

Felix came out of his semi-stupor with a start and was about to make a reply when we heard Penbury clap his hands in what I thought was a distinguished, Oriental, despotic sort of way. Felix and I re-entered the dining room. I looked with a new interest at the man Radcliffe. His head was lowered and he was gazing with his intense, humorous eyes into a half-empty glass.

We played with a will for we felt the eyes of the people around the table urging us to expel with the mounting volume of our melodies the foggy preoccupation that had come upon them during the interval of talk. We must have played for fully half an hour. Then we were dismissed and Jabez, smirking at Felix and myself as if we had had a triumph, led us back to the kitchen where the ageing maid Agnes stroked Felix's hair in a motherly way and even looked in a way to be sisterly to me. She told us a long story of a visit she had once paid to London when she had worked as a seamstress in some establishment that had done commissions for the Royal Court itself; perhaps, said Agnes, for the very gentry before whom Felix would one day be fiddling on the highest possible plane. From the way that Agnes nearly fainted with pride as she told us these things we could see that she set great store upon such experiences as touching the royal hem, and so on. Jabez had clearly heard the tale before but he was respectfully dumb as Agnes brought out the worn, fragile details, each for its careful caress, and he nodded at us from time to time as if to say that we were in rare company. This talk of nobles and high patronage was the last straw of excitement that looked like breaking Felix's moral back. He was swaying on his feet and saying Goo-goo as his eyes goggled at Agnes. She had now taken Felix's hand, and as I thought that Felix had enough to put up with in the way of cruel pressure from his father, I said it would be better if we now left. Jabez thanked us gravely on behalf of his master and said that there would, no doubt, be other engagements, news of which would be brought to us in due course.

Felix and I left the house. As we made our way down the drive, I looked back and saw Helen Penbury and the captain, their backs towards us, walking on the terrace.

At the gate which brought us to the main road Felix's father, an incandescent, hopping little man with a voice like a strongly blown flute, was waiting for Felix. He snatched the violin case from his son. He kept dancing about like a sheepdog in his excitement and between him and the shadows thrown by the tall roadside hedge it was a hard tricky bit of walking that we did.

'For God's sake, Felix,' I said, 'ask your old man to make up his mind about the side of the road on which he's going to walk. He's got us both surrounded and me uneasy.'

Felix went on with his description of what had happened up at the mansion, still too deaf with pride and astonishment to heed me.

'They were there, all those nobs?' asked Mr Jamieson.

'All there.'

'Mr Penbury, Mr Bowen, Mr Radcliffe?'

'And Mr Jarvis.'

'Oh yes. Fancy me forgetting him. Felix. Me forgetting Mr Jarvis. Me forgetting the man with the smartest head on him in all Moonlea.' He pulled me by the arm and began to laugh embarrassedly, and I told him, in a low voice, not wishing to

110

be unfriendly and in a mood to broaden the quiet night for the admission of the widest possible manias, that he seemed indeed to have made a bad lapse in this matter of forgetting Jarvis.

'And Miss Helen,' said Felix, 'she spoke to me.'

'Miss Helen? Spoke to you? An angel, that girl.'

'And Captain Wilson, a soldier.'

'A real soldier?'

'Oh, real all right. Dressed up to the nines, red and everything. And smart. Straight as a line.'

'Sparking Miss Helen, no doubt, Felix,' said Mr Jamieson, his voice suddenly serious and solemn as a tombstone.

'Sure to be. He was eyeing her off and on in that warm way, you know.'

'Less of that talk about warmth. You're still a boy. What else is there to tell?'

'Jabez said Mr Penbury is sure to help me on now that he's heard me, sure to help you too by giving you some easier work now that he has seen all you've done to help me.'

Felix's father stopped. We all stopped. There was a promising finality about the way his boots came together with a sudden click. It was good, restful to see this elastic gnome at ease.

'He said that?'

'Exactly that, dad.'

'Jabez said that, Jabez who is the very right hand of Mr Penbury?'

'Just as I said it. Ask the harpist.'

'Oh gracious God, gracious God,' said Mr Jamieson, and he began to tremble like a man in a love-climax. Then he began a fresh brand of laugh that was more than half sob.

111

I listened and made up my mind that it would be a waste to try pointing out to Mr Jamieson that life would feel less clogged and inflamed in Felix's pipes if his old man would not keep pestering him at night, but I could see that these two were off on some private comet of longing and delight and I said goodnight to them. I reminded Felix also when there was a lull in the gale of his father's gladness that we should probably be seeing each other again if Penbury kept to his plan of pouring a little music on the fibres of Moonlea to soften them into a relaxed and harmless rest.

8

The following evening, Katherine, John Simon and I set out on a walk up to the summit of the South Mountain. We shouted goodbye to Davy. He was humming out a vague ineffective harmony with the song that Wilfie Bannion was singing in his garden. Mrs Brier had gone down into Moonlea to a meeting of prayer which was to be held in the chapel of Mr Bowen. She would pray for us all, she said, and John Simon and I had thanked her, gravely.

We made our way across the valley. The evening air was very quiet. We took a rough sheep track that led twisting through the tall ferns to the top. My hand rested lightly on the fern tips, cooling my fingers as I walked. The grass underfoot was soft and odorous. I walked quickly ahead. Katherine and John Simon brought up behind, a steady ten yards in my rear, alongside each other and talking in low voices. Now and then I turned my head to look at them. There was a certain shyness about them as their eyes met, yet they seemed deeply pleased to be near each other, and once, as I glanced at their heads, both rounded, pensive, dark, at a moment when a bend in the path blotted their bodies from my view, I felt that there was a wonderful rightness in the meeting of those two lives. Whatever the end and however cunningly contrived the bitterness of their passage, it was good that those two people had had the chance to ponder on and long for the substance of each other. A richness had been added to them; to me, and to whatever remote, uncommunicable part of existence benefits from the anguish of the unfulfilled. The thought saddened and I quickened my step to a breath-cracking lope to expel it.

From the summit was an admirable view. I turned away from Moonlea of which I had already seen and guessed too much. I turned my eyes towards the endless hill ranges of the south and west. My spirit surrendered all its whimpering questions, yawned over on to its side and slept. I sat with my back to the side of a knoll and deliberately drank every drop of serenity I could distil from the sight of those hills of which the furthest were already losing their outline as the evening thought of its return.

John Simon and Katherine came and lay at my side against the knoll.

'You're fools,' I said, my voice as loud and angry as I could make it for at the sight and sound of them I was raw again and on edge about tomorrow.

'What's up now, boy?'

'Unless you get your neck broken in the meantime you'll be here in twenty years' time, you and Katherine, chaste, restrained and in a busy itch from tip to toe with regrets, footing it down to the conventicle for a session of pious forgetting with Mr Bowen when they bite too deep. And the hunger which you won't satisfy will put you both into sad shabby graves a couple of decades before time. But don't worry. Davy will be there with his smile and his patient hoe and a fine armful of cabbage plants to beautify each plot.'

'Please, harpist,' said Katherine, 'don't talk like that. For the clown you say you are, you hurt too much.'

'He doesn't mean to hurt us, Katherine. Alan is the best friend we'll have. He sees too little of the whole picture. He

114

still shouts where we've learned to whisper.'

'You mean,' I said, 'he still insists on living when you've learned to die, each day a slow loving sip at the notion of the grave. You're going on like a pair of clay-boned fools. But don't brood about what I said on the subject of the conventicle and lining your middle age with prayers. You won't have the chance.'

'Why not?'

'I was at Penbury's last night. I should have told you this before but I wanted the chance of telling you while Katherine was with you and you were both out of sight of Moonlea which seems to put some kind leprosy of acceptance on your minds.'

'What did Penbury say?'

'He's got a team of jokes lined up for use against you toilers that will break the laughter record for this age. Either he arranges for you leading thinkers and critics to be picked off like so many partridges on the estate of Plimmon or the furnaces close down, the people starve and they either avenge their empty guts by mangling you false prophets into a stopgap pie or, if they stand firm, the whole issue of you gets smashed under a cascade of soldiers. There was a man there last night. He took the furnace-closing line. He talked as if he had hunger on a leash, trained to leap at selected throats and bring home selected gullets at his whistle. His name was Radcliffe.'

'I know him. A forceful man with dreams of greatness.'

'Who wouldn't get a bad case of them with you boys stooped like dwarfs all around. There was a soldier there too. He looked full of muscle and wholesome tradition and a sense of duty so vibrant it made me feel no more than half born and made his moustache bristle. He pledged Penbury

115

the support of his whole strength in defence of his smoke-holes and rent collections. Jarvis the Clerk piped up to promise the King's Justice and Mr Bowen pledged the support of the Lord by proxy. Their statements were all up to the level of the food and the music, which were high. They are ready for a tidy bit of pruning. By the time they finish with you, John Simon, you will be a part of the autumn's compost. There'll be no loophole for you, no obstruction for them. They can afford to concentrate their genius and their wealth on that one little township, get their fingers around the red inflamed spot and squeeze it clear of all its humours of dissent. You may bite a finger here and there, John Simon, because there is great talent behind that brow of yours. You might give Penbury's ankle a wrench as his foot comes down to make a fresh impress on the soft dirt he has made of you other people's lives. But the foot would go down to its elected depth and you'd be a bubble in the mud, no more. These new mighty ones are just easing themselves into a new frame of living, John Simon, and the collective agony of all who might persist in resenting them would be the shadow of a growing pain and that would be all. Up there in the North you and Katherine could lead lives that would add up to something gleaming and glorious. Just think of it, boy. A solitude, wrought to one's shape, fitted to the body of all one's desires...'

'From now on, Alan, there could be no solitude that wouldn't clang like a cave with echoes.' He stood up. 'Look down there to the south, Alan. What do you see?'

I lifted myself from the knoll. Katherine rose, too, and stood at my side. I gazed into the distance.

'I see the light thickening as the sun sets. I see a stretch of earth wrinkled into hills and valleys and between the

116

wrinkles I suppose there are little legions of things breathing hard and trying their best to make, or believe that they have made, their breath immortal.'

'Nothing else at all?'

'Nothing, and my eyes are good.'

'You see no occasional smoky patches behind each line of hills?'

'Those, yes.'

'Under each smudge, there is a town like Moonlea, a centre of new work, in mine, mill or foundry.'

'What of it?'

'It bears on what you were saying.'

'I see no link.'

'Strings of towns, just like Moonlea, separated as yet by short hills, long ignorance and a little fear. If those townships were once to act together we'd be more than a bubble in the mud. As far as the eye can see from here, Alan, a dozen hill ranges and behind each range a score of Moonleas. And in each Moonlea, a few thousand people whose pattern of feeling and experience, whose impulse of misery are precisely as ours. The number of times I've stood on this very spot, fondling that notion, chuckling as I felt my spirit grin at Penbury and Radcliffe and the arrogant set of their eyes. When once one's mind has gone to pasture on the field of a thought that is bound one day to startle the whole ugly yawn out of living, nothing much inside one's life matters. You can feel expectancy nibble at the days to come and they are full of juice.'

'I can believe that, boy. You've taken the whole jugful.'

'In all those towns to the south, I have friends, men the people know and trust, men who have seen the slow ravelling of faith and patience as conditions have grown worse

117

and winters have grown more biting. I and they have thought long about this thing. We have agreed that the time may come when we would have to fuse our small scattered mutterings into a single voice, to tell the ironmasters that theirs may not be the only wisdom. We promised that if one should call, the others would come to his side.'

'Has the call come?'

'I'm giving it.'

'When?'

'The minute I'm certain that Penbury means his threat about raking out the furnaces.'

'Where will they rally, these crusaders of the lean guts?'

'On this very top where we are sitting now.'

'Like an army?'

'Something like. The contingents will assemble from a dozen valleys.'

'Armed? Where would you get guns or even pikes from?'

'We won't need them. We've had quarrels about that, my friends and I, bitter quarrels. But most of us know force would be mad. Numbers and the gift of making iron, they are our only weapons.'

For a minute I said nothing. What John Simon had said had staggered me. I had for so long been accustomed in my timorous traffic with human life to think only of men and women singly or in tiny groups that this suggestion of a great multitude marching forth from their caves of frustration at the command of John Simon took my mind off its balance and made me feel that despite all the kicking incredulity with which I had so far received John Simon's words there might be the making of a miracle in his intentions. But the stain of my belief was soon absorbed and my mind was once more whitely unpersuaded.

'And when you've got all these boys marshalled like a million sons of Moses upon this Sinai, what then? What will they do? You've got to see the end of these things, John Simon. To pass into history as the greatest assembler of paupers in the history of bread riots will avail you nothing, will not even be worth the grass of this hill which will be trampled down in the course of the procession. You are dealing with men who are accurately horrible in their spite and mania for power.'

'If you were I, Alan, do you think you'd do any differently?'

'The whole rhythm of you has changed. New winds have been playing on your hillocks, John Simon, and I'm not sure that I could find my way inside you any more. Go on with your plan. I can guess how you feel. You see the shadow of a degrading nastiness spreading over the hills. You want to see if there is anything on earth that will make the shadow yield. You were always more curious than I. The fullest triumph over all these louts who take and make oppression would be to turn your back on them, but for a lot of reasons that are rooted in a soil that is quite alien to me that is something you will not do. I'll stand by to watch. According to life's book of forecasts of which I sell copies to all who wish to take a course in terrified blinking, you and Katherine are moving into a slow-baking oven in which you will attain a crust of crisp futility pleasant to the teeth of doom and its butler, Penbury. I'd like that not to happen. There's a hint of great unrealised delight in you, John Simon, which makes me sick to see you footling about with these boys in their wainscoting.'

'The wind is coming up with the darkness. Come on.'

We made our way down the path towards the valley-bed.

119

The shape of Moonlea declared itself raggedly in the gloom from the tiny lighted windows. We walked for many minutes with no sound at all save that of our feet on the dampening grass. We were soaked in our thoughts.

9

I walked with Lemuel Stevens through the early evening light of the following day to a spot where I and my harp were to help bring a sense of cool refreshment into the clinkered existence of Moonlea. The place, directly opposite Lemuel's store, had been well chosen. It was the place where the main street of Moonlea had been cut almost exactly in half to make room for the new splendid chapel in which Mr Bowen had built up the greatest single following of any divine in Moonlea. There were still twenty clear yards between the chapel and the first of the small, constantly similar houses that trailed right along to the very foot of the hill on which the Briers had their cottage.

'Where do I play, Lemuel?'

'See the trees?' He pointed to a curtain of oaks that stood in a semi-circle at the point of meeting between the flat ground and the slope that went upward to the Penbury house. 'There's a small wooden platform there. You'll play on that, you and Felix.'

'He too?'

'Oh yes. Mr Bowen was telling me how sweetly he played at Mr Penbury's. He said there's genius in that boy. He said you can see that from the way his eyes burn when his bow is crossing the strings. That, says Mr Bowen, is genius as like as not.'

'That's sickness as like as not. Felix wears a suit of

damprot buttoned up with fears. He's a tall bruise.'

'Are you saying something, harpist?' asked Lemuel coming closer and looking puzzled.

'Keep your ear in, Lemuel. This isn't your idiom.'

'Mr Bowen says he'd love to have Felix play while he preaches. Then, truly, he said, he would be within the very core of God's inspiration.'

'Together, those two would be unbeatable. With Felix's sobbing melodies tickling the passion of this prophet into a fever, the Devil would be ashamed into feeling boyish and would run back for his short trousers within the hour.'

'He also said that all Felix wants now to make him a great artist, truly, is the custom of seeing the spirits of folk before him regularly, prostrate and willing to be stroked.'

'Speaking as an old stroker, Lemuel, there'll be no lack of those things for Felix to practise on. People bring their spirits along in buckets and baskets to anybody who looks as if he's running a stall for anything higher than boredom or filth.'

'All this music is going to sweeten Moonlea beyond recognition. It might even help you, harpist, to speak more plainly and less in riddles that not even a spaniel could follow.'

'I hope so. This is a crab-apple of a place.'

'Did you talk to John Simon?'

'For a long time. My jaw still twitches at the mention of his name.'

'What did he say?'

'Not much that you could take in without a lot of training.'

'Is he beginning to see reason?'

'Beginning? He's got the thing trained like a bear. He sees it marching around him all day long. You mean to ask if he's beginning to see life in the sort of light for which you serve as one of the cheaper wicks.'

'You know what I mean, harpist. Don't provoke a man. Does he understand yet that he will cause only misery and even death if he stays on in Moonlea?'

'I don't think so.'

'Did you tell him he is only tempting fate by staying here?'

'He hasn't started to see it like that, Lemuel.'

'It's that Katherine. She's got the man helpless and numb with her dark witcheries.'

'You're wrong there too, Lemuel. When John Simon and Moonlea have played each other out and if there is anything left over of us except a little ash and a little night, remind me to discuss this whole matter with you once more. The whole feel of life gives him no peace, and you and I, Lemuel, are part of the feel, all the moving thoughts that rest with a cutting edge on other people's freedom. If his only ail were the witchery of Katherine Brier the thing would be simple. He'd resolve all his troubles in the honest pleasure of being a goat full time and I'd be there at the railing of the pen urging him on and giving him the beat when he flags and getting a bonus from you and Penbury on every day of sated stupor in which I could persuade him to stay. To John Simon, you and I and Penbury are a squalid lot of intruders, and we are, too, you with your pennies and I with my constant and deafening chime of selfish moods. He isn't happy about us. He's part of a new disease of awareness that'll kill us off like flies on some distant day. You were born too small and I was born too loud to be able to do much about it. But tonight we are free to buzz and pollute to our heart's content. Where's my harp?'

'Two men are bringing it down from the mansion.'

123

'There they are now. And a big crowd with them and all with an air of jubilee about them that does my eyes good to look on.'

Into the clear space came a procession of people following the two large men who were carrying Penbury's harp. They carried it with a gentle care as if it were an object of reverence, and the people behind seemed to be walking quietly as well.

'They've never had much music here, have they, Lemuel?'

'Not much. The first Mr Penbury, he was against it. It's always been a serious hardworking sort of place, Moonlea. Until a year ago there wasn't an iron town in the country to compare with it.'

Many of the people had on their best dark suits and there was a quality of restlessness in their faces and limbs that could not be wholly explained by their eagerness to hear me perform. Felix, with his father at his side carrying his violin and in as bright a glow as ever, appeared and was given a loud cheer. Felix was frightened by this, but Mr Jamieson bowed and grinned and seemed clearly to be feeling the vitalising unguent of a new joy on his frame. We were hoisted on to a little platform and were about to make a start when Mr Bowen came into sight. He was wearing a black suit that hung well on his body with lapels of a deeper jet that shone with a lovely intensity. He walked towards the platform, carrying in his hand some thick volume, a Bible or a Prayer Book. At the sight of him I realised for the first time that the crowd could be divided into two clear sections. There was the large body of men and women who stood nearest to the platform; these were carefully and respectfully dressed as if for a high-class burial, and once they realised that Mr Bowen was making towards them they opened their

124

ranks to admit his passage. They were timid, amenable folk, distressed by the swift black rumours of impending crisis and fight. They appeared to be hoping that by their own smiling welcome to all things and all men they would cause the idiocy of conflict to vanish through a hole in the ground. Behind them were the vaguely undecided, their eyes constantly turning to the sides, to the back and front, for some reliable point of reference, sick with a new unwelcome consciousness, watching every moment and tasting it for any sign of significance that would give them an emblem of stability, a hint of direction. The outer fringe of the crowd was overtly hostile. They viewed the pleasant platoon in the front and Felix and myself with plain impatience and contempt. Their faces darkened and their lips moved but there was no clear unmistakable sign of dissension. They like the first and second factions were waiting with a desperate intentness.

Mr Bowen mounted the platform. He explained in a voice that was gently strong, that he was very glad to see so many of the folk gathered together for the simple pleasure of listening. Some youths and maidens tittered and Mr Bowen and the black-clad brigade in the front had to do some hard looking and nudging before they fell still and solemn. Mr Bowen said he could not let the occasion pass without a word or two and I bet myself that in this matter of Mr Bowen's words a careful count would be interesting, if too long for comfort. I leaned my head against the strings of the harp and winked at Felix who frowned at me. Mr Bowen said it was the time of harvest. He said it in such a way that many of the older men and women nearest the platform nodded their heads and smiled at each other as if to say that it took a man like Mr Bowen to home in the manner of a pigeon to such facts as that about the harvest. Harvests, said Mr Bowen, were the token of faith, knowledge and strength. Every wain that lumbered along a lane with its great golden load was a token of the unity in action of these three forces. This was the team of human genius, blessed by the holy sweat from every ploughman's limbs. The faces of Mr Bowen's listeners grew sorrowful at this, for they, like him, still had the smell and feel of the earth on their minds. They, said Mr Bowen, they with their patient labouring hands were the seed that Mr Penbury, acting for God, had placed in the furrows. Unless some wicked wind blew through the earth and stripped it to an obscene nakedness the time of peace and abundance would come once again for him and them. But let them not forget that he without them would be little the poorer: they without him would be fully destitute and damned. That is only the essential skeleton of what Mr Bowen said. But as it came forth from his mouth there were harps and clavichords, angels' wings and God knows what of persuasive beauty festooned around it. Most of the folk in the front were crying with a kind of tremendous joy. The neutral zone was stirring uneasily, looking upward as if in search of some planet where there would be no mind to make up. The crowd's refractory crust hardened; their muttering grew distinct.

'So the big man could live without us,' bawled a wrathful clear voice.

'Let him try. Give Penbury and Radcliffe a turn on the shovels.'

'He plans to bury us, Bowen,' shouted another, 'but not in a furrow, boy, not in a furrow.'

Mr Bowen looked at his supporters, startled. I could see the agitation of the quiet older folk as they were pressed nearer the platform. Mr Bowen gave us the signal to start playing. As at the mansion I padded behind Felix, initiating no melody but only thickening the mixture. Some people near to the street complained that they could not hear well. A dozen men came forward and carried the little platform with Felix, myself and our instruments still on to within about ten yards of the highway.

Our first items were all hymns. At first it was only the frankly pious who sang and it was wonderful for me to watch the fervent melancholy that rose in them wring all boldness and earthly desire from their faces. But as the best-loved hymns were repeated the groove of their simple assertions deepened, the great majority of the crowd slipped out of whatever thicket of aloofness and dissent they had been tearing their flesh on and moved smoothly into the cavern of dark formless yearning that opened out within the shell of soft harmonising sound. At moments when the harping left my mind free I wondered if God, or the fulfilment of whatever tall presence it was that whipped the senses of the multitude, would find a habitable corner to stand in in all that low-roofed ecstasy. The people before me were banging their heads against a long reef of loves and terrors, but the reef was soft as pap and their heads would still be in excellent trim for the next chorus. I shared for a few instants the gladness of quiescence, of standing consciously equidistant from life and death and finding them equally intrusive, untimely and in the worst possible taste. The hymns, the glugging absorption of the singers, pulled Felix's emotions to tatters and the fragments of him were in every corner of the crowd. He was close to toppling off the platform from depletion when some of the people out on the road called for an end to the purely devotional part of the rally. Mr Bowen lifted his hand reluctantly in signal that we could now take a brisker tempo. I tapped Felix on the shoulder and told him to take a rest or the next hymn would be played strictly and slowly over and on account of him. He shook his head, flushed and stupefied, and we watched the audience wincing as they groped their way back to thought that knew itself to be paying a heavy rent on a finite skull, back to a programme of bread and daily survival. I felt that Felix and I could have been crowned then and there as two of reason's leading lullabies. Over the road Lemuel's wife, Isabella, wearing a richly brown pinafore that caught my eye, sold off a crock of nettle beer to the thirsty singers. I looked around for Lemuel who had been standing at the side of the platform but there was no sign of him.

There was a shout of welcome from the people on the fringe, and the crowd opened, as if automatically, once more to admit John Simon who walked slow and smiling towards the platform. He seemed embarrassed at the notice he had received and kept his eyes fixed on me. I felt that crowds would always open for John Simon and that he would always be astonished and made to feel awkward by this attention. He leaned his arms on the platform and told Felix very courteously how glad he and his friends were to see him do so well with the fiddle. Felix kept his back to John Simon, his neck in a flush, as if the praise of John Simon and his friends was the last thing he wanted. Mr Jamieson was also leaning on to the platform tugging at Felix's trousers and humming some tune he wanted us to play, obviously eager to get John Simon out of the way and the curtain rung down on this pensive, quiet interlude.

'You going to make a speech, John Simon?' I asked. 'If you could make your notions clear to those people after their session at the graveside peering through the clods, you'd be a wizard. I'd kiss your feet.'

'No. I'm not going to make a speech. They know all I know. Some of them, a lot more. They're happy, and I like that. The evening's calm and the music's sweet. For a moment no wind to make the face sting. Carry on, boy.'

'You sing then. My fingers have an urge to play that song you used to move people to weeping with in the old days, "All Lost and Lonely Hearts on Earth"; remember it? That song on top of those salvation chants and they'd be so numb Penbury'd have to rake his fires right out on top of them for them to know that anything's different in the iron trade.'

'I don't want to sing either. I just want to tell you that I've got to slip over to Westlea. I'll probably be back before the end of the festival. If not, wait here for me.'

'Going alone?'

'Yes. Why?'

'Oh nothing. Just be careful. Penbury might wish to try a few private manoeuvres before closing down the furnaces.'

'You're getting quite a tactician, Alan. But don't worry. Westlea's no distance at all. Goodbye.'

As he moved away my eye was caught by a sudden movement of the curtain over the glass-paned top half of Lemuel Stevens's shop door. The curtain was drawn back. I could see Lemuel quite clearly but could not distinguish certainly the man who stood at his side. Lemuel was pointing at John Simon. His arm was rigid as if with excitement. It moved as John Simon made his way swiftly out of the crowd. I kept my eyes motionless on Lemuel's door. When Felix plucked my arm and asked me what about a resumption of the music, I told him to be still or do what the devil he liked. I kept on with my staring. It lasted no more than a minute. The man Bledgely, one of the two who had caused my bruises that day on Plimmon's estate, his high coat collar turned up around his face, stepped out and without looking to left or right began walking in the direction that John Simon had taken.

I jumped down from the platform, wanting to run and warn John Simon. I would have liked the chance of being with him to give Bledgely a formal official welcome and send him back to Penbury or Plimmon as black and blue as coal and sky. But the people crowded around me, hundreds strong, breathing thanks and gratitude right into my face as if I had brought them each a sack of gold. I felt sucked down and helpless as I swirled among the women with their little curtseys and the men with their interminable 'Thank you, Oh thank you, Mr Leigh.' I was on the point of screaming at them to leave me alone when, through an opening between two heads, I saw the face of Wilfie Bannion. I shouted to him and in three or four moves of his arms he was at my side. He asked me what I wanted.

'John Simon's gone off to Westlea alone.'

'I know that. Some of the men from the mines beyond Tudbury are coming in to talk with him. We have a friend at Westlea whose cottage we use for these meetings. There's no reason for alarm.'

'There is, though. You remember what you told me about your brother, your brother Sam, and the man who was seen in the town just before he died?'

Wilfie made no reply. He looked at me with his eyes very quiet in his head, waiting for me to go on.

'A man with a couple of fingers missing, the very man who put me in the shadow over at Plimmon's. He's here, in Moonlea. I saw him coming out of Lemuel's and he started

130

off after John Simon. His name is Bledgely and he's a great bear of a man. Come on, let's start.'

'You stay here, harpist. The people like you.'

'But John Simon…'

'I won't make any mistakes. I know the way.'

'To Westlea?'

'To Westlea and to Bledgely.'

He dashed from the crowd like a flash and ran westward along the highway as fast as he could. I would have followed him had not hands grasped my arms to bear me back to the platform where Felix was already trembling his way into a jig to which some of the younger people were already beginning to dance. The elder folk objected at first and refused to make room for the dancers to perform their movements, but Mr Bowen drew them off to leave an adequate clearing for the dancers. He said in a voice that everybody could hear that laughter and joy too belonged on earth, and he said it propri-etorially as if he were the very man who had just told sadness and death to move on to the next parish. But there was no real certainty in his tone and it sounded to me as if he had just been told that fact about joy about an hour before and had accepted it for publication only after he and joy, both buttoned up to the ears because of chills, had been properly introduced to each other.

Down a lane through the trees under which we had begun our playing came Helen Penbury and three or four other women, fussily dressed. Behind them came Jabez and a small troupe of retainers bearing hampers. These were set down together with chairs for the ladies on the spot where the platform had originally been set. Then the hampers were opened, showing a miraculous variety of cakes. Helen Penbury announced in a voice that made everyone's head turn towards her that she had brought a little something for the children. A great wave of children came forth from the crowd, so many of whom I could not remember having seen around the platform that I suspected some of them of being elders on the crouch, shortened by years of ironmaking or a sudden wish for cake. They lined up at the hampers and Helen and her assistants gave each one a smile with his dainty and looked as if they were sure that with such a full force of urbanity now being thrown behind simple kindliness the world could now start bringing back most of its regrets from the laundry. The children, chewing hard as they came away to fit themselves into the procession at a new spot and with a different look, seemed to agree with Helen and her companions. I stopped my playing to look at her. I could not help contrasting her brilliant, beautifully tended surface and the lit glittering chambers of her confident interior with the raggle-taggle of spoiled tormented shadows that met me in most of the cottages of Moonlea, that of Katherine Brier above all and that of the widow and children of Sammy Bannion. Sammy had lived in one of the older, immensely thick-walled dwellings of Moonlea's earliest village period. John Simon had taken me to see it. Since Sammy's death his wife and children had been living in what was virtually an excavation in one of its larger walls while the authentic rooms were occupied by some more numerous and more solvent group. The faces of Mrs Bannion and Katherine moved out of my mind, took their places alongside Helen's, and an interesting gallery they made of it. I saw her smile at me, the kind of smile that appears to come easily to tall women as if the grimace becomes fringed with a knowing frost in the course of the extra distance it has to traverse on its way up from the heart. The smile infuriated me. It made

132

me think on the instant that she might have worn that identical, scient look an hour or two before as she heard her father or Radcliffe give orders to put Bledgely on the scent. All my senses called her and her tribe a pack of evil ones, smugly vile, bald of all those waving feelers of insistent mercy that keep most others in a tingle of comradeship or pain, as I imagined John Simon dead, the whole essence of his rich sweetness kicked down the hole by people to whom he had been only a brief and wretched hindrance. I saw too the ravaged waste into which the life of Katherine would enter if the dead John Simon turned the last key on her twisted silent wants. At that moment I hated silence. I had the taste of too many silences on my tongue, my own, silkenly familiar, others, rough and mortally acrid. I gave the harp a bang with my feet and hands.

'Why doesn't life shout its morbid silly bloody head off?' I asked Felix and got no answer. I stood up, leaving Felix to carry on with the jig. Through a gap between two houses at the far end of Moonlea, near the great black-brown stain of the works yards I saw Wilfie. He was walking very slowly, making me think that John Simon and Bledgely in turn must have slackened their pace.

I was on the point of jumping to the ground when the butler Jabez came to the foot of the platform. He gave a short bow in a way that showed he enjoyed this bowing, would indeed have been flat on his face most of the time and enjoying every submissive moment of it if his job did not require an upright human to handle some of its functions. He said that Miss Helen wished to serve refreshment to the musicians. We stepped down and walked slowly towards the elegant smiling group between the trees. Felix walked behind me dabbing away at his wet face with a kerchief and blowing hard into it at intervals to distract his mind from its central theme of timidity. When I reached the group Helen offered me a cake. She was in a mood to charm and was doing deliberate things with her mouth and eyes that did no more than anger me after those moments of panic and sickening thought about John Simon.

'Frankly,' I said very quietly to her, 'I don't care if your father never sleeps. I'm sorry to my bones I ever decided to come over Arthur's Crown. For your cakes, keep them please. I've no wish for sweetness.'

'What's worrying you, harpist?'

'I couldn't explain. A fleet of blacksailed thoughts. The smell of damp, turned clay that came up from those hymns. Grisly. Tears in the eyes of the death-ridden, then sweat on the features of young lust. All liquid, all pumped up by plucked strings. I've got to get out of here for a bit. So long.'

I ran through the trees, swerved and set my face towards the road that Wilfie Bannion had taken. A half mile out of the town I took in my stride. I was ill with the lack of breath in my body and the surfeit of forebodings in my mind. I stared at the dark length of track in front of me and saw not a soul. I grew calmer. I reassured myself about John Simon. Bledgely, I told myself, might have set out merely to watch his movements. It was fantastic that even these over-assertive princes of pride like Penbury and Radcliffe would have sunk so low as to direct stranglers and head-breakers to curtail opposition and change the shape of critics. Fantastic. I recalled my meeting with Bledgely on the Plimmon estate. That had been different. I had been trespassing. The word made pinging quizzical echoes in my mind, but I told them to hush and let me get on with my job of consoling myself and sealing up the rot holes of my fears.

134

Bledgely had been a keeper, and even if I regarded enclosers of land as maniacs, still it was a widespread mania and apparently blessed by the Parliament in London and by whoever it was who sat upon the throne. And even if Bledgely meant harm to John Simon, Wilfie Bannion had worn a nimble vindictive look when he left me. Again I felt this whole traffic in hatred and violence was an ugly polluting intrusion to me. I should have jumped clear of it at the beginning and stuck to the modes of feeling and living, the easy genial unhurried step from day to day which I had adjusted perfectly to the sum total of my desires. I sat on a hillock by the roadside. As the energy flowed back into my body and a sportive fancy dragged its green over the patch that had been blackened by my earnest brooding, I pondered the look that Helen Penbury had given me as she offered me her cake. There had been a willing warmth in the corners of it. Perhaps she was attracted and beguiled by the total strangeness of me as I was by that of her. Perhaps there was a point at which mere oddity came as a pleasant change even from the ample possession of wealth, power and the right to have whole populations toiling away like beavers at your behest. We might have a few moments of interested staring one at the other as we passed in the space of our mutual remoteness. If only as a lover of long walking, it would be good for me to sound the hills and valleys and clefts in the landscape of that woman's heart. If the landscape turned out to be dead flat and even repellent all the way in and out it would not be the first time I had known that kind of blank boredom in my traffic with a woman. And even if she lured me in an inch or two only to beat me over the head with her riding crop, that too would be a rich item to reflect on and narrate when my teeth fell out and my stiffened joints put

135

an end to my roaming, showing all my gums to nothingness and not caring a suck...

I leaped from the hillock. From the wood a furlong ahead came the drawn scream of a man in crucial pain. I stood, then began my running again. I made towards the trees. As I came nearer, my legs slowed down once more, not this time from fatigue but because from within the wood came the sound of blows so quick and so horrifyingly suggestive in their muffled dampness that they made part of me faint.

I walked through the trees, slowly and with caution, conscious of having my fingers judge the feel of bark. The beating stopped. I came to a clearing. In front of me I saw the face of Wilfie Bannion who was leaning against the boll of an oak, his face twisted and half smiling with a crazy delight, his throat rising and falling to the stroke of a painful sobbing. At his feet lay Bledgely, his head bloody, his teeth bared, his limbs hugely strewn, his fingers deep in the leaf-covered earth.

'God, God,' I said, 'this is a horrible thing. Look at him, Wilfie, look at him.'

'I've looked. Don't shake, harpist. We've got to get rid of this. I feel better now, better. It was awful when I met him and started. One is full of noise at first and then the noise grows less and that is better.'

'Where's John Simon?' I wanted Wilfie to be quiet for a few moments, to heal the violent break in his voice as he spoke.

'Westlea, I suppose. He doesn't even know this man was following him. I took a short cut and waited for him among the trees. As he came into the wood he started to run as if he wanted to come up with John Simon before the wood ended. I got in the first blow. That was the only way.

Otherwise he'd have slaughtered the both of us.'

'Yes, yes.' My head was spinning like a top with all this talk and sight of slaughter. Wilfie was like ice now, cool and attentive, moving his eyes around to find the best place to dispose of Bledgely. He pointed to a shallow trough about eight yards away.

'We'll put him in there. We'll cover him with leaves, boughs, earth.'

'But they'll find out, Wilfie. People are not daft. You've played into Penbury's hands.'

'By the time they find about this there'll be things going on in Moonlea a lot bigger than Bledgely or his death.'

We lifted the dead man and carried him, Wilfie at the arms, to the shallow ditch at which Wilfie had pointed. The distance we carried the burden was short, but it had been long since I had lifted and supported the weight of anything that looked as grotesque or was as heavy as Bledgely. By the time we laid him down in the ready-made grave my senses had taken on a kind of drunken clarity and the least stirring of our feet among the drying leaves was like the banging of a drumstick on my inner ear. I dropped my half of Bledgely a second ahead of time and Wilfie gave me a sharp, impatient glance. I rested my head against a tree and hated the cold practical pressure of the moment which did not allow my spirit the pleasure of expanding voluptuously as it liked to do at the thought of death. This was vulgar, low-grade death, which left the mind a muddy fearing lump, and I did not like it.

'Why can't all you people be cosily dead?' I shouted, and the look in Wilfie's eyes as he received my question showed me that there must have been a fair seam of madness in my tone. 'Or stupid as hell like those weeping chanting loons

137

back there who listened to my playing.'

'Shut up, harpist. Get back to Moonlea.'

'What'll this mean, Wilfie? Will it mean something terrible?'

'Not to you. It'll make Penbury throw away any doubts he might have had about closing down the furnaces. By Saturday night they'll be cold and the battle will be on. Did I once hear you say that Penbury couldn't sleep?'

'That's it. He likes a drop of music on the eyelids before midnight.' I was dazed by the contrast between the memory of the quiet perfectly appointed room in the mansion where Penbury had told me of his weakness and the clearing in which Bledgely and black calamity both kept grinning at me. 'Why?'

Wilfie stared down at Bledgely and laughed.

'That's funny,' he said, and started dropping things on Bledgely that would soon have the body hidden from sight.

'You coming back, Wilfie?'

'No. I'm going on to Westlea. I've got to tell John Simon. From now on he'll have to know everything that goes on.'

'Why don't you guess it all and then have a good long swoon?' Wilfie had paused in his scooping of earth and leaves and was looking up at my face. 'You're glad this happened, aren't you, Wilfie?'

'Glad that it's this man on the ground and not John Simon? Of course. But there's more in it than that. It'll bring a lot of boils to the break. I've been sick of being like Bledgely is now, still and having things dropped on me from above.'

'The danger doesn't worry you?'

'After ten years in Moonlea and what happened to Sam, I'm as numb to it as that tree over there. And having a dead

Bledgely thrown down as a kind of gauntlet will be good for John Simon too. It'll pull him out of his shadow once and for all. He's a great lad, the only one of us who has just the right words and just the right feelings to get hold of the whole heart of a multitude and fill the thing with light. But he's soft too often with sadness, too fond of laying his hand on the sand of the arena he should be fighting in, fingering it to have the wonder of its fineness, its warmth or coldness on his flesh. Ever since he had that quarrel with Jeremy Longridge when we had our meeting with the men from the southern valleys, John Simon has been drifting into a queer sickly sort of Quakerish fancy that a peaceful kiss laid with sufficient pressure on each of Penbury's cheeks would see the people better fed. He's too much like you, harpist, but you have no responsibility and you have no great importance save to those idle ones and sleepless ones who wish and can afford to have you near to keep their senses in a tickle. But this will put an end to John Simon's peculiar cramps of the will. From now on, harpist, there'll be great songs for you to sing.'

'You have a fierce wisdom, Wilfie. You make me feel very small and very insecure. Can you manage this burial task without me? I'm not at ease in this kind of ceremony.'

'Get back to Moonlea. The people will be missing you.'

I turned away and walked back to the town. It was late dusk as I went down the main street. The larger part of the crowd which had been assembled when I left was still there, as if clinging desperately to the harmless geniality of the moment. A dozen thick storm torches had been lit around the platform, and in the faint light the young couples were still dancing and the older folk were appealing to Felix to start them once again on a round of slower and better-loved

139

melody. One of the youths became angry at these constant interruptions and pulled roughly at the coat-tail of an old man whose protests had been incessant and loud and whose voice seemed to be set in a frame of sobs. Mr Bowen who was standing near Helen Penbury saw the incident and cried out:

'Shame on you, Nathaniel Perry, to be so inflamed with these antics of the devil as not to know when you have had enough and to make you offend the grief of our old friend Gideon Mathews who has lately lost his wife and wishes to lay the songs of God like an ointment of healing on the sting of his deprivation.'

The lad Nathaniel spoke an oath to his companions and they laughed. Mr Bowen straightened and looked as if he were going to advance on them, but Helen Penbury pulled him by the arm. I heard her say:

'No unpleasantness, Mr Bowen. You remember what my father said tonight. The people can be given their head in anything inessential. There are no real troublemakers here. A few over-amorous oafs, little more. Let them dance till dawn if they desire. It will use up energy they might be storing for less pleasant purposes.'

'Of course, Miss Helen. My temper is hasty. I hate to see the old treated without love or reverence. It irks me to see members of my flock pushed to one side in the course of the celebration. Would you mind if I were to take a party of them to that patch behind the chapel where they could have their own measure of joy in a service of prayer and song?'

'That would be an excellent diversion, Mr Bowen. Take them.'

Mr Bowen went over to the old man Gideon Mathews who shook with pleasure as he heard the tidings. He explained

Mr Bowen's wishes to those around him and soon he and a large body of the older people were walking away from the platform. Mrs Brier was among them. She came up to me. Her face was fully lighted by one of the torches. Her eyes were red and large, and I could see that she too, as Mr Bowen had said, had been laying on the ointment to all the parts in her that had been rutted and maimed and it struck me that there must have been many like Mrs Brier in that multitude, little megaliths of deprivation.

'Where's Davy?' I asked. 'He's always singing up there on the hillside. I thought he would have been down to such a rally as this like a flash.'

'He gets excited. He loves singing as you say, and he's a treat to listen to in quiet songs with Wilfie Bannion and those boys when there's nothing to take his mind off the singing. But down here with so many people around him he'd be all right for a bit, singing like an organ, then he would wake up to where he was and then he would find the people sitting on his brow, and that makes him wild.'

'That's a wise way to feel, Mrs Brier. People on your brow. That's a thing to run from. People are a plague.'

'The last time we were all gathered in the open for song and prayer Davy was ill for days after. A man at his side kept telling him that he was singing too loud and off the note. He told Davy that five times. Then Davy hit him and he was ill for many days.'

'The man?'

'No, Davy. I don't know about the other one. It was Davy who suffered most. He was too ill even for his baskets. He just sat in the corner, saying nothing. Is John Simon all right, harpist?' Mrs Brier had brought her face close to mine and I could see the extra brightness of her eyes.

141

'Why do you ask?'

'I saw you run after him and Wilfie Bannion. I thought there might have been trouble.'

'No trouble. The place is full of peace. As far as I know he's all right.'

'Oh.' Her eyes were full of hesitation and conjecture. 'So long, harpist.'

She followed those who were bound for the patch behind the chapel. I could hear Mr Bowen pour his breath into the feeble flame of the first hymn. The younger folk bawled their contempt and shouted on Felix to play louder. The lad Nathaniel Perry caught sight of me. He was dancing with a stout girl thick in the lips and hanging on to Nathaniel as if her bout of full expression had now opened. The heat and perfume of the maiden had evidently inspired Nathaniel to a mood of uproarious daring. He grasped my arm and pushed me towards the platform, saying it was more of my music that they wished to hear. I took hold of his neckerchief and pushed him away.

'You go to the devil, Nathaniel. I've played my last tune for the night.' I pointed to his companion. 'She's tuned and ready for the right player, boy. One single note will do and no need to fiddle with scales. You'll find her fuller of rich melodies than I have ever been and the performer won't need too much subtlety in his touch.'

Nathaniel guffawed and soon dragged the maiden off into the shadows and I envied the quick unselfconscious simplicity of the manoeuvre. I heard a soft chuckle from behind me. It was Helen Penbury.

'In this moment,' I said, 'there is much to laugh at. Of these items, what do you choose as your particular fancy?'

'You.' She drew a dark-blue shawl closer around her

142

shoulders. 'It is the connoisseur of absurdity who is at bottom the most absurd.'

'I'm not in the same class as these Moonlea performers. Think again.'

'I still take you. After the company of Moonlea's leading matrons, I find your tone refreshingly salacious.'

'Just give me the wink. I can be downright filthy on demand.'

Some moves were now being made to bring the evening to an official end. Mr Jamieson and his friends were helping Felix down from the platform. Helen Penbury went on to Felix, took him by the hand and thanked him in a way that seemed to put him at ease and make him very happy. I was glad she had done that. The same men who had brought the hamper and chairs down from the mansion were now returning them. Helen was saying good night to the ladies.

'But, Helen,' one of them was saying, 'you really are very daring, you know. To walk along that path through the trees, alone, at this time of night, that's shocking. With things so disturbed...'

'Jabez will be with me.'

'This is where you miss the Captain. Where is he tonight?'

'Tudbury. Some business at the barracks, I think.' She raised her arm and signalled Jabez to approach, which he did in a way that I was slow to fathom. 'A mess dinner, I think I heard him say. But I'll be quite safe with Jabez. He's quite fearless and he's been far too long acquiring the shape of a butler to have any impulse of impropriety in the darkness with a lady.'

'Oh, Miss Helen, you are terrible.'

There were trills of excited laughter from the ladies. It was clear that Helen's outlook drew a tickling finger across their

143

senses; their emotional gardens were small, enclosed, and a shudder in the shrubs during Mr Bowen's longer perorations was about their maximum in the line of ecstasy. Also, as wives of the senior officials at the foundries their conscious-ness that night would be ground to a sharper edge by the suspicion of danger and tension that was hardening throughout the whole air of Moonlea.

Helen began her walk up the path through the trees, Jabez doing his duty as escort a few yards ahead, puffing already after so brief an exercise. She turned around and I believed I saw her arm perform a gesture of invitation towards me. I was not sure, but I wished to believe that that was what she had done. I wanted to talk to someone after that tableau in the woods with Wilfie Bannion and Bledgely. Those moments had put too many strange flavours on my palate for comfort, and, even if she had not beckoned, it was a good cause to be wrong in.

I heard her shout to Jabez that she wished to walk slowly and to be alone and she told him to go on to the house and tell her father that she would be back shortly.

'But, Miss Helen, the master was most stern in this very particular. He told me to be quite certain that you get home early and safely. The hour is no longer early, and as the ladies said these woods and these times are not altogether to be trusted.'

'Don't be a grandmother, Jabez. I'm no more than a few yards away from home now, and I've always been as safe in these woods as in my own bed. Be off with you, there's a good fellow.'

Jabez, muttering his complaints, vanished around a bend in the path. Helen branched leftward and walked in the shadow of the tall, beautifully laboured wall of Penbury's

Italian garden where the only vines that Moonlea would ever know grew. I followed her. I found her standing in a deep archway, closed by an intricate gate. Her dark cape was one with the shadow, but her face was vividly plain. I stood about a yard away from her, as amazed by her stillness as by the tide of evening scents that came forth from the garden. The walls of this woman were still steep and smooth to me and at that moment I was in no mood for bounding climbs.

'You didn't mind my following you?'

'Had I minded I would have taken the straight path.'

'I suppose so. You could always have run or screamed for Jabez if you had objected to my padding behind. Why do you want to talk to me?'

'We both have things to say that the other will listen to. Right?'

'Right. At some points there are several worlds between us. At others we are close as flesh and bone. God knows why, but I knew that at the very moment I saw you up on Arthur's Crown. I'm glad you're letting me talk to you. Any more of Felix and Bowen and that crew and I'd have been ready for Bedlam and a ring in my nose. I bet that captain would take this as an opportunity for some sword-play if he could see me here standing in front of you, even standing so still and distant and respectably appreciative of you as if you were a painting.'

'He might do. He has a fine line in pride.'

'What's he to you? His eyes light up the valley every time he looks at you. I saw that much even with strands of Felix's hair getting in my eyes that night I played your food down.'

'We've been friends for a long time. I think my father has considered the idea that some day we should be married.'

'There's a coolness in your voice. Don't you want to marry

the man? He looks as if he has life firmly under control.'

'My programme has always been vague. Each day I change my government of ideas.'

'But just at the moment you don't warm to the idea of the captain.'

'No. You can tell what he intends to see a year ahead. He's either taut with a sense of duty, which bores me, or squelchy with tenderness, which sickens me.' Her hands moved beneath her cape. 'He's something of a musician. He tunes himself each morning and he remains the livelong day exactly and sensitively in pitch. That degree of fitness can become as tedious as its opposite.'

'And Plimmon, the moustached chieftain with whom I saw you riding? Where is he to be located on the love map?'

She laughed. Her hands came forth from the cape and played with the vine strand which curled around the grey, perfectly fashioned stonework of the archway.

'Nowhere. He thinks it enough that he should ever ride with the daughter of an ironmaster. Plimmon has his dreams pitched on tighter strings than you have ever known on your harp. When he thinks of mating he might even take a fling at royalty.'

'And he considers you and your father to be of little account.'

'As far as I know, he endures us, no more.'

'Good God, fancy that. And there was I imagining that from you upward life would be a nice solid wall of ivory with not a fissure of any sort to break the even surface of your contempt. And now I find this Plimmon acting the iceberg to you as well as you do to the people of Moonlea. He must be a very exceptional maniac. The more I hear of you all the less I envy life its job of fitting you within the framework of one

146

species.'

'You're full of savour, harpist. Have you had many women in your wanderings?'

'Oh, quite a number. And not more than a half of them out of passion. The rest I followed with pure pity twitching in my hand like a dowser's rod. I've been in a thousand little poverty-bitten places on the bare slopes of unkind hills where men and women lead meagre bitter lives. But from what I've seen and felt, too, it's mainly the women who suffer. It's only their souls that have the quality of silk that allows them to be stuffed into the smallest and furthest folds of hell.'

'Isn't the fragrance of this garden superb when evening falls? Smell it.'

'Leave the fragrance be. I'm hanging myself out on the line on your account. So listen to my talk of souls and hell. It's special, and it makes me giddy to think that any human being can be as free from interest in such topics as you. Let me tell you a little more about those lonely places. The lives that most of the folk lead there are brief and black. Perhaps your father in his sleepless wisdom may iron out these folds of agony one day, but I doubt it. And when I pass through these places or pause there to play them a tune I ask myself by what miracle of showmanship the beauty of life can ever have made itself manifest to these people. For the men it is not so bad. When they find the sense of beauty withered and dead and tough as a piece of old beef they can always sandwich the thing between two slices of work and ale, then ache and belch their way to quietness. But women don't do that. In them there is always the kindly hope that the image of beauty will come knocking at their doors, bow politely to them when they open, take their hands, however gnarled, and lead them to some certain paradise.'

'And you, in your homely way, have been the image of beauty from time to time?'

'Something like that.'

'An inter-shire stallion.'

'Not quite so crude. A kind of suggestion of it, with my harp. In my mind now I have the picture of at least a hundred women whom I have called for an hour or so beyond the power of dirt and want.'

'You're quite apostolic, tonight, harpist. You disappoint. You've been giving too much of an ear to your radical friends on the other side of Moonlea.'

'Sorry. Normally I'm not like this. Ask John Simon Adams. He'll tell you that often I'm a selfish poetical loon more concerned with a sunset or the pitch of a song than with all the chromatic pain of man. It's the nearness of women that provokes this vein in me. They seem to tear the stone away from some spring of quick compassion and the nearness of you is in a stone-tearing class of its own. After one look at you, as you stand there now, I could do the rounds of earth licking all the wounds of man and bidding them be healed.'

'Forget such weeping projects, harpist! The wounds of man are tailored. They are requested, measured, paid for by the wearer. To found a religion, even a mood, on a wish to go around selling bandage to the afflicted is an authentic form of madness. You may kiss my hand, harpist. I'm in a mood to be excited.'

I kissed her hand. The vine-smell of her fingers was sharp, provoking. Her flesh was warm. A rolling wave of light from opened furnace-doors rose and washed the darkness.

'Something has made you very happy tonight,' I said. 'You think you are sitting on some tight little hill of triumph or you would not have consented to play the fool with me. Although I suppose that by Moonlea standards I am, as you stated earlier, a comparatively interesting freak. Did you have the idea that something has happened or will happen tonight that will make it easier for your father to keep on treating the neck of Moonlea as a footrest?'

'Possibly.'

'Perhaps somebody was to die.' I heard her foot kick against the woodwork of the gate as if in a gesture of surprise. 'Tell me, tell me, because I do not understand the timetable of hate and conflict that you people are laying down for the conduct of life. I and the goats are baffled and I want to make up for the awful wear and tear on my mind and heart by being able to make them happier about not being human on my return. The wind and a curious tickle in my heart drove me here and before I leave I wish to know, were you happier because you thought that someone might die tonight?'

'Perhaps.'

'And you were hoping perhaps that the someone might have been John Simon Adams?'

'Why not?'

'Why, for Christ's sake?'

'He's interfering with the happiness of a lot of people. He's a fool. But like the rest of us he will no doubt distil his own brand of hemlock at the required strength. But why talk of him, anyway, harpist?'

'That's it. Why should I care a damn? If John Simon wants to let himself into the stew he's welcome to whatever slice of onion comes his way. The night's soft. You're warm, Helen.'

The gate yielded behind her. We entered the garden. A few

yards from the gate there was a gently sloping turfed bank. We lay upon it. Our hunger for each other filled the night. Our passion swung into the deliberate beat of the tear-ecstasy of the hymn singers who were still at it below. We scorched every shadow beneath the trees. From moment to moment my nerves were scraped painfully by the guess that her mind might well have been hoisted on to its lofty peak of desire by some excited prophetic glimpse of John Simon bludgeoned out of life, harmless.

She rose, trembling and embarrassed.

'Someone died,' I said.

'How do you know?'

'After an experience like this, in such a garden, I am always fey.'

'Why do you tell me that now? she asked, and there was a pettish anger in her voice.

'I tell you because I want you to know that whatever happens to John Simon, however shrewdly poised your anger when it strikes, he'll always be your wound. He and his kind want so little for themselves and think so much about others they will bleed you and your old man with your cautious nut-gathering lusts to death. And all because he's not terrified like the rest of us. I wonder what will grow when there are no terrors left at all. Good night.'

I left her. As I came out of the trees into the clearing alongside Mr Bowen's chapel, I looked back and saw Jabez come down the path from the mansion, swinging a lantern and calling insistently and discreetly for her.

10

I lay back beneath the beech tree at the bottom of the Briers' garden. Davy was at my side sucking a pipe and staring impressed at the stillness of my limbs. All the afternoon I had been helping him with his basket-making. I had found the work enriching, but my hands were sore after the hours of concentrated carefulness. From inside the house I could hear the deep sweet voices of Mrs Brier and Katherine singing in a simple harmony. I had torn a young swede from the soil and was chewing it. John Simon had not slept at the cottage the night before. I had not seen him from that moment when I saw him vanish along the road to Westlea, followed by Bledgely. At the thought of Bledgely I shivered and bit harder at my swede. But I had decided that these things, John Simon, Bledgely, Katherine, all desires that sat ill upon me and smelled in my memory of vines, would worry me no more. I would spend one more evening at Moonlea and in the morning I would be once more on the road.

'Where's John Simon?' asked Davy.

'About his business.'

'He's often away.'

'He has a lot of business.'

'I like John Simon.'

'So do we all, Davy. He's all right.'

'But I like you even better.'

'Thank you, Davy. I like you too. You've taught me a lot of things about plants such as I have never before seen grow in the soil of gardens. And when my hands grow too cold and slow for strings I'll have the magic of basket-making to fall back on.'

'You sit down with me, harpist, and talk with me. John Simon often sits and says not a word with me.'

'I'm lazier than he is. When he sits down he wants to rest.'

'Will you be here for ever, Alan?'

'Tomorrow I go.'

'You have business too?'

'A sort of business.'

'And will you be back on the day after?'

'I expect so.' I saw no point in not lying to Davy. It would do him no harm that could hold a candle to the rich passages of maiming to which he had already been treated. I did not wish to be questioned, by his mother or by Katherine. But I was determined that even if they should know they would not dissuade me. I could feel the whole place moving at a gallop into midnight.

Through the bushes that hid the garden wall I heard someone make a hushing sound. I stood up and walked to the point from which the sound came. It was Wilfie Bannion, still streaked with furnace dirt. The sight of him reminded me once again of Bledgely and my knees went hollow.

'Where's John Simon?' I asked.

'Still at Westlea, lying low.'

'Why didn't he come back here?'

'The people who sent Bledgely after him probably think he's dead. I suppose they gave instructions to Bledgely not to return when the job was done, so they'll see nothing amiss in his absence. We didn't think they would make a definite move so soon. In the few days before they find out the truth about John Simon he'll have the chance of doing one or two things which they might otherwise have prevented him from doing. So he's staying at Westlea.'

'What's he got to do there?'

'Making arrangements for the food as like as not.'

'Food? What food? What for?'

'Forty miles to the west of here is open country where they still farm the fields. Penbury, Plimmon and Radcliffe will try to starve us. We've been in touch with the people who led the movement against the turnpikes and the workhouses in the western counties. They haven't got much food to spare, but if the iron-towns go dead they've promised to send us as much as they can. That'll help us hold out for a little while. There'll be enough for the kids, anyway. If Penbury's got a grain of sense it won't last long. He'll see we've reached the point where we won't live on his terms any longer. And once it starts we have good friends who'll speak up for us at London.'

'I've been there. It's a noisy place. They'll have to speak very loud to make anyone hear. I don't see what you're driving at at all. Penbury'll have the town cut off. It'll be isolated like a plague case. Not a potato, not a bean will come through.'

'We've got the numbers and we know the land. John Simon says we'll win without a blow. I'm not as calm about that side of it as he is but I'm not worrying. We'll get the food. Now this is what we want you to do, harpist.'

'Oh no,' I said, tapping Wilfie's hand to make my words more emphatic, 'I'm going without fail tomorrow. Tell John Simon goodbye for me if he's not back by the time I start out.'

153

'You won't be going.'

'Since when have you been standing guard inside my head making plans? I say I'm going. Do you mean by that nodding of your head and that wise-looking smile that you will find some way to stop me? Now look, Wilfie...'

'You look, harpist. It was no whim that brought you down from the hills in the North to find out how it was with John Simon. You came because he was in danger and you and he are of one piece.'

'Not any longer. He's in his closet and I'm in mine. It's dark and the perfumes are mixed, but I have a strong bolt on the door and I feel safe.'

'You won't leave. You'll say you will. You'll keep on saying you will, but when John Simon needs you you'll be by his side.'

'From the way you say it I have the feeling that his side is going to be the centre of some gloomy actions.'

'This is what you have to do. Find out all you can from Penbury and his spaniel dogs about what they intend to do.'

'I can tell you now. Bark and bite and they'll charge you for all the teeth they can't get back.'

'I want the details. When the furnaces will be going cold, when the soldiers are due to come in, where they are to be stationed. Will you do that?'

'I promise nothing. Ever since I came here I have been going on from minute to minute. If the good clear sense in my mind manages to get in touch with my feet keep your eye on the path up Arthur's Crown. You'll have a good view of my vanishing backside.'

'I don't think so. You have a shadow in the eyes. Moonlea's got you on the hooks.'

He turned and went towards his cottage, leaving me with

154

my full reply still a good ten minutes short of birth.

I told Davy I would soon be back and climbed over the garden wall at the spot where Wilfie had spoken to me. I walked quickly down the rough hillside. It occurred to me that Katherine should be told about John Simon. I stopped and looked back at the cottage. I decided not to go back there. From now on it would be even less wise for Katherine to be plaguing herself with the thought of him. He had chosen his own private doorway of destructive anguish and he would vanish through it. I watched the smoke rise from the chimney; below it I could still see the wisp of smoke rising from the pipe of Davy, ironically straight and serene. The sight of it brought me a sudden regret that almost made me weep. I continued on my way.

I reached the shop of Lemuel Stevens. I opened the door and was startled by the loud bell that Lemuel had suspended above the door to give him warning of unwelcome visitors. Isabella was there. She was happy, excited and called me into the kitchen. I accepted the offer, sat down on the plain narrow fireside chair she drew up for me and swallowed the jar of herbal beer which she poured out for me. The table was covered with the enormous china pieces which she had been taking down from their shelves for cleaning. The sideboard, looking vaster than ever with all its partitions sombrely empty, stared towards the window. She hummed and smiled as she watched me drink and I could see that she had come as near as she ever would to challenging the mould of melancholy into which her being had flowed.

'You're happy today, Mrs Stevens.'

'Can't a body sing if she has a mind to?' she asked coyly.

'A body can do what she pleases. Where's Lemuel?'

'Up at the mansion.'

'From the look of you I should say that Penbury has the mutiny well in hand.'

'They tell me John Simon Adams has run away. You'd know about that, wouldn't you, harpist?'

'He didn't sleep in his bed last night.'

'Then he must have run away. I knew his insolence would some day crack.'

'Just as well. Let all things crack. That's good music when you've seen so many queer things all in one nice lovely piece. I could have wished that John Simon had come away from Moonlea with me, but as far as he's concerned any place out of Moonlea is a good place for him.'

'But not for that bitch Katherine. She'll miss the great hot body of him.'

'That's a pagan statement, Mrs Stevens. You shock me.'

'Oh, I didn't mean anything wicked by it, harpist. You ask Lemuel. I've got a mind like snow. He's said so so many times. You'll never find the devil's mark between these four walls.'

'Keep trying. It's not so bad.'

I looked at her. Her face was moving to a morbid rhythm. Some elemental shoots were breaking through the stone hard surface that she and Lemuel had laid down upon their lives, upon their allotment of diligent desolation.

'Tell me, harpist,' she said, dragging her words out, 'is it true what they say, that Davy has nothing of the man about him at all, that she sickened of having always a sleeping man at her side and that is why she rushed in an adulterous fashion to the arms of John Simon Adams?'

'I'm only living there for a short space. I only talk to Davy. I don't look him over for flaws. I'm ignorant about these things. Men and women could be after each other in

156

the open manner of cats and dogs, and I have an inkling that they would be no worse off than they are now. I don't like the look of you when you speak about these things. What kind of well have you and Lemuel been crouching in to give you such thoughts as those? How would you like it if I asked you what kind of a performer Lemuel is? It's all right. I won't press for an answer and there's no need for you to totter into a faint.'

'You're disgusting, harpist, disgusting. Lemuel Stevens and I have led the cleanest lives in Moonlea.'

'Don't carry on about it. I can smell the soap.'

'If Lemuel hadn't told me to be kind and nice to you I'd call the neighbours to put you out. I'd run and tell Mr Bowen what kind of a man you are, what kind of a monster we have let into the town.'

'Mr Bowen knows. He puts me on the scales each Sunday. He can tell you about me to the last quaint, damned ounce. All the things I love make him spin like a top with sickness. You've lived too hard, you two. You've kept your eyes fixed so tightly on the prospect of a bliss that will never come I can feel your sockets ache. When will you find the quiet pasture you set out to find?' My voice was quiet, kind and calmed her irritation.

'Soon, harpist.'

'Tell me about it.'

'When all this trouble blows over and Moonlea will be busy and prosperous once again, Mr Penbury is seeing to it that Lemuel is set up in business at Tudbury. That's my home, you know, and my mother, who is a widow and not well, will be glad to have us back there. She says I've given too much of my life to Lemuel. She says I married beneath me.'

157

'Beneath you? How was that? Where was Lemuel?'

'I mean he was so poor. Poorer than a church mouse, with nothing but his character. My father was the richest butcher in all Tudbury. Oh, I'll be glad to leave here. There's not been much pleasure except for the wonderful meetings with Mr Bowen. And there are so many people who don't understand Lemuel, who envy him too bitterly.'

'The people who don't understand about the famine and the millers? A crass lot. Don't worry your head about them.' I looked at her drawn, swiftly ageing face, wrinkled with the strain of trying to make terms with a weariness and dingy self-restraint that had become chronic and without end or palpable solace. 'In Tudbury there'll be a fresh start. You'll bloom like things in spring.' The lie boomed into my nettle beer glass.

The door bell rang again and Lemuel came in hopping rather than walking. He was blither than I had ever seen him before. I told him I was glad that Mr Penbury had once more shown his gratitude to him for his willing services and I prophesied, having nothing better to do with my tongue at that moment, that before he had finished Lemuel would probably be one of the wealthiest factors in the kingdom.

'Life's a dark sort of conflict, Lemuel,' I said, 'but you are the boy who knows the corners into which the soil drifts, the soil where a seed needs only the warmth of an attentive hand to make it sprout.'

'I think you're right. Isabella and I have given up a lot since we came to Moonlea. We were like a pair of slaves when we were in that first bakehouse. But we are beginning to see the light. I've got some good news for you too.'

'Penbury has given up sleeping altogether and I'm now on full time.'

'Don't joke, harpist. Be humble for the sake of God or you'll be spoiling the fine impression you've made so far. There is a big ball at Lord Plimmon's place tonight. He has heard of your skill with the harp and he has sent for you. There aren't many minstrels like you left now and Lord Plimmon has some noble friends from London who are staying with him and they said how interested they would be in hearing you. You can never tell what the end of these things will be.'

'A soreness in a couple of my fingers and another long strange night added to my collection. That'll be the end of it.'

'You're a bit sad and bitter tonight. What's up?'

'Oh, it's nothing. That nettle beer casts a little shadow but really I am full of joy for the way in which things are turning out for you and Mrs Stevens. What happens to John Simon doesn't interest me any more.'

'That's the way to feel. John Simon was never a scrap of use to anyone.'

His voice could almost be seen to lean over and kiss that past tense. He turned his head aside to hide his flushed satisfaction as he saw my eyebrows lift and my eyes rest inquiringly upon him.

'You've not heard from him?'

'Not a word, Lemuel. He saw the danger light. He's no fool.'

'That's it. He cleared out while the going was good.'

'No doubt about it. What time do they want me to play at the lord's place?'

'Eight or somewhere near. I'll be going along there with you.'

'What's your role?'

159

'I've got a basket of cottage loaves to deliver to the kitchen of the Plimmon Hall. Cottage loaves are the best I do. They melt between the lips as you probably remember, harpist. It isn't often I get the chance to do them as they ought to be done. The Moonlea folk like their tack plain, hard and cheap. But if I can make a permanent connection with Lord Plimmon's butler I'll be made.'

'Let's start then. We'll make our way quietly on foot.'

He loaded his basket and we started out. When we came to the town's end he was already gasping. He had overloaded the basket. We paused outside the tavern The Leaves After the Rain. I said it would be better for the both of us if we rested inside and took some ale to strengthen us for the journey which would be quite long with such a weight on his arm. At the moment I made the suggestion his face lit up, for the evening was warm and golden in a way that invited a joyous repose but the moment after his face was blank with terror.

'Me, go into that place and drink ale? Don't be daft, harpist. You don't know who you are talking to. You want to hear Mr Bowen about the alehouses. He'd burn them down to the last stick, that's what he'd do.'

'Ach, come on, man. The days are surely gone when you need to be thinking of your every action in terms of what Mr Bowen and Mr Penbury will say. You've served them well, and you're a made man. Somebody told me there was a time when you were quite fond of your stoup.'

'And what was I in the days when I was? Little better than a beggar hanging around the Northgate Arms and the Mitre Arms in Tudbury, holding the horses for a lot of tosspots. It was then Isabella and her mother got hold of me and look what they've done for me.'

160

'A fine bit of laundering. Every wrinkle perfectly ironed and in place.'

'She's a wonderful woman, Isabella. She's been behind me all the time.'

'As the kid who died of shock in the forest said about the king of the elves.'

'What was that?'

'A song I heard. Come on, man. You've got something to celebrate. This is the day of your ascension. Plimmon treats his stomach to some of your cottage loaves and John Simon Adams has slipped from the life of Moonlea. Soon you too will be saying goodbye to Moonlea and all its memories of hard jet days. Besides, I've got some thoughts I'd like to soak and slacken. There's no one about to see you go in, and if you do it'll be on my conscience and I'll remind Mr Bowen to add me to the ashes on the day when he starts kindling the alehouses. Your good name won't suffer at all.'

'It is hot and that basket is heavy.'

He looked up and down the empty road. I entered The Leaves and he followed me, pulling hard to get his burden through the narrow door. I helped him.

'Tell me, Lemuel, why didn't you get somebody with a cart to help you take this contraption along?'

'And have the smell of horse on Lord Plimmon's cottage loaves? That sort of thought, harpist, explains why you haven't got on any better than you have.'

There were about a dozen men seated on the benches and settles within. They stared and fell silent with surprise when we came in.

'You see?' said Lemuel uneasily, 'they've only got to lay eyes on me and they act as if I was some kind of man from the moon.'

161

'They've heard good reports from the moon, these iron boys. There's as much love as anything else in the way they stare at you. Sit there.'

I led him to a roughly designed alcove where we could be alone and talk with a minimum of distraction. He breathed relief and even gave me a quick smile as he found himself free from the attention of the other men, several of whom I saw leaving the room with disgusted grimaces. I approached the heavy studious Abel and bought two pints of his dark ale and took them back to the concealed bench. Lemuel drained half of his in two gulps and I could see that the thirst of this man for ale during his years of intense effort and repentance must have been deep and painful. After he had finished the first pint he rose to go.

'No, no, stay for a second,' I said. He remained standing, his finger curled around the handle of his basket ready to lift it and be on his way. 'Don't worry about the price, boy. I'll pay for the lot. I've got some money. I've got no business, no ambition, and I'm grateful to you, Lemuel, for all you've done for me in bringing me and my harpistry to the attention of such notable men as Penbury and this lord. You won't have to pay a penny and you deserve to have the forgotten dewponds of old delight refilled for a few minutes. This treat is on the improvident and feckless. Drink up, boy.'

When I went to the counter again I leaned over and said softly to Abel who was drawing the beer in the tiny room behind.

'If you have any hemlock there, Abel, with which you might be intending to stiffen the drink of Lemuel, don't do it. He's worth keeping alive on all counts.'

As Lemuel began his second jar he put his uneasiness to one side.

162

'I've done all right,' he said, slipping down on his seat, making himself comfortable against the dark-stained woodwork, smiling broadly and rubbing his fingers along his small darkening teeth. 'What did you say I'd one day be?'

'One of the richest factors in this area of the land.'

'Factor? What is that exactly, harpist?'

'Kind of king among shopkeepers; no serving, no standing for hours, no smiling and bowing at a lot of silly devils you'd rather see dead.'

'I get the idea, harpist. Your language, as always, is terrible, but the idea is plain.'

He took a long violent pull at his drink. His smile wore thin and vanished.

'But even so, harpist, even so, I had some wonderful times back there at the Northgate Arms in Tudbury. No worries, see. Nobody to keep prodding at me from behind.' He put his glass down and laid his hand on mine.

'There was always some good sport around the Northgate. Some very handy little maidens around there, I can tell you. May and Violet and all those, real good sorts. A gill of ale and they were there, boy, ripe and ready for the job, see? Oh, they were good days, harpist, as I look back on them now. A waste of a man's substance, of course, but often, when I get careless in my sleep my dreams go back to them and I can smell that old yard in the Northgate and I can smell May and Violet too, for they were strong and lingering on all the senses, those two.'

'Good to you, were they, Lem?'

'Oh, very kind, very willing...' The drowsy complacent yearning dropped from his face. He took a hold of himself and he put his hand over the top of his three-quarters empty jar. 'But what I'm saying, harpist, is repellent to the Lord

163

God. Terrible things I'm saying, with you putting that hot evil inviting look upon me. Let's drink up and go.'

As he was draining his drink Abel walked up with refills.

'We've not always been the best of friends, Lemuel,' said Abel, 'but I would like you to accept this offering of ale from my hand and drink to the future. May it see you prosper greatly and may it be less full of cloud and confusion than the past.'

'Thank you, Abel. I'm very glad to hear you admit at last that you misunderstood me. And I'm glad to hear you take an interest in the future too. You've spent too much of your time with your head sunk in books handing your heart over to the dead past and letting the present go curdled. To the future, Abel.'

We drank. Lemuel drank noisily. Abel and I watched both him and each other with solemn interest over the rim of our glasses. When Abel left us, Lemuel said:

'I'll be freer in Tudbury than I've even been here. Don't get the wrong idea about me, harpist. I believe in decency. I believe in the clean life and the profits it brings. But Christ, a man can get so lonely when his life is all effort, and memory is the only food, the only fire.'

'They'll happen again, Lemuel. You'll soon be a big man in Tudbury. You've covered the hard part of the course. When the fancy takes you you'll be able to nip up to the yard of the Northgate, and I bet time makes a great point of standing still there and you'll find May and Violet still laughing, still kind, still on fire for you.'

'On fire? You think so?'

'Of course. In the patch of everybody's past there is the tiny row of joyful living things into which went most of one's essential longings, which have defied the wheel of our

164

desolating days and wait for one's return. Don't mind if these words make you giddy, Lemuel. They are meant to do that. I am the drink's right-hand man.'

He pressed his fist between his legs and groaned. He put his head down and drank from his pot as if it were a trough.

'But you surprise me with this talk and this groaning, Lemuel. I thought you had worked out lust from your being as neatly as you had worked rebellion. I always thought you were a burnt-out little performer who had sold off his bit of passion as charcoal long since. Isabella's a pretty woman. Doesn't she soothe you any more?'

The mention of Isabella frightened him. He raised his finger to his lips and sent suspicious looks around the alcove at the same time.

'Isabella's a good woman.'

'Saint, first class.'

'Isabella's a pretty woman, too, harpist.'

'The rose of Moonlea.'

'Clever as a lawyer with the books. Never a penny out.'

'She's been a godsend to you, boy.'

'But in the matter of love, harpist, she has kept her ear for far too long in the mouth of Mr Bowen.'

'That's one way of keeping the ear hot even though the rest of you goes icy.'

'Mr Bowen is a fine man, harpist.'

'God's own gaffer.'

'The host of angels sing and speak through him.'

'I've heard them, boy. The angels have really been letting go since they started paying the rent on Bowen.'

'But...' Lemuel put his teeth over the rim of his pot and bit hard in his embarrassed efforts to find the right word. 'But he's out of touch with the simple pleasures. To hear

165

that man talk about the flesh on a cold rainy Sunday is to make you wonder why he bothers to wear his own at all.'

'It's all right for him. He stands up there and preaches. The fire he puts into just one sermon would serve us poor bastards for a whole year of hard whoremastering.'

'Ssshhhh! Keep it low, boy, keep it low. Isabella heard him soon after she came here. It wasn't so very long after we got married either. We had listened to Mr Bowen from five to seven. And halfway through supper that night as I was edging around the table towards her, full of meat and fresh after the long, idle Sabbath, she foreswore the flesh even more loudly than Mr Bowen. God, the Devil must have ached that evening, the way she beat at my face and called me an animal and dedicated herself to the chaste life. She said we should have to give ourselves entire to the business, not only to make money but to keep the inside of the skull wholesome and free from sin's alloy. And we have, harpist, we have.'

'And you've both shrunk. Making a rough measurement with my thumb I'd say you still have about a third of what you were born with in this matter of skill in living and squeezing joy and grace and fulfilment from the business. Your natures will come slowly back to warmth, but there'll be an edge of spite in every embrace that'll keep you nicely scarred. You'll have to turn your back on Isabella and grow your own blooms, Lemuel. And you can do it, too. You're a made man. You don't need Penbury or those boys and their odd drops of honey any more. If you want ale, drink it. If you want women, take them. If the only thing that comes from my long journey from the North is to see that desiring light come into your eyes, Lemuel, it will have been worth it.'

'You're right, harpist: I was like a man buried alive. I'll

teach them to look down on me and cage me in wickerwork drawers.'

'God! Did she actually fit you up with a garment like that?'

'It was an idea of Isabella. She was fiddling about with the wickerwork one night when something stoked my fire.'

The front door of the inn opened and in came Floss Bennett. She looked as ruffled and sullen as ever, as if she had found her own private gale to stand in. She stood by the counter and Abel served her impassively. She caught sight of Lemuel, stared unbelievingly at him for a few seconds and smiled at him. After a short spasm of embarrassment he returned the smile. The presence of the woman seemed to have transfixed him. His eyes did a quick patrol from the loose breasts inside the crimson shawl to the enormous legs and strong shabby shoes. Her red, love-eaten face turned to wink at him from time to time. Each time she winked he gave a short cough as if his wish for this woman were operating some kind of lever in his lungs.

'Do you remember I was telling you about a girl called Violet?'

'And May. Your field of glory at the Northgate Arms in the long ago.'

'She's the image of Violet, that Floss. God, funny how I haven't noticed it before. Funny how my mind has stuck just like a burr to the thought of Violet all these years and not noticing how like a twin of her this Floss Bennett was. They've blinded me. Penbury, Bowen, Isabella, they've blinded me. The bloody Samson of Moonlea. That's me, harpist. A blind, deluded bloody Samson.'

'There, Samson,' I said, nodding my head at Floss, 'is one temple who wouldn't mind being taken up and thrown

167

down. She's partial to you, too.'

'How do you know that?'

'She told me. I heard her say in this very room that if you had Penbury's advantages, if your old man had had the gumption or the luck to do the right things with ore and furnace blast you would be another Penbury today.'

'She said that?'

'Just look at the way her eyes burn when they glance at you. It's clear, boy. Can't you see it?'

'Yes, I can. But give me time, harpist. I'm still a bit timid and trussed. I've still got a lot of coffin to get out of before I'm properly back in the light.'

'Keep tunnelling, Lem. Floss is ready for the taking. You can leave your siege guns at home.'

He drank his ale rapidly to get his will on to the plane he desired. Halfway through a gulp Floss herself came up to the table and asked him whether he would like a chat about old times on the hillside behind the inn.

'Old times, old times?' said Lemuel in a voice that squeaked. He clambered with painful shyness out of the alcove.

'What about some of those in case our mouths get tired of just talking?'

'The cottage loaves?'

'They look lovely, Mr Stevens. Bring a pocketful.'

Lemuel filled his pockets and invited me to help myself until he returned.

'Won't be long,' he muttered in my ear, 'then we'll continue our journey.'

'Take your time, Lemuel. Life's got a lot to make up to you. Approach the job with a gradual frenzy. Floss's trade mark is heavy wear and tear on all flanks.'

'Shut your brazen bloody mouth, harpist,' said Floss, beginning to bite at one of the loaves.

Floss opened the back door of the inn and walked out into the cool dark yard where I had sat with John Simon on the first evening of my stay in Moonlea. Floss jerked her finger to the right and they made their way out of sight along a steep difficult path. Lemuel stooped and gasping with the crazy surge of his longings and the sudden exertions of the exercise.

I left the alcove and waited by the counter.

'Things are quiet tonight,' I said to Abel.

'It'll do the men of Moonlea no harm to stay away from places like these,' he answered without taking his eyes from the brown-covered book he held in his hands.

'That's funny talk to come from you.'

'There are more important things than getting rich out of ale. A nice quiet trade keeps me alive. And too much ale has made too many men easy game for the ironmasters.'

'You're a quaint one, Abel. What are you reading?'

'*The Age of Reason.*'

'When is that due to dawn?'

'We're edging into it now.'

'Who wrote it?'

'Tom Paine. Ever heard of him?'

'Up in the North there were some boys who were very fond of books and gave me the benefit of what they read, but for myself I've never had much to do with them.'

'The old man who kept this place for years and asked me to help him run it before he died was a fine old scholar. His books made him the target of a lot of suspicion. As a server of beer and having no job connected with God or the law he was marked down as a Jacobin. Things were going great guns in those days with every ounce of iron being bought up within an hour to feed the war with France. Then some slow-witted lads from Tudbury full of loyalty to Church and King made trips out here from Tudbury and smashed the place, the inside of it, anyway, to a ruin. The second time they came they burned part of it as well. Look at the wainscoting to your right there. No, a bit higher. See the black burn stain?'

'I see it. Just because he read books about reason?'

'That's it.'

'I was shrewder than I thought when I decided to stick to a programme of noise and movement. What happened to the old man?'

'They left him senseless on the floor to roast, as soon as the fire had got a grip. I got here just in time to drag him out. I was a fugitive myself at the time, just a kid though. In the part of Kent I lived in there'd been a bit of hunger and a bit of rick burning to singe the landlords into a state of sympathy. The flames didn't touch them. The phoenix learned from those boys. Our cottages burned twice as fast as the ricks. They organised a kind of badger hunt right through the county. We were the badgers, just right for size, too large to go crawling unfairly into small safe holes. The local corps of Yeomanry, strong mounted lads, hunted us for practice. I can still smell the ditches I spent a few days hiding in. It was a parson who found me when I crawled out and looked for food during my journey to the west. He handed me over, and a few others as well who were running away with me. He told us how sure he was we'd land in hell. After the ditches and a long look at him I said it would be a pleasure. They didn't hang me, nor did they deport me. I was too young, they said. They let the young warriors flog

170

me in a village near Rochester with a few extra lashes in honour of Pitt the great liberator who was staying nearby. Then they let me go with a caution and a laugh. You want to see the marks? They're faint now but very interesting.'

'No.'

'Old Barnes who kept The Leaves took me in after I failed to keep my mouth shut outside the Moonlea church one Sunday morning. When he died I took over. It's been very peaceful and satisfying but some part of me never got outside those ditches and their heavy green-water stink. And my feeling about folk who like the feel of humans under their boots, pawn their pity for an extra pair of woollens in our longer winters, is still the same. If ever John Simon Adams is driven to do something big and open to show that he doesn't like them either I'll be behind him. Would you like to read some of these books I have here, harpist?'

'No, thank you, Abel. I'm simple. I want to live and I want to die and I don't want to pull the notion of either out of shape with thought. I want to shrink neatly, without fuss.'

'You'll be lucky if they let you alone to do that.'

'I'm fleet. You know where John Simon is?'

'I know most things. He's in Westlea.'

'You know they sent that strangler after him?'

'I heard that too. I also knew the strangler did no strangling.'

'No, he didn't. What do you think of John Simon, Abel?'

'That I'd give everything I have to him if he wanted it, that goes without saying. But I wish he'd been born with more luck.'

'Luck?'

'A man can be born to trouble because he has something in him that will not let his spirit sleep in the presence of

171

unkindness or fraud. He may be born to trouble because he comes too late to the place where he would have found his due ration of love and contentment. No man should have both brands of trouble. In all the life of John Simon Adams I see no hint of consolation and in whatever age a man lives, however dark with stress, a man should at some time, in some way, be consoled.'

'And Penbury, what about him?'

'Richard, our Penbury, he's a soft one.'

'Soft? What standards have you around here, Abel?'

'It was his father John who carved out the kingdom. He travelled Europe and the whole of this land making absolutely certain that there would be no furnaces stronger, more efficient than his. You've seen the six great chimneys that paint the sky scarlet as the furnace doors open in the night, they were the first of their kind. They made the purest iron in the world. He was a strong man, John Penbury. It wasn't that he wished conflict; he didn't get far enough outside himself to see that peace and conflict might be opposed. He wanted to leave his mark and if it was a deep and bloody one he was not likely to bother his head with thoughts about the people who provided the blood. He saw Moonlea as growing out of his own head. He felt no doubt, suspected no ugliness, and in that measure must have been a happy man. If to be wretched is to be tormented by the rub of other people's defects on one's own, then he was as free from wretchedness as any man born. The long war with France was nothing to him but an opportunity from God to push on with fresh furnaces until he had the biggest ironworks in the world. He was the man to burn out any grumbling on the part of fainthearts and traitors against the war. He was the man to order an instant ducking party for any of the Free Preachers who came around to protest against the conspiracy of Church and landlord, chapel and ironmaster. I've never known a man whose moral universe ended so utterly at his own fingertips. When he was old and his grip was slackening I've seen him on a Sunday morning in the main street of Moonlea stopping dead in his tracks to stare astonished at some group of walking people as if becoming aware for the first time of other human beings. He even tried to get his own coinage so that he could freeze and fix the life of Moonlea within the limits he wanted to set for it, and he only gave up the attempt when the Government in London told him they wouldn't order any more of his ironwork if he wasn't a good boy and didn't keep buying his coins from the King's shop. He was a Caesar.'

'And the son isn't?'

'Richard went as a young man to France to keep an eye on some foundry works at Toulouse which is a place in the south of that country. He spent his time in Paris painting a lot and even writing poetry, and I've been told he was a friend of some of the followers of Rousseau. You've not heard of him? He believed men should experiment as boldly with ways of being free as Penbury experimented with ways of blasting dross out of iron ore. Richard came back hating Moonlea and wishing no stone or smut of it. He made these views known to his father and the old man beat him senseless on the night of his return. They never spoke to each other again, but Richard fell into step. He's carried on but he's still out of place. And the war has long been over. There've been troubles here that the old man might have ended with a week of private hangings and a few clever tunes on the wits of the dolts who hearkened to his every word as if it were Holy Writ. But Richard's gone on from

173

year to year, blowing hot and cold, strutting with great effect at odd intervals plagued by mercy and tripping over his own early dreams at others. It's a tricky business failing to deteriorate in time with one's fellows and along the lines laid down by one's own thoroughly degraded fathers. You know he doesn't sleep well at nights?'

'He pays me to play the harp to him at times when his thoughts make circles around him at midnight. It makes the circles slower and broader even if he doesn't drop off.'

'But his daughter'll be old John all over again. She's young yet and her father in his moments of weakness and regret reminds her that beauty and peace should be pursued on earth even at the expense of having fewer people doff their caps to you in the process. But watch her body, harpist, watch her eyes as she looks at Moonlea and the people in it. She's got no tenderness in her at all. She'll consume a whole stream of lovers and enemies to feed her own will-force. Richard will soon grieve or stammer himself into a stupor or death. She'll marry Radcliffe or somebody else free from her old man's groaning and subtle reservations. There'll probably be another war and then there will be no muttering in Moonlea, no more talk of equality. There will be iron, there will be lives rotting into profitable slime in Penbury's cottages, there will be silence and a more confident whiteness in the columns that flank the master's hillside home.'

'And for you, who crouched in ditches, for John Simon who cracks his skull against the stone, no victory.'

'We don't aim to win.'

'What the hell are you out for then?'

'To break silence, that's all.'

'Another drink, Abel. You frighten me.'

'What game are you playing with him, harpist?'

174

'Him? Who?'

'That housefly, Lemuel.'

'Oh him. I'd almost forgotten. Partly to lift his lid and see what kind of stew is bubbling. I've seen. It's odd how little the essential vegetables of a man's experience change even though the name of his garden is changed from heaven to hell and back again.'

'That wasn't your only reason.'

'No. Like this, turned upside down and hung out to dry on a line of ale and Floss he might say things that will be of interest, if not to me, to you.'

'Keep your ears open. Here they come.'

I could see them through the window. They were slithering down the steep rocky embankment. Floss was braking herself now and then and adjusting what she probably thought were blatant signs of disturbance. Lemuel, just behind her, had the palest blankest face I had ever seen on a creature whose blood was supposed nominally to be warm. He looked as though an earthquake had singled him out. They did not immediately re-enter the tavern. They sat on one of the large flat rocks at the back of the yard, nibbling voraciously at Lemuel's bread. Lemuel rocked slightly on his perch, his short legs well up from the ground. He was clearly still feeling the effects of the ale, although, after the interval with Floss, he must have been feeling that he had given up almost as much for her as he had for trade. Now and then he would glance at her, throw his head back as if struck by some sudden thought or rich, vitalising memory and giggle. She had put her hand into his sack of days and made the tied neck gape.

When they came in Floss did not linger. She muttered something to me about having to see her mother, and after muttering back that I understood but did not believe, I wished her a courteous good night. Lemuel did not look at her. He almost ran back into the alcove. I had a drink waiting for him on the table.

'You won't tell, will you, harpist?'

'Tell whom? Tell what?'

'Isabella, of course. She wouldn't understand. She'll never understand the way it has been with my longings, the way my body has moaned for another in the heat of that bakehouse.'

'I'll never tell. Even if Isabella found out it'll be a lesson to her never to keep a willing donkey short of oats.'

'You've had the longing too, haven't you, harpist?' He crinkled his eyes cunningly.

'For Floss, you mean. Not that I know of. She's too much for me. I'd rather lie directly on a furrow like those boys who think it makes the crops grow faster.'

'Oh no, not her. You wouldn't have to think of anybody like her, having a fine body and being able to play the harp, and that' – he lifted his pot and winked his right eye confidentially – 'you could do yourself a lot of good with a certain party, harpist.' He had dropped his voice and brought his mouth across the table near to my face.

'What are you talking about?'

'Jabez told me about it. I was excited when I heard. And pleased, harpist, pleased for you. He saw. Jabez was by the Italian garden that night. You would be all right there, harpist, you could be very jocose there, boy. I always said she was a hot-blooded bitch, that Helen, for all the cold ways she put on in front of Mr Bowen and the others. And if she takes to you you'd be able to do a bit of good for Lemuel, I wouldn't doubt.'

'Shut your small mean mouth, boy. You're hacking at my ears. Any more of that winking and whispering and I'll be pulling that woodwork down on you.'

'No offence, harpist. Glad to see you getting on. Delighted. What a fine bloody laugh that would be. Radcliffe with his eye on her, that dandy captain with his eye on her, half the huntsmen in the county with their you-know-whats barking tally ho every time she passes and a poor bloody harpist nips in the backway and steals their tidbit.'

I leaned over the table, my arm drawn back to hit the wits right out of him and I could see Abel lean over the counter, his eyes hanging eagerly on my gesture. But I remembered what I wished to do with Lemuel, remembered too the blasting storm of novelty that had just rushed through the stuffy little inward closets of the man and I smiled.

'That's right, boy. My sun's coming from behind the clouds with a vengeance. I know the secret will be well kept with you. Let the lady have her sport. If there's any talk of a service fee I'll ask her to double it so that you can have your bonus as a reward for rooting up all these facts.'

He rolled on the bench with glee at this sally.

'That's the way, harpist. Diddle the high and mighty bastards. That's the way to get on. No point in diddling the same poor sods all the time.'

'Have you forgotten about Plimmon Hall?'

'I don't forget anything. I've got as good a head for ale as you. You don't know the apprenticeship I served in Tudbury in the old days. God, if Mr Bowen could only have seen me then. Brother Sink the boys who hung about the stabling yard of the Northgate used to call me. They were fine, cosy, filthy days, harpist.'

'I can believe it, boy. Here's a last drink.'

'Two gulps and you'll be wondering where it vanished.'

'How was Floss?'

He stopped halfway through a swallow and quivered.

'Oh God,' he said, 'there's a woman for you.'

'I bet you've had her plenty of times before. I can see through you, Lem. You're no dedicated monk. Strikes me you've kept up a pretty steady pace since Tudbury. You could see that from the way she looked at you. You're a king for her, Lemuel.'

'Well...' he started, wondering in what direction to lie next.

'I bet you've wanted her plenty of times,' I said, quietly and coaxingly. 'I bet you could have had her that time when Bledgely banged Sam Bannion's head in, when you got Floss to give that false evidence.'

His pot rattled on to the table boards. His head banged against the back of the settle as he drew back from me, his face fearstruck, bleached, ugly.

'Don't say those things, harpist!' He tried to shout but he was hoarse as a frog and his voice would not lift. I bent over him and my voice was lullingly low and persuasive still.

'We all have these little secrets, Lemuel. The Penbury girl and me, you share that item and I think it good that you should. It makes us friends. There's you and Floss...'

His mind dropped from its ridge of doubt towards me and he smiled, drooling, his eyes lit with triumph.

'She was ready for me that night up on the hillside, that night Bledgely went up the mountain after Sam. I was there to make sure that she was in position to give that evidence about Sam. One look at me and she could see my mind dry and chapped with longing. So she decided to kill two birds with one stone...' He began to laugh in a soprano frenzy.

178

'Did you hear that, harpist? Two birds with one stone... and Sam there in that bloody dingle. She was pulling me into her, into the hot welcoming friendly darkness of her, when we heard Sam scream and that frightened me and I ran home, harpist, because I don't like roughness in any shape or form.'

'That Sam had no tact.'

'Ever since that night I'd been thinking of her. That was a nice little job, that of Sam, and Flossie kept her head cool right through to the end, even when that madman Wilf Bannion went beating and bullying her. She made a tidy bit out of that, and you and me will have many a chance to do the same before we're finished with Moonlea, won't we, harpist?'

'You can trust me, Lem. Any little job you want done, say the word.'

We left the inn. Lemuel was unsteady. I carried his basket. The dusk was moving into a deeper blue. The night air made Lemuel drunker, more carefree. Less than a minute after we left the inn he was plunging into a description of what Sammy's widow had said, how she had looked in the first unbelieving madness of her grief.

'And that Katherine will look the same too. That dirty bitch Katherine will look the same too, won't she, harpist?' He grasped me with both his arms. My grip tightened on the basket and my eyes, as they stared at the darkening skyline, half closed.

'When?' I asked.

'When she finds that John Simon has had what he's been asking for all this time. Don't you think he's been asking for it?'

'Asking for what?'

'To have his head knocked in. Now that you are getting on

179

so well up at the mansion and in that garden you ought to be the first to say that John Simon shouldn't be allowed to live. You're no friend of his, harpist. I've never had any doubt about that since you came back to Moonlea. You're more my kind, keen, cautious, you know.'

'That's it. He's too miserable for my liking. He's against music, he's against love. All he's for is trouble, and I don't like chaps who get mixed up with married women, either. I may not strike you as much of a Christian, Lemuel, but I'm all for respecting the home and the vows and all that. A little bit on the edge of the roof now and then with somebody like Floss who is elemental like the wind and not likely to figure in the final count unless you brought part of the roof down, but not with married women. I'm for peace and getting on and iron and wars, off and on, and law.'

'That's a fine sentiment, a beautiful axiom. You've been listening to Mr Bowen.'

'I probably got the idea from him. I do no thinking except in leap year.'

'You wouldn't miss him?'

'If I had two hearts I wouldn't worry even one of them about him. I'm on my own, Lemuel, out for myself. Where is John Simon?'

'We've heard the last of him?'

'Is he dead?'

'He'll trouble Mr Penbury no more.'

'Is he dead?'

'He'll set no more tongues wagging about the price of bread, about the profits of trade.'

I stopped, took hold of Lemuel's collar and shook him.

'I'm asking you, man, is he dead?'

'I think so. He ought to be.'

'Who did it? You?'

'God forbid, no. I'm not that sort of man, harpist. I'm against roughness, I told you. A fair profit on my labour, that's all I want.'

'Who killed him then?'

'A man. You wouldn't know him.' Lemuel began to sniff noisily, as if suddenly smitten by the fear that he might have spoken too much.

'A big man?' I asked. 'Fingers missing?'

'How do you know?'

'I followed him when he went after John Simon. We all marched out of Moonlea like a procession but unbeknown to each other. Have you seen him since, that man with the maimed hand?'

'Bledgely? He had orders to keep straight on. He was told it wouldn't be wise to come back to Moonlea.'

'Did he tell you John Simon was dead? There's been no talk of a body being found.'

'We've not heard from him yet, but we will, we will. He's a great one, Bledgely. Strong and cunning like we all ought to be. You ought to have seen Sam Bannion. You should have seen him. Oh, he was a sight. How far did you follow Bledgely, harpist?'

'They went into that wood over there. Then I came back. It was the night of the singing and dancing. There was work for me to do in Moonlea.'

'And in that garden, too. Don't forget the garden, harpist.' He chuckled and seized my arm again.

'Keep your mind on John Simon and that wood, Lemuel.'

'That's right. The wood. That's where he'll have done it, for sure. Trust Bledgely to have picked somewhere nice and quiet. Strength with cunning, isn't that a wonderful thing to

181

have, harpist? Come on, let's go in there now and find John Simon. I've been itching to break the news about him to the people for a long time. He'll be there just as Bledgely left him, in the state he should always have been in, quiet and in no way to trouble anybody.'

'And you think he's really in there among those trees, dead?'

'I feel it in my bones. There's a wonderful happy glow in my bones at the feel of it. He's said a lot of wicked things about me, has John Simon. And you know what you said about married women. If he's dead, heaven is smiling.'

'And there's no sorrow about him anywhere inside you?'

'What has sorrow about him got to do with me?' He grasped my arm once more as a vast upsurge of wind rattled through his body. I could feel the storm vibrating disgustingly through my own frame. 'Forget sorrow, harpist. It's mostly a nuisance. Handy for you with the harp when you want to make people cry. But when you are trying to get on, a nuisance. Think of those little jobs you said you'd like to be doing and forget you ever saw Bledgely. Forget sorrow too. Off and on when I had those longings on me, the longings I told you of, I would feel sorrow and every time I did the dough went sour. That shows, doesn't it. Sorrow is mostly a nuisance.'

'Easy now. We are really alone in the night now. That racket you made just then drove even the birds away. This way into the wood. If John Simon Adams is really in here this is going to be a golden night for you. Penbury will badger the Parliament in London to make you a prince, at least a prince. You have deserved well of the master.'

'He loves me. Penbury thinks the world of me. Sometimes he's looked at me, especially in his tired spells, half crying with what looked to me like sorrow, and he's said, "Why can't everybody be like you, Lemuel? Why can't everybody be kind and helpful like Lemuel Stevens?" Tell you another thing, too, harpist.' He was hanging on to my shoulder and I could hear the last details of his warm beer-gurgles as he got his speech into shape for discharge into my ear. 'If I was a bit younger I'd have stood a chance with that Helen. More than once I've wanted to follow her when she's gone up the mountain on her own. I'm not big, but I've got real style about me, a master's stroke. Ask Flossie. Just you ask Flossie.' He stood quite still, lifted his head in the silver green-edged light and laughed wildly. 'I've got skill. God, what that chilly bloody Isabella's been missing!'

'Look around for John Simon, Lemuel, and forget about your artistry or you'll find your dough getting sour under melancholy hands again.'

He fell serious once more. He bent down as if to start the search in real earnest. He lurched in swift swerves as the blood went to his head and thickened the beer. He hung on to a tree for support, and as I came near to him I could see he was close to being sick. His face was chalk white and strained.

'That John Simon!' he said. 'Even dead, a trouble. Even dead he won't lie where a decent man can find him. Keep your eyes sharp, harpist. You'll help me find him. If you saw Bledgely come into this wood this is where Bledgely left him. I worked it all out. All the details they left to me. I told Bledgely that one evening John Simon was sure to go to Westlea alone to have one of his meetings and this wood was the perfect place the lovely place to put a stop to anybody who goes to too many meetings. Did you see the muscles of that Bledgely?'

183

'No. But he was clearly a bull.'

'A treat to see. A miracle. He had one at the top of his arm, big as my leg. Why does God give such things to some men and not to others? What's the matter with God? Doesn't God know that it's little things like that that cause so much bitterness, needless bitterness?'

'We'll get Bowen to take it up. It's a big issue, big as your leg.'

'Isabella looked a lot at Bledgely. She was a bit afraid of him because he had a way of talking that was only half human. You notice how clear and plain I talk?'

'Like a bell, boy, a treat to hear.'

'Well, Bledgely wasn't like that at all. More like a grunt. But Isabella stared at him all the time and once or twice it made me thoughtful. Isn't it pretty in this wood. Mostly I'm afraid of the lonely dark, but this dark is pretty.'

'It is. We are sharing a lot of beauty between the two of us here.'

'We two, and John Simon wherever he's managing to hide himself.'

'A secretive sod. Always was.'

'Did you ever have picnics in the woods when you were a kid, harpist?'

'Off and on. I was never much under roofs.'

'What I remember is the bluebells and getting blinded by the smoke from the dampwood fires. Did you ever have that?'

'I was often blinded. I got in the way of more smoke than anybody else of my age. I must have had eyes at just the right height. I like it though. Anything that stings I like. Any sign of John Simon?'

'Not a trail.'

'Keep your eyes on the ground. You'll not find him where you're staring. Even Bledgely wouldn't be so daft as to stick him on top of a tree.'

'That moment I was thinking about something else... Tell you what we'll do, harpist. When we find John Simon we'll have a little spit on him. I always felt I'd like to do that to John Simon. By his side I always felt so small, so shrunken with wanting so much. He never said much to me. He always looked at me and said nothing as if the sight of me made him very thoughtful. I wished I could have spat on him when he was able to feel, harpist. But we've got to do the best we can. We're little blokes trying to do the best we can and look as big about it as we can manage. Why the hell couldn't he have been nice to me. He wasn't such a bad chap really, not behind the quietness and that bloody awful thoughtfulness.' He rubbed his sleeve across his eyes.

'Because he had no love for you. Why look so sad all of a sudden? This is your night of glory, Lemuel. You ought to be rolling with laughter.'

'I will be. Give me a minute. It was that Flossie. Dragged my guts out, that's what she did. Like when I was a kid in the days where there was no food for us in Tudbury. I've had a lot of sick hours in my life, harpist, sick hours. Oh Jesus God, you wouldn't believe. And that Isabella too. Once I had the food to fill my insides she had to go and make them hard and frozen. It was like digging myself out of the earth when I started with Flossie.'

I took his arm and guided him to the spot where Wilf Bannion and I had laid Bledgely.

'The ground about here looks as if it's been disturbed,' I said. 'Look at those leaves, the heaped leaves. They are not as they fell off the tree. No wind would work in that way.' I

185

kneeled down. I could feel Lemuel's eyes luminously protrusive with dread as they peered over my shoulder. I remembered to the inch the part of the rough concealment under which I would find the face of Bledgely.

'I'm getting near to something, Lemuel. The flesh of man has a way of announcing itself. You don't have to see it to know that it is near.' Lemuel's nerve thinned and he turned his head away. 'There's nothing to fear, Lemuel. This is your work and a new life in Tudbury will be a fine reward. The end of all hunger, boy, think of that. I've seen any number of dead folk in my wanderings. In the far, lonelier villages there'd often be a cottage from which the strong ones would all have gone to the towns or to softer fields. But the older and weaker would stay and I've often wasted good days warming their hearts a little and easing them into a painless acceptance, as they went downward. Here we are now, boy. Take a good careful look, Lemuel. This is really a sight.'

I had removed the last of the earth and leaves. The face of the dead Bledgely was clearly to be seen, open-eyed, jaw-dropped. Had the man meant anything to me the juncture of silver-green shadow, the lovely tree sounds and the horror of his ugly stillness would have made me reel. Lemuel looked at him and broke into a low cry.

'God, he's changed.' He peered through his wet unclear eyes.

'Look closer. You've got to be certain it's him.'

Lemuel moaned and gritted his teeth as he lowered his head for the examination.

'It isn't him at all! It isn't him at all!' And he gave a long jagged shriek of terror and broke away from my side. I tried to hold him back. I fancied an additional turn of whatever vice it was I had put the man's head into. But he was too swift for me and without any trace of the unsteadiness he had shown since leaving the inn he raced back to Moonlea.

I left the wood and made towards the ridge that separated me from Plimmon Hall. I saw no reason why I should still not present myself there as a witness of whatever bit of elegance and splendour might be going forward, and it would have been a pity to send those gentlemen back to London without a sight of a native minstrel. It would be instructive too to watch the scene with my mind still coloured by the memory of Lemuel stammering out his small shabby prides, fears, evils in the shadow of the woodland. As I made my way through the difficult thickets and trees of the slope I thought of Bledgely and what his discovery might mean. It would not affect the issue of the struggle between John Simon and Penbury one whit. I might, in making my revelation to Lemuel in that way, have terrified him into his shell where he would be charier than he had been in the past of taking an active part in the events that were impending. Or was that a wish meant merely to heal my own doubts? Or might it not have been better to have left Lemuel himself at Bledgely's side and in the same condition? There was hardly any case for Lemuel as far as I could see. Of all the men I had ever met he was the one most painstakingly committed to life. In the course of my rapid, irrelevant skirmishings on the flank of my time I had often seen life wear a griped and stricken look. But Lemuel was the first close-up portrait of the tiny liver fluke, with no root in brotherhood or passionate courage, which caused life to wear that expression... I had been daft to bring him to the wood at all. I should have left well enough alone. But the man's yearning forlornness had fascinated me. I had wanted badly to enrich his fabric with a few strands of pure crimson. Nothing more would be heard of Bledgely. Another tool had broken in Penbury's hand. That was all. The world would stage another of its long strategic silences and we would shuffle back to our first positions under cover of it and we would try to forget, all of us, that that intrusive oaf was there, rotting. As I stood there still on the hillside I would dearly have loved to transmit the evasive simplicity of that notion to the whole planet.

Halfway up the ridge I felt the full recoil of my spirit from the obscure foolery in which I had been engaged with Lemuel. I rested against a tree. I felt once again that impulse of itching remoteness I had so often felt in the stream of lives and desires between which there would be no peace, which created in their endless flights and pursuits a lethal and amazing whirl.

As I reached the hilltop the view surprised me. Some of the Moonlea furnaces were being tapped and the night was a light red over the town. On Moonlea's western edge, nearest to me, the black scar of tip on which the still burning refuse from the furnaces was thrown glowed as if with a sullen will to burn its identity into the hill's loveliness. I turned my eyes, resting the anger in them, to the inert shadow of the woodland below. I walked on. Ten paces more and I had a full view of Plimmon's valley. The mansion was blazing with light. It was more beautiful than ever with its outline picked out in golden windows. I branched to the right, finding a path which would bring me down to the back of the hall. The sight of it made all the more odious to me the crass cruel glare of Penbury's ovens behind me and I wished, with a vehemence that broke surface at my lips with a dozen oaths, that desolation would quickly fall on these shrewd polluting fools.

Between the hillside and the rearquarters of Plimmon Hall was a gravel area. Walking along it I could see through the windows the bustle of the cooks and serving-men as they laboured at the ovens and tables. Food was being carried in and out of the kitchen. I stood quietly at one of the windows watching a servant load on to a serving dish two chickens cooked and dressed in a way I had never before seen but a way so beautifully elegant the chicken would have been consoled for the curriculum of death, heat and loss of fat. I was bewitched by this sight of what genius went into the production and allaying of gluttony at this level. Further on I could see Jabez, looking as knowing as a priest decanting a stout, dusty bottle of wine, sniffing at it, laying the bottle's glass against the flesh of his face, making some subtle judgement on the wine's fitness. I could not make out for a moment why he was there. Then I remembered that he himself had told me, that first night I had gone to the Penbury house, that his real speciality was the care and presentation of wines and when any of the neighbouring mansions staged some supernormal celebration they would often request the loan of Jabez to have their cellars primed for the event. Jabez had looked shocked and disgusted when I said he probably jumped at the chance of these outings with their prospect of hours of free drinking. Jabez, apparently, had an honourable contract with his palate to swallow nothing but air during his hours of duty as vintner-elect to the great. I was just going to tap on the window and ask him to come and show me the way to wherever it was I was supposed to go when a surly snarling sound made me turn around quickly. I had a second in which to see one of Plimmon's hunting hounds leaping toward my head. I raised my arm to ward it off. It got its teeth around the fingers of

189

my right hand while I beat at its eyes with my left. I shouted as loudly as I could and two servants with staves came and beat the animal away. It made off, still snarling, to the far corner of the yard, and the two servants, thinking me a thief, closed in with their sticks at the ready to do as much for me as they had done for the dog. I showed them my bleeding fingers and told them not to be fools.

'Who are you?' they asked.

'I'm a harpist. I'm due to play here.'

'Who can identify you?'

'Jabez, the fat butler. Get him out here and he'll tell you who I am.'

Jabez was brought out and he gave me greeting. The men apologised for the trouble I had had.

'Can't be too careful with trouble brewing up over the hill there. Rather you got bitten than His Lordship.'

Jabez was sorrowful about my hurt hand and sent for a young strong girl who tore up some white fabric to serve as bandage.

'There'll be no harping for you tonight,' said Jabez as soon as he got me seated in the kitchen and gave me some slices of chicken to eat. 'That's a terrible pity, a great pity.'

'Oh, I'm not as good as all that,' I said, thinking that a little modesty might ease the smart of my hands.

'I wasn't thinking of you or your skill,' said Jabez with a snap of his teeth that put me in my place and almost brought him into the same class as that hunting hound. 'I was just thinking that this was the very night when you should have been prepared to play your very best. This is the greatest night we've had in any of the greatest houses for years and years.'

'Why?'

'Come and see.'

He led me once again into the gravel yard. He called over to the stablemen that it was we and that they could keep their hounds on the leash. He tiptoed and shooed for all he was worth and we advanced like a pair of middle-aged cats around the corner of the building. The two men with staves came towards us again, one of them leading the dog that had come at me. The dog was growling thoughtfully as if it had been well pleased with its first taste of me. Jabez told them in a tone of whistling impatience to go about their business and not to be so fussy. We reached an immense window and Jabez invited me to peep in, warning me to do so with care.

'For God's sake don't show yourself.'

The room into which I looked was a massive ballroom. I found the light that burst through the glass intense and hard to bear. The floor was full of dancers. Many of the men were uniformed; the women were a cool little regiment of pinky whiteness mobilised to a rhythm of blithe expectancy.

'Isn't it wonderful, harpist?'

'Light, lust and gleaming fabric, and plenty of it. If this is their recipe for heaven they are making a good job of it. I see Felix there too in the far corner.'

We left the window with the same stealth and made our way back to the kitchen.

'The greatest night for years,' said Jabez still breathless from the excitement that had been communicated to him through the glass.

'Tell me why. Have they all paid to come in or what?'

'Haven't you heard the news?'

'No.'

'Lord Plimmon and Helen Penbury, their engagement has just been announced. What a glorious pair they make. Both

191

so tall and masterful-like. They'll make Plimmon Hall the very centre of the land.'

I chewed steadily and watched the dancing joy and eagerness on the face of Jabez. The man was riding the highest wave of happiness and at that moment, looking at him, I was glad that there were those among us whose nerves find a field of harmless, hurtless adorations.

'It was a surprise?' I asked.

'Surprise? It nearly bowled us over.' He looked cautiously around at the other servants and came closer to me. 'Of course there were a lot of ill wishers on both sides of the hill who kept saying that Miss Helen would never have a chance, who said she was aiming at a region where the daughter of an ironmaster had no right to climb. And then news came that Lord Plimmon was paying steady court to one of the greatest ladies in London, grieving his heart out for love of her. I got that news from a friend of his valet who was an eye-witness of all this. There have been whispers that if Lord Plimmon's suit with that lady had gone smoothly the marriage would have brought him near the throne. Did you hear that, harpist? Near the throne. But it was not to be.'

'No?'

'No. And don't look so blank, harpist. I don't think you understand the full importance of what I'm revealing to you.'

'Oh, I do, Jabez. Carry on. This is high excitement. Near the throne... Who'd have thought that I'd be hearing almost directly from that quarter. That, and being bitten by Plimmon's dog, all in one night. I'm living to the full, boy.'

'It was not to be. The lady rejected Lord Plimmon. According to my friend, she is infatuated with some poet, a scandalous fellow, who is the rage of London but scarcely

192

bon ton as they say. As soon as the parents have disposed of the poet they plan to marry the lady to one of the older Scottish peers.'

'Poor bloody poet,' I whispered into my chicken.

'What was that?'

'Nothing. Carry on. This is even better than Lemuel.'

'Speak plain for God's sake. The wind makes more and better sense than you. You can imagine how furious Lord Plimmon was. He's as proud as Lucifer. He looks a bit like Lucifer, does Lord Plimmon. Tall and black like and stern, hellish stern. He rode down from London this morning. His horses were nearly dead when they arrived. He went almost at once to Mr Penbury's and asked Miss Helen if she would consent to the announcement being made tonight.'

'And she didn't say no even once?'

'Why should she? She knows what her due is. She was born for the highest places in the land. She has never set her hat at Lord Plimmon like some others I could mention. She knew her father was no great lover of Lord Plimmon on account of certain scornful things the latter has sometimes said about the ironmasters. But Miss Helen has kept her own ideas clear at the back of her head and now we see where they've been leading. There won't be a lady in the land greater than she when she finishes. Her grandfather was a farmer's son who played with fire and iron and the family have lived near their furnaces ever since. That shows character and I don't know whether I've told you this before but without character there is nothing. There are some people who disagree with it. They say it's base to have the smell of puddling too near the mansion, that a man who has the wealth of a noble should have the place and the name of one too.'

We went to sit in a window recess where a servant, at a signal from Jabez, brought us a great jug of ale, pewter pots, a loaf of fresh white bread, knives, a round of cheese and a lump of hot tender meat. Jabez who had finished the last of his duties connected with the wine ate and drank. He lost no time in repeating the story of the betrothal. I was interested to hear the new details that had come oozing from the folds of Jabez's mind for this new version, how this person had smiled, that one curtseyed, this one sweated, that one nearly swooned, when Plimmon had swung through the doors of Penbury's mansion and made clear his new decision. Between the heat of the kitchen and the melting zeal of Jabez's reverence I counted myself among the near-swooners.

'But there's one thing in all this,' I said with deferential friendliness when Jabez had screwed in the final period, 'one thing that I don't follow.'

He smiled at me indulgently as if I were an aborigine who would have to be wheedled slowly, over the years, into a state of passable urbanity.

'What don't you follow, harpist?'

'I know little of this Miss Helen, but she strikes me as being a girl of fierce spirit, as proud and resolute as Lord Plimmon himself, even if not so dark and Lucifer-like. She must, I take it, have known of the assault he was conducting on the lady in London who is near the throne. Women reproduce and perpetuate that kind of tidbit even better than they do the species. He comes shooting back from London, a spent, rejected force, and offers himself to her. One would have thought she would have sent him packing and picking bits of the door out of his nose. Explain that.'

He laughed at me, rocking delightedly back and forth as

194

big men do, as if I had just made one of the richest jokes of his time.

'Love doesn't enter into these things, harpist.'

'What does then. What's the mechanism at this altitude. Tell me, because I've got the traditional approach, simple and bestial, you know.'

'We don't always get what we desire, not all we desire,' said the butler, his voice profound and slow as if he had just seen the full extent of the thought he had propounded. 'Lord Plimmon flew high. It would have been a fine thing if he could have had the lady of his choice in London. Miss Helen might have married Mr Radcliffe who is her father's partner, and that would have been a fair match too. But the way it's worked out is best of all. Soon there won't be any life in this county at all except what Lord Plimmon and Mr Penbury are willing to give it. There are a lot of the old cottagers who think Lord Plimmon is after nothing but their land; out to grab all he can and pack them off into the workhouses or the iron-towns. But they're wrong, harpist, absolutely wrong.' He banged the side of his hand on my arm as it was on its way to my mouth and I smiled at him, agreeing and trying to suggest that I did not need all this underlining. 'Lord Plimmon is going to bring more wealth to the land than it's ever had before. He's studied the question. He's been sending bailiffs all over to look at the new methods. He's going to replenish the herds that have been getting thinner ever since I can remember. He'll nurse the furrows out of which the old cottage farmers have tugged the last gut of goodness. He's planning to establish a chain of key farms right across the country and he's going to see to it that the older folk are allowed to keep on as many of the cottage crafts as possible. I heard him and Mr Penbury talk about

195

that a year back and they've both got their heart and soul set on it. If they can get the older folk working at their looms and other trades families will have something to fall back on when things get slack in the iron centres. Isn't that a wise move, harpist?'

'Wise enough. It is good to have all this thought going on.'

We drank silently for a while, then I bade him good night. Outside I paused once more outside the great window behind which the dancers moved. I saw Plimmon stand in a corner gravely accepting congratulations from a pair of older men. Of Helen I saw nothing. Slowly and without deliberate thought I picked my way back to Moonlea.

11

The night had become quite dark when I arrived back in Moonlea's main street. I had no wish to share the company of Mrs Brier and Katherine until John Simon had returned to lighten the load of their premonitions. I had been all my life too much alone to be able to stand with ease the impact of three so different sets of desires upon me. Katherine for days past had been almost unceasingly sad. Mrs Brier had seemed happier, as if desperately optimistic that some event, whose nature she would never have the courage frankly to conceive in terms of a hope, would spring forth and spirit away her anxieties. Davy had been edging into an ever closer companionship with me as if his wish was that I should fill the gap caused by John Simon's absence.

I walked along the empty, soundless, ill-lit street. It would not have disagreed with me to sleep out of doors. I sat on the steps outside the shop of Lemuel Stevens, resting my back upon a wooden support. Along the street came the rattle of a carriage and four making towards the Penbury house. I heard the laughter of people from within the carriage. A gentle wind from over the foundries brought me a sulphurous and disquieting whiff. That, together with the laughter of the well-wined people who had just rolled by, broke up the surface of the peace that had come upon me, since I had been resting against Lemuel's woodwork. I thought of the walled garden near the Penbury home and the smell of vines that was its thematic phrase in my remembering. The hint of warm ecstasy that rose from the thought made me averse to Lemuel's steps and the nearness of Lemuel's body. His frustrations had the same smell as the foundries and did not wait for a favourable wind to come your way. I wondered whether at that moment in one of the upstairs rooms he was gibbering a digest of his fears into the ear of Isabella.

I walked towards the green patch where Felix and I had accompanied the singing and the dancers. I made my way up the path along which I had followed Helen Penbury. A watchman, one of several private guardians paid by Penbury to patrol the streets of Moonlea after dark, came into the circle of light cast by the storm lantern that hung from the wall of the building next to Lemuel's, peered up into the shadows where I stood and shouted to know who was there. I remained still and said nothing. He passed on. I continued my walk. I reached the gate of the garden and entered. I lay down on the slope of soft turf. With the high, leaf-covered walls around me, I felt secure, serene. I felt once again a bitter impatient regret that Katherine and John Simon had not heeded my appeal that they should both leave Moonlea and come North with me. I heard the carriage roll back down the hillside and make its return journey through Moonlea and towards Plimmon Hall, its rattling clamour even more offensive to me now. I waited until the silence had wiped itself clean again and looked carefully around the garden once again. Secure, serene.

I must have lain there fifteen or so minutes when I heard the gate open. I looked up. Even in that shadow I knew it was Helen Penbury. Vaguely I could make out her face but her long cloak was dark. I greeted her in a whisper.

'Who's there?' There was only the slightest trace of surprise in her voice.

'The harpist.'

'What are you doing here?'

'I wanted quietness. I had some ale, walked and talked a lot, then got bitten by Plimmon's dogs. So I wanted very much to quiet myself and give the world a rest from me. And you?'

'When I want to think I often come here. The ball left me with a headache. The fights were strong and the wines were mixed. I would have stayed to talk with my father but he has a species of philosophic migraine. I wanted a few minutes here.'

'Shall I go?'

'Go or stay. It's of no moment.'

'Thank you. I'll stay. I'm a little giddy too. I told you about the hound, the dog of that lord. It chewed at my finger tonight and my spirit's still sick from the smell and feel of it.'

'I was sorry to hear about that. Jabez told me. Jabez got very drunk and he became very sentimental about you. Said you had a hint of nobility.'

'He ought to know. He's a great fancier of form among the elect. You've had a good evening of it.'

'It was good to dance again.'

'I mean Plimmon. That was a good stroke.'

'Oh that. It should please my father.'

'Jabez said he and your father were not happy about each other. Why should he be pleased now?'

'Plimmon's in deadly earnest about life. Not like you or my father for that matter. My father's responsibilities have always irked and upset him. Since his health started to ravel

199

he's been willing to settle with life on however low a plane of satisfaction. This marriage will be enough of a triumph to console him a little. There'll be no lack of purpose or programme with Plimmon. There won't be a ha'porth of room for regret.'

'Why do you say these things to me?'

'I'd say them to the garden if you weren't here. Don't be too flattered by my confidences. I often hold dialogues with the night out here. Consider yourself a part of the vines. Besides, to my view you are a totally unreal person, a sort of midnight visitor with whom guile and pretence would be little more than a waste of good wit.'

'It will give you power, this wedding?'

'Yes, much power.'

'That Abel was right.'

'Who's Abel?'

'He keeps a tavern. He gave me a sketch of your character.'

'A tavern of the higher class, no doubt. What did he say?'

'He said your dreams had an imperial edge. That, given your way, you would restore the graveyard peace which was established here by your grandfather.'

'I wouldn't trust the prophecies of pot-men.'

'Your other lovers will be disappointed.'

'Who are they?'

'Radcliffe, the captain. I suppose this Plimmon dwarfs them.'

'He does, and they know it. Radcliffe will be content with his foundries, the captain with his ideal of discipline and duty, the one hotter, the other colder than I, but they will be content.'

'And you'll look forward to ruling jointly a kingdom from

which melancholy and strife will have been driven for ever.'

'We shall act for the best welfare of our subjects. Good night. You may stay here if you wish. I think the grapes have matured beyond the point where they can be unsettled by the presence of an alien body.'

'Good night.'

'And keep out of harm's way, harpist. I should hate to see you in need of the whip.'

'I won't be. Soon I shall be too busy stitching a few damns on to my last farewell to be plaguing the hearts of princes and their freezing ladies. Don't bite off more than you can chew. I'm not thinking of you when I say that. I'm thinking of the folk who are going to be bitten.' I held up my right hand with its rough casing of bandage. 'It's a hell of a thing, being bitten.'

The gate opened and she was gone.

12

Two nights later Penbury gathered together the most reliable of his workers – there were not many of them now – and raked out the furnaces. We watched from the hillside. It was an impressive sight. There was a pungent sense of finality as we watched the great mounds of raked embers cool and vanish into the blackness. Radcliffe had timed the ceremony of extinction well. All through and around Moonlea anxious eyes had watched the cooling and in many hearts no fire of contempt or defiance had been kindled to replace the glow that had slipped into the night. There was only a queasy flicker as they saw arrive the moment of which so much had been whispered that it had acquired in the minds of many a lowering apocalyptic terror.

John Simon was at my side. Behind him was Wilfie Bannion, the brothers Andrews and five or six others. John Simon had come back from Westlea that morning and ever since he had been receiving the reports of messengers who came and went continually with information about the arrival of the Yeomanry and the mounted county Militia, with small numbers of newly recruited infantry from Tudbury. The soldiers were being quartered at the Town Hall and the inns of Moonlea. Twenty had already moved into The Leaves After the Rain. A group of four had been stationed at the foot of the path which led down from the Briers' cottage.

John Simon gave a short whistle as the last fire down in the works' yard was doused.

'That's the first part completed,' he said. 'Come on in, lads.'

We followed him into the cottage. Mrs Brier was seated in her fireside chair, her face white with worry but her eyes fixed on the grey garment she was knitting. Davy was at his endless basketwork and smiling at us all. Katherine stood by the fire recess brewing some tea.

'Before we separate,' said John Simon looking at me, 'we'll have to ask the harpist what he intends to do. Look, Alan, we don't want any trouble to come to you in any piece of conflict for which you didn't ask. If you want to clear off back over the mountains, goodbye, and here's hoping that we'll see each other again when there's a bit more time for singing and for long sweet talk about the soul of man. What about it?'

Katherine turned to look at me. Without studying her face closely I knew she did not want me to go. I knew that in some way I had come to stand between her and final isolation. I thought of Plimmon, his long, grave, assured face, so free from all those things that nourish doubt about the goodness and rightness of living. I thought of his oiled, expanding dreams, checked at this point only to run more fluently at another.

'I might be of some use. I'll stay.'

'All right. Wilfie, Lewis, John, you know the rallying points to which you are to go and give the word. Tomorrow night we shall gather at the top of the Southern Mountain within sight of Moonlea and the whole county. That will be to show Penbury that we here are not alone, that we shall support each other to the end, whatever happens.'

'How many of you will be armed?'

'None.'

'None. With Moonlea looking like the day before Waterloo? What daftness is this?'

'Harpist,' said Lewis Andrews, 'we've been over that a hundred times before. Penbury is an ironmaster but he is not such a ruthless fool as most of his tribe. Show him moral force and he will relent, make our labour lighter and our pockets heavier with coin. John Simon has told us that, God knows how many times, and we believe him. So we'll gather on the Southern Mountain at night bearing torches, endless thousands of us, and the great glow of our patient might, brighter than ever Penbury's furnaces were, will paralyse even the ferocity of our friend Radcliffe.'

'It's a gamble, John Simon, that's what I say. Plimmon and Radcliffe have been itching for a bit of military glory ever since the war with France ended and cheated them of the chance to be heroes on a national scale. A nice cheap easy slice of glory they'll have if they decide to cut us down as we stand like cattle on that height.'

'They won't dare,' said John Simon. 'The whole county would explode if they did. This is different from the days when they never had to deal with more than a few dozen workers at a time.'

'I still say,' said Wilfie Bannion, 'that an array of weapons, any weapons, in the hands of the strong would have been worth a whole mountain of argument and appeal. The men in the South valleys had a plan to break into the garrisons for forty miles around and get hold of arms enough from there to make the masters respect us. It was John Simon who talked that plan out of countenance. He said it was folly.'

'And it still is, Wilf. Penbury would need only to have

Jarvis the Law clerk speak of the King's Peace and that would have been the end of us. The ironmasters think well of the King and the King is no doubt grateful to the ironmasters for it. Within a day of our being called armed traitors we would have had a thousand soldiers upon us all convinced that we were dangerous vermin and in no time at all we'd be trampled back to a point lower than that from which we started. Killing's none of our business.'

'And being killed?'

'We'll consider that when it happens. Have any of you seen Eddie Parr?'

'Not yet. Why do you want Eddie?'

'I sent a message to him to come back here by today. Any idea where he is?'

'Three days back he was in one of the villages to the west of Tudbury. But you know Eddie. You never know where the devil he's going to turn up next.'

'He's a queer one. Thank you, Katherine.' Katherine had brought some mugs of tea to the table. 'We'll need a drop of something warm for our journey. Come around here, lads, and drink up.'

'Are you one of the messengers too?' I asked John Simon.

'Of course.'

'Be careful. They'll be keeping special watch on you. Since the soldiers arrived this morning they've had a constant patrol moving between here and Moonlea. They'll swoop on you the moment you appear. Can't understand why they haven't been up here to get you before now.'

'They probably want to find out what the pattern of resistance will be first. It's no good putting me in the basket until they find out who the other leaders are and what plans they have.'

205

I withdrew into a corner with my tea and Wilf Bannion followed me. I had exchanged no word with Wilfie since he had put his head over the garden wall and had that brief chat with me in the early evening of the day I had gone over to Plimmon Hall. Wilfie had never been altogether convinced of my worth, and it was clear that now he had even sharper doubts of my stability. As we stood there, poised to meet whatever might be coming, I could see that he still regarded me as utterly a stranger.

'Wilfie,' I said, grimacing at my first sip at the thick rancid tea. 'You know what you told me about your brother Sammy?'

'I remember.'

'I got it all out of Lemuel. I got him on the ale and it flooded him into frankness. Good ale. He and that old life-beaten blouse Floss, just like you said, they were together in it.'

'We don't need to give Lemuel ale to know things like that. Moonlea sharpens your nose for the whiff of evil. But I'm glad you're now quite sure about these facts. It might make you less ready to go fawning around with such gewgaws as harps. Why do you mention Sammy now?'

'They brought Bledgely's body in yesterday.'

'What about it?'

'It just struck me. Radcliffe and his friends will be looking for something to hang around John Simon's neck. This moral force and rallying the boys up on the mountain like a choir are vague sorts of crime for their purposes. They'll see that Bledgely was killed. Men don't look like he looked after a chill. They'll get a whole covey of Lemuels to say they saw John Simon making these changes in Bledgely.'

'That won't happen.'

'What makes you so sure?'

'Because the moment any innocent person is accused of killing Bledgely the guilty person will make a point of stepping forward and he'll be very glad to do it and very proud too. Don't worry about that, harpist. Keep your eyes on the hours ahead.'

We rejoined our friends at the table. As soon as they finished their drink they took their hats and sticks and went on to the porch of the cottage.

'Keep clear of Moonlea and all known paths,' said John Simon. 'Stick to the higher slopes and don't talk to anyone on the way.'

'What about the soldiers at the bottom of the path?'

'I've got little Lenny Foster to play the fool and fox them. They'll be too busy chasing Lenny in and out of the thickets to notice us.'

He wished them good fortune and they all started walking quickly up the hillside. John Simon spoke a few words to Katherine and followed them. We waved them goodbye and re-entered the cottage. Davy came and sat near his mother in front of the fire.

'It's late,' she said. 'Go to bed, Davy.' She was morosely on edge.

Davy made a neat heap of his basket-making materials and went off into the curtained recess where he slept. Mrs Brier plunged angrily into the fire with a rough iron bar.

'No good will come of all this,' she said.

Katherine stood up and gathered the mugs on the table together with a jangling clatter.

'No good has ever come out of living,' she shouted with a bitterness that made Mrs Brier fling her head up with surprise.

Mrs Brier stretched out her arm and I helped her rise from the chair.

'I haven't much strength tonight,' she said.

'You rest, Mrs Brier. Put your mind at ease. Everything will be well.'

She looked at Katherine but Katherine kept her back turned to her and I could hear the self-conscious rub of her fingers over the white table boards. Mrs Brier went towards the small door beyond the sideboard where her bed was. As her fingers began rattling the latch and as Katherine and I were waiting with a kind of desperate curiosity to hear what she might say a gunshot sounded nearby, tearingly, terrifyingly loud.

'God alive,' said Katherine.

Davy's head appeared from behind the curtain, his heavy lips trembling with shock.

'That will be one of them,' said Mrs Brier. 'John Simon, Wilfie, Lewis or one of them. First one, then all.' She opened her door. 'And when all have gone, there may be some peace.'

I could see Katherine begin to sway, supporting herself against the table. I went to stand close to her.

'Faint?' I asked.

'I can't stand this much more.'

'Grit your teeth and close your eyes for a few more days. For God's sake don't try to be wise or brave. Let the days go past you like water. Be a stone, a round stupid stone. Don't make your notions of time and place bleed with your awareness. Moonlea and Plimmon and Radcliffe will stage their little minute of applied daftness. When the blow falls John Simon will be a fugitive. These boys are just making faces at something that has them measured for the boot, the whole boot. When John Simon starts to run I'll see to it that he runs in the right direction. Will you be ready to join him?'

She glanced at Mrs Brier's bedroom. Its door was still open. In the total silence of the kitchen we could hear Mrs Brier's breathing.

'Yes,' said Katherine. 'Tell me and I'll be ready.'

13

At dusk of the following day I sat on the Southern Mountain waiting for John Simon and his army of protesters from the valleys which I could see radiating like wheel-spokes for twenty, thirty miles around. I felt more settled, assured, tolerant of the trouble I saw shaping before me, less fractious about the intrusion of others into the cool little closets of my normal solitude and unconcern. I had been helped in this by what had happened in Moonlea during the day. I had been rejected. The eyes of those who sided with Penbury had viewed me, unfriendly. I could feel from the glances of those in authority that Lemuel had made his report and had branded me as a menace, not perhaps a positive, active one, but one to be looked at doubtfully by the friends of order. I had gone to the Penbury home and had found the main gate barred and guarded. I had asked for Jabez and after a lot of hesitation he had come down to tell me that Mr Radcliffe had insisted that I be treated as one of the enemy and forbidden access to the house. Penbury, said Jabez, who went wandering from room to room moaning and complaining that things should have come to such a ghastly pass, had tried to intercede for me and said there was no harm in me at all, and even claimed that I was one of the very people in the whole of Moonlea who were reasonably sane and decent. But Miss Helen had supported Radcliffe, and I was told, through Jabez, to stick at John Simon's side and take the medicine that was shortly to be administered to pests of our insurrectionary stripe. Jarred, I had come down into the main street in time to see a group of workers bringing in the body of Lenny Foster. It was Lenny, left by John Simon to distract the soldiers, who had been shot by a sentry the night before. They said he had refused to halt when called upon to do so and Lenny was now being delivered to the home of his parents with half a head. A few hundred furious people gathered near Lem. Stevens's store in protest. Plimmon came galloping up at the head of his Yeomanry. Foot soldiers took their positions and encircled the group. Plimmon told the assembled people that he would give them five minutes in which to get back to their homes and put a stop to this hysteria or be cut down. He repeated the last phrase thunderously. The man was obviously at his most tensely excited, and he looked as if he could have been sick with disappointment when the people silently dispersed. The sounds of their dragging feet, the jingle of harness medals, the screaming grief of Lenny Foster's sisters came with distinct clearness to my ears. A guard of six soldiers was left on the steps outside Lemuel's shop. I saw Lemuel, waved my arm to him, but he dived back into the shop to avoid me. I noticed groups of workers drifting in twos and threes towards the edges of the town. I got some food and made my way to the Southern Mountain to wait.

The time was long and I was too conscious of the empty plateau for comfort. I sucked some plucked, long-stalked grass that numbed the hunger for food. I wondered what had been going on in the mind of Lemuel when he had taken such pains to avoid my tongue and eye. I felt no fear, not even a planned disquietude on the subject of Lemuel; only a vague general impatience with man and nature for having made Lemuel stoop so low under a load of striving malice.... John Simon had told me that contingents would start converging near Moonlea from dusk onward. I stood up and stared in every direction, but I could see no movement in the thickening light. For several minutes I was afraid that something had happened to turn John Simon's intentions to pure ash.... I walked away from the beautifully rounded mound against which I had been resting my body and made my way briskly towards the lip of the mountain from which I could see better anything that stirred below.... There were many things that could happen to make John Simon look a fool. I recalled something that Mrs Brier had told me the day before, about gifts and promises of bread to the faithful who would have no truck with the doctrines and doings of John Simon. On this earth there is a legion of automatic bread-takers. Given the assurance of life for even twenty-four hours to come and they become as passively uncritical as trees. Mrs Brier was a good sample, an oak of the species. She had struggled too hard for too many years for the little security she knew. Her days had gone mad with their own meagreness. She was easy prey now for any fool who might wish to wiggle a threatening sceptre or cajoling bribe in her face. Idiot toil, idiot need, idiot love, had created around her a menagerie of uncaged dilemmas, all savage, all flesh-eating, ready to snap her every timid assertion into a pulp. She and the thousands like her would enter into any cunning compact with the Penburys and Bowens to make the ground under John Simon's feet soggy, full of deathly traps.... Or the Yeomanry might have made swift strategic visits to all those centres from which John Simon thought to gather his host of compassionate protesters....

I shivered. There was no mark in the gloom. I made a step

212

downwards. It would be better to sit with Abel at The Leaves After the Rain and between the sodden outbursts of soldiers' songs and the rustling bodytraffic of Floss Bennett working to a scherzo beat since the military occupation, we could talk with ale-softened hopes about the rights of man in the age of gold. And I could think between my cups of the smile on the faces of Helen Penbury and Plimmon as the tricked and whipped slipped quietly back to their cottages and forges and I would go out to the cool mossy cave-like yard, bang my furious fist upon the ice-cold rock and curse the ill-chance that had sent the healing passions of John Simon Adams to dwell in a crass unripe age which would not allow his fingers to find the nerve of action that would allow him a peaceful harmony with the men and things around him, that would have Plimmon, with all his stupid self-mad dreams stretched out in an elegantly fertilising stillness along one of his own furrows.

Then, below me, five great veins of redness pressed to the surface of the night. The legions were coming up from the south, men bearing torches in their ranks, making for the foot of the mountain on which I stood. I looked fascinated at the broad streams of brightness that came closer, clearer. John Simon had been right. In the hearts and minds of the folk who had been gathered in from their quiet fields to labour in other ways between those hills there had been a ripeness I had not seen, a fullness I had not felt. But it was I in my tiny acre of pride and sufficiency who was coming to flower, very slowly, testing, suspecting, even hating the petals that would grow ruthlessly into the pattern of a more merciful, more exacting, more hazardous understanding.

As the first wave of torches touched the foot of the Southern Mountain and began their slow orderly climb I

213

began to cry and shout, exultantly, like a madman, as if all the lovely loving gentleness of man on earth had been gathered up into one symbol and presented to me for the first time.

'A quiet raising of hands against those who know they have taken wrong painful paths,' I remembered John Simon saying. 'The look of reproof on the face of a multitude, long ill-used yet strongly patient, knowing itself to have powers of life and death over the malevolent and fiendish who have contrived its misery, yet wishing only life, for itself, for others.'

For two hours the men and torches poured in flickering waves on to the plateau. The district leaders, strong-voiced incisive men, had their movements well prepared and the mass fell without hesitation or disorder into place. I looked across the valley. Moonlea itself was in darkness. The Penbury house was a blaze of light, neat, symmetrical, consciously confident light.

I could not see John Simon, but I soon picked out Wilfie Bannion, quick, grim and lithe as death's own dog loping from group to group. I approached him.

'Any trouble on the way?'

'Not much. We are a few thousand short. A lot of the men in the Southern valleys backed out at the last moment and refused to march. Said they wouldn't go out against the ironmasters without even the means to defend themselves. That was a blow to John Simon because he really thought he had talked them out of that attitude.'

'Anything else?'

'No. The soldiers were quiet as mice.'

'I bet they never expected this.'

'Did you?'

'No, honest to God, Wilfie, I didn't.'

'How did you feel when you first saw us?'

'Hard to say. Very moved, as if the whole earth were stirring.'

'That's what's happening. The whole earth is stirring. You should have heard us singing on the way.'

'Plimmon will take several hours getting over this.'

'More than that. This is a side of life that monarch has never seen before and we're out to rub his nose into it.'

'When do you disperse? Before morning?'

'At dawn we march into Moonlea.'

'Into Moonlea? John Simon said you'd show yourselves on the mountain and then break up and go back home.'

'No. We are going down into Moonlea. John Simon wouldn't have it at first and the other leaders had to argue like hell to make him see that they had given in quite enough to his mania for peace and persuasion by consenting to come here unarmed. We're going down into Moonlea and we're going to put our demands to Penbury or Radcliffe or whoever else is there to listen and make decisions. They tell me Penbury is ill, weakened under the multiple stresses and strains of being a master of men.'

'He isn't so bad. In certain moods, tender as a mouth.'

'Hush your merciful fuss, harpist. We are the great cleansing rain for his type of foulness.' He laughed at the pensive bewilderment on my face as I stared around at the throng. 'We'll put our demands. When we feel sure that they'll be met, that we won't have any more years of seeing wages go down and rent and prices go up while the whole tribe of us swing and choke in a rope of debt and dirt, we'll go home.'

'There's a lot of soldiers down there, Wilfie. What if they start trouble?'

215

Wilfie looked straight into my face and smiled.

'There are some of us, lower in the scale of hope and charity than John Simon Adams, who'd like to see them try. The way we've lived for the last ten years, a little sharp agony might do us all the world of good.'

'That's a tricky thing to want, boy. Agony's an odd broth, any way you look at it.'

'If it breaks the surface of a calm that's rotten, bad and spreading death beneath, it's good.'

Wilfie left me. For an hour I walked among the groups. The mountain, with all those torches and bodies upon it, had ceased to be cold. I wanted someone to talk to but I was a stranger, and they had been told to speak to no one but to those they knew. My mind worked in curious waves. One moment I would be caught up utterly in the vast rhythm of decision to which every one of those men had contributed his quiet part. Then the present would fall away from me and I was shaken by a shudder of futility and fear, ashamed that I was no longer wholly my simple, dirigible self, cool and malleable between the fingers of my moods but only a fragment, a shrinking threatened fragment of this great hot array of clowns. They were only vaguely aware of what they wished to do and as the night wore on and they grew to realise as they stared at each other the full extent of their grotesque passivity and danger, they lost even that wrath which in its intense absent-mindedness might have prompted them to make their gesture well. As I walked around I saw hundreds who stood quite still, their strong shoulders stooped towards the torches, their bodies inert, their eyes thoughtlessly solemn.

At first light all torches were doused. They fell into rank and marched down the hillside towards Moonlea. In advance of the main column a dozen lads ran tirelessly to give warning of any barricade or ambush they might find on the road.

The sun was well up as we entered Moonlea. My ears started at the sudden sound of our moving bodies between the buildings of the main street. Beyond the black acres of the furnace yards the hillsides were a brilliant green, their feet gangrenous with the streets of cottages. Not a soul was to be seen along the first stretches of the town.

As the road turned, about fifty yards from the spot at which the gravel drive to Penbury's house began, we found the Yeomanry drawn up. The patch of intense ominous colour they made caused many of the men to gasp. Plimmon, on a bay, was at their head looking more like a leader of men than any man has the right to look. I was near the head of the marchers. Standing on some raised ground at the roadside the whole of the street as far as I could see was full of men, in ranks of four, five, six. Twenty yards from where Plimmon stood we were called to a halt. John Simon stepped a little ahead of the front rank. It was the first time I had had a good look at him since the night before. His face had lost most of its old sense of inward assurance. He was feeling the incoming winds more strongly. His eyes were worried and strained.

'We want to see Penbury,' he shouted. 'There are men from twenty towns assembled here and they speak with one united voice. Where is Penbury?'

'Not here,' said Radcliffe who was on Plimmon's left. He too was in the uniform of a Yeomanry officer. He rode his horse with less ease than either Plimmon or Wilson, who was on Plimmon's right hand. Radcliffe's face was red and fierce, and his hand kept opening and closing on the pommel of his sword as if in haste to be at us and done with it. Wilfie Bannion was watching him intently, his hand stroking the rough cord of his breeches, the movement clearly audible in the stretched sensitive silence that had followed Radcliffe's first words.

'Not here,' he said again. 'And not likely to be to talk with you, Adams, or with your friends.'

At a sign from Plimmon Mr Bowen, wearing a black top-coat buttoned up to his neck and smiling pleasantly at us all, stepped from behind the leaders of the uniformed body and began to speak. The early morning cold and his amazement at having to deal with so assorted and alien a congregation made his hands to tremble and his voice to fade. John Simon raised his hand courteously towards him and said:

'Few of us can hear you, Mr Bowen. We have heard your message often in the past and are familiar with its outline. Its real substance lies in the scabbards of the gentlemen behind you. So those of us who can hear do not especially wish to listen. For decency's sake, Mr Bowen, stick to the quietness and divinity which are your proper field and leave us to worry in our own ways at the bone of our bread and butter questions. Where is Penbury, Mr Radcliffe?'

'At his home waiting for this vulgar bit of heroics to pass over.'

'Then we'll go up there. We shall be very civil, Mr Radcliffe. No one will be hurt or offended.'

As John Simon was lifting his hand to give the signal to advance, Plimmon made a brusque, disgusted gesture and Mr Jarvis the clerk of the town appeared from between the cavalry men in the same manner as Mr Bowen. He looked sick with misery and foreboding. His brown, austere suit, thin hair, short body, his fingers yellowish and curled at the edges like old paper, made a poor showing against the frame of fit, fluorescent warriors. He took a document from his pocket, and when he had succeeded in holding it steady enough to be read, he began to speak in a mumble that made no sense to us. Radcliffe stopped him with an irritable bawl and told him to read louder. Mr Jarvis lifted his eyes as if he were in total despair and tried again. This time we got most of his words clearly. It was the Riot Act and in it we were promised punishment if we did not forthwith stop being a menace to the King's Peace and go back to those places and occupations where we had first got the idea of being a menace to the King's Peace. John Simon waited for Mr Jarvis to finish, his head on one side, as if being consciously polite. He smiled at Mr Jarvis, and the older man smiled back delightedly thinking that his efforts with the law had done some good. Then John Simon shouted:

'That's enough. March forward, lads.'

Mr Jarvis scuttled out of harm's way into the deep roadside ditch, I following him. I saw Radcliffe's stallion leap forward and his sword swing towards John Simon. The heavy blade caught him in the temple and he went down. Wilfie Bannion, drawing a short knife from beneath his coat, sprang with a wild curse at Radcliffe. He fell back with Plimmon's beautiful sword in his chest. A cry of mad rage came from the hundreds of men in the first detachments. Many of them produced short staves, knives, even a few pistols. The sheer animal weight of their pressing bodies caused the horsemen for a few minutes to fall back. Then there was a deafening rattle of musket fire. The windows of the cottages along the main street had opened and the foot soldiers were firing carefully into the packed mass of bodies that filled the highway. The men in front fell

219

back. Plimmon ordered his men to withdraw a space to give them momentum for the charge. I found Lewis Andrews at my side in the ditch. Between us we pulled John Simon through a gap in the hedge and dragged him across the short field that divided us from the woods around the Penbury house. From there we saw Plimmon stage his field-day. It was brief, it was simple. Horses are stronger than men and the Yeomen had thrown in their lot thoroughly with the horses. It was a triumph for strong insensitive minds and bodies. A group of very young cavalry men whom I could see clearly, for they seemed to do only a little moving about, kept shouting hurrah, hurrah, in time with the brandishing of their sabres in a way that made one faint and sick and unbelieving. The foot soldiers in the houses were still firing and the closing up of demonstrators as Plimmon's charge exerted a fierce pressure from the front kept them ceaselessly supplied with a thickening target. We saw some of the men climb up the cottage fronts to try and tear the guns from the soldiers' hands but we did not see one who got as far even as the upstairs window. From inside the houses I heard the screams of women raised in terror and I was aware of a horrifying rightness in the sound of them. Inside ten minutes there were fleeing men on every road and path out of Moonlea.

We continued our way up the hillside, keeping low, taking advantage of all the cover the trees gave us. John Simon was still senseless and it was heavy work bearing him up that slope. We reached a small quarry, quiet, seemingly disused. In a corner of it we took refuge. A drip of water had formed a tiny pool and from it we bathed John Simon's head. He opened his eyes, saw the grey blank menacing face of quarry rock and closed them again.

'We'll be safe enough here for a short while,' said Lewis. 'But the huntsmen will make good sport of combing the hillside for laggards so we must get away as soon as we can.'

In fifteen minutes John Simon was able to stand. His face wore an expression of quiet bitterness and astonishment and we did not talk. We began walking cautiously towards the summit of Arthur's Crown. From there we could see the rapid distracted movements of people in the street of Moonlea looking for their dead and wounded.

'Wilfie Bannion will be one of those,' said Lewis.

'One of those?' asked John Simon. 'Those what?'

'Dead.'

'Wilfie? Dead?'

'Aye,' I answered. 'Plimmon made very sure of Wilfie. He got a lot of noble sword and he's dead. I saw that from the ditch.'

'There was no cunning in Wilfie. He was never one to wait.'

'Oh Jesus,' whispered John Simon and thrust his face into the thick whinberry bush on which we lay. 'I was wrong. I was as wrong as I could have been. And we were stepped on.'

'How's your head?'

'Aches. I wish Radcliffe had used the sharp side. Then I'd have had no head to ache and I'd have been no worse off. I was a loon to lead them into that butcher shop. They tried to tell me that, Jeremy Longridge, Wilfie, but I was sure of my wisdom and wouldn't listen.'

'Forget about it. They'll be after you like a ferret when they can't find your body. But the road to the North is open and bloodless. This is it, boy. Down the other side of Arthur's Crown and away. Shall I go and tell Katherine that you've started the journey?'

'I suppose so. But give me a bit of time to think.'

'Time to think! God in heaven, of all things to ask for!'

14

We stayed that night in a tiny village at the northern foot of
Arthur's Crown, the whole massive mountain between us
and Moonlea. We were fed and sheltered by some cottagers
who knew Lewis Andrews and they lied with great good will
to the cavalrymen who came around at evening in a sportive
and careless mood making inquiries as to whether anything
had been seen of fleeing rioters from Moonlea.

Before turning into the beds that our hosts had arranged
for us in the attic of their cottage, I had nearly succeeded in
bringing John Simon completely around to my way of
thinking.

'Leave it to me,' I said. 'Just sit there and be stupid and
dumb, boy. People get wise in season like fruit gets ripe. This
is the world of Plimmon and Radcliffe. After that performance this morning the people will be sick with shock and
pain for months to come. Penbury, whose feelers were once
dipped for a space in poetry and are the more shrewd for
that, will have the sense to treat them a little more gently
than usual for some time to come and by the time Bowen
and his brothers of the burning brand have done equating
you with Satan and the ungrateful son he'll have them
believing that you were responsible for every single murder
committed on the other side of the hill today. It's not even
a good joke. Let's get away.'

'They made me look a fool. They made me look a terrible

fool,' was all John Simon said. But from the way he nodded at the opinions I expressed I was sure that on the following morning he, Katherine and I would be showing our backs to the stricken, peaceless valleys, and to make my assurance double I told John Simon once again, with a glowing persuasive rapture on all my words, of the freshness and beauty we would find in the northern dingle that had become mine.

At about nine, as we were sitting in the kitchen of the cottage, the door opened and a man of about my own age, a man graceful in his proportions, with an immensely broad brow, deep humorous eyes, a costume that mingled the garments of an ironworker with those of a woodsman, came into the room. His face as he came into view had been deadly grave, but at the sight of us his mouth puckered into a smile of greeting, though his eyes were as vacant and sad as before. John Simon waved his hand at him.

'Alan,' he said, 'this is my friend, Eddie Parr. Where've you been, Eddie?'

'I got delayed in a village fifteen miles to the west of here. I got back as soon as I could. I landed in Moonlea in the middle of the morning.'

'What news?'

Eddie looked around at us, pausing at each face in turn, staring finally at the aged cottager who sat smoking a long clay pipe in a fireside chair.

'Oh, it was bad,' he said, moving nearer to the fireplace, glancing at me as he moved as if he had heard of me and wished to confirm some impression he had made.

We waited for him to go on. The grandfather clock kept dusting the silence. The old man's lips popped around his clay, over-noisily, as if he wished to isolate himself from us. The pressure of the silence was beginning to irk him, and I,

224

to help him, tapped with my toecap the thick, clumsily carved leg of the stool near which I stood.

'All this morning,' said Eddie, 'I walked up and down that main street. No one challenged me. All this afternoon I was in a field, sick, sick and rolling like a dog. I've never seen dead people like that before, heaped.'

'It's a terrible sight,' said John Simon. 'But some people like it. There must be some kind of beauty, some kind of deep consoling beauty in it for some people or they wouldn't be at such pains to arrange it.' His speaking voice was only a whisper's shadow above breathing. The whole being of John Simon was a painful bulge of thought and feeling. I cast around in my mind for some means of tearing at and destroying the mantle of grieving, helpless anger and remorse he was stitching around himself.

'I saw Plimmon,' said Eddie. 'He was happy. He was smiling. Especially when they carried the body of Wilfie Bannion to join the others. He's got teeth like snow, that Plimmon.'

'Has he now?' asked the old man, and I could have wished the whole talk of these lonely desperate men could have slid off into some serene backwater of harmless gossip about all the trivial issues of existence starting with Plimmon's teeth.

'He's a handsome enough chap, no denying,' I said. 'Like the pictures of gods, only with a keener sense of business in his eye.'

'The whole family was like it,' said the old man, nodding at me with the makings of a grin, he, too, relieved at the prospect of hearing no more for a while of those dead folk beyond the mountain in their quiet shabby street and of the things that would need to be done for the affair to be

225

rounded off with an intelligible comment. 'Just like a woman with the seed fixed right in here. They swell, the Plimmons. Like bread to us are fields to them. They gobble and swell.'

'Like frogs,' said John Simon. 'They'll swell and they'll burst.'

'In their sort of pool, John Simon, the education and the grub are good. They do nothing so daft as to burst. You might. They won't.'

There was a kick on the door.

'A friend to see John Simon Adams,' said the voice of the woman of the cottage. 'Benny Cornish, my nephew, from Westlea.'

'Unbar the door, Eddie.'

Benny Cornish was a young, flat-featured lad, with dark eyes and a monkey-like way of keeping them big and fixed on you when he spoke. The skin of his neck kept moving to the rhythm of some muscular tic beneath the coarse grey flannel of his muffler.

'Hullo, grandfather,' said the lad to the old man in the corner.

'Hullo, Benny Cornish. How is your mother, my daughter, Louisa Cornish?'

'When I saw her last she was well,' answered Benny, and I liked the grave courtesy with which these two spoke to each other. There was a feeling of security in the earnest fullness of their questions and answers.

'When did you see her last?'

'Two days ago.'

'What have you been doing, Benny Cornish, that you have not been home for two days?'

'At headquarters.'

'Headquarters?' The old man's voice had risen querulously. 'What headquarters? What kind of a place is that for a shaving of a lad like you, Benny?'

'The headquarters of the Western Valley men. You've surely heard of them, grandfather. We are prepared.'

'Stay at home and mind your mother, for mercy's sake. This strife is work for men and your mother has been unwell for many months. What's happening here? Why is all the quietness going out of life? In my young day if people didn't like it anywhere they just moved on and made themselves content. Now there's a loudness of trouble on every wind. Where is the quietness I knew once?'

There was a frank, challenging distress in the old man's voice and manner, and I would have liked to sit down and talk that question over with him because it had a fresh promising sound. But the boy Cornish approached me and made an awkward, solemn gesture of lifting his finger to his temple in the manner of a military salute.

'I was sent to speak to John Simon Adams,' he said. 'Him who is leader of the North Eastern valleys. Are you John Simon Adams?'

'Not I, boy. I was blown in by the wind. There's your man there sitting beneath the lamp.'

'What do you want, Benny?' asked John Simon.

'I come from Jeremy Longridge, our leader in the South Western valleys. He has sent me with a message for you.'

'It was good of Jeremy to send. Was your journey easy? What did you see on the way? Did you pass through Moonlea? What was it like? What were they doing when you passed through?' John Simon was distracted and trembling again, as he had been when he recovered consciousness that morning. He caught hold of the boy's hand. 'What had they done with the dead people, Benny?'

227

'I don't know,' said Benny. He pulled his hand away from John Simon's and stepped back. He was clearly ill at ease in the presence of the whole, writhing tenderness that he could feel coming out in waves from the heart and mind of John Simon. 'I didn't pass through Moonlea. I was no such fool. I kept to the hillside paths. Two soldiers spotted me just near the top of Arthur's Crown. They ran to catch me and even fired a shot. But I was faster than a hare.'

'Good lad, good lad,' said the old man to his pipe bowl, chuckling and patting the side of his chair. 'I was the same, when I was a kid, just the same, like a stag, like a little stag.'

'What did Jeremy Longridge say?' asked John Simon, slowly and with difficulty, as if not greatly wishing to hear the answer.

'He said Plimmon's victory this morning will mean martial law throughout the whole region. He said if we fail now we fail for ever. He said the best thing you can do if you've learned nothing from what happened this morning is to make your own way to America where there are plenty of empty spaces for empty heads, or turn up in front of Plimmon with the rope already in your hand to save him the trouble of buying one.'

'Jeremy said all that?'

'His very words. I learned them off like I would learn verses.'

'I can believe it. He was always a bitter one, was Jeremy. He should have come as I told him to, when the signal went forth. He should have added his thousands to ours. It might have made all the difference, the last ounce that would have turned the scale. Whatever he thought privately about my notions he should have come as he said he would. Then no one need have died, no one, no one.'

228

'Don't torment yourself about it,' I said, taking John Simon by the arm and forcing him back into his chair. 'Blood was wanted, that was the programme. Plimmon wanted blood. That's part of his growing method at the moment. You were fool enough to bring him the game without his having to beat the bush for it. That's all.'

'Nothing is all. There's a hell of a lot more to it and I want to hear it. What else did Jeremy say, Benny?'

'He said if you've learned your lesson we can really make a start, a fresh start. We in the Western Valleys are ready. If you wish to see him go to The Leaves After the Rain the night after tomorrow night. Abel will take you to him.'

John Simon made no immediate reply. He rested his head between his elbows on the table. His head sank until his lips played with the stained crust which remained from the last meal.

'I'll think about it,' he said, and left the kitchen. We could hear him pacing beneath the broad elder trees that shaded the cottage's entrance.

'He shouldn't be out there,' I said. 'After what he's been through today he'd be better off in bed.'

'Let him be,' said Eddie Parr. 'There'll be no peace or rest for him until he makes up his mind one way or the other. Let him pace. It's a soft clear night and it will do him no harm.'

'Benny Cornish,' said the old man, 'you'll be hungry after all your gallivanting and talk of headquarters and so on. Go to your aunt outside and tell her to fill you with bread and milk.'

'Jeremy Longridge says we're soldiers in a sort of army now and will be until the ironmasters make a decent peace with us. And as soldiers we must learn to suffer many hardships.'

'Less of these bloody speeches from you, Benny Cornish, and drink your milk. It makes my teeth drop out the faster to hear a shaver like you carry on as if he were the old Wellington Duke himself.'

Benny turned from his grandfather and winked at me. The grandfather turned away from Benny and winked at me. I winked back at both of them and was glad to be stroking the inner lining of these two lives.

'Who's Longridge?' I asked Eddie Parr. 'For what are his men prepared? What lesson exactly does he hope that John Simon has learned? Don't tell me this Longridge is going to ask John Simon to walk up for another dose of being butchered.'

'Longridge is a clear seer. I ought to know. In my brief days as a Free Preacher I did a fair bit of seeing myself and I'm a good judge. Jeremy doesn't believe in persuasion by peaceful example any more. He says it's like putting your head in the lion's mouth before pulling the heart out of the lion or the teeth from its head. He says the rich are a small army which keeps the whole nation of the poor besieged within thick filthy walls by guile and terror. He says that for men to live in their thousands simply to enrich the Penburys and Plimmons is to betray life. Therefore, he says, let the nation of the poor be rid of its besiegers and make its life a serene and clear and fruitful thing. He says it is good that those who forge the iron should be the masters of the foundries in which it is forged. He says it is likewise good that the fields should belong to those who wish to till them, as once they must have done. He says that if the workers are to be slaves in the new towns, a prey to hunger and to diseases they didn't know before, then it is better that the foundries and mines be destroyed now and we with them and the valleys made empty and quiet once again.'

'Tell me more of this Longridge. When John Simon came down from the North my absence left a gap within him. I know he must have found many things to fill the space. I want to know the flavour of the things and people he used to do the job of filling.'

'Longridge? There's so much to say. If he thought his dying would leave our bodies freer to straighten he would die and think as little of it as he would of a short cough.'

'Has John Simon been a great friend of his?'

'When they first met, that was in the bad winter of two years back, we thought they must be the two separated halves of a thing that had always passionately wished to be whole. They might have come from the far parts of the earth to be joined together between these hills so perfectly did they seem to make the idea and the force that would show us the way through these years. At the beginning it was Longridge who was the moral persuader, the mild and gentle one. You should have seen the way in which the whole body of him seemed to glow when he spoke of the water of merciful thoughts in which even the most callous of the ironmastering oafs could be dipped and made responsive to our wills. As long, he used to say, as the workman's knowledge of the world in which he lives is small and defective for so long will all his desires be clumsy, stupid and doomed. It was he more than anybody who got us to study and read and always for a long time after Jeremy Longridge had been in a town there would be fewer to be seen in the taverns although he never had the time to say anything against ale as such. However dark the day he lit a wick of purpose that left no shadow.'

'I've heard of such men, Eddie. I'm not like them. The feel

231

of other men's lives is rough as sandstone on my face. I dodge away from it, that's the great aim of all my breathing. I give as little of a damn for whether they find salvation as for whether they find gold or dung or amethyses or smallpox or whatever it is they feel will belly out their lives. But I'm glad such men exist as feel the fever of a boundless misery. Somehow, somewhere, I suppose they keep the root of something watered, something that off and on serves as a magnet even for the slowest, daftest feet.'

'The root of all life, harpist, all existence, goes to suck at their hearts.'

'Did they quarrel, this man and John Simon?'

'In those days it was Longridge who called John Simon rash and John Simon who called Longridge a saintly fool. It was Adams who said that only a furnace with all its scalding, changing force could be a symbol to guide men who had been tried by too much wretchedness, that the fires we tended so well for Penbury should be laid and lit beneath the owners to make them jump towards reason a little more quickly. Longridge said only a conviction of wrong in the minds of those who had erred and a conviction in the minds of the wronged that a fixed limit must be set to the term of endurance on this earth would avail us. Had we listened to John Simon we would have left our cottages that winter and burned the courts of law, the poorhouses and the mansions of the mighty.'

'And now they've changed places altogether. That's uncanny. I've never had any ideas myself long enough in the arm to stretch down inside and pull me inside out for curing. I've always tried to sidestep things big enough to make an abiding image on my mind. But I always thought that such ideas, when a man did have them, sprang from some deep

232

soil and changed as little as trees. What happened?'

'I can't say exactly. Both were sincere; they had magnets in them. They might have drawn each other to the opposite pole. Jeremy married a girl called Iona from Tudbury. She was a beauty and as wise as a woman ever will be. She thought just like Jeremy because she too had been all the way through the mill. Her father went to Van Diemen's Land on the ship that took the first batch of boys who were dragged into the Assize Court for mentioning wages to Penbury's father. But Iona was calm and taught Jeremy how to make the fire of his desires run through him when he spoke without burning the lining of his veins. She nursed him well, for he had been always like to die from a weakness in his chest, and we saw the trace of blood in his skin for the first time. Then a group of publicans and other types of patriot at Tudbury who hated to see their neighbours thirst for anything but ale consulted with the masters and the parsons and got their sanction to treat Jeremy as anti-Christ. They soaked a band of hooligans in their strongest brew and let them loose on Jeremy as they would hounds on a stag, one night when Jeremy was coming over the hillside from a talk with us here at Moonlea. They beat him to within a bruise of death. It took Iona months to get him strong again, and when he was managing to walk once more she herself died in childbed.'

'The whole course,' I muttered. 'Not a lesson missed, not a single whipping made briefer by a second.'

'That changed Jeremy. It was as if the whole cool pool of gentleness in the man had come under a savage heat leaving only the hard bitter mud. Had John Simon remained then what he had been until that time the fighting would have started that winter. But John Simon had changed too. His

233

spirit had flown or crawled, depending on the way you look at it, on to precisely the same hillock of patient passivity which had just been left by Jeremy. As each commanded the devotion of about half the ironworkers who were ready for revolt the whole surge was held in tension.'

'Why did John Simon change? What was going on in the man?'

'Longridge had been a better preacher than he thought. During those months when Jeremy was on his bed his notions of moral force had been making a deeper and deeper rut in John Simon's mind. Then when Jeremy started wanting to drag the ironmasters from their golden perches with the bare hands of necessity and put Plimmon to do a little ploughing for a change, he was faced with the ghosts of his own dead convictions whenever he tried to recruit John Simon's active support. It was just as if some creature had come along and snapped off John Simon's mental sword arm. It was about the time he went to live with the Briers. It was then we noticed it most. Mind, I'm suggesting nothing. What happened or happens there is John Simon's own business. All I'm saying is that it's a tragedy when two minds like his and Jeremy's cease or fail to work in harmony. The people have few leaders and the thoughts of those leaders should be in a straight and simple line if they are to be understood, cherished. The people have little awareness of the many subtle winds that can turn the vane of a man's thoughts. They understand the kind of change that can turn a life from fair to foul between dawn and night. They understand the cold and hunger and smashed bodies that can tear the bowels from all bliss, but they've had little chance of getting the measure of those quiet worms of doubt and indecision that make their hollow nests in the soul and brain

234

of a man. I understand a bit, but not all, not all.'

I felt I had the picture clearly in my mind now. John Simon's unused body love for Katherine Brier had created in him a gentle corrosive pessimism which had ruined his belief in the power of decisive action in any sphere, had lured him into a treacherous peacefulness in the face of men who, by every canon of his experience, his early diagnosis, were incurably wolfish, aggressive. He had succumbed to a gradual sardonic paralysis of the will, his innate mercy taking him firmly by both hands and locking them behind his back. If the process could be reversed then healing might be achieved.... I looked out of the window. The night's darkness was lightening. I expected to see John Simon pacing like a maddened animal up and down in the shadow of the elder trees, biting at the red, rotten flesh of his delays and indecisions. He was sitting down with a boiler between his legs, a small open fire a foot or so in front of where he sat, a short soldering iron in his hand as he did some quick skilled job of salvage on the boiler's bottom. The cottager's wife stood at his side smiling at the deftness of his fingers, and at something he must just have said, for John Simon's lips were happy too and looked as if they had just come back to rest after shaping themselves around words he had been glad to utter. The whole of him gave me that impression as he sat there in the darkness, lit by the dancing, unworried firelight. It was not often since my coming to Moonlea that I had seen him looking like that. Some stone had been lifted, some door opened, some light let in, some wound closed and taught not to throb.... The process in reverse. He would join Longridge in a wind of fury and that would set his whole life in motion once again, redemptive, selfish, cleansing action. Mrs Brier and Davy had their being in a world of raptures

235

that knew themselves maimed, brooding upon the mystery of their own mutilation in a round of numbing prayer and almost total imperception which had its own laws of satisfaction and fulfilment. If John Simon should kick at them in clearing the hurdle of his desires as he would now most certainly kick at Penbury and his money-spinning peers, and thrust at the stoppage of stupid squalor in the lives of his neighbours, they would find as little hurt in that as they had found in tolerance and meek unanimity.

I said some of these things to Eddie Parr who had put his head down on the table boards and was ready to sleep.

'Once,' said Eddie Parr, in a voice I could hardly hear, his mouth almost pressed into the table's woodwork, 'in a northern town, I saw a kid, about eight he was and a machine-minder. He looked about eighty, as wise and cold as eighty. I was looking at him at the very moment when his head tumbled to one side and he was dragged into the machinery. Some time I'm going to write a long, great poem about that, a poem that will be as hard for people to read as it will be for me to live and write it. But every time I've saved up enough to buy the paper I see that kid, and he keeps looking at me and telling me he said it all, so why the hell should I bother.'

Benny Cornish came in, buttoning his coat, hoisting his trousers and chewing his last mouthful of food. He left the door half open and we heard John Simon drop the staunched boiler to the ground. He came towards the door and we heard him tell the woman:

'You try it now. It'll be as right as ever it was. I put a bit more lead into it than was needed, but the boiler couldn't be much heavier than it was. I don't know how you lug things like that on and off fires.'

John Simon came in and put his arms around the shoulders of Benny Cornish.

'Listen, Benny, these are the things I want you to tell Jeremy Longridge. Tell him that he was right and I was wrong. Tell him that at the moment I'm half pain, half wisdom and that I aim soon to be all wisdom and to pass the pain on to somebody else, like Plimmon. Tell him that as yet we have no arms in our valleys but with or without them we shall be by his side when the time has come to burn out the impurities. Tell him I shall be waiting for him two nights from now at The Leaves After the Rain. Will you remember that?'

'I'll be able to say it to him just like verses. That's why they sent me, because I can hear things and then say them again, just like verses.'

'That's good. So long, Benny.'

'So long, John Simon Adams.' The boy glanced at the old man whose head had toppled forward on his chest and he winked. Then he opened the door and was gone.

The lady of the cottage showed us where we were to sleep and we slept, I in a chamber of the darkest dreams.

15

It was the afternoon of the next day when I walked through the main street of Moonlea again. John Simon had told me, before I set out from the Cornish cottage, that there would be no danger in my going down into Moonlea because I had not yet done anything which would tie me in their eyes to him. He said he would not have asked me to go had he not been afraid that something might go wrong with his plan to meet Longridge at The Leaves After the Rain. He did not want to go down there and find Longridge taken and the place an ambush. I was to get in touch with Abel, and unless he gave me the all-clear signal, send a message over the hill to John Simon. When he first made the suggestion I had not been happy. I could not possibly have been blithe with old man Cornish viewing me from his other planet of mute disquietude and foreboding. But when Eddie Parr said he would go if I felt uncertain about the prospect I told them I would consider it a privilege to help them in this way.

I had called briefly in at the cottage of the Briers. There I had met a girl called Phoebe, a niece of Mrs Brier, who was a servant at the Penbury home. She told me that Plimmon and Radcliffe were preparing a gibbet for myself and John Simon, a tidy legal gibbet, for the murder of Bledgely, with Lemuel as chief witness and principal assistant to the hangman. She also gave me a long and interesting account of the passionate clash of tempers between Plimmon and

Helen Penbury when Plimmon had stalked into her room and reproved her in a voice that could be heard right up to Arthur's Crown for having had the imprudence to consort even for a space of seconds with such a performer as I. Plimmon, on evidence of my perfidy supplied by the butler Jabez who was seeking Plimmon's favour, had come to regard me as an even longer thorn than the freeholders. This news had made me feel no warmer. I let them feed me, gave them no news of John Simon's whereabouts and left as quickly as I could.

As I walked through Moonlea in the late afternoon quietness, I saw that the place was even more of an armed camp than when I had seen it last. At every few yards there was a group of soldiers, mounted or on foot. About the foot soldiers there was an unwilling displeased air as if they wanted to remind the inhabitants that they were there under duress. But the horsemen, sturdy, bovine lads, sons of rich farmers for the most part, enjoyed every pungent, dramatic moment of it, sat their horses with an expansive ease and were clearly impatient to show their mettle once again. I walked unobtrusively along, keeping my head bowed. Captain Wilson was there, accoutred for every type of slaughter, and his brows lowered as he saw me, but he made no move to halt my progress. His head kept turning from time to time to look at the new flag which had been run up on the roof of the Town Hall. Some young women came forth fitfully to offer food and drink in a pleasant enough manner to the soldiers, particularly the horsemen. But of men or older women I saw nothing.

I caught a glimpse of Lemuel Stevens. I waved my arm and hailed him. The moment he saw me he ran and dived into his shop. I tried to catch him but when I reached his door and found it bolted fast, I rattled it angrily and called him by name, but not too loudly. Through the glass I could see Lemuel and Isabella standing in the half-light. They held each other by the hand and were chattering like a pair of magpies through whose tails a shot has just whistled. I could feel their excited panic coming at me even through the barrier.

I edged furtively around Moonlea for the whole of that day. There was much to see. There was a memorial service for the slain in the chapel of Mr Bowen, and I saw Helen Penbury in a dress of profound mourning walk into the chapel to hear the sermon of high beauty which Mr Bowen delivered on the majesty of death and the folly of man. After the service a large crowd assembled in the main street to receive the bounty of loaves which was distributed at the command of Richard Penbury. Penbury himself was there, carried down in his chair, looking more dejected and diaphanous than ever. I spent the night in a barn on Penbury's estate.

In the early evening of the next day I found my way to The Leaves After the Rain. In the yard outside a large group of foot soldiers were lying about, bored, talking in snatches with no seeming interest even in their own voices. The hands of some were plucking away at tidying tasks on their packs and guns, but without haste or enthusiasm. The faces of all of them were sullen and full of a dangerous fretfulness whenever their eyes lit on the door of the tavern. Twenty or more horses were tethered along the right-hand wall of the inn yard. The soldiers growled back an answer to my greeting. I tripped over a musket as I picked my way towards the entrance of the house and had a fist banged on my leg by a black-haired irascible giant who bawled a filthy curse on me and Moonlea.

The large room of The Leaves was monopolised by the officers of the regiment of Yeomen. Seeing them, close up, I was more than ever impressed by their enormous size and strength, more than ever astonished by the imperturbable contentment on their faces. I was pensive as I tried to calculate the quantities of good food taken in, clean air breathed and never questioned doctrine assimilated to labour them to such a fine equine finish. Their gay talk did not finish as I entered the room. Abel was serving out drink, as expressionless as his counter, and gave me no immediate sign of recognition. The officers must have put me down as a serving man of the tavern and did not spare me a second glance.

When Abel caught my eye and beckoned me I ducked beneath the woodwork of the counter and went to his side. We were facing into the tiny room where he kept the barrels and the pots.

'Don't say anything yet,' he said softly, and then in a louder voice, 'the pots in the corner are dirty; get a clean dish of water and swill them out. You'll find a wiping-cloth hanging on that line there.'

I sat down on a stool in the dark further corner and enjoyed the simple swishing of the vessels through the tepid water. As I wiped them I took pleasure in breathing upon them and making them shine with the hard cloth. The task was so clean, obvious and easy, that an expression of little-witted delight must have come across my face because when I came out of my mood of far, unheeding detachment, I found four young officers, their faces glowing and full, leaning over the counter and bawling their laughter at me.

'A clown,' roared one of them, 'a sweet bumpkin to divert us at the revels. Did you ever see such blankness? God,

241

God, couldn't we shake the dolt until he gave us the recipe for such idiot joy as we just saw on his face?'

'One of the three wise men who came out of the East Midlands to give these flea-bitten helots news of their new Messiah,' said another.

'Drag him out here for some sport,' shouted a third who was swaying visibly and was apparently the drunkest and fiercest of the group.

'You're right, Herbert,' said one of his companions.

His request that I be dragged forth and made to perform as a kind of circus item was taken up on varying planes of eagerness by his friends. I remained seated, giving some thought to their words. I was tired. During the past days I had thought much and my body had moved rapidly from one place to another in steady rhythm with my brain. I had been fidgety, even afraid, and one fear had followed so closely upon another my conscience had been too busied by the successive stages of this dark entertainment to have savoured fully the obscene mildew of this mood of uncertainty and trembling. My few hours with Katherine in the Brier cottage, grave, assured and, in so subtly comforting a way, intelligently hopeless, had smoothed my scags a little and restored some part of my torn calm. Sitting there in that cool retreat, making an elemental rapture of warm water tides in the smooth caves of pot and pewter ware, had ironed out the last wrinkle in my trampled self. The last discord of alien experience had died. I was myself, the dignified unsullied solitary. For a moment I could not associate that covey of oafs, beef-fed, replete and confident, with the artfully contrived mechanism of dirt, danger, cruelty and oppression that lashed them and John Simon Adams into a black living column of cursed and cursing effort. When I heard their voices and understood what they were saying and asking, I was conscious only of snouts being poked into all the silent, fair places of feeling and knowing that had contributed to my being. For the first time since I had come to Moonlea I felt the utter unquestioned, beautifully assimilated hate that must have hardened the veins of John Simon and the Bannions to the unbending majesty of dead bone. I smashed a pot against a barrel top, leaving the handle with a spiked fragment of pot in my hand. I had the wish to wound someone.

'Ach, he's a simple lad,' I heard Abel say. 'Don't make a sport of him, gentlemen. Left alone he is quite without harm. We've all got rights of a sort.'

'What do you say?' asked the man they called Herbert.

'I said we've all got rights of a sort.' Abel and the officer stared at each other. Abel was calm, cool as one of those mossy rocks outside, his face without anger, his hands gripped on the counter. A voice from the fireplace shouted over:

'The Colonel will not be obliged to you for baiting the local imbeciles, Herbert. I suggest you leave them alone.'

Herbert laughed and turned away. Abel came hurriedly to me, wrenched the jagged weapon from my hand and forced me to sit down again on the stool.

'Careful,' he said. 'That's daftness. Close your ears if you're too touchy. You'll hear worse things than that.'

As dusk thickened, the troops and their officers settled down to the business of eating and drinking. Four women, among them that mistress of mixed frolics, Floss Bennett, had come in from Moonlea to prepare the feast. Tables had been arranged outside for the rankers and although some of them complained of the frosty nip in the air they were told to leave it or lump it. The hot meat lumps and the beer soon put an end to their muttering. Inside the tavern the air of banqueting had reached a high level of delight. I had seen little of men wolfing in substantial bodies and at that tempo. Life ran back a whole series of curtains as I watched the gut-filling proceed. My eyes went from eater to eater, my mind full of an awed and even terrified attention. I would have been content to stand stock still and take in all the dripping details or saunter around and congratulate the swifter wolves on the way their teeth appeared for a flashing second around a piece of meat before it vanished behind a bloated triumphant grin. Some of the officers, notably Herbert, took exception to my fixed inquisitorial eyes.

'Is it some damned idling ghost we have among us here?' asked Herbert in his bull-voice, and there would have been trouble for me if Abel had not fitted me into the ranks of his serving staff. He furnished me with a snow-white apron, the snowy, starched stiffness bemused my sensitive limbs in a trice. I was set to marching around the tables with a great wooden tray full of such things as gravy bowls. The gravy's curling steam made an intoxicating smell and my eyes and lips were quickly wet and heavy with hunger. The ecstasy did not help my movements to become any more nimble and the habit of some of the officers of jumping up and pushing their chairs back as the talk grew more excited was an impediment to me. But as my task wore on I got into the way of determining my path between the tables to within an inch, of singling out those of the diners who were likeliest to be fiddling with their chairs as I came along and soon I was spilling only a minimum of gravy and only down selected necks.

The eating had all been done when Abel nodded to me

from a corner and I went up to him.

'Take off that apron and come with me.'

'This is a warm, agreeable scene,' I said, and Abel and I swept our eyes around the room. Some of the officers were now eyeing Floss and her companions with precisely the same glare as earlier they had used on the pork. I would have liked to see the chase when it began. It was not likely that nature had ever thrown such a cooperative quarry as Floss and her friends in the way of skilled huntsmen. But I was interested to know whether rape among gentlemen had evolved any little coating of specialised technique or followed the same method of foaming cut and thrust that I had noted among the lads of the pasturage and the sheep-cotes.

'Come with me,' said Abel. 'They've sent word. John Simon is on his way. He wants you to be present at the meeting. He thinks you may be able to help.'

'I? He should know better than that.'

'John Simon is a sick and lonely man, harpist. In the coming days he will not grow less sick or less lonely. If you are his friend he will never need you more than he needs you now.'

'All right. Take me to where he wants me to go.'

Abel left the counter and the drawing of the ale in charge of his wife who was looking markedly invalid in a white frilly bed-bonnet and a reddish robe. Her face was sallow and bored, not unlike the woodwork of the barrels in point of colour and mobility but without their saving suggestion of a pleasant stupor. Life, in Abel's wife, had been rubbed to a toothy wakeful vigilance, and whenever she had filled a pot or glass she shot a glance of splintering hatred across the counter at the revellers. The senior officer, a major, looked

245

pensively at her from time to time as if weighing the chances of having the whole company poisoned and rendered black in the face. He drank his ale more slowly than the rest.

I followed Abel through a small door which opened out at the back of the barrel room. I found myself in an annexe of the kitchen. Abel, walking ahead of me, set two large hams swinging with his passage. They caught me, cold and moist, on the side of my head. The surprise and sadness it caused me distracted my mind briefly from the question of what earthly use John Simon would find to make of my presence at the meeting which was now to be held.

We came to the broad back yard of the inn. The roaring sound of the foot soldiers from the front yard was louder now, and we could see the glare of their torches over the inn's roof, but apart from one belching, urinating fellow propped against the wall ten or so yards from where we stood, we were alone and unseen. I listened to the cool flow of the mountain stream through the green rocks. We wished the soldier Godspeed. He must have accelerated in some wise, for he mumbled a few words and lurched away. I followed Abel to a small shed in the left-hand corner of the yard. It was half full of sacks and a mouldy smell of potatoes and swedes left too long. He pulled away five or six heaped sacks and revealed a door not three feet high. He pulled the door open and a creaking frowsy stairway came into view. He led the way and at the top of about eight steps we came to what appeared to be a broad attic in which one candle guttered. After the fragrance, the light, the animation, the shaking, sharpening hungers of the inn parlour I felt sad and solitary.

'This is a dark and undesirable place, Abel,' I said. 'This place doesn't suit my spirit at all. Lift your candle a bit for

246

me to see.'

'You can leave the light,' said a deep voice from a corner which was not reached by the failing flicker of the candle.

The voice was soft and friendly but startled me none the less.

'Is this the friend of John Simon Adams, the harpist?'

'This is he.'

'You think he can be trusted?'

'John Simon says so. In Moonlea, Mr Connor, that's enough. John Simon thinks it would be useful for the harpist to see you and know you.'

'If he betrays us he'll be one of many with a wish to do so,' said another voice, lighter in quality, fiercer in tone, than that of the man Connor.

'Are the windows masked?' asked Connor.

'I boarded them up days ago in readiness for such an occasion.'

'Quite certain.'

'Quite certain. I'll have had as much experience as you, Mr Connor, in pitting my wits against such gentry as we have below, I'll venture.'

'No offence, Abel.'

Abel set his candle down alongside the one that was fast dying on the floor. In the better light I examined the two men who were sitting on a heap of straw and sacking about six yards away from me. Connor was about fifty, dressed in a dark green topcoat which was tightly buttoned to his chin. He had a long nose, sunken eyes. As he smiled assuringly across at me I observed how tiny and pretty, like a set of miniatures, his teeth were. One felt that here was a man to whom the world was infinitely smaller than his mind, who measured out his feelings in small drops, who held his life

247

eternally and securely between his own two hands. There was a whimsical hint in the slope of his head as he looked at me, as if I were a curio, a human product whom he would find it hard to fit without discomfort into his prim neat book of purpose and method. The man at his side was different. Leaner by far than Connor he wore the dark loosely fitting clothes of the foundry hand, a discoloured kerchief around his neck. His eyes rested on me in a critical distrustful stare and my eyes got caught by the great knot of his hands which he held motionless on a level with his throat. A man, I felt, with as special a knowledge of utter solitude as I, but solitude from which sweetness and joy had been drained by as beautifully jointed a system of pipes as stupid calamity and frustration would ever devise.

'I must go down now,' said Abel.

'How long do you think John Simon will be? We mustn't linger here too long.'

'He won't be a second longer than he can help. You ought to know that.'

'It's not too cosy here with the den of lions immediately beneath.'

'The ale is going well. You'll find that the lions will shortly be asleep or very genial.'

'I hope so.'

Abel made his way down the stairs, holding his powerful broad body stiffly as if relieving his legs of some part of the weight that might have made the woodwork creak unduly.

'My own office at Tudbury would have been more pleasant than this,' said Connor.

'With a dozen police spies on each side of the door? I wouldn't trust even that chief clerk of yours.'

'I don't. There is not a tittle of written evidence in that

office of mine which would link my activity as a thoroughly respectable solicitor with my activity as a citizen of radical views.

'You've been a great aid to us all, Mr Connor.'

'This is the only part of me that lives. Conveyancing and tidying up the fraudulence of the propertied serves only to get one used to the coffin.'

'I often think about you.'

'To be in your thoughts, Jeremy, is something of an honour. What do you think of me?'

'I just wonder why you offer up your neck for a cause that looks so little like succeeding for a long time to come.'

'There are some, Jeremy, who have a sense of the future as acutely developed as a sense of the past or a proneness to greed in others. I had a wonderful ration of purely mental activity when I was young. My father was a snob in matters of study. Had he not been irreligious he would have clamped both him and myself into Holy Orders, preferably a monastery. But he was a great-nephew of David Hume and he wished me to become the philosophic Napoleon of the day. He gave me everything except the hard tinder of real experience against which my gift of logic could strike a spark and start to live.'

'And we are the tinder?'

'More than the tinder, Jeremy. You are the whole of life. You and your kind represent in the flesh what a perfect movement of ideas to a perfectly coherent end would represent to a dusty and isolated philosopher.'

'Are you Longridge, Jeremy Longridge?' I asked the younger man.

'Yes, I am. What of it?'

'I heard about you. I wanted to meet you. Once I knew

John Simon Adams very well.'

Jeremy looked as if he were going to make me some reply. He said nothing. I felt he had divined the thoughts in my head and found them good. His hands dropped. He even took his eyes off my face and his eyes and mine joined in watching the little sea of grey soft tallow around the base of the shorter candle. Then he looked sidewards at Connor again.

'Even so,' he said, 'it's a great mystery.'

'What is?' I asked, feeling out of it in the company of those two with their air of potent self-knowledge and assurance. 'What's the mystery?'

'That some men should raise their fists without being driven to it by bare need. Some of us seem to have no choice.' He looked over at me and smiled as if glad that I had elected to break the silence between us. I could see at that instant that he was very shy and I felt more akin to him.

'We all have a choice.' said Connor looking uneasily about him, as if eager to be continuing the conversation and keeping the silence at bay.

'I don't know,' said Jeremy Longridge. 'Men like John Simon Adams and myself, we are not much more than leaves in the wind, bits of painful feeling that gripe the guts of the masses. From the cottages, the hovels, the drink-shops and sweat-mills, anger rises and we are moved. No choice, Mr Connor, save perhaps the last-minute privilege of adjusting the key of the scream we utter. Like Wilfie Bannion. He picked a high note.'

'We all have a choice. You and John Simon Adams could as well have chosen a replete and sodden silence. You could have made a bed of weaker bodies and settled on them. You are wiser than the rest. You could have done quite well if

250

your minds had opened out on the piggery. But some of us are cursed with the urge to be making assertions that are either too big or too deep to fit into the box of current relations. So we have to broaden the box or whittle down our assertions.'

'Have you a choice, harpist?' Jeremy asked me.

'I don't know. I've never seen life as you boys seem to see it, a distinct, separate thing like a detachable shadow, to be examined and kicked or kissed. It's just flown around me, not hurting too much, and I've never given a conscious damn. No, I've never thought about this business of choosing. I wish I were far away from here. I wish John Simon Adams were far away from here. I wish he were still full of the joyful singing that was in him once and which has now died. But I'm here, and so is he. And his joy may still be in him, but it is singing in a key that my ears are deaf to hear. I feel the hate and fret that fills the ground between you and the mighty. The mighty have me by the leg too, and my leg kicks to be free, but hour after hour I stay here, like the rabbit stays by the weasel. That puzzles me.'

'The whole instrument of your passion is being retuned. We all have a set of special pities which we work off in different ways. Harping is the simple way of doing it. But to look for and find the strings of significance that today hang loosely between men and which must be drawn tighter before any real sweetness of melody will be heard in living, that's the job, harpist. Do that and you will see the very face of the joy whose mere anus you have been fiddling with to date.'

'Is that what I've been doing?'

'Something like that.'

'I thought I kept rather stooped.'

'It's only when you become really and horribly aware of men and women that the authentic torment and rapture of art swing you to the hilltop.'

'Sounds like a hell of a fate to me,' I thought of Katherine and John Simon and my mind filled too of a sudden with the vision of the girl to whom this Jeremy had been married, who had made his hot, savagely maimed life calm, cool and good. 'Anything that links man to man, man to woman, is bad and bitter, the way I taste it. I'd like to go away from here, safe, daft, forgetful, my ears full of music and arms full of an animal contentment. I'd like to be running like a stag to my glen in the north. With a growing world putting on such black muscles as Moonlea, running is a very sensible thing.'

'We'd all like to run, harpist. But some brand of love speaks through us and we are doomed to listen.'

The floor beneath shivered as the singing of the two sets of soldiers rose to a peak. There was a hint of red-lined frenzy, especially in the singing of the foot soldiers who were obviously trying to drown out the sound of the officers who, under the strain of the challenge, were laying aside the gentility of their earlier effort. The officers were singing a patriotic song which was stiffer in the joints than that being bawled by the rank and file who were rubbing the dirt out of the singing-tale of some long, fornicating joust that seemed, from what little I could hear, to involve the swift defloration of a whole village by some past member of their regiment. I listened intently to the few words that were clearly audible and to the clash of the song-waves that came hurtling from the two sets of strong, inflamed throats. There was a hint of complete anaesthetic daftness in the mounting pile of sound which made me, as I glanced at the darkened, over-pensive faces of my two companions, intensely covetous. I would not have wished to be with the men downstairs; I would have taken an armful of death any time as a neater and more comely billet, but I would have liked their immunity at that moment from the pained and paining wishes which seemed to be the fabric on to which we were to be painted. I was haunted more and more by the feeling that I was being contributed, slipped like a tiny coin through the tricky fingers of creative events to an offertory whose sum total I would not have the satisfaction of knowing, even if I should have the wish.

There was a movement from downstairs. There was a quick whispering of voices from the outhouse and a few seconds later John Simon appeared at the head of the stairs. He was out of breath and held on to the flimsy woodwork for support. He grasped me by the arm and smiled at Connor and Jeremy who rose to greet him, eagerly and with questions in a cluster around their mouths.

'Just at the back of Penbury's place,' said John Simon, 'some trooper came out from the trees. I don't think they were after me, I don't think they saw me but I ran for it all the same.' He put his hand to his head. 'It made that spot ache, the spot where Plimmon hit me.'

'We heard about that,' said Connor quietly.

'Tell us about it, John Simon.'

'Some other time, later, a lot later. We haven't much time tonight and there's a lot to be done.'

'You see the thing the way I saw it now, John Simon?' asked Jeremy.

'Most of my mind always did. There was something that put me in the dark. I'm sorry, I'm sorrier than my tongue will ever tell. There's no need to talk about it now.'

253

'No need at all. Let's talk of what's to come. Will the men who followed you from the mountain top into Moonlea rise again?'

'Armed, yes. They might never forgive me for putting their heads between the jaws of those gentlemen butchers but they'll never need to say that I didn't give them the chance to answer back. They've had no drill and they have no arms. You know that.'

'The guns and pikes I offered you three months ago are still in their store places,' said Connor. 'They can be brought and distributed whenever you say the word.'

'I say it. Plimmon and Radcliffe are nicely purulent and proud on their midden. Let them be lanced. I say the word. We'll be waiting. And when we have the arms, what?'

'Jeremy's men in the Western valleys and Evans's men to the south will take the lead.'

'You don't think much of us at Moonlea, even armed and cured of delusions?'

'It's not that. The biggest concentration of troops is here at Moonlea. In time as other ironmasters have to add bayonets to their old goads of fear and want to tease their workers into obedient silence, they will be spread more evenly over the county. But at the moment they are here and they seem to be easy in their minds about the other areas. The large majority of the men who followed you the first time may be in a fighting mood for any new assault you make on the masters, but they took a deep wound and a good many of them have cleared off out of Moonlea. I know more about that side of it than you. Our enemies have made good use of their initial surprise. The minds of many are still reeling and your Mr Radcliffe and Mr Bowen have been busy among the wavering, spreading the tale that at the moment of danger you bolted to a place of safety and left them to lick the blood. In some quarters you are even being denounced as a King's agent, a provocator.'

'They know me better than that, Connor. They'd never believe such a lie.'

'It suits a lot of people to believe it. It absolves them from the responsibility of doing anything more than to look resigned and wait for Penbury's terms. If you can manage to swallow poverty, lies are not so bad in the gullet. And I told you that most of your best lads have already fled and have joined Jeremy down in the southern valleys. They'd like you to be with them, John Simon. Join them and supplies will start reaching you in three or four days time.'

'Do you think we'll succeed?'

'We'll make a noise and an echo. Success changes flavour as soon as it passes the portals of each man's mind. No one can tell exactly where we are going. We might just be trying to keep the promise of movement alive until such time as the road becomes clear. The soil of effort grows tired and we may be part of the manuring period. Oppression's a fine, deep-rooted tree, John Simon. We'll make a notch on it. It's not likely we'll make it fall. Goodbye.'

They waved their hands in greeting to us and left, Connor leading the way down the stairs. Jeremy, as his head was vanishing, gave us a final wink and grin. The expression sat oddly on his lean severe face and it was with a real relief that I smiled back at him, as if glad of the hint that our next phase of assertive activity might be a bit less portentous and foredoomed than Connor's words led us to assume. We heard the departing pair knock out a signal on the woodwork and then heard Abel's low voice as he took away and then replaced the sacks and other material with which

255

he had concealed the entrance of the stairway.

I looked around the loft and made a face.

'Come on, John Simon. What are we waiting here for? This place is as cheerful as a draughty tomb. Where do we go now? To the Cornish cottage? We can't stay about here. We are practically standing on a solid bed of soldiers. And several times today I saw two shrewd, keen men dressed all in black eyeing me up and down. I heard someone say that they are agents sent all the way from some such place as London to track people down and prepare them for hanging. Those two looked vindictive, as if they had found against humanity on all counts. One way and the other this place puts people off being born. What are you doing now?'

John Simon had lain down on the pile of sacks and straw on which Jeremy and Connor had been sitting when I first came into the loft. He seemed enormously tired. His eyes were closed, his hands pressed upon his forehead.

'What's up, boy?' I asked. 'Don't tell me you want to spend the night here. We'd better get started before that party downstairs stop celebrating the death of the human mind and start nosing around the premises with a view to badgering any thoughts that might still be ghosting about.'

'Just a minute.'

'You ill?'

'That smack made sad music in my skull. It played a doleful tune just then. And the journey down the hillside expecting a trooper to come out from every bush didn't help.'

'All right, then. Rest. I'll listen to the singing. The minds of those boys downstairs certainly root like nimble swine among the offal heaps. Just listen to the words of what they're singing. Each verse a jubilee song for man's first sin.

256

How can a brain stare permanently in the direction of that topic? What caught their eye about it that we omitted to see? It must make life simple and very easy to pour out, brooding on so simple-witted a thing.'

John Simon nodded, as if he wished to hear no more talk from me. I could smell the grey musty despair of his reflections.

'I came down here tonight expecting a stern accounting from Jeremy Longridge,' he said. 'But he didn't say a word. We're not like him yet, Alan, but we may be. He has burned himself hard making the light he lives by. There are no frills upon his fist. He has a clear knowledge of vileness and all it can accomplish and a patient conviction that it will never accomplish what it most desires, our extinction. How was Katherine when you saw her?'

'Quiet and a bit afraid.'

'Did she say anything?'

'Not much. There was a woman there I didn't know. She was a nice quiet sort of person who was fond of Wilfie Bannion. She tried to make out that I stand in some sort of danger from Plimmon.'

'What have you done to him? Played off key?'

'No. I've had three or four chats with the woman he's to marry, Penbury's daughter. And he doesn't like being cuckolded, even in theory, by a harpist. So Lemuel the baker's going to swear he saw you and me butchering that oaf, what was his name?'

'Bledgely.'

'Have you ever heard such stuff?'

'Quite often. What they hang you for doesn't much matter. And perjurers are cheap to come by with rates of pay so low in other trades. Lemuel will perjure with passion and skill.

257

If truth had been that man's cruel stepmother he couldn't be meaner towards it. He really loves the masters. He must have had all the juices of independence steamed out of him by the heat of the ovens he bakes his bread in. If anybody can talk me on to a gibbet, it's Lemuel.'

'What about me, don't I qualify?'

'No. They've no real quarrel with you. Plimmon is out to frighten you, that's all. If you wanted to get out of Moonlea tonight I don't think they'd try to stop you.'

'Ready?'

'Yes, I'm better now. My head's clearer. I felt stupid as an ox when Jeremy and Connor were here. Connor's a good man. He'll see us supplied with everything we need. He's in touch with the movement in all the big cities, London, Manchester, Birmingham. When we stir here he'll see that our friends do their part there.'

'Fight, you mean?'

'No. Just remind the King and his Government that their soldiers could be passing on the time more usefully than they are doing here, that we are sick of these Yeomen gentry who are mentally the twins of the horses they ride, that the skies won't fall if they let us have our own unions and give us a say about the way in which we want to live.'

'Aren't they hard to persuade, these Kings and Governments?'

'They have been. But as we change, they will. To them, at present, we are of no more moment than the life in soil which makes their wheat. Come on.'

We blew out the almost dead light on the floor. We started down the stairs, listening intently for any sound that might tell us of danger. The singing in the main room of the tavern had died away completely, but in the front yard outside and along the road there were snatches of song from the foot soldiers. They were still trying to stretch out the night and the time of revel. A woman's scream followed by the same woman's laughter made me jump and the old woodwork to creak. John Simon gave three quiet raps on the board above the entrance at the stair's bottom.

'I hope Abel will hurry,' he said. 'We have a long walk back to the Cornish cottage tonight. Then tomorrow for the southern valleys.' He turned and touched my arm, 'Are you coming with me?'

'Yes. Since we have both equally offended Plimmon, I think I will. I'd like to see that interesting gentleman getting his hide tanned. I'd like to make him a wedding gift of a harp with his own dried intestines fitted in to do service among the smaller strings.'

'Keep the issue impersonal, Alan. It pays.'

We heard a voice, a muffled angry voice from behind the door saying 'Open.' It was not Abel's voice and we moved away from the door two or three steps, puzzled. Then Abel's voice, unmistakable, loud, as if in torment, bawled out:

'John Simon, harpist, you're trapped. You're...'

There was the sound of a blow and Abel's voice fell silent. We climbed back up into the loft. Gun butts began beating at the small frail door. There was an efficient swing to the violence of the attackers and they would not have been more than a minute in smashing their way through. The banging ceased suddenly as if at a word of command.

John Simon and I stiffened, then leaned our bodies forward, eager to hear what was meant by this silence.

'Adams and Leigh!' a voice shouted. The voice was loud, but neither rough nor brutal. I recognised it at once. It was that of the senior officer, the major, who had been sitting at the head of the table. 'Adams and Leigh, we know you are up there. Come down and surrender in the King's name. If you have weapons throw them down before you walk down the stairs. If you do not come out, we'll simply burn the place. That will save me the trouble of sending any of my men up to fetch you. I'll give you one minute, so be sensible and come along with us.'

I was going to ask where it was they proposed taking us, but John Simon hushed me to silence. We could hear other voices breaking in beyond the door, angry impatient voices pitched in a clear tone of death or glory. They seemed to be appealing for a chance to come charging up the stairs and drag us forth at their swords' ends. The major's voice rose above the babble and there was silence again.

'Where's that light?' asked John Simon. 'Let's see what we are doing.'

We got down on our knees and began searching with intense vigour over the rough splintering floor and half a minute had gone by before we realised that we had no means to light the candle even if we should find it.

'There was a window here,' said John Simon. 'If we could find that we could make a run for it, anyway.'

We went our way around the low ceiling. We found the window recess that had been boarded up by Abel. He had done his work well. We prised and tugged until our fingers bled but it availed us nothing. I was crying with fury but John Simon stayed calm as a hill, showing nothing of his rage or impatience. We heard the major's voice again. We went to the head of the stairs to listen.

'We are setting a light to the sacks around the door,' he said. 'In a few seconds you'll be able to smell the smoke that will have choked you before the flames reach you. You'll be doing an ill turn to your good friend Abel who is at the moment stretched senseless at my feet, to let his tavern be reduced to ashes on your account. If you come down promptly I promise you no further harm will come to him or his living.'

Wisps of smoke curled up towards us.

'I'm against being baked,' I said. 'It's no new thing. Always was a poor one with heat. Let's go down and talk with these efficient bastards.'

'As you say,' said John Simon. 'We are coming out,' he shouted.

There was a commotion outside as if a body of men had been sent swiftly forward to extinguish the flames. Another volley of blows fell on the door which fell inward.

We walked into the small shed, full of smoke and the stench of burned sacking. Two soldiers with bayonets fixed, prodded us towards the yard. They grunted as they did so as if they were as embarrassed as we at being in such a tiny place with complete strangers.

The air was sweet in the yard. The lights of the tavern's main room were still blazing bright and storm lanterns had been set at regular intervals around the yard so that there would be no corner that could not be supervised in detail by the major who stood in the centre. Soldiers were ringed around and the first thing I noticed was the thin glint of light from the bayonet blades. But my eyes soon left them and rested on the brilliant fringes of water that welled over the rocks in the steep bank behind the inn.

I heard the major speak to us and my attention came back to the men who were closing in on us. At the major's side were the two men in black, the policemen and Lemuel.

'So you see I was right,' said Lemuel excitedly. 'Wasn't I right, major?'

261

'You've done well, Stevens. I'll see that Mr Radcliffe is informed. Bring manacles for these two men.'

The taller of the two police agents produced the manacles, one pair from each of the two pockets inside his greatcoat. The touch of them on my skin made me feel cold and shrunken.

'Once I set eyes on the harpist in the main street of Moonlea yesterday afternoon,' went on Lemuel, 'I knew that Adams would be coming down presently. So I stayed in my bedroom window, with my father-in-law's telescope, which was once at sea with Nelson, fixed on Arthur's Crown. And sure enough after an hour's waiting just before nightfall who should I see skulking from bush to bush on the hilltop but Adams himself. I shouted so loud with glee I nearly frightened my wife Isabella to death. That's how I came to catch him.'

'Be quiet, you,' said the officer Herbert, pushing Lemuel out of the way. 'You'll get your reward whatever it is.'

'What are we charged with?' asked John Simon. 'As far as I know it is not yet a penal offence to be hit flat by a landlord's sword. Or did I in some way offend the sword?'

'Listen to the man,' said Lemuel. 'He stands there manacled and has the impudence to ask in what way he has offended.'

'Leaders of riots should know better than to speak protestingly when brought to justice,' said the major.

'There was no riot and you know it. Fortunately for you we didn't have the foresight to see that you'd want to kill us.'

'The specific charge is that on September 10th of this year, you, John Simon Adams, and you, Alan Hugh Leigh, did kill Josiah Bledgely in the Thrushes' Wood near Westlea.'

262

'I saw them,' said Lemuel, 'with my own eyes I saw them.'

'Don't forget your father-in-law's telescope, Lem.,' I said. 'You're a dim, peculiar human, boy, and I'm going to give you a lot of serious thought just to spite my brain which has never been too kind to me. If they manage to hang us and my ghost comes playing the harp in and out of season under your bloody bed, don't try to argue with me because I'll be adamant and tireless.'

A pair of horses came into the yard. Spencer and a fellow officer mounted them and two soldiers attached John Simon and myself by means of stout cord to the back of the saddles.

'We have been told to secure you beyond any possibility of escape,' said the major. 'You'll pardon the crudeness of this extra precaution.'

'We'll try not even to think about it,' said John Simon.

As these arrangements were being made we heard a moan from one of the corners. A soldier held up one of the lanterns and moved it. In its light we could see Abel, his face pale and sickened, rubbing his forehead with the fingers of his right hand. As soon as he saw us he came to our side.

'Keep your distance,' said the soldier with the lantern, grasping Abel's coat-tail.

'I'm sorry for everything that's happened,' said Abel. 'I did what I could but they got hold of my wife and threatened her with punishment if she did not tell them what she knew. She's ill and frightened and she knew you'd be coming here tonight.'

'That's all right, Abel. Don't sound so sorrowful, man. This isn't the end of the world. This isn't the end of anything.'

'What about the innkeeper?' asked Spencer. 'He's surely an accomplice and we know enough about his political views from that report that was brought in by the agents. A fine bit of Australian fodder if you ask me.'

'Leave him here. He'll be under our eye. That blow you gave him, Spencer, when he cried out will be chastisement enough for him for a while. He can't do any harm.'

'Whatever you say, sir.' He spurred his horse and our little convoy started on its way. John Simon and I were about two yards from the rump of the animals to which we were attached, two foot soldiers walking a few feet behind us. We could feel the ruthless strength of the horses as they jerked our manacled arms into abrupt, awkward angles.

'My God,' said John Simon. 'All the way to Tudbury gaol like this?'

'To the Penbury mansion,' said Spencer in a tone harder and more sullen than he had used in the yard.

'Why there? There's no judge or gaol there to my knowledge. Or is there?'

'You'll find out. The order is that you be taken there before transfer to Tudbury.'

'Plimmon wants to gloat,' said John Simon to me. 'And Mr Radcliffe, no doubt, will put on a memorable session of snarling. He loathes every hair on my head and not on strictly political grounds either. Not long after I came here he came roaming around the foundries and I told him something about ironmoulding that he didn't know. He fancies himself as an artist in that line and he didn't like it. Since then his hatred has matured under various kinds of sun.'

Spencer and his companion, at a word from the latter, spurred their horses and we found ourselves running at a rate faster than we could manage. My breath grew so short I could hardly get out my words of swearing protest. John Simon fared better than I, for he was stronger and even through the painful confusion of my breathlessness I could see the staring fury of his eyes as they were settled on Spencer's thick back.

'Easy on there, you red-coated ruffian,' he bawled.

Spencer sent his horse into a gallop. John Simon went hurtling over a mound and for ten yards he was dragged along in Spencer's rear, his body convulsed and rolling in his efforts to get free of the steel and rope that secured him. Spencer's companion spoke a few urgent, half-angry words that I could not hear and they halted. Spencer's face was crazy with malice as he turned to look at us. It softened somewhat as he saw John Simon's face, cut badly, bleeding. They walked us through the long main street of Moonlea, dark as a wolf's mouth save for the weak gleam of the occasional lanterns that had been hung from walls as a police measure years before by the order of Penbury. The night was massively silent and a part of the great wash of John Simon's disgust came swirling my way. My eyes travelled up and down the seemingly endless rows of small, ill-formed cottages.

'Ahoy there,' I shouted, loudly as I could. 'Moonlea! People of Moonlea! John Simon Adams is here. He needs you.'

One of the foot soldiers escorting us brought his gun butt on to the nape of my neck and I dropped forward on to the ground, quite conscious and lucidly sick. The other soldier stood guard in front of John Simon, his eyes, like those of the two mounted men, sweeping the street anxiously.

'For that,' said Spencer, 'I've a mind to give them another gallop.'

'You remember what the major said,' answered his companion. 'A gentlemanly calm, that's the recipe.'

'A great good that'll do us,' growled Spencer. 'A suspiciously considerate fellow, that damned Welford.'

We stopped again and listened. At points all along the street we could hear darkened windows opening and at some I could see the moving smudge of a face, expectant, terrified or pitying. But there was no more than that. A pale white stir of compassion in the further shadows, but no more than that.

We entered the great gates of Penbury's mansion. The lights in the house burned from all windows and it was a gallant sight, standing there on its beautiful bulge of hill, set to the last perfect inch in its frame of tall dark trees, consciously well planned. The sight of it, coming suddenly, cut my eyes as I tried to steady them in my jolting aching head, made me feel endlessly more forlorn, dirtied, abused, and I shouted a richly dripping oath at the soldier who had hit me. He answered back in a smooth black flood and between us we made the darkness chafe and wonder with our spite.

Spencer and his friend dismounted on the gravelled square in front of the house.

'In a way,' said Spencer in what for him must have been a thoughtful tone, 'in a way, it's a pity.'

'A pity? For these fellows, you mean?'

'Good God, no. A pity if the whole affair is going to fizzle out like this, hauling a few of these scoundrels before a magistrate for a round of quiet boring hangings. I think they could have arranged a more satisfying bit of hunting after putting us to the trouble of getting our uniforms on once more. Life's getting hellish dull, Banbury, hellish. You there!'

266

He shouted to one of the soldiers, 'Rap on that door. We don't want to be shivering out here all night.'

The soldier marched swiftly to the door, watched by his fellow. Spencer and Banbury stood close together talking and looking up at the sky. Banbury must have been some kind of star-gazer for he was pointing at various formations in the heavens and inviting Spencer to take an interest. Spencer did no more than grunt and shrug his heavy shoulders as if kept only by politeness of the ingrained sort from telling Banbury what he felt about such fleshless hobbies as these. John Simon walked with brief noiseless steps towards them. Before either of them could turn to stop him he had kicked Spencer's legs from beneath him and even as he was falling dealt his head a loud thud with his bare fists. Banbury dived at John Simon and the foot soldier did as much for me with the fierceness of men wishing to bring a long night to a definite climax. Then the doors of the house were thrown open and there in the brilliant light stood Plimmon and Radcliffe, magnificently dressed, erectly proud as young stallions and smiling out at us as blithely as if we had been their brides.

We were ushered into the large reception room, the room with the crimson hangings into which I had gazed that very first night when I had seen Penbury for the first time and heard him speak in his quaking voice of his dreams and fears. Penbury was not in the room; nor was Helen. Jarvis the clerk was there, looking as uncertain and full of timid reservations as ever but trying with an occasional forced smile to do justice to what was supposed to be the jollity of the occasion and match the wine-flushed pleasure that glared from the eyes and teeth of his masters. Also present were some sleek, dark-clothed functionaries and their assistants whose names and natures I did not know but who all looked so urbane and efficient one felt there was little to be said since it was clear that this band had been discussing the matter of their self-protection all evening in a vein of masterful shrewdness. They all took seats except Plimmon who stood in front of the high-banked spluttering fire, looking down at us from his great height. I studied the man with interest. He had the most beautiful flesh I had ever seen and a back whose shape had an inexpressible loveliness of strength and assurance. He had been well looked after, nourished with a purposive care for some significant passage of self-revelation. The world's grisly sickness had secreted a real pearl in this man. His voice when he spoke was obviously made for the finest eloquence. I could well believe that his ambitions had eagle's wings. I almost had an impulse to ask him whether, after the good work he had already done in growing and draping chains on the socially obscure, he would not like to take harp lessons so that there would be no possible chink in his ivory facade through which some subsequent flaw might crawl. But I made no such offer. The sun of my selfishness had not yet altogether set. Despite the torture of pain and humiliation I had felt in the course of that trip tied to a saddle, the forefront of my mind was still lit with the certainty that some joke, a nightmarishly tasteless one to be true, was being played out at my expense, and that if I behaved with a proper show of confident innocence these power-fanciers would see that they would be doing no more than dulling the edge of their excellently horrible laws in directing them with all this thoroughness at a lonely minstrel who would never produce anything more profitable to them than an elegy of shame and bitter regret in the hearts of their existing, self-wasted helots. But

I had not been in the room more than a minute before I realised that Plimmon was looking at me with an even more vindictive contempt than he did at John Simon.

'Why bring us here?' asked John Simon. 'This is no gaol, no court. What game is this? Does the law now begin and end here?'

'Clearly not,' said Plimmon, his voice almost a coo, his whole being in deep harmony with circumstance. 'We wished to see you, to make certain that no mistake had been made.'

'Satisfied?'

'Fully. A pity that we hadn't chastened you to a point where you would not have been able to commit that final folly upon the person of Captain Spencer. But you were perhaps due for a final fling. Your projected condominium of beggars will serve in odd ways to manure my fields more richly. Lazy scoundrels and thieves will doze at their work no longer; nor will they pilfer on my estates with your doctrines of equality on their lips to give their conscience ease.'

Plimmon swung his glance around the room at all his listeners except John Simon and myself. They smiled broadly back at him as if on the edge of applauding.

'Is the trial to be here?' asked John Simon. 'Where's the judge, who's the hangman? Radcliffe?'

'I'd be delighted to oblige,' said Radcliffe while Jarvis the clerk was wagging his head furiously at this light taking of the law's name in vain.

'That would be right and proper,' said John Simon. 'The men who give us our law are all in this room. No judge will tell us anything different from what we'd hear from you.'

'You'll be fairly dealt with, have no fear; as fairly dealt

with as the plague carriers of envy and unrest can be dealt with.' The word 'dealt' stuck in my ears. It broke up into cyclic variants, death and belt, belt and death. 'You'll be taken to Tudbury and lodged there until your trial.'

'The charges?'

'Murder.'

'Bledgely?'

'The same.'

'Let me say this quietly. Neither I nor the harpist laid a finger on that bear. Seeing that you set him off the leash with a view to strangling me it would have been a pleasure for us to do so, but we didn't.'

'I suppose he fell asleep and rolled into that hole by error, smashing his own head in *en route* to make his sleep the sounder.'

The men sitting around laughed. I looked at them and saw how intensely their clean pink faces shone as if their whole conviction of righteousness had come glowing to the surface to make us timid.

'It won't do Wilfie Bannion any harm to say it now,' said John Simon. 'He killed Bledgely. Bledgely killed Sam, Wilfie's brother. Even you gentlemen must have heard the one about an eye for an eye. We are very simple down in the foundry yards. We still think it a pretty good axiom'

'Bannion is dead.'

'The harpist saw him. Didn't you, Alan?'

'I did. He flattened the pate of Bledgely. He was defending himself. Bledgely had left Moonlea to kill John Simon. I saw it all. It was the night of the singing.'

'Bannion is dead,' said Plimmon again, 'and the word of men who have stirred up trouble and brought tragic catastrophe to a happy, prosperous town is not likely to count for much.'

'There are witnesses,' said Mr Jarvis.

'Tell us how much you'll pay them. The least you can give us is the satisfaction of knowing to the penny how much our necks are worth to you. Now take us out of here. I've had enough for one night and I've no fancy to be entertaining you vultures till the dawn.'

'You'll entertain us a lot more before we're done, Adams.'

'This isn't the last of it, Plimmon. The men you'll be facing from now on will not be so daftly trusting as I. You horsemen must be taught humility. I'll be sorry if it can be taught only by serving up the same type of butchery that you love to dispense. We think it an awful waste of good humanity but you are laying down the rules. Hanging us won't make you a scrap safer.'

'But it will be a contribution to that end. No doubt of that. You are the head of the abscess. We squeeze you and the rest of the impurity will come swiftly to the surface, to be dealt with in our own time.'

'Your thoughts have the same quality as the drapings here. Thick, crimson, lightproof. Go ahead. To me it doesn't matter all that much. But the harpist's done you no harm. Turn him free.'

'He's been by your side from the beginning. It was he who in a mood of feckless vainglory led Lemuel Stevens to the very spot where you had buried poor Bledgely's body. Looking at him it's hard to believe he can ever have been a real danger. But we've been told of his cunning. It wouldn't surprise me if he turned out to be a more sinister figure in the revolt than even Adams himself, one of the master planners from outside of whom our police tells us.'

'What in hell's name are you talking about?' I asked, trying to reduce my face to an even fuller blankness. 'I,

271

sinister? Why don't you call Penbury? He'll tell you I'm just a harpist, a good one, never off the right key and so daft in my ways of doing and thinking you high humans ought to wear me on your watch-chains as a mascot. Call Penbury and get me out of these manacles, for God's sake.'

'Mr Penbury is ill. Ill and near to dying. He can't be disturbed. Odd that all the people to whom you make appeal should all be so uniformly inaccessible, dead or dying. I hope it will remain like that to the end. You'll find all our witnesses splendidly alive.' He pulled a silken bell-cord. The butler Jabez appeared, his eyes huge with interest as he stared at me. 'Are the horses ready?'

'Yes, my lord. Quite ready. The men are awaiting your orders.'

'Captain Spencer recovered?'

'Fully recovered, my lord.'

'Good.'

We were marched out into the hallway. Glancing to the left I caught a glimpse of Helen Penbury's face through a door half-opened. She had been watching, and she vanished from view as we appeared. Plimmon saw too, and he shouted an angry order to the guards. John Simon and I were lifted up on to the backs of horses, our legs as well as arms tied. Six troopers rode with us.

We rode through the night. The darkness was trembling with day when we crossed the ridge below which lay the county town of Tudbury.

16

The magistrates' hearing was held early the next day in a
large hostelry in Tudbury called The Crimson Feather. John
Simon stood weary, numb and indifferent, while the
ceremony went swiftly on its way to completion. The place
was full of busy, tipsy men and even tipsier arguments to
which we paid no heed. Lemuel Stevens perjured in magnificent harmony with their every wish. It was amidst a real
exultation on the part of about forty of these portly, loud,
coherent fellows that we were committed for trial at the next
Tudbury assizes.

It was an October morning when we were taken out of
Tudbury castle where we had been lodged, for trial. It was
a day of brilliant sun and through the high broad grating
which gave a glimpse of the courtyard from both our cells we
could see a flimsy mist breaking up beneath the light and
warmth. The gaol was the most ancient building in all
Tudbury, part of the vast, well-patched castle that had been
the heaviest knuckle in the looting baronial fist through
many centuries of border war. It dominated Tudbury. We
could not see it from our cells, but we had long accurate
descriptions of the town, the thickness of the walls, the
habits of the old dead looters whose shield they had been
against the tiny marauding teeth of the hill foragers, from
our chief gaoler, Bartholomew Clark. Bartholomew was not
officially a gaoler but caretaker of the wing of the castle in

which we were lodged. The castle had recently been condemned as a gaol and we should have been taken to the new prison which had been built at Chungford and which was serving as a temporary home for Tudbury's felons until such time as Tudbury completed the building of a brand new bastille of its own. But Plimmon, as High Sheriff of the county, had insisted that we be held at the castle, a lodgement that he considered more fitting for men who were traitors to the King's Peace. Bartholomew had recounted all this to us with great relish as giving him a greater dignity than usual and besides he had been going half-mad with loneliness in his abandoned section of the castle until our arrival.

Bartholomew was a notable man and he had leavened a large part of my misery's lump since I had been brought into the gaol. He was a bulb-nosed, cheerful, waddling man, about fifty, wrapped in a huge, sack-like coat which he never seemed to put off and fond of drunkenness in any shape or form. Anything that would change the key of consciousness suited his card. Ale, wine, gin poured into the gaol in a steady stream and he made it plain to John Simon and myself that as a liberal-minded turnkey he would always be willing to turn part of these supplies over to us if we could arrange with him for payment from somewhere outside. John Simon told him that he was not interested and was so intent on listening to the existing melodies in his mind that Bartholomew looked upon him as an unpleasant freak. I was more sociable. I took all that Bartholomew had to offer and we often sat in my cell and split a bottle while I told him endless tales of my wanderings among the hills plucking my harp and my lusts. After a few drinks he would often tell me that in his early days he had been quite a radical and he

274

knew a lot of revolutionary hymns which, he said, he had often sung in bitter burning protest beneath the walls of Tudbury castle which he had always regarded as emblematic of oppression at its most crass. But his strings had grown slack, tuneless and filthy. Tudbury, he told me, was a town of serfs and hangers-on. The livelier spirits had been deported ten years ago after a riot in the surrounding countryside against rack-renting on the part of the town's chief landlord. It had been touch and go for Bartholomew for a while and he would have gone down to the Pacific with the rest if three or four souses of the town had not come forward and said that Bartholomew had spent the night of the trouble with them, dead drunk. The other rebels who had remained uncaught drifted off into the new mining and foundry areas and had left Tudbury with such penitent dregs as Bartholomew, dreaming God knows what darkling dreams of freedom when a few pints set the mills of wrath turning once more and falling glumly in line with the Church and King mobs who could always be relied upon to tear the hide off anyone who looked unusually pensive or struck an alien note in behaviour. I told Bartholomew he should be ashamed of himself for having lent his life to such a piece of fraud. When I said that he would look at me with a terrible sadness in his eyes as if I had dug my finger into some aching patch of corruption within him. Then he would drink a little more, peer outside the cell door to make sure that there were no spies in the corridor; then he would bring his head close to mine and whisper those rusty antiquated songs of revolt that lay strewn along the gutter of his fine, abandoned self, and after a night or two I got to know them as well as he and we made an impressive sight crooning this rhyming litany of defiance and revenge against the walls in which I was imprisoned, against the men who paid Bartholomew to keep guard over us, while the tears ran fast down his face into his nearly black cravat of greasy immemorial linen while I smiled up at the oblong of sky I could see through the grating, pleased by the rich gravy of absurdity this scene seemed to pour over the black dollop of what appeared to be our forthcoming doom.

There was a small opening, formidably barred, high up in the wall, between John Simon's cell and mine. I had heard but few words from him since our arrival. A comment on the smell of the straw, a curse when his distraught body banged into the wall when the cell was dark and his body mad to be free. We had been allowed no visitors and he was half crazy with the desire to know how things were with Jeremy and Connor in the valleys and countryside to south and west of us. Sometimes in desperation he asked Bartholomew but the latter only winked and belched and tried to look solemn, telling John Simon that such talk was traitor's talk that only served to bring a man nearer the worms and that John Simon would be better employed trying to fix his mind on something narcotically unpolitical like God or drink. Each evening following such a request from John Simon, Bartholomew would drink and sing and weep with more passion than ever. In the main he stood in deep awe of John Simon and respected his sullen silences.

'He's a good lad,' he would croak into my ear, jerking his finger towards John Simon's cell, 'with a heart bigger than this,' patting the magnificent outswell of his stomach, 'but a fool, a great fool. You can't beat these, nobody can beat these.' He banged his fist on the immense stones of the wall behind us. 'And there are worse things than stones and the men who pile them one on the other for their own power's sake. It's those swine down there.' He pointed with stiff arm down in the direction of Tudbury. 'Poor folk all, but they'd as lief hang you both as look at you if Plimmon threw them a penny from his saddle bags and told them to get on with the job. There's too much autumn, harpist, too much autumn for anybody's liking. And the falling rotting ones among us are never trodden properly into the ground.' At that point he would make a long pause and stare as if in wondering worship at the wall that separated us from John Simon.

'Someone's always paying, harpist.'

'Paying what, Bartholomew?'

'We soft ones who see life as a night to be got through in the cosiest sort of fuddle, who drink the very slime our hearts are squeezed into, we think we are bringing off a very smart deal to be soft as butter and beyond the reach of pain when kicked, quit of all the agony that goes with decent hardness. But nothing's free, harpist. Somebody's paying all the time. Even with a free bitch to bed on the straw in the cellar of Slaney's gin shop down in Caroline Street and stupor at twopence a time it's still too hellishly expensive. That's only the down-payment, because for radiant boys like you who are setting your faces towards the dawn and keeping fresh the parts of life that we defile, breaking the silence in our acre of degradation, the paying's never done.'

'You go to hell, Bartholomew. Don't call me radiant. So far I've done as little glowing as you. You treacherous benighted ones can't rot fast enough for me. There's no dawn. There's the act of getting drunk again and finding some fresh fool to betray and I see no more in it than that. I came like a guile-less idiot out of my woods and hillsides. You made a trap for me. You've got me by the leg. I hate the way I'm being

277

pawed and I can't even scream. You are a part of Plimmon's detachable backside. John Simon's a fool. Would you lift a finger to help him?'

'My fingers are very numb, harpist. Carrying keys about this castle has been a chilly life for charitable thoughts. But things change in a man's inside. Forgetfulness and change are the only miracles. The glory may come to me. The very dirt of me may stir and become new life to amaze me and you. Having you two boys here with me has knocked a lot of rust from the hinges of many doors inside me. And there are thoughts walking in parts of me that have not been trodden by thoughts of pity or hope for a long time past. But don't bank on me, harpist. For God's sake, don't bank on me. I'm bedded down deep in my soft corrupted days. I've stared at these walls too long. They've thickened my fears and the fingers of all my goodness are numb.'

Occasionally we were disturbed by a superior official, some envoy of the castle warden who half-brained Bartholomew if the latter were caught being lax in the conduct of affairs. But usually we were either warned in advance of the official's coming by Bartholomew's assistant, Little Jacob, or because we were the only prisoners in the castle and there was no great sympathy felt for Plimmon's pretensions, the official left us in peace.

It was a fine sensation when the cell doors opened and John Simon and I were allowed to walk out into the corridor, up the ten stone steps and through the little room where Bartholomew slept, out into a vast hall which had once, the gaoler told us, been the banqueting room of the castle in days when the point and purpose of the place were more festive than they had since become. In the hall there were eight soldiers, fully armed, who fell in at our side and served

278

as escort. Under that high ceiling, in the flood of light that came from the fantastically tall windows, every footstep resounding along the stonework of the place, I had, for an instant, a dramatic and important feeling, and as I walked in front of John Simon, I straightened my back and held my head up high for all the world as if a gallery of spectators had been watching the performance. The great doors were dragged open. The inrushing air was clear as crystal and there was a moment's giddiness as we got our first lungful of it. Our cells were meagrely ventilated and had the personality of a drain. In the courtyard, a closed black van was waiting, as small and glum a thing as I had ever seen. Around it were twenty or more lancers, their horses uncannily still. I asked the soldier at my side what was the point of all this turnout. He gave me no reply, absorbed in looking stern. We were bundled into the van with two soldiers. There was a small window in the van's door and through this I was allowed to peer. The lancers formed two columns, one on each side of the van, and we began our progress slowly down the castle hill and towards the centre of Tudbury.

'To how many more novelties are we going to be treated?' asked John Simon. 'First they take us on a social call to the ironmasters before locking us up. Then they give us a gaol to ourselves and forget to supply air. Now we form part of a carnival through Tudbury. The assizes are held in the same building as the gaol. Why this outing?'

'It'll be a fine sight for the folk of Tudbury,' said the elder of the two soldiers, a thin-lipped, blue-eyed fellow who seemed eager to make his unpleasantness felt. He thrust his face forward as he spoke and pressed his heavy chin fiercely into the stiff collar of his scarlet tunic. He had an air of impressively articulate stupidity. He had thought himself into a true regard for the institutions he was being paid to defend. He was earning his keep every inch of the way. He would have treated us with joy to his whole stock of ball-cartridge if we had attempted a leap out of the conveyance. I smiled at him, in case he decided not even to wait for the leap. 'You've been keeping the decent people of this neighbourhood terrified with your chattering and muttering and meetings and conventions long enough. There'll be no more of keeping honest workmen from their toil. They'll be glad to see you getting your desserts.' His voice rose and he even banged the bench that ran alongside the side of the van to make his point more formidably.

'Oh, shut your rattle, Rolf,' said the other soldier.

'This boy has thought it all out,' said John Simon.

'He's got us taped,' I added. 'He'll probably turn out to be the judge.'

'Got a bonus from Plimmon when he handed in his brain as salmon bait as like as not,' said John Simon.

The soldier Rolf got up, his nostrils wide and gaping as his mouth.

'How would you like me to crack your head open?'

'I wouldn't at all. This van is no place to die in. And if you're showing off in this way to work yourself up to be a general, you're doing the wrong thing. Your masters have a special show worked out for us and they wouldn't thank you for spoiling it by delivering us at the court door mangled. What exactly have we done to curdle your gall, anyway? Are you an ironmaster?'

The second soldier pulled Rolf back on to his seat when he glared at us furiously, his mind clearly failing to provide him with the next page on the programme.

'He thinks you're godless,' said the second soldier pleasantly as if trying to explain away and apologise for the hard-bristling wrath of his friend.

'What of that? I didn't think you soldiers went in much for theology. Is he some kind of dervish?'

'Most of the time he doesn't give a damn about it. But he had a fever in India last year and he hasn't been the same since. When he was a kid he worked for a parson who was a sweet man, so he says, and who was about the only person who was ever good to him. So Rolf goes mad every so often against anybody who runs down the parsons like you boys do.'

'Not all parsons,' said John Simon. 'The sweet ones we're for, just like Rolf is.' He leaned over and touched Rolf lightly on the knee. 'Take it easy, boy. I'm sorry the sight of us makes you sick and wild. Those fevers are bad things and so are worlds where sweetness is so rare that one bit of kindness can go echoing around a life to its end like a long song. I've never come within a thousand miles of offending you. You are not so daft or cruel as we think you are. We are not so bad or troublesome as you think we are. We don't know each other nearly well enough to be wanting to bend each other's teeth in. People have poured some odd poisons into your brain, Rolf, but don't be fooled, boy, don't be fooled.'

John Simon's voice had become soft and persuasive and the anger had more than half vanished from the face of the man Rolf. He sat quite still, his face expressionless but tending towards a vague, embarrassed sadness. I felt that the second soldier, a more genially imaginative man, had a fair measure of control over the moods of Rolf.

The van was travelling now through cobbled streets and there were sounds of cheering, uneven, a little forced, all around us. I looked out. We were in one of the shopping streets of Tudbury. Clumps of people had formed around each doorway. I saw maidens waving at the lancers and the older folk frowned, muttered or shook their fists at the van. There were a few, and my eye even through the tiny grating singled them out swiftly, who stood silent and their faces expressed things that ranged from idiot indifference through disquietude to a compassionate terror. The sight of them had an upsetting effect on me and I was glad to sit down.

The van was climbing again. We were ascending the castle hill on a road other than that which had brought us down. We stopped on the narrow path that wound around the castle's foot. The second soldier looked out and said that a procession was making its way into the assize court. I joined him at the peephole. Straggling up the hill was a file of people, many of them brilliantly dressed as if for some day of merriment, judges, clergy, law officers, burgesses, and their servants and retainers.

'This,' I said, 'is a reception of the first class. My life has never before been whipped up into such a foam of colourful fuss as this. Those boys are dressed to kill. But why don't they give them a carriage like we've got, brighter in colour, of course, and with more windows. Some of those old ones in the crimson robes look bent double to me. This is a steep hill and those robes must be as heavy as the men underneath.'

'They've been to church,' said the second soldier, taking off his cap to scratch his thick black curls. He smiled again with his pleasantly bitter mouth. 'They do that at the beginning of each fresh assize to invoke a blessing on their justice. So when they come to pour it on you two you'll know there's nothing wanton or pagan about it. It's been blessed. There's the church there, bottom of the hill. It's very ancient too, like the castle.'

'You sound all right,' I told him. 'You seem full of light to me. What's your name?'

'Jarman.'

'You on our side?'

'God no. I'm on nobody's side. I'm a soldier. I just keep alive. That's my religion or most of it, anyway. I'm just sorry you haven't got more of a chance, and looking at you close, I can't see that you're very much different from me.'

'So you think they've got doom wrapped up for us in there?'

'Sure of it. Some of those judges are very winded and bitter and eager to be finished with the job when they've done climbing that hill.'

The van proceeded. It stopped outside the court. We dismounted. Jarman said 'Good luck' to us very quietly and the man Rolf stared at us with a fixed curiosity as a fresh escort hurried us through a small door some twenty yards to the left of the main entrance. We went down a flight of twelve steps and through a long whitewashed corridor. We entered a small room where we were kept for some minutes. A white-bearded man relieved us of our manacles. Then we were taken up another flight of stairs and into the court itself.

I had never felt so luminous or horrifying an isolation as I did when I stood in the black-painted wooden contraption they called the dock at John Simon's side. I felt at once the cold slap of hostility, of critical unkind awareness that came towards us from every corner of the room. At the people sitting at the back of the court I glanced hardly at all. Their part of the room was dark, lit by a few feeble tapers, and I

283

could not bother my eye or mind to find out what their individual faces and bodies looked like.

It took them just a few hours short of two judicial days for them to finish with us. With the help of a bored judge, Lemuel, an eloquent and ambitious prosecutor called Sir Horace and a strangely nervous young counsel called Collett whom Connor had sent to our aid, we heard in the poor light of the second afternoon a doleful rigmarole from the judge which told us that we would be hanged.

17

The three days after the trial were dark sultry days and we took our mood from them. We lay back on our straw palliases and said little. John Simon hummed a tune now and then, and once or twice I even heard him laugh quietly as if the slipping earth of calamity had uncovered some source of gaiety that had been closed to him before. It was halfway through the third day that I seemed to realise to the unimprovable full the precise nature of what had befallen me. The flow of events into which I had entered had not wholly found room for me, but something in the shifting of my thoughts, something in the evil staleness of my bed, admitted me into an acre of merciless clarity and my fingers sank into the straw as if for support and my lips kept saying softly, softly, so that John Simon in the next cell would not hear: 'A bloody thing, a bloody thing.'

But the fourth day saw a brilliantly blue sky again and it helped me to prod some of my fears back into a corner.

'It's Sunday,' said John Simon.

'I've lost count,' I found it easier to speak after the long silence than I thought it would be. 'Is it?'

'I've got a feeling for days. Anyway, I've noticed that the buzz of sound from the town goes quiet on a Sunday.'

'The day of rest,' I said, letting my mind and its curious wheels sink into the first rut they found. I did not want John Simon to talk solemnly about what had happened to us, the air of that court suffocating with human breath and perjury, about what was likely to happen to us. At that moment I could have wished that Bartholomew would shuffle in and do a little genial strangling so that I would not again know the shock of absurdity I had felt the day before when I had made the mistake of standing aside from my immediate situation and feeling myself ridiculous, tricked, strung in respect of all my hams.

'Alan Hugh,' said John Simon in a low voice.

'I'm here.'

'You listening?'

'Of course.'

'I want you to listen.'

'Why so earnest, boy?'

'I suppose you know there's a chance they may change their minds about you.'

'What makes you think so? You heard the judge. His words were very clear. Two lots of rope, that was the order.'

'That was part of the ritual. They wanted to make a show of being ruthless. But I have a strong feeling that in your case they might think twice.'

'Why talk about it? Let's look on the black side. It's smooth, cosy, and doesn't strain the eyes. I'm trying to be serene and I'm finding the road steep. You're not making things any easier by these doubts and prophecies. If the people in that court had had any sense or reason I wouldn't have been tried at all. They would have asked me to play a short funeral tune while they put their brains under the clod and then sent me about their business. They can't find Longridge or Connor so they have to be content with a sample from the lightweight division. That was me.'

'Don't be too downcast. There's nothing like being due to

be hung to make people think more seriously about you. That judge smelt the truth even if his long years of loyalty to Plimmon and his tribe prevented him from seeing and telling it. He'll set a wheel or two going. Penbury might put in a word or two unless he's dead by now.'

'Why do you talk like this? Once you said there was a fitness about my being here. That's a good epitaph. Why try to change it? I'm bearing up. I wouldn't want to be here alone. I wouldn't want to be here with anybody else. But with you, I don't mind.'

'I don't want you to feel like that, Alan. If the slightest chance comes your way, take it with both hands.'

'I'm trying my best to smother hope and you go pumping air into the damned thing. I had it within an inch of the last twitch and here it is again mewing like a cat and keeping me awake. For the first time in my life I can't even raise enough wind to tell people to go to hell. Once I could see men as a tribe of quaint and forgivable comedians, but I am beginning to uncover a seam of dull and horrible earnestness in their antics. They really like to be foul, don't they? It's an activity, they put art into it.'

The door of the cell was opened and Bartholomew brought in a young clergyman, a red-faced, sprucely dressed young man who looked as if he had pitched his sympathy in the highest key. He carried a large leather-bound Bible in his hand and he was smiling at me as he entered with an intensity of brotherliness that went so far beyond the normal as to jangle inharmoniously in the small cell.

'This,' said Bartholomew, 'is the Reverend Claude Mayhew of the Parish of St Mary's in Tudbury. He is also Chaplain Designate to the castle. He's here to give you comfort, harpist. He's got a fine line in comfort. Judging by

287

the low looks you've been wearing since the trial you'll need all he can give.'

'Thoughtful,' I said. 'That's all my trouble. Trying to measure the exact weight of my thirty years, trying to find out what my moments have meant in the sum. I am glad to see you, Reverend Mayhew. You are free to practise on me as hard as you like. I like the thrust of other people's wishes into my soil. We'll toss for the biggest compassion.'

'I am here to help you, Leigh.'

'Help yourself,' I said sniffing. 'Pinch away and I'll come to any shape you like. I'll give you so much confidence in yourself as a changer of men you'll be able to set up shop as the land's premier improver.'

'Oh, he's a nice chap, this harpist,' said Bartholomew delightedly to the visitor. 'You'll be able to work off any text you like on him and he'll take it all, quiet as a baby. He's obliging. But the other one in there, Adams, he's godless. I'm glad he said nobody was to visit him, not even you. You'd only have drawn him into arguments that would have made the place unpleasant, and him surly. But you'll be able to enjoy yourself with the harpist. He's polite. Right to the end he'll be sweet as sugar. We've had some good bouts of singing and talking together, the harpist and I.'

'We have and all,' I said.

'I'll leave you to it then.'

'All right. So long, Barth. Sit down, Mr Mayhew. On the little stool there. I'll lie down. My thoughts come easy and are milky white when I lie down flat.'

The clergyman opened his Bible and began to read. His face had lost the smile that had given it such youthfulness when I saw him first. He was reading with an inflection of grave urgency which made it clear that he thought he was dealing with something obstinate and fearful within me. His tone made for sleep and I fixed my eyes on a point high in the wall and heard not a word he spoke. I was not even aware of it when he closed the book. He coughed to attract my attention.

'I trust that you were fortified by that,' he said. 'It must be the most beautiful passage of human hopefulness in all the world.'

'Yes, yes. It sounded very lovely. Why should the hopers have to breathe so hotly upon hope in every age? You are young, aren't you?'

'I have never before had the experience of visiting a man in your condition.'

'What does it feel like?'

'Painful and chastening.'

'It'll do you the world of good. Looking straight into the eyes of the damned must be fine rich soil for one who wishes to grow a few fresh slogans with which to hearten mankind.'

'I hope in the next few weeks to turn your mind away from any follies you might have yielded to in the past, and towards God.'

'An exchange of essence between you and me, a kindly exchange, should benefit the world greatly. I shall see more of you, I hope.'

'You will not put me off. Before I came here I spoke with the man, a wise, sweet man, who has been my teacher and adviser for many years, and he told me that when dealing with those who would need me most the gap between them and God would at first sight terrify and discourage.'

'Don't be terrified, boy. We play a fine fascinating game, we soul-watchers. Keep your end up and I'll provide you with a first-class target before we're done.'

'Do you think there is anything I might do with or for your silent friend, the man in the next cell?'

'Leave well alone. With me you'll just barely survive, with your brain hanging on by a thread. John Simon would finish you off. God has let him off religion altogether to get on with the real job of persuading us to lay aside our napkins and grow up.'

'I'm sad to hear you say that. There will be a service in the castle chapel later this morning which you and your friend will be expected to attend. I hope that it will leave your spirits, if not lighter and more Christian, at least reconciled and at peace.'

'Reconciled and at peace. There's a lovely magic in those words. It's a pity their meaning is so dim.'

The young chaplain left me. Half an hour later they came to fetch us to attend the service. I had shouted in to John Simon that it would be silly to neglect the opportunity even of a short walk and a change. Bartholomew and his assistant fixed the chain to our leg before taking us on our walk through the damp, narrow, dark corridors. He apologised for this and said that he personally would get into the deepest trouble if he allowed us the slightest chance of misbehaving ourselves. I told him that we understood about this, and that, reduced as our scope now was, we would do all we could to keep him out of trouble. He was still mumbling his thanks to me for this thoughtfulness when we shuffled through the narrow door which led us into the chapel. It was a larger place than I had anticipated. We had a brief glimpse of thick pillars and the warm glow of the altar which made me almost drunk after the smallness and drabness of the cell. We were put to sit behind a dark grey screen from which we could see little of the chapel's interior.

'The place sounds empty,' I said to Bartholomew who had taken his place, standing, behind our bench.

'This is especially for you,' he said. 'It's a kind of privilege.'

'Oh.' The discovery that so much serious thought went into the arrangement of these details in the strange chilly margin where we found ourselves gave me the same kind of shock as one would feel on finding evidence of a pious respectability in a nest of stoats.

The officiating priest was Mr Mayhew. His voice seemed stronger than when he had spoken to me privately. He was helped by a choir of boys and men who appeared to be feeling the solemnity of the occasion and singing in a more powerful boom for that reason. John Simon paid no attention to the intoning. He told Bartholomew to move out of the way and spent the whole time reading the inscriptions on the stone memorial tablets, mostly of past Governors and Sheriffs of the castle and their wives. Some of the tablets were extremely old and went back into periods of history with which I had no acquaintance at all. They gave our own dilemma the enrichment of a mossy tradition, and John Simon seemed quite pleased as he pointed out to me the Norman quality of most of the folk commemorated. I nodded without intelligence to show him that my knowledge of the Normans was small and not yet breeched.

'They were the ironmasters of their day,' said John Simon. 'Their crown was made up of such castles as these. They crumbled.'

'They seem to be hanging on here.'

'Look, friends,' said Bartholomew almost pettishly, 'all this service is for you. Yet you go staring at the wall and chattering. You don't appreciate what's being done for you.'

291

'You go to the devil, Bartholomew,' said John Simon in an amiable, contented way. 'And look at this one here, Alan. This is a beauty. The grandfather of Plimmon himself. They tell me he was very tight in the fists. The family fortunes had been allowed to run down and he was the first of the Plimmons to skin the rats who were nibbling at the last treasures and to fight their way back into the higher flight.'

I thought of Helen Penbury, reminded of her by the mention of a Plimmon in the motion of flight. I could smell the cool green of the glen where I had seen her for the first time, the rare, uncoarsened whiteness of her skin, the delicate blue of her cloak, the feel of the hard breadcrust on my teeth as I had chewed at it and meditated upon her softness.

'What does it say about old Plimmon, John Simon?'

'It's Latin, a tongue I never knew. The usual things, I suppose. Full of good works and wisdom. It's no wonder these mighty folk find it so easy to believe only the best and most charitable about themselves. They've certainly presented these myths to the public in very clear print.'

I listened to the choir singers who were aloft and sweet on a series of high clean notes.

'Tell me, Barth,' I said, 'if this ceremony is so very special, who took the trouble to provide it?'

'It's one of the old Plimmon bequests. The money for a whole service on each waiting Sunday for the condemned was given about a hundred years ago by one of the Plimmon women. She was Scotch and one of her kinsmen was executed. So she felt a kind of fellow feeling, so to speak, and she was out to refresh the doomed with as much holiness as possible.'

'If she still haunts this part of the building, thank her.

292

That was a constructive thought. God help us, the fur-lined gestures that people make. Fancy thinking of a thing like that. You should tell the world about these special benefits. Properly announced, they'd get a lot of boys coming in here if only for the singing.'

The service ceased as Mr Mayhew's voice was heard again and the slow difficult walk through the unlit corridors was repeated.

Not long after being returned to our cells, one of Bartholomew's assistants brought us a meal of lukewarm broth that was of exactly the same colour as the screen behind which we had sat in the chapel. I could not eat it, but I could hear John Simon spooning it out with vigour and even tapping the dish as if in rhythm with an inward song.

'You sound happier,' I said.

'That little journey got my mind out of a sorrowful rut. Coming back there was no black border on my thoughts at all. I wondered why.'

'I'll tell Mr Mayhew. He's the chaplain. He's young and he'll be pleased to know he's doing a bit of good. He's worried into a palsy by the gap between us and God. You ought to talk to him. He's fresh as a daisy.'

'It wasn't him. All I can imagine Mayhew doing is to put a few fresh tassels on the mourning fringe. No, it's probably because I haven't any choice to make now that will be painful, that will leave the unchosen thing festering in the flesh.'

'Speak clearer, boy.'

'Either I die or Longridge smashes this place from around us. I can see rich possibilities in either.'

18

It was on the following Tuesday that we got our first visitor. It was Katherine to see John Simon. She spoke to me through the grille. I could not see her but it was good to hear her voice, although I could feel the texture of it stretched almost to breaking in the frame of her sickness. I asked her how Davy was and she said he was very busy about his basket-making and asking after both of us.

'Thank him for that, Katherine.'

Then all I heard was the whispered speaking of her and John Simon.

Bartholomew came into my cell explaining that he was sorry I had no visitor to bear me company and he hoped that his presence would bring me some solace.

'It will, boy. You are a real companion to have, Bartholomew, one of the nicest I've known. You do nothing whatever to my heart, for good or ill. It's like being friendly with the weather.'

'Isn't there anybody on earth you'd like to have visiting you?'

'No,' I gave it some more thought. 'No, nobody on earth.'

'No one at all? Not even some woman you've wept over?'

'No. I've created the conditions of a moulting but satisfying peace between these walls, Bartholomew. I wouldn't want it shattered.'

Bartholomew left me, returning along the corridor ten

minutes later to let Katherine out. I heard her weep incon-
solably and, natural as it was that she should weep, I was
surprised to hear the sound.

There was complete silence for an hour or so. Even the
prison rats whose movements my ears had learned to follow
with a precise exactitude seemed to have fallen still. We
were given our evening meal and then we were left alone
again. As the darkness was coming on, I heard John Simon's
voice speaking to me through the grille telling me to come
near.

'I don't want anybody to hear this. There might be
somebody outside there. I wouldn't trust Bartholomew far;
his moral sense drowned an age back. He's sorry for us, but
I think he'd sell us twice over for a quart of ale.'

'What is it?'

'Something Katherine managed to tell me this afternoon.
She's got word from Longridge. He tells us to keep hoping,
that everything is not yet lost.'

'I'm glad to hear of anybody who thinks that. But that's
not much to go on. Where is he? What's he doing?'

'Katherine only had scraps of news to go on. Connor was
arrested at Manchester a fortnight ago and is awaiting trial.
The soldiers captured a lot of the supplies he was sending
down to the men in the Southern valleys. Plimmon and
Radcliffe have ordered a combing out of all the men who
have not gone into hiding and whom he thinks might be
sympathetic with us. Longridge is still hiding, but he tells
Katherine to tell us that everything is far from lost, that we
are not to despair. The men at Moonlea have gone back to
work at less pay, the ones who are staying on there, that is.
Radcliffe has brought in a lot of workers from the Eastern
counties and he's been evicting the people from those tied

295

cottages by the score. The ships for America'll be doing a roaring trade for a while to come.'

'I suppose they will. There's a lot of movement up, down and across. Plimmon and Radcliffe are staging a painful revel. They are the wind in a peculiar autumn. They blow and the leaves drift. Wish we could drift too.'

'Longridge said that if we wished to get any word through to him there will always be one or two men we can trust in that tavern in Tudbury, The Flag.'

'Did you give Katherine a message for him?'

'When she was here there was nothing I could think of that I wanted to tell him. I was sorry she'd come and told her not to put herself to the trouble again. My God, she's ploughed a deep furrow through me, that Katherine. I wish I had kept as remote from that sort of feeling as you, Alan.'

'What message could you possibly have for Longridge? What have we to tell him? Short of a miracle that never happens to boys who are so out of favour with the preachers as we are, we are finished.'

'I'm beginning to think not. Until Katherine came, I would have agreed. When she was here I'll admit I thought about it for a few seconds and then dropped it in the well. No point in asking her to tell Longridge we are glad he's alive, and that we still believe in the dignity of man and have her risk gaol just to go along to The Flag to communicate those facts to Longridge's friends. But when she left I had the feeling that nothing could be left as unfinished as whatever it is that has grown up between her and me. The whole cold river of acceptance is breaking up and there might be a floe for me, Katherine, you.'

'We'll have to be nimble jumpers, John Simon, and we haven't got much space here to take a good run.'

296

'Longridge is a bit of a genius. His hatred has a hammer-head of pure steel. Losing Connor and me for what I'm worth will not daunt him at all. He, like all our lads, knows that if they go down in defeat now, the only thing left for them will be to queue up for a new suit of chains, with Radcliffe and Penbury having the last say in the matter of shade, weight, cut. When Longridge comes out of the shadow he'll come for us and he'll enjoy smashing to atoms whatever comes in his way.'

'And your message to him?'

'That we'll do every mortal thing we can to help. That I'd rather my last act on earth be to create a wilderness for foxes than a kingdom for Radcliffe.'

'And your messenger? Katherine?'

'She won't come again.'

'Who then?'

'Bartholomew. There's always the chance that he may not run true to form. Hasn't he been telling us that sometimes in his talks with you and me he sees the ghost of his dead decency stumbling about among the ruins of his ancient dreams. A man who can see that can do anything. I'll sound him tonight. There must be some part of the man that's fought off the weeds.'

'Not an inch. Amuse yourself with these notions but don't try to build anything on them. Give Bartholomew a few more showers and he'd sprout any weed you like freely at both ears.'

'The air's full of change. It might strike him as well as the next man. If the lads outside try to get us free it will make it simple for them if we have only a grain of help and sympathy from Bartholomew.'

'The air here is full of something, but it isn't change. I've never been in any place where things seemed to be so much on their haunches. Let's sit quietly and let's try not to please these great granite lumps overmuch by tearing at them. Let Longridge make his bid, and if a few sessions of hopeful swearing by us will fertilise his wrath to a finer flower we will swear. Let's try to be reconciled and at peace, as Mr Mayhew says, and think of those warm sunlit summers we knew as kids spinning out each day lying on that grass slope by the blacksmith's listening to the old men talking of the varieties of contentment they had known or would never know. The fullest joy is probably in that recollection and there is nothing worse or better than that I can think of to say about living.'

'We'll see. For some reason I'm excited. I could shout about it. My spirit's on the move again.'

Bartholomew came in to see us that evening. He carried his large lantern and after locking the door with slow hands and hard breath he laid it down in a corner. He seated himself on the bench and produced a bottle and a cracked dirty cup. He was reflective to the point of melancholy, and I asked him what had been going forward to put him in this state.

'There are times,' he said, 'when a man realises that the best thing to be is a shepherd or anything simple like that.' He sighed, poured himself out a cupful of wine and sipped. 'This is not simple, this job.'

'Not particularly. Not as simple, as you say, as looking after sheep.'

'Today, the County Sheriff's clerk was here to talk with me. An officious, clever little sod if ever there was one. Eyes stretched right across his rump, if you follow my meaning.'

'I know,' said John Simon who had drawn his bench up to

298

the grille and was standing on it to be one of the company. 'Out to make a homemade tartan for his clan with bits and pieces of other people's pelts. What was this clerk on about, Bartholomew?'

Bartholomew made no immediate reply. He glanced up, smiling at the opening from which John Simon's voice came.

'Glad to see you so cheerful again, Adams. There was a real shadow on me from the thought that you would be sorrowful after the visit of your beautiful friend. It's terrible to see a man helpless like you are, terrible. That's why I say this isn't a simple job. What sheep would ever get itself in such a bloody mess as you boys are in? What sheep would risk their necks because some of their fellows are not getting a fair share of the fatter pasture?'

'A good many, I bet. Perhaps sheep would be quicker to do it, being straighter in their ways.'

'Maybe too. I haven't thought enough about these things. I haven't observed enough. I'm tiny and shrinking with ignorance and there's nothing you can wash the fabric of thoughts in, is there?'

'Wine, like you do.'

'There is that. Like a drop?'

No, thanks. You fill up, Bartholomew. Give your mind a real wash-day and talk to us about simplicity. It's a good theme in this setting, none better.'

'That clerk said they had their eye on me, said I was losing my grasp on my functions fast and that he would see me out of the castle if I didn't stiffen my spine. They were the words he uttered in a thin but loud voice with his hand right under my nose, which is a way he has of intimidating people. Stiffen your spine, he said, and even as he spoke my spine was like a stick of sugar inside me being sucked at by all the years I've lived. He said I'd been too free and easy with you two for a start and he talked of doubling the guard. He thinks I've gone so daft and slack you might try to use me for an escape. Personally I thought that little red-headed assistant of mine, Jacob, had been making a report to Danvers about me. That's the clerk's name, Danvers.' He fell silent again and drank. 'An hour ago I lost my temper with Little Jacob and put my boot into him so far it took me five minutes to get the thing back again. Little Jacob is sitting in the office there, his backside a bit raised above the level of the chair because it's still sore and sobbing hard and saying he looks on me like a father and it would never dawn on him to do any such thing as talk to Danvers. One day I'll do something right. I must remember to give Little Jacob some of that soothing ointment I keep for my leg to dab on his backside. But most of the time Danvers was on about the gate.'

'What gate?'

'Can't tell you. You mustn't ask me things like that. Never ask a turnkey about gates or doors. That's almost like a proverb. I'm glad the visit of that young woman didn't upset you, Adams. She's a fine-looking young woman. Every day she was here. I got sick of seeing her so near to tears. I'm glad I let her see you now. Perhaps that's one of the right things I've done since birth. But I'm glad it brought you no more grieving. Why the hell can't people be free to come and go, all people. What kind of flavour will the meditations of that young woman have when you are gone, Adams? Ever thought of that?'

'I think about it all the time. I'd prefer not to. I'd rather talk to you about something neutral like gates or doors. It can't do you any harm to talk to us about doors. It won't benefit us much. Whatever that Danvers says I think you've kept a fine set of fingers on us since we've been here. You talk about your argument with that man and just treat us as part of the wall, and it'll ease your kidneys or whatever it is that ails you to show us the thorns that Danvers left in you.'

'All people on the castle staff are supposed to go in and out by the main gate and give the password to the soldier they have stationed there and a hell of a rigmarole it is too for a man who has passed the zenith of his years and clever-ness, like me, and who dearly loves to be nipping out for a jar and a few moments of remembered manhood in the lap of a friendly whore. So a long time ago I found a door at the end of corridor number seven which isn't used any more on account of the damp. Through there is a small tunnel and that brings you to another door through the main wall of the castle which you can't see from the outside on account of the ivy which hangs down thick like a curtain at that point. So sometimes I slip out through there and nobody's the wiser.'

'You leave it open?'

'Nobody knows about it but me. The tunnel's filling up with stones now, but it's been a lovely secret to have. Danvers doesn't know about the door and he's puzzled because he reckons some of the soldiers have seen me down in Tudbury when there's been no record of me passing through the main gate. So for a bit I'd better be using the main gate and giving the password and God knows what just to show willing. I wish I hadn't abused Little Jacob like I did. He's a shy boy and I've put him right for solace with some of the most splendid bedmates in Tudbury, women who have mastered the whole business of delight and who can stroke out all the shakes and shudders in under five minutes, easy. I've sinned richly. I've trodden the approaches to iniquity

301

flat and smooth with my feet, but now my feet are like lead and I have shudders that cannot be stroked to stillness. I'm in a poor way, friends.'

'What's up, boy? You ill?'

'Sick to a hair's breadth of dying. All last night I gasped and sweated. Little Jacob says I screamed a bit too. I might have done so because I was very frightened.'

'Did you have a pain?'

'Such a pain, I would not even have wished it on that bloody Danvers. All the inside of me from the chest to the privates, a wood with its branches bent with agony. Oh, it was awful. Little Jacob laid a stone bottle full of boiling water on my stomach, and having this vessel perched heavy as death itself on top of my guts gave me the trembles worse than ever, and I woke out of a shallow dream in which I had been lying half drowned and threw it at Little Jacob.' Bartholomew laid his cup down and drank in frantic gulps from the bottle itself. 'If I had fetched him one with that, Little Jacob would have had more than a sore rear by now. I've been brutal with that poor little sod. Last night might have been some punishment from God. They say God's got more eyes than that Danvers, but I don't think so, although I'm not nearly so flippant on these topics as you two.'

'I'm sorry to hear you were so ill.'

'This notion of God slips in and out of me in a curious way. Mostly I've tried to keep it in the anteroom because in me there is a power to go the whole hog about something or another and the only time I've come anywhere doing that is with women and the whole hog with them leaves a man so tired it fills his life with big full stops that ache like gallstones and prevent him getting much better or worse. But what if I went the whole hog on this notion of God.

Before you knew it I'd be showing horror at such ungodly games as keeping you boys locked up and hung, and so on. So I keep God in the anteroom and hang on to my pay in a way so eager it must be really baffling to God if he is there to look and be baffled at all. I was talking to the Reverend Mayhew about you, harpist.'

'What did he say?'

'He says that you are an agreeable sort of chap. He likes you. But he says that in matters of the soul he thinks you are a bit careless and unripe.'

'I'll get steadier and riper as time goes on. Time is all I want, Barth. That is why I say this whole wish to be hanging me is so foolish.'

'That's what he says. Men, he said to me, are sure to see the clear outline of their own doom.'

'He's right there. We dawdle on the job. Doom waits, just like a faithful dog, panting and eager to be seen, fed and patted and here we are, not caring a damn.'

'These are bad topics, harpist. For the first time in all my years I cried this morning. After the pain I was bleached and weak. I even told Little Jacob of the old churchyard where my father is buried, although it's fifteen years since I last disturbed the old man with even a thought. Weak, weak. That's why I let the young woman in to see Adams. I'd rather die than have another night like last night. I've washed off most of the topsoil and what's left isn't deep enough for the idea of death and God to grow and not look awkward, out of place. That little tunnel at the bottom of number seven was the only secret I ever had and now even that is filling up with stones my arms can't move, and soon it'll be blocked and I won't ever again go through the door in the wall behind the ivy and see the light in Slaney's

303

window staring at me from across the moat. It's been such a comfort to me and now it's filling up with those great bloody stones my arms are too weak to move. I'll tell Mr Mayhew about that because I think it makes a fine image for a man who is in his line of business and has to argue with pagans. Life, I'll tell Mr Mayhew, is just like the low tunnel at the bottom of number seven, and it's filling up with great stones that my arms can't move. Sing that lullaby to me, harpist. I like the harmonies we get on that tune. It's like velvet. As a kid I once had velvet breeches, very fancy. They did more to steer me into a steady devotion to sin than anything I know.'

We began singing, Bartholomew in a distracted, tuneless howl, John Simon and I in a thoughtful vigilant croon. Halfway through a long note Bartholomew's head fell back against the wall, his mouth hanging open, his eyes staring and a powerful sweat upon his skin. A soft panting sound came from within him. I raised the lamp to have a clearer look at him, but he told me in a deep plain voice to put the thing down and carry on with the singing. He said something too about those velvet breeches, but his tone slithered and I could not make out all the words. I launched myself on the song again when John Simon's voice, urgent, commanding, broke in and made me quiet:

'Bartholomew,' he said. 'Listen to me, Bartholomew. That thought you had, the one you call God, wasn't such a bad thought. It tells you in a queer way that you could have been more dignified and useful and that's true. You can make up for a lot of things, Bartholomew, if you wish. Deep down in your heart you believe as we do. That pattern of a new brotherhood we speak out for, you've glimpsed it too. But you're tired and prefer to shamble in alleyways to walking swiftly in the light. Not even alleyways will be much use to you now. You're full of pain and you might even be dead before Plimmon and his friends have put the rope on us. Help us to get out of here, Bartholomew. Just get us outside these walls and the rest you can leave to us. We'll not forget you,' John Simon stopped, drew himself up and looked into the dim light of my cell. 'Why don't you answer, Bartholomew? Is he listening, Alan? Does he understand what I say?'

'His eyes are open. But he looks blown-out and remote. Some storm has passed his way.'

Bartholomew nodded his head vacantly as if inviting John Simon to go on. I supported Bartholomew's body, thinking he might topple off the stool in his weakness. I could feel the pain go through his body with the contemptuous rhythm of waves on a quiet beach.

'We have friends,' said John Simon. 'You'll find them at a tavern in Tudbury whose name I'll give you. All you have to do is tell them we are waiting and they'll see we have the means to get clean out of Tudbury and to safety in a trice. And they'd see you were repaid for your trouble, Bartholomew, if that means anything to you.'

Bartholomew made no answer. His head fell back convulsively once again. His skull sounded on the granite and his eyes closed.

'I think he's fainted.'

'Get the keys.'

I fumbled inside Bartholomew's old stale-smelling great-coat. I could hear the jingle of the keys hanging from a belt around his waist but the man was wearing such a confusion of clothes it took my fingers minutes to get down to the correct layer. I was just closing my hand around the bunch

305

to get it away with a violent tug when there was a banging on the door and the voice of Little Jacob was heard telling Bartholomew to come out and have his supper. Bartholomew opened his eyes, his face still grey and wet, staring at us with a rib of irony in his expression.

'Come in here,' he shouted.

Little Jacob came in and looked inquisitively at us. Bartholomew stretched out his arm.

'Lift me up,' he said, 'I've had another of those turns.'

Jacob did as he was told, examining the old man's face solicitously. Bartholomew was on his feet again, resting himself clumsily against the open door, his breath a series of rattling gasps. He dismissed Jacob.

'It's no good,' he said quietly, his face upturned towards the grille where John Simon was still listening. 'You said – deep down in your heart. There is no deep down, honest to God, Adams, there is no deep down. It's a thin slice of a thing, gone dark with age, dampness, cold, not fit even for my own teeth. I'd agree to get you out because I believe you stand for some things that are right, that you are good, that you are better at least than the people who put you here. I'd agree to go to that tavern and tell your friends. I'd wish them well. But I'd betray them too. Every day I must have my bit of betrayal or the night would be too strange to be borne. The only really thorough and constant ones, Adams, are the corrupt ones. That's why people like you will always manage to get yourselves hanged whenever you crop up and try to make men blush. I'm glad Little Jacob came. I wouldn't like you boys to see to the very furthest corners of my sty. Good night.'

19

The next day Mayhew came to see me with an expression of joy upon his face more radiant than I had seen before. It crossed my mind that when our climax came the look on his face would be dazzling. He told me in a low voice, looking almost conspiratorial, that I had a visitor.

'Send him in,' I said.

'You are requested to come to the Castle Warden's office.'

'Oh, somebody special. All right. I'll come. Wait till I tell John Simon.'

'Please don't bother.' His voice dropped even lower. 'Perhaps it would be better if he didn't know. This might concern only you.'

'You're very mysterious, Mr Mayhew. After the time I've been in here I find it hard to stand all this whispering. There's something so very frank about gaol. Carry on then.'

Little Jacob was waiting for us in the corridor. He walked behind us.

'Where's Bartholomew, Jacob?' I asked.

'Oh, he's bad. He's a dying man.'

'I knew he wasn't up to the mark. Last time I saw him he looked like a brother to the plague. From his chest to his privates, he said, a forest of pain.'

'Leigh!' said Mr Mayhew, and for a few seconds I did not know why he sounded so appalled.

'I'm only repeating what he said. He looked deathly.

Where have they put him?'

'He's in his own room. The doctor said he might die, but on the other hand he might get well again.'

'That's what I call getting right to the heart of the question. Keep the bottle away from him. He's drunk so much his main gut must be wondering whether Barth is a man or a vineyard.'

'I'll tell him that. He's very partial to a chat with you.'

The dark corridor lightened as we reached a tall barred window. A yard beyond the window the corridor ended in a broad oaken door. Little Jacob nipped ahead of us and knocked upon the door three times. The door was opened from inside. Mayhew took me by the arm and pushed me in. The light from the window in the corridor had my eyes inept to cope with the darkness of the room into which I had entered. I could distinguish nothing of the people or the furnishings which might be before me. When my sight improved, I made out a large round table in gleaming wood and, sitting down on the side of it opposite to where I stood, a woman. The set of the shoulders and head was familiar to me at once. I recognised even the pale blue cloak which I had seen her wear the first time we met.

'Sit down, harpist,' she said.

'What's this for?'

'Displeased to see me?'

'Neither pleased nor otherwise. One becomes slow and blunt in this place. Gracefulness perishes. Why all the shadow?'

'I had a fancy I wouldn't like to have the place fully lit. The Warden of the castle humoured me.'

'Embarrassed at the sight of me, perhaps?'

'That's a kind of feeling I could never have. I see you well

308

enough. You look ill and sad, harpist. You suffer from the clipping of your wings.'

'I'm sick to be here. I'm sick at all that's happened.'

'I know that. You belong among mountains and trees. You are a misfit here.'

'If you imagine that there are some who take to it as ducks to water, that is a myth that breeds only in large mansions. This is a hell for more people than mountain lovers.'

'You don't belong here. You know my meaning.'

'I suppose I do. But you'll remember there was a trial held in these parts about a week ago. You might have pointed out my unfitness for this kind of darkness to those dunder-headed loons who made me out to be a social menace, a bad enough one to be hung for safety's sake. But don't worry about my being a misfit. I've lost most of the interest I ever had in mountains, trees and harps. This place looks a bit stiff from the outside, but it's coming nicely to my shape and if I find the death they propose for me as cosy around the shoulders as the rot-hole where they have me now, I won't complain.'

'Don't be bitter, harpist. An example had to be made of you. You tripped over the rules and had your nose put out of joint. You were never without friends who keenly felt the misery of what you went through. Keenly.'

'This talk of friends baffles me. I sent a lawyer to see you, a man called Collett to see if you or your father would step in and persuade them to see reason. At the moment I have one friend only and I'm making do with him. He's in the next cell to mine.'

'I told you about that. Once you were arrested the law had to take its course. My father was ill. I had to conciliate Lord Plimmon who is a hard, stern man. But your friends have not been idle, harpist. We don't want you to suffer for something you never did.'

'You mean killing the man Bledgely?'

'Yes.'

'How do you know I didn't kill him. Why shouldn't I have killed him? Why shouldn't I have some satisfaction for having strayed for my sins into this damned dingle?'

'Because it isn't in your nature to kill, harpist, because since you came to Moonlea you have been nothing but an innocent victim of circumstances.'

'So is John Simon Adams.'

'My friends could not be made to take such a view of him. Moonlea knows him only too well.'

'What does all this end in? What are you trying to say?'

'That you can be free.'

'Escape, you mean?'

'A free unconditional pardon.' Her gloved hand moved along the table. 'I too have been sick in my own way at the thought of your being here, harpist. My father is better now. Since he heard of your plight he has not ceased to bestir himself on your behalf. There must have been a magic quality in your harp playing, for I've not seen him so active for years. Radcliffe was a little difficult at first but he came to see that he would not be risking or losing overmuch with you at freedom. In any case, my father is really having his last spurt saving you from the gallows. Radcliffe didn't wish to refuse the last wish of a dying man. With his help the matter was simple.'

'And Plimmon? I can't imagine his mind being changed about the man who dared to exchange a word or two with his chosen one.'

'He's been in London since the trial on his own business.'

'Do you have any love for that man?'

'That question is without meaning for me.'

'What about John Simon Adams?'

'Hopeless. He dies.'

'I couldn't leave him. We've always been close to each other. More so than ever now.'

'Don't be a fool, harpist. He was born for hate and misery. He doomed himself the moment he started to meddle in the affairs of a town that had known only peace before he came. Such men are meant to be stamped on. You were born for joy and freedom. He could have died in a thousand ways in which you would have been powerless to help him. I've thought much about you, harpist. I would be grieved if you refused this offer of my help.'

'Thank you. I mean that. Thank you. There's no one I would have wished more to be helped by than you. It's a pity that our ways and thoughts should be so unlike. It's a pity you know as little about John Simon Adams as I know about you. Oh, the blank untouchable sides of us all. I want to say yes, yes, of course, yes. I want to live. I wonder has the world ever heard that before.'

'And you shall. Go back over the mountain where I saw you first. Go back to where you belong and forget about Moonlea, forget it ever existed.'

'I'd like that.'

I stretched my arms out on the walnut table and laid my head upon them. What I had heard had startled me, destroyed what little balance I had managed to achieve since arriving at the castle. In the forefront of my mind was a clamant urge that I throw myself at Helen Penbury's feet, act the liquescent idiot, drivel out my gratitude for what she had done and then act on her advice as fast as a pigeon. But in the mind's back was the bitter insoluble devotion to John Simon that I had always felt and that was now strengthened by a kinship in experience greater than anything we had before known. Even as I was telling myself that decency would compel me to stay at his side my mind was spinning out its busy cosy web of consoling counter-suggestion. Free, I could move heaven and earth to free John Simon. I could become the vital point of contact between him and the forces that were massing under Longridge. I would, with a fullness of will new to my being, be heroically devoted to the cause of freedom for which John Simon was ready to die. I would really become, proudly become, all those things they had said I was at the trial. I even managed to throw into my delight a tremor of defiant hatred. And Lemuel... Of course there was Lemuel. I would be an avenging angel. A single inefficient noose for Lemuel and Isabella. Life would wipe its nose and come forward to thank me. I could see it all. I could see every tremendous detail as clearly as I could now see Helen's face, astonishingly white and calm. John Simon would understand. He understood everything. That was the man's great trade, a merciful understanding. He would not mind being left alone. His was a nature that genuinely seemed to sustain itself on those very forms of loneliness that corroded and killed the spirit of others.

'When can I be free?'

'Within a few days. One or two small formalities and you will be free to leave.'

'Thank you. I will always be grateful to you.'

'Goodbye, harpist.' She rapped on the table.

I rejoined Mayhew and Little Jacob in the corridor. My knees were shaking and I rested on the broad sill of the window.

'Good news?' asked Mayhew.

'I'm to be free. A pardon.'

'God's gracious will has been done. I was never without hope.'

I nodded my head in the direction of my cell.

'I don't want to go back there. After this I couldn't stand to talk with John Simon. It wouldn't be the same.' I was talking with a painful effort. 'It would be terrible. He'll understand. You tell him, Mr Mayhew. He's wiser and stronger than I am. You tell him. Tell him not to be afraid, that there'll always be friends.... You tell him.'

'I'll do that, Leigh.' A slight solemn quiver was running through Mayhew. 'You're quite right not to wish to return to a place that has meant so many days of melancholy horror to you. He'll understand.'

'You don't think he'll imagine I'm betraying or deserting him?' My voice was high and uncertain, my mind in a night of nervous confusion.

'He'll think nothing of the sort. He'll be overjoyed. Corridor 2, Jacob.'

We began walking in a direction that was strange to me. We came to a block of cells that were cleaner but no larger than the one I had left. I leaned my head against the cold stonework. I sought Mayhew's hand and wrung it.

'Thank God, thank God,' I said softly, and I would have kept on saying it for a long time as a substitute for thought had not the grinning delighted Jacob pushed me in and turned the key, leaving me at once more nakedly alone than before.

313

20

Three days later I was led again into the office of the Castle Warden. The Deputy County Sheriff was waiting to speak to me. It was odd to see this gentleman sitting huge and clumsy in brilliant light on the same chair that Helen Penbury had occupied in shadow when she had brought me the first news of my pardon. The slightest sounds of that interview had been running back and fore in my mind since it had ended.

The Deputy County Sheriff greeted me cheerfully. My suit of grey prison sackcloth, my general air of having been hit over the head with my own right leg, must have made the man feel the more glorious and resplendent. He was wearing a suit of a fawn shade. It looked to me like a riding suit and his face looked as if he had just come in from a gallop. He told me that my release had been arranged, that I could leave the prison, if I wished, that day. He did not go so far as to slap me on the shoulder, but it was clear that he wanted to strike and keep a note of cordial bonhomie. He kept booming out from time to time that I should consider myself a very lucky man indeed in having had this brilliant stroke of luck, of having had friends who had exerted themselves so valiantly on my behalf. I guessed that he found his occasional brief duties at the castle either tedious or disquieting and that he was deriving a rich enjoyment from extending these congratulations, with their relatively festive air, to me. I viewed him with a serious interest. I recalled that not since John Simon and I had arrived at the place had we caught a glimpse of him.

'Pardon me,' I said, interrupting his trumpet voluntary in a quiet polite way, 'We've not seen you before, have we?'

'What do you mean?' There was a break of bad temper in his voice.

'You've not come to see us in our sleep or anything like that? I thought you might have been interested, the rest of the gaol being empty, and we being in the situation we were in, and so on.'

'There's been no need. No, I've not been to see you. Did you have any complaint to make?'

'Not in terms that you could have followed. But this place is drab. A cheerful word from you would have improved things greatly.'

'Are you being insolently humorous, fellow?' He was leaning over the table and showing all his upper teeth in a well-wrought snarl.

'God, no. And if I had been hanged, would you have come along then?'

'Of course, of course. That is one of the regrettable but unavoidable functions of my office. To see justice properly executed.'

'I'm glad of that. One doesn't like to feel neglected.'

'What is the point of all these questions, Leigh? I know that you have undergone a trying time but I tolerate impudence from no one.'

'No point. I'm talking because I'm afraid to be quiet. I'm sorry a busy man like you has to be the target but people have put up with worse things. Back there, in the half-dark, one gets touchy about trifles, about points of dignity that never bothered one before.'

315

'Well, you don't have to worry about that any more. You've been lucky, remarkably lucky. Get out of the district, far out of it, there's a good fellow. And see that from now on there is not even the remotest connection between you and the vortex of trouble-making into which you were nearly sucked down. It isn't enough nowadays for the citizen to be passively good. He must be active in resisting the contamination. Have you a livelihood?'

'I'm a harpist, without a harp.'

'Get work of a solid useful kind, my man, and keep your harping for a harmless hobby. The country's full of fine work for strong arms like yours. Here are two guineas. They will see you over your first period as a free man.'

'This is a gift from you?'

'No, from friends.'

'Thank them.'

'I will, indeed. The turnkey, Jacob, will be waiting with your clothes. Goodbye, Leigh, and good luck.'

I went back to my cell, dressed, prepared to say goodbye to Mr Mayhew and Little Jacob.

'What about Bartholomew?' I asked. 'Can I see him?'

'He's in a very bad way,' said Jacob. 'Leave him alone, that's what I'd do if I were you. He stares ahead of him and stares behind him as if he's afraid someone is coming at him and most of the time he mutters. It's a terrible place in there with him, terrible.'

'I'm sorry about that. In this place he's got plenty to mutter about. Tell him I wish him well. Who's he expecting that he stares so?' I turned to the young chaplain: 'Look, Mr Mayhew. This is something that I'll never be able to explain to myself or to anybody else. But I can't go back there to say goodbye to my friend John Simon Adams. I know he'll

316

understand, but I don't, not altogether, and that makes me ache. Do it for me, will you?'

'You're wise. Make the parting clean and abrupt. If you were leaving someone who needed your support, it would be different. I don't claim to understand the material and quality of his beliefs and I hardly think I would sympathise with them even if I did, but we must admire the iron quality of their foundations. There is a gift of softness, of tears, in you, harpist, which has never been present in your friend. He fills his own solitude and he would not wish to have it any other way. I doubt whether he will ever miss you.'

I took the black, broad-brimmed hat which Jacob was holding out to me.

'You know little of me, Mr Mayhew, and even less of John Simon. For not knowing the chain of things that has made us what we are you might be less wise, but I don't think you'll be less happy.'

'You have the address of the farm I gave you, where my parents live.'

'Yes, I have it.'

'Try to go there some time, harpist. I've told my mother and father about you. They'd like to know you. They have great happiness and we'd be glad to share it with you if ever you feel like breaking with your wandering and coming to see us.'

'I'll bear that in mind. Thank you. Goodbye.'

They walked with me as far as the great hall of the castle where the pair of soldiers on duty opened the doors to let me pass. I waved to them, still feeling half pleased, half uneasy at Mayhew's suggestion that I retreat into the genial recesses of his privacy. I made my way down the steep hill that led away from the castle into the town. I jingled the pair of substantial guineas in my pocket and glued my eyes hungrily on the hills that loomed up to the north, the hills of my destination, the hills to which I wished instantly to home.

'I shall eat,' I told myself. 'Then I will walk, northward. I will walk until I drop or die, until the last taste of memory has faded. I wish to God my lump of mind would come away from its moorings to be tossed aside. It's been dirtied; when shall it again be laundered?'

I kept walking through the main street of Tudbury. It was a market day and in my moments of hesitation as I tried to deal with the new situation of facing wide spaces and crowded streets I came close on several occasions to being hustled off my balance by running messengers, tradesfolk with their handcarts. I kept to the side of the road and walked cautiously. Near the end of the street a vividly painted Union Jack on a signboard caught my eye and I found myself outside the tavern called The Flag. I remembered what John Simon had said and made my way, very slowly and hesitantly, over its threshold. In the deep fireplace, as I walked in, a large sirloin of beef was roasting on a spit. I sat down on a bench inside the fireplace, enjoying the intense heat and smell of the meat. The landlord, a man in late middle age, approached me and I asked him for some ale and a helping of the beef. After the stale cool fodder of the gaol I found my whole body crying out for a few slices of the hot, fresh, clean meat. He sat at a window seat and served me. He stood at my side as I began my eating and drinking, smiling, twisting his napkin dexterously around his hands. Through a mouthful of food I told him that if this was the provender of the gods then there would be something to be said even for being immortal. He obviously did not understand what I had said, but he looked none the less pleased. Three or four men, one of whom I had the feeling of having seen before, but whose face I could not place, came to occupy the bench by the fire which I had vacated. They looked at me intently, smiling from time to time, one of them winking, as if wishing to show their friendliness, to hear me say something to them. I averted my eyes from them, watching the stream of people and things in the narrow street outside. Over the roof of a low building on the street's opposite side I could catch a glimpse of the castle's eastern wall, with its elusive, saddening pattern of light greys among darks where the wall had been restored. The sight of it made me as jumpy and fretful as the eyes of the men who had come to sit by the fire. I knew who they were, without having to think deeply about it. There was something about the set of their dark broad faces that reminded me of John Simon. They would be his friends. They were clearly waiting for me to make the first sign and approach. They would know without doubt who I was. In however small a way I was a figure at whom the public had gazed. I dipped my lips into the ale without drinking and listened to the liquid flow back from my flesh into the dark pot. I had been hoisted from a well and the world was gathering around to watch the details of my dripping. I grimaced embarrassedly into the brown mirror of my drink.

I finished my meal, making a great play of rinsing my plate with a fragment of bread, finding the silence of the long room harder and harder to bear. I called for more ale. I drank it more swiftly than I had the last. My mind softened to a pitying pulp. At the thought of John Simon I could have wept into the pot, and on my tongue was a flood of words, hot comradely words that would have invited those waiting men by the fire to make me one with them in any venture, however desperate, which would erase the indecent wrong which had been done to John Simon and myself, give him the new lease of daring splendid opportunity which his spirit would achieve, if freed. To cut at the proud, bloody heart of Plimmon and his clan, make him and his ancestor-ridden guts a sacrifice for once in a while to the world's queer appetite for change and give the oppressed a few minutes' respite from being so grossly and tediously baited by their masters. I banged my pot on the table. There were tears in my eyes and my face was twisted by a crazy sorrow. The three watchers had their heads bent forward. I was cold with fear. I knew that at that moment I had no wish to be breaking the passionately waiting silence between us. I did not want John Simon to die. I did not want the thing that scarred the lives of the unfree and the weak to escape my contempt. But I had as I sat there as little as I had ever had of the conviction that gives a man defiant valour. My compassion had been wrought to fit a smaller frame. I had none of the guile that makes occasionally malleable a man's relations with those who can destroy and enslave him. I was inept, vagrant, helpless and sick with the dread that I should know once again the incomprehensible, retching horror of being trussed, laughed at, filleted and hung up, the dread I had shared with John Simon. I wanted to be somewhere where I could talk to myself for a long time alone, to see no other, to have a peace, whatever its deprivations and flatnesses, in which I could slowly learn again to see the world as a bearable, acceptable thing, sufficiently a wilderness to be unimportant. I beckoned the landlord to my side. I asked him for the tally. He changed the first of my guineas. The watching men smiled at me once more. I smiled back at

320

them and then bolted from the tavern, vanished into the thickening crowd, eager to put between myself and Moonlea and Tudbury as many hill ranges and as many acts of sullen deliberate forgetting as I could. I glanced back at the tavern, from behind a tall box on which sat a blind boy with a misshapen diseased face. He was holding a collecting bag on behalf of a girl who was playing a small stringed instrument which no one could hear in the middle of the street. The boy sensed my presence, leaned over and, letting his hand trail downwards, stroked my cheek. In my distraction I felt only a simple gratitude and a pleasure in relieving, however obliquely, his desolation. I nodded at the girl too who had glanced around to see if all went well with her friend or brother and with her too I felt an access of authentic brotherliness. Above the boy's head hung a pawnbroker's emblem executed in gigantic and gleaming bronze. The man who had come out to the portal of The Flag to see where I had gone shook his head and went inside. I slipped some coins into the boy's collecting bag and went on my way.

Around the corner, in what looked like one of Tudbury's larger squares, a coach was being loaded with luggage. There were several passengers already inside. Two more were preparing to ascend. The slight of the big restless horses slipping on the greasy cobbles made me pause for a few moments. Then I approached a postillion.

'Where to, friend?'

'North.'

'How far?'

'Short stage only. Wenlake.'

'Where's that?'

'Nineteen, twenty miles. Pretty place, Wenlake.'

'Any room?'

'One vacant seat.'

'How much?'

'Get your ticket over there, the small window with the old man poking his head out waving to that kid, and you'll have to hurry.' He turned away then suddenly faced me once again. 'Any luggage?'

'No, just me.'

'Good enough. We've got too much in the boot as it is. All in, please!'

I obtained and paid for my ticket. I climbed in. I was lodged between two men, one large and surly, wearing a beaver hat, the other lean, hollow-cheeked and apparently light of heart. There were some women in the corner places with their eyes turned sedulously outward. I tried hard not to examine the situation too closely. I had done the right thing. I shaped my mind and even my lips around those words until the lean man started to keep his eye on me. I knew I was full to the brim of doubts, hesitations, regrets which would be capable of impelling me forward and pulling me back every other second if I gave them the chance. Wisdom was whatever put miles between me and the southern slope of Arthur's Crown. It was then the tentacles of a pity and a doom I wished no part of would stretch out most fiercely. Had I walked northwards, my first intention, thoughts would have pulled at my muscles, tormenting my feet towards the west, towards Moonlea. In a swift coach, closeted with nameless strangers whose unconsciousness of me was as complete as that I wished for myself, my resolve would be taken for me. When I alighted there would be no question of return. I would go back calmly and without recall into my tomb of hills.

The journey began. The thin blithe man at my side was

322

delighted to have at least one neighbour who looked less like death's twin than the man in the beaver hat. He would be as good an antidote as any, a bushel for the creeping light of my reflections. The women in the corners had spotted me and seemed glad that they could look at me with scorn. It was my clothes that prompted the peculiar fixity of their contempt. If there had been crops in the carriage they would have been safe from the birds. The thin man was now talking of his youth and of the prosperity that had come to the area with the pits and foundries. He was a merchant, a seller of hardware, and he told me the moulders of Moonlea would be world famous by the time his firm of vendors had completed their selling campaign. I told him I was glad to hear this. I remembered that John Simon was a moulder. I recalled the fervour in his eyes as he had tried to demonstrate the details of his craft on that patch of brown earth outside Katherine Brier's cottage, with me leaning back on my elbows listening to Davy's high monotonous croon from the bottom of the garden and wondering what all John Simon's talk and fervour were about.

'Beautiful hills here,' said the hardware seller. 'I like these low soft hills. The high rugged ones further north repel me. Rather too much grandeur, I say. But these round little foothills, they are perfectly to my taste. Man might have made these.'

'I like all hills.'

'Even those tall, rough, rugged ones?'

'I can't have too much grandeur.' I stared at the tall crown of my silent neighbour's beaver hat.

'The lack of urban amenities does not bother you then?'

'Not at all. I live right in the middle of the mountain, so far in, the goats chew at us in protest when we are too human.'

'I fancy the autumn hues have been richer this year than for a long time past. Would you agree there, sir?'

'I'm glad of that. I'm not much for autumn as a season. It bids me too insistently to be still and shut up. But it's nice to see the trees having a change, even to being naked.'

'You have a discerning eye, sir. Could I make so bold as to inquire what line of business you might be in?'

'At the moment, listening to you and trying to be numb. Go on with your remarks, sir. I get few chances to converse with real travellers.'

'Thank you, thank you indeed. It is gratifying in these public vehicles not to be peremptorily dismissed as a chatterbox.' He glanced at the beaver-hatted man and dropped his voice. 'Frankly, sir, my errand here was a rather grave one.' He looked at me, eyebrows up, lips in.

'Somebody dead?'

'Worse than that. Deliveries of the ornamental lines in which we specialise from the Penbury works had almost ceased as the result of the strike and the threat of riot. Of course our orders with them are not so large as they would receive from the Government of His Majesty, but I say it's the articles of peace that are going to sustain the commerce of this land in the long run. Tumult, commotion and blood-shed have only a limited duration on this earth. Domestic hardware is eternal. Its external forms will change but its principle is deathless.'

'You think that?'

'Emphatically. But, thank God, Mr Penbury can breathe again. You heard that two of the leaders had been con-demned for murder?'

'I heard about it.'

'One of them has been pardoned, I read in today's press.

324

The other one, Adams, is undoubtedly the real malefactor. The pardoned one, so my newspaper put me to understand, was little better than an idiot, a catspaw whom Adams used to deflect suspicion from himself. It is only to be hoped that Adams in his present solitude will spend the period to good effect, make his peace with God and issue a full statement that will turn his fellows aside from similar courses in the future. This Adams must be a real scoundrel. Thinking about him made me cross during the whole of my journey down. Causing the military to be brought in, causing loss and inconvenience to the community's trade, furthering his own ambitions by playing on the wretchedness of some of our labouring poor, using some wandering half-wit of a minstrel as a decoy and scapegoat. I'm not a hard-hearted man, sir, but I could with little effort bring myself to hope that they will deny this Adams every solace material and spiritual. I hope that his every hour of waiting for the gibbet will be made by fear and remorse to seem like a year. I hope he will be given to taste, in full measure, that bitterness of heart which is and always will be the due of those who fail to pull at the oar in harmony with their fellow men.'

I beat on the roof of the coach.

'Are you ill, sir?'

'No, forgot something. I've got to go back.'

'They are unwilling to stop between stages.'

'They've got to stop. Driver, driver!' The ladies were pushing their fingers in their ears. I banged louder on the frail wood of the coach's top. 'Stop, will you?'

The coach slowed and the angry voices of the driver and postillion were heard roaring to know what was amiss. I clambered over the knees of the man with the beaver hat and his neighbour and jumped down on to the road. I touched my hat to the thin, talkative man.

'Don't talk so glibly of bitterness, brother. It's a queer and terrifying land, one not to be wished on anybody until you yourself have looked into all its corners.'

I slammed the door shut.

'How far back to Tudbury?' I asked the driver.

'Six miles.'

'Moonlea?'

'Cut over those hills there due west. Ten miles, perhaps more.'

'Thank you.' I nodded once again at the thin man. 'As one half-wit to another, boy, keep thinking. Even I hope one day to break through the fog.'

I walked slowly off the road and towards the path that led west. I gave only one short glance at the coach as it rolled again along the straight climbing road.

21

Even before I reached the summit of the hill from which I would be able to see Moonlea I saw the heavy smoke cloud which showed that the foundries had resumed work. On the hill's top, I sat down to rest, still twitching with anger at the quirk of mind that had sent me hurtling out of the coach and brought my steps back to a place that I wished only to forget. Below me were the four cottages of which the one on the extreme right was Katherine Brier's. The sight of it caused me a sharp ache. A plume of light smoke hung above its chimney. From the other three cottages no smoke came. They looked quite deserted. I debated whether or not I should call in to see the Briers there and then. By now Katherine would probably have heard that I had been freed and the sight of me would not cause her too fierce a shock or mood of distress. But I had no stomach to face her or Mrs Brier or anyone who would have the wish to go poking deep into me and find out how I thought and felt after being lifted from the ditch of killing shadows in which John Simon still lay. I jumped with an oath to my feet and turned sharp right to the carriageway that would lead me into Moonlea.

I passed The Leaves After the Rain. The place had changed in no way. Along the right-hand wall of the big front yard horses were still tethered and, in tidy heaps at regular intervals, was soldiers' equipment. Three soldiers, their scarlet jackets off, were seated on one of the window sills. It crossed my mind that Abel might be playing for safety, might be unwilling for that reason to have public contact with anyone who had fallen under the eye of the law, even someone like myself at whom the law had taken a second quick look, about whom it had had a second clement thought, causing it to blink and say it had only been joking. I did not look at the soldiers and sauntered past.

The main street of Moonlea presented a striking sight. Along the pavement moved occasional soldiers, but there was no air of caution or urgency about them. They were clearly conscious that whatever danger or disease might once have threatened the tranquillity or mental health of the iron town had now passed. But in the street itself was a great convoy of carts filled with furniture and smaller domestic articles. The first cart I came to and into which I peeped had two small babies asleep in baskets that had been placed between the legs of a table. I approached a man who had come to the side of the cart. He pulled at a brownish woollen covering that one of the children had dragged up over its face. He muttered some words about the trouble he had always had with children. I asked him what was the reason for all the activity I saw from one end of the long street to the other. He said they were moving in to take the place of workers who had left for reasons he knew nothing of. Then he turned sullenly on his heel and spoke no more. I walked curiously from one cart to another, watching the people who were grouped around them but asking no more questions. I heard my name called. I turned and saw a sergeant walking quickly towards me. He put his hand on my shoulder and took up a fistful of my coat cloth. He asked me if my name was Leigh.

'That's my name.'

'You left Tudbury Castle this morning?'

'You people ought to know that.'

'I don't want any insolence.'

'And I don't want any pawing. Get away from me, for God's sake. I left Tudbury with a pardon and a few shillings for all the fun I had given you boys in letting you land me at the foot of the gibbet. That means I've ceased to be a criminal. So keep your hands off me.'

'You'd be well advised to keep your temper. You've been lucky once. The second time may be less pleasant.'

'You're enjoying this. I can see that. You must have been short of somebody to put the fear of hell up for days past. But where I've just come from I overfed my fears and they burst and died. It's a pity that couldn't happen to all people who tremble at the sight of you performers. I may not look it, friend, but I am now fearless and you strike me as plain comical, no more, no less.'

'We're watching you.'

'Stop watching me. Watch somebody else who's liable to blanch at the touch of your eye. From now on I'll make a very poor victim.'

'Move out of here.'

'What for?'

'Moonlea doesn't want you. You can only find trouble here.'

I watched his big red face with interest.

'What did you say?'

'I said you can find only trouble here.'

'What do you think I've been finding up to now? I don't need an invitation to leave here. I just called in here to tell you and the other defenders of the right how glad I am to be seeing the last of you. Radcliffe seems to have things well in

329

hand. By the way, was it he who gave you orders to welcome me back with this little warning?'

'That's no business of yours. Take my counsel, harpist. You're still a learner as far as trouble is concerned.'

He left me. I divided myself into the usual zones of fear and disgust. The drilled efficient vindictiveness for which these uniformed men stood was still something for which my mind and body had not even the rudiments of an answer. I was thinking of that point when, about fifty yards ahead, I saw Lemuel. Even at that distance I saw him change colour. He had a soldier on each side of him. He plucked the sleeve of the soldier on his right. He then turned swiftly around and walked in the direction of his shop. I followed, half running, calling Lemuel's name. By the time I reached his door he had disappeared inside leaving the two soldiers on dumb truculent guard on each side.

'I only wanted to tell him not to feel alarmed,' I said. 'I hate alarm. Tell him to be serene and stop regarding me as the signal for a sprint. Tell him I bear no malice. I'm too tired to bear anything more than an inch or two. I just wanted to know what he's got planted for next spring in that rotting compost he carries about between his ears in lieu of a mind. That was all. If you two can work out the code of signals he uses pass it on to him.'

I wandered about Moonlea for an hour more, greeting and being greeted, mostly by people who had no wish to give me more than a perfunctory smile and a handwave. Then as night began to fall I made my way to the cottage of the Briers.

Mrs Brier and Davy wept helplessly at the sight of me. Davy laid aside his eternal basket-making and sat at my knees and listened to me as I put wind into a great galleon

330

of lies about the strange places to which I had been since I had seen him last. Katherine was, as always in the presence of Mrs Brier, impassive and silent. She prepared a huge meal of broth for me, watching me as I ate with bright consuming eyes, mad with a wish to have me alone to speak to. Mrs Brier began to talk to me, scalloping the edges of our dilemma with references to the fine sermons calling for peace and brotherhood that Mr Bowen had preached since the day of our removal. She spoke too of the fine work that had been done by Mr Jarvis the clerk who had gone around the homes of those greatly indebted for rent and bread, mitigating and even, in an exceptional neap tide of goodness, cancelling the debts of those who were willing to let bygones be bygones, renounce all thought of defiance, and resume work at the new rates.

'And some,' I said, 'did not let bygones be bygones?'

'Only a few. And they were people who never seemed properly to have settled down in Moonlea. They moved off.'

'I saw the carts.'

'A lot of carts,' said Davy, smiling.

'Aye, a lot. Looked to me as if somebody might have been tearing out the heart of Moonlea and fitting in another. My eyes might have been a bit too tender, having seen so little for so long, but that's what it looked like to me.'

'Only a few, only a few,' said Mrs Brier obstinately. 'It's nice and peaceful now.' And she continued to talk, warily and with some skill, making her way thoughtfully inch by inch to that centre of the whole theme where her mind had never ceased to be. She waited until Katherine had entered the larder.

'And John Simon?'

'No hope.'

'No hope at all?'

'Not a scrap. He was the one they wanted. I was a decoration.'

She gave a little sob, raised her hand to her mouth, but I could see the relief rise in her eyes just before she turned her head away. I watched her with absolute calm. I was glad that at least the torment of one of our number had been resolved. The weariness of my body was yielding slowly to the warmth of the fire and the feel of food. What small pool of ill will had been distilled from the day's events was evaporating fast. I patted Davy affectionately on the arm and smiled with what I thought was an expression of melancholy understanding at Mrs Brier.

After the meal Mrs Brier and Davy went early to bed. Katherine drew her chair up close to mine. I looked at her with surprise. There was no sorrow or resignation on her face. Her eyes and mouth expressed a hard, almost exultant resolution.

'I'm glad to see you, harpist.' There was something in her tone that unsettled me with a quick inexorable thoroughness.

'Thank you, Katherine. I felt I had to see you before getting out of Moonlea for good.'

She smiled in the way they call wise and I did not like it.

'I never thought they'd hang you, Alan.'

'Why not?' There was a suggestion of contemptuous sureness in her voice that piqued me absurdly.

'You were never more than the trimming. You know that. They knew who the deadly enemy was. John Simon.'

'Trimming? Then why did they hang on to me for so long?'

'They were never quite sure of how the people would take

the conviction of John Simon. For all they knew at the time it might have started a wave of trouble that they could never have ended. So they thought it wise to have someone in reserve, someone harmless to whom they could put on a show of mercy. Mercy's always popular, however small and silly the dose, especially when shown to such an idol of the fools as a minstrel. You are a strange man, harpist, a better man than you think.'

'Oh, I don't know....'

'Yes, you are. You still won't admit to yourself why you came back to Moonlea today. Yet the truth is there for you to look at if you wish. When fate knits a coat for you it spends a lot of love and time making it just your fit and it can't be dragged off as easily as you'd have liked. You'll never be free because you're as much inside John Simon Adams as I am, and it's a queer home to have. And you'll never feel that mercy has been shown to you as long as they continue with their plan to butcher him. When you came to Moonlea this summer there were parts of you growing that had never concerned you before.'

'That's daft, Katherine. I know what you're suffering and I don't want to hurt you. But don't think things about me that are not true. Don't drag me into any dreams you might have. Don't rely on me. There's nothing in me to rely on. Not a fibre of me has changed. I want to be left alone.'

'You are the one who said he had no feeling about the ironmasters, who said all conflict and rebellion were childishness.'

'Not childishness exactly; no concern of mine.'

'But now you hate the ironmasters as we do. You'll deny it, but it's there. If it weren't, you wouldn't have come back to this cottage today.'

'I came here to say goodbye. Don't stir me into any cake of courage and goodness, Katherine. I'd spoil the mixture.'

'You came here because the old roaming harpist you used to be is dead, and you're still too busy crying over his grave to know where you go next. The last breath left his body in that stinking hole where you left John Simon. You might have wanted to get away, to get back to your old freedom, but there'd be no life there for you any more. You came back here because you have no intention of letting John Simon die, of seeing the people who hurt you, Penbury and the rest of them, get off scot free.'

'Now, Katherine,' I stood up, leaned against the mantel-piece, stared down amazed into the blazing fire. 'Grief is a wild strong horse. You're hanging on to its mane and it's taking you for a long painful ride. Let it go and be at peace, for God's sake. You don't know me as I know myself. I want a dark solitary corner, and I'll find one. You and John Simon belong on your particular kind of summit. The air would be too cold for me to breathe up there. John Simon's finished. The movement he led has fallen into pitiful fragments. Nobody'll lift a finger to help him. Just bite your lip and forget him. You've had a long enough training in regret. You won't find it hard.'

'It's my regrets that are finished. I'm not being patient any more. I'm answering back, as loudly as I can, and you are going to help me. Tonight, at half-past eleven, after the last patrols have gone by, Eddie Parr, the Humphries brothers and three others are coming here. They have a plan to get John Simon out of Tudbury, alive. You'll help them. There are certain things about that castle that they must know and don't know yet. You are the only one who can help them.'

334

'Katherine, I'm asking you this as seriously as I can.' My voice was solemn as a tombstone. 'You can't rely on me. There's nothing in me that even I can rely on. I can't even trust my own teeth to bite into the right thing at the right time. All I feel at the moment is a gladness that I'm not going to die. What I feel about John Simon is still a black numb patch. When the colour and feeling come back into it it'll ache like the devil. But my heart and nerve have been beaten to a pulp. Not even by a miracle could I lift a finger to help John Simon.'

'You will, though, you will. You've been remade all over, harpist.'

'Oh Christ...' And I was going to embark once again on a round of querulous protest when there was a knock on the door. I drew my breath in sharply and was terrified. Katherine's words had drawn me tauter than I had imagined.

'You're like a ghost,' she said. 'This isn't Tudbury. You're free. Anyway, you think you are, and that's a good start.'

She opened the door. The tall servant girl, Phoebe, came in. I remembered that she was the girl who had been friendly with Wilfie Bannion and I expected her, at the sight of me, to burst into a flood of tears, I being alive and Wilfie being dead. But she looked at me with a calm intentness as if I provided her with matter of great interest for her thoughts. About her, as about Katherine, hung that air of dispassionate resolution which confused me. I was in a mood that could have done with a shower of endless compassion. I did not like this bold objectivity.

'You've altered but little, harpist,' said Phoebe pensively, as if she had right in front of her mind's eye a full portrait of me emaciated, me dead. Her lips trembled slightly as if she could not decide to give me the details of these portraits.

'And John Simon?'

'Well, within the limits that you know.'

'Good. I have a message for you.'

'From whom?'

'Penbury himself.'

'Thought he was dead or dying.'

'He nearly was. He seemed to lose all interest, then he came to life again. Funny how people do that, some people, anyway. Others don't, do they?'

'No. I don't want to see him. I want to get some food together, say goodbye to the people I know, and then home by way of the North star to nibble the bark of whatever tree it is that makes a man incapable of remembrance.'

'There is no such tree. Nor should there be one. That is the only valuable thing about being a man, remembrance, and making the spear of memory hard and sharp.'

'You're full of programmes. Everybody's full of programmes. Why can't I find somebody as cold and empty as I am to exchange horrible echoes with?'

'Penbury knows you're back. He was told less than five minutes after you arrived at Moonlea. He must have taken quite a fancy to you.'

'They say huntsmen shed quite a few tears over the fox. When does he want to see me?'

'Tonight.'

'What hurry is he in? Is death knocking as hard as that upon him? Won't tomorrow do?'

'He doesn't believe in tomorrow any more. His heart is feeble. You'd better go and see him. He made a great fuss to get you free, so they tell me. You can lose nothing.'

'All right. I'll go.'

336

I picked my hat up from the chair in the corner on to which I had thrown it. At that moment I had no intention of seeing either Katherine or her cottage again.

'Goodbye,' I said.

'Till about midnight,' said Katherine.

I left without another word. As I walked through Moonlea's main street a few of the carts that had stood there earlier in the day were still in the same position. Men and women swung lanterns and shouted directions that seemed to make little sense to me or to them. The carts were being unloaded and the furniture and other articles being carried into the empty houses. A bitter noisy quarrel between two men who were laying claim to the same house was going on and abated only when a group of soldiers sauntered unobtrusively by on the other side of the road. I saw other groups of soldiers in the thicker shadows of the side alleys.

I approached the Penbury home by the back entrance which I had always used. They were a long time answering. There were only a few rooms of the house lighted. Below me in Moonlea the furnaces were being tapped and the great flames of red and blue leaped up over the eastern side of the town. The smell of them was faint up on the hillside where I stood. The door opened. The old butler Jabez stood before me. His face was impressed, his lower lip hanging with surprise. Clearly, having nearly been hung had put me up so high, or cast me down so low, in the estimation of this man that he found it hard to express himself with me as easily as he had done in days gone by. As he ushered me into the kitchen and into the presence of the prim ageing maid whom I had met before, there was an uneasy smile upon his face, loosely hung for quick removal, as if his master had decided to take up social relations with a clothed baboon. I was given a pewter pot of strong ale with foam upon it smooth and cool as marble. The maid also pressed me to some cakes while Jabez went off to another part of the house to find out what was to be done about me. I made no attempt to be pleasant. I found the atmosphere constrained and hurtful. I sat on a stool, my back resting against a huge, dark-brown sideboard, and I chewed absorbedly.

Jabez returned and beckoned me to follow him. The maid was looking at me sorrowfully and I relented in my churl-ishness.

'Do you remember the little fiddler, Felix?' I asked her, and we both laughed. 'There was a man in the gaol who reminded me a lot of Felix. He was very young and very earnest.'

'Was he a... a prisoner too, Mr Leigh?'

'No, he was a minister of the Lord. A Mr Mayhew, a rosy, smiling young man whose parents loved him dearly and made the whole universe fit him cosily like a greased glove. His job was to prepare us to be hanged.'

Jabez supported the maid as she began to sway over the table.

'You shouldn't say things like that, right out, all of a sudden, to the innocent and inexperienced, Mr Leigh. You don't know what it may bring on.'

'Tell her I'm sorry. I really am sorry about making Agnes or whatever her name is rock like that. Once I was very delicate about these things, kept shut up for years on end if I thought that any word of mine would bring a bruise. But you see how it is with me now, blurting things out and not caring a damn for the torment of my fellows. This phase has made my manners corrupt, and no mistake. That reminds me, Jabez, speaking of corruption. I'm sorry you didn't get that steward's job at Plimmon's.'

'Steward? Plimmon's?'

'You know. They told me that you gave him all sorts of interesting information about me that didn't help me at all. Didn't help you either by the look of it. You're still a butler and I'm still a harpist. But we live, boy. That's the important thing.'

'Don't believe those things, Mr Leigh. I didn't say anything about you. I know nothing against you.'

'Only a beginner would let that stop him from working up a full head of evidence, Jabez. You should have heard Lemuel. Now there's a man who'll reach the very top by doing no more than wheeling truth to the boneyard at a low whistle from his master. Get yourself a barrow, boy, and a key to the boneyard. There'll be no lack of profitable trips. Don't look so worried, man. I've no intention of hurting you. You can lie about me to the top of your bent and I won't even charge a commission. I can imagine some, fiercer ones than I, who would take you in earnest and be worried about the strange shapes you make, who would take pleasure in arranging you in a bow knot around that black memorial pillar to Penbury's father down in the cemetery, but I am only interested in picking out the rhythm of events as they come in a steady stinging hail upon my skull. One day I will play an impression of all this on my harp, with the strings dyed jet black and cut in three places especially for the job.'

We had arrived at the door of the room where I had seen Penbury on the midnight occasions when I had played him his sedative melodies. Jabez slipped me in, then withdrew. The room was not in darkness as it had been before. A lamp, turned down, gave a faint light from a far corner. The ebb and flow of flames from the furnaces could be seen on the broad glass panes of the window. Penbury was sitting in the same chair which he had occupied on that first night months before. He appeared to have shrunk considerably, his hair had lost the last few shreds of darkness. His eyes were protrusive, still sleeplessly intelligent, but even so they did not seem to give any convincing show of life to the sunken devastated features of his face. His body was tensely drawn up, as if expectant from second to second of some new and crippling hurt. He beckoned me to a chair and I sat down. When he spoke he did so very slowly, approaching each word as if it were a separate world of thought and effort.

'They have done terrible things to you, harpist.'

'I think so.'

'I did my best for you. For a long time now things have been getting out of my hands. I can see myself being one of the useless rejects of my own age, like you, harpist. That is a rather amusing idea, don't you think?'

'It doesn't amuse me. I'm in a poor state for laughter. No one should be rejected. No one should be hurt. Who's so big he has the right to put anybody on the rack?'

'Right, quite right. But we've failed, you and I. And the rack-makers probably think they have as much right to make a living and ply their curious craft as we. I, too pensively, undecided; you, too errant and idle, both unfit for conflict. There was something about the ambitions of my father that had a vague rough poetry and I consoled myself with that for a time. But there is no beauty in the sound of fist on face or whip on back. There is a mixture of pride and cleverness and utter clarity in these Radcliffes and Plimmons that will make of them some superlative and horrifying animal before their days on earth are done. They'll be deaf as stones and they won't hear the dreadful drying rustle of other people's lives

340

at all. It's cost me a lot, not being like them, but I'm glad I wasn't. Tenderness is the whole of life, tenderness is the only science worthy of pursuit. I'm glad I've been stricken into silence and uselessness. It would be bad for the earth if all dissenters were as you and I, harpist, soft-cored, courteous, haunted by a sense of lost and recoverable beauty. Fortunately or unfortunately, there will always be John Simon Adams, changing his name, his precise longing and his mode of agony in each generation, making his poetry from mad resistance, almost numb with confidence in his own courage and rightness, chanting the unspoiled promise of our kind, dying with good cheer to shame the plunderers, the ungentle and the bad. I say fortunately because this fanatical identity with the multitude may wreak some miracle of decency among the great herd and its scoundrelly drovers. I say unfortunately, because all this endurance and greatness may be doing no more than prolonging a note of fruitless pain. How is Adams, harpist?'

'As you say. They'll not make him wince.'

'I have often thought of you, often, too often during these weeks. Even when I was at my sickest, deliriously ill, my mind gripped with my narrow concern for my own thinning hide I kept seeing you and that wretched hangman. I thought at first that the insistence of the image was some kind of harbinger of death, like a raven, but it must have given me some sort of strength to make my affirmation on your behalf.'

'I'm glad you believed in my innocence.'

'You mean you didn't kill that fellow Bledgely?'

'Of course I didn't. Are you saying you helped to free me thinking me guilty the whole time?'

'What is the difference? When men start putting their

hates to the test, harpist, butchery becomes mechanical and meaningless. One tries to rescue the few things and people that have individual significance. That's all one can do, except that short cut through the hemlock field.'

'And John Simon? You wouldn't stir a finger to help him?'

'Not even a finger. I have worn out one half of my reserves of strength for you. Had I exerted myself for Adams I would have attained nothing more than a word of reproof and you would both have gone up on the roll of martyrs. No, I felt no great qualms about Adams. When men set up as symbols, harpist, they must be prepared for treatment which will be rather less or rather more than human. But I confess that the thought of him waiting there torments me at night as much as it ever did. There must be something in my imagination especially susceptible to the rub of this particular bit of barbarism. I'll be glad when he's gone. Then my dreams will either vanish altogether or wear a smile. Do you dream about it too, harpist?'

'I only came out this morning. I haven't yet experienced the dreams that go with liberation. In there I was not bothered. I had John Simon. He always had a way of making me feel that I had it in me to be fearless and full of contempt for all that was alien to us.'

'You hated to leave him?'

'I try to think I acted for the best.'

'You are not convinced?'

'No. No part of me is convinced, more's the pity.'

'You will leave here now?'

'Tomorrow.'

'I'll let you have some money.'

'Thank you. It may help you with those dreams to think of me flashing gold in the world's eye.'

His eyes turned to the large gleaming harp in the corner. 'Have you a wish to play?' he asked.

'There isn't even the ghost of music in my hands. There may never be again. Latterly I have met too many men who were more than expert at mutilating the spirit.'

'Have no fear. You've been bitterly struck, but the ache will pass. The spirit absorbs everything, makes everything its food: it's an idiot thing that doesn't know when it's had enough. Mutilation of the urge to fashion loveliness it gobbles up as a special titbit. Would you like that harp for yourself? When you go there will be no one to play it.'

'Too big.' I walked to the door. 'Too heavy.' I saw his eyes turn away from the lamp, towards the flame troubled shadow that pressed upon the window. Then his head fell slightly forward. 'Goodbye then, and I wish you much happiness.'

'Goodbye, harpist.'

Back in the corridor I saw Jabez at the further end of it, crouched and motioning to me with his hand and head. I thought he might be wanting to apologise to me once again for having passed that information on to Plimmon and I pouted my lips outward as if to tell Jabez that he was to give the matter no more thought, that we were all, with varying degrees of backside, subject to this strange mania of desiring a golden throne; in his case a throne of respite from the tedium of being a butler, suave and soft footed, in mine, the throne of a passionate interest in finding something or another that would make my mood fixed, painless and immutable. But Jabez kept signalling and I walked up the corridor towards him. He opened the door near which he had been standing and, mumbling something which I did not completely understand, pushed me into its recess as he

343

tapped lightly on one of its panels. I let myself be pushed without resistance. I had no wish to hasten my departure from the house. Outside was cold darkness, merciless understanding, the need to move or be recognisably still, the urge to some decision that would grin at me like an idiot or slash at me with a realised sense of my deep, long-laboured significance. Even during those few seconds when I entered into the thick shadow of that part of the corridor where Jabez stood I could see the face of Katherine, hear her voice, feel my own wretched writhing helplessness in the face of her, her way of making you feel that the future as interpreted and demanded by her was inescapable, wanted, magnetic with the angry wisdom of her projected longings, however formidably foul its first touch might taste on your lips.

The room into which I entered must have been lighted by several lamps of stronger power than any I had seen before. Their brilliance hit my eyes dizzy, and I paused, half blind, at the doorway for a few seconds, breaking my vision into this new discipline. It was a room that had streaks of gold leaf let into the wall against a smooth stone of delicate grey. The carving of the woodwork, of an intricate fantastic beauty, had an oriental air. The chairs were short-legged, sumptuous, deeply cushioned. Helen Penbury was sitting on one of them. A low table with a top of gleaming yellow metal stood in front of her. On it was a tray bearing a silver coffee pot and tiny cups. I sat down on one of the chairs at which she nodded. I let myself down carefully. I was at home fully sitting on the ground. I could not approach without disquietude the tall formal chairs that seemed currently to be the fashion in urban communities, but these yielding dwarfish articles struck me as quaint and I had to smile as I reached bottom and found myself so sensuously cosy. I ran my hands delightedly over the velvet cushions that had vivid black and white designs worked on them, designs that contained the motive theme of veiled women.

She passed me the tiny cup of glimmering jet-black liquid. The first sip bit at my palate and she laughed at the way I jumped away from it.

'I never had a taste of that before. It's got a fierce wise edge on it.'

'It keeps one awake.'

'You mean there are people who wish to keep putting off sleep?'

'Many.'

'They must find their days varied and charming.'

'Not always. They might find dreams bad and unwelcome.'

'I suppose they could.'

'My father has dreams.'

'He said something about them.'

'About you and Adams being hanged. He used to wake up screaming. He got to a point where he did not want to sleep at all.'

'So he drank this to keep his dreams at the side of the bed. Handy, that. But the best way not to have screaming dreams about the hanged is not to hang them. That might sound simple-witted, but I'm simple.'

'Yes, of course.'

'But he's all right now that I'm free?'

'He still broods about Adams.'

'But John Simon doesn't warrant a scream?'

'Yes, he does. My father has a greater hate of crude violence than any man living. His whole being is a vote against the need for agony on earth.'

'He should have been in that castle. He'd have done something more than vote.'

'Was it bad?'

'The very headquarters of agony. Wet, dark, and the broth was horrible. And the gaoler was a sentimental madman who made my coat wet even faster than the walls when he recalled the clean days of his virginity. The nights were dreamless because the brain grew so weary of thinking about that broth it didn't have a breath left over for visions.'

'Poor harpist. You must have suffered.'

'Oh, I don't know... I'm the lucky one. I have a way of thinking about other things. It's worse for John Simon. He had tried to do something and failed, and there's nothing worse than that for keeping the mind tied to a ring in the floor waiting for the axe. I've never tried to do anything. So the man with the rope would not have been achieving much one way or the other with me except to make the place a bit quieter. But it would have been easier if we had a room like this to do the waiting in, with all those gold streaks in the wall and all this softness for the body.' The coffee flicked some nerve of anger in me. 'Why do you have to keep such places as that to go shoving people into?'

'We didn't invent that castle, harpist. We're sorry you were put there. We're sorry it was grim, but it was something we had little say in.'

'I'm sorry too. But for a second I caught a smell of that place once again, even in this hollowed jewel of a room, and it made me mad, blind mad, against you, your father, your husband-to-be, and all the other folk who might have had a hand in doing these things to John Simon and me. Just bear with me for a moment while I get this off my chest. I've been trying not to think about it. But the whole memory of it, one

346

of these fine black hours, is going to come right over the rim of me, and it'll make me scream louder than your father has ever done. Perhaps not with the mouth but with the heart, and I'm afraid of what I'll do then because I've never been terribly and earnestly committed to the job of loathing before now.' I tensed my body to raise myself from the chair and go, then changed my mind and relaxed my limbs with a low groan. 'That's better. It's this coffee that did it, slapping the promise of sleep black and blue. Tell me, why did you want to see me again? Why didn't you let me go without another thought?'

'Because I wanted to tell you how glad I was you accepted that offer of freedom. The earth would have been heard to mutter sadly in its many autumns if you had been allowed to perish in that prison.'

'I like that about the muttering earth. You've heard it too. First the little shudder like teeth clicking, then the brief words as if the earth cannot really bring itself to believe that such a life is going on.'

'This little bit of devastation won't put you off your stride. You'll come to a rich flower, harpist. You have it within you to make your days glow like this room. You have something that will disconcert life a lot more than it will disconcert you. And that's good. There are too many of us who agree to dance to prearranged rhythms.'

'Plimmon is such a rhythm?'

'There are things I can do as his wife that I could not do otherwise. And not all bad things either. There have to be some who'll keep themselves free from hatreds. I think there should be garden borders of men and women allowed to exist only for the fragrance and sum of rapture they commu-nicate.'

347

'There are too many for whom the flower-beds would have no point, who have not been taught to know the meaning of fragrance, whose rapture drowns in the mud. If you're thinking of me as such a bloom, I don't smell it at the moment.'

'Get as far from here as you can. Even in those mountains of the north where you say your home is, sounds and echoes of all this hurt and squalor would reach you through the years, causing you grief and regret.'

'And why should I be immune? Why should anyone be utterly secure when some are so utterly doomed?'

'If we have sinned, preserving you might be our way of mixing atonement with pleasure.' She smiled at me but my face as I looked across at her was consciously unmoved.

'That should console me, but it doesn't. Let the dose be shared, I say. Filth will endure while some never see it.' I looked around the warm rich perfect room, in something like pain at the thought of how strangely and swiftly I had come to know it, how swiftly and strangely it would within a few minutes be left and cease to be known. 'It's good, this immunity. But no one on earth is worth it, no one.'

She rose and went to a small walnut-wood table in a corner, opened a drawer that slid beneath her hand without a sound and drew out a long white envelope.

'This will help,' she said.

She handed it to me and I took it, weighing it curiously in my hand.

'What's in it?'

'Money and a passage to America. There you might find yourself a new beginning. Here you'll be badgered until you fall. You've lost your struggle. From now on you are only a nuisance who will grow shabbier and quieter. In the law's eyes you will be a species of vagrant; for Plimmon and possibly for me when my crust hardens, a species of game to be hunted with more or less vigour.'

'And if the crust does not harden, if you too need a change of root?'

'Ships run for all. And if I looked hard enough for my kind of soil I'd probably find you there.'

I got to my feet.

'That isn't a promise, is it?'

'Not even the promise of one. The crust will probably harden and a root as well-tended as mine will probably want to lie still.

'I think so too, and I'm glad. A promise is a gag in the mouth of all the days to come. And I like my days to sing. I've never promised or been promised more than a tune or a scrap of food or simple loving. There can be no promises. Life kicks and sooner or later we land with fewer teeth than we had before. You've been good. I'll remember you. I'll think of you. If ever I come face to face with you again, I may look quaint and quaint may be my words, but in my mind I'm sure there'll be a wonderful chant of gladness. I think some portion of my fervent nights will always be dedicated to you. I'll say no more than that. Goodbye.'

Jabez showed me out of the house. I crouched in the doorway for a while to let my body make terms with the cold. Then, grasping the long white envelope, I made my way towards Katherine's cottage, with only one of my legs and one-half of my will wanting to.

22

There was no light shining in any of the cottage windows as I approached. I knocked quietly and Katherine opened to me. There was no light inside save that which was given off by the well-banked fire. In the half-breached dark I could make out the forms of about ten men, some standing, some seated. The small kitchen seemed crowded. I recognised the man who came forward to shake my hand. It was Eddie Parr. The rest of the men came around too, adding their excited sounds of greeting and congratulation, but there was an especial quality about the sound and touch of Eddie. There was a sensitiveness, an undaunted alertness of limb and nerve in him that made me feel that life would not be forever the dirty and oafish lump it had been to date. I was glad to see him, with a gladness that gave a richly singing tone to my insides. I sat down by his side near the fire. Katherine was going to say something when she leaned her head to one side and hushed us to silence. I heard nothing for a few seconds then perceived the clump of horses' hooves on the pathway leading up the mountain. We remained still and silent until they had passed.

'They don't usually come as late as this,' said Katherine. 'I suppose the Captain gets a fit occasionally to send a patrol to the top of the mountain to enjoy the view and find out if any ironworker has set fire to his own cottage in any of the surrounding valleys.' There was a savage acridity in her tone.

I moved my stool nearer the fire, resting my head against the warm oak surround. I knew that if anyone were to speak for many minutes in a soft lulling voice I would quickly be asleep. I hoped with a vague pouting in my mind that nothing would be said to make me prickle with fear or uneasiness... I knew from the whole air of the room that the hope was as foolish as any that I had ever entertained. I wondered if Mrs Brier knew about this meeting and, if so, what she felt about it. I was too curious on this point not to ask.

'What about the other people in the house, Katherine?'

'Mrs Brier knows. Each time we meet she lies awake, terrified half to death, with the clothes pulled around her head so that she'll hear nothing. She will not inform. Davy sleeps through it all. He sleeps through everything. Why do you ask? Are you afraid they might give something away?'

'Oh, that didn't worry me at all. I just wondered how they felt, lying there in the dark with all this solemnity lying like a snow bank out here.'

'I see,' said Katherine. Her voice was flat, impatient. She clearly saw no point in my little campaigns of wonder.

'Are we all here?'

'All of us,' said Eddie. 'All except young Benny Cornish who was one of the messengers from the Western valleys. The soldiers caught him yesterday.'

'Where is he now?'

'In one of the cells beneath the court at Moonlea.'

'We'll not let him stay there long. Will you tell them the news, Eddie?'

'No, you do it, Katherine. I think you've got more information than the rest of us.'

'All right then. Friends, the day is near at hand. Many

have grown sick during these weeks of waiting. Many of us had feared that after our first defeat here at Moonlea the cause would go down to silence without even a whimper. I can tell you that we are going to do much more than whimper. Connor, before he was arrested at Manchester, was able to arrange for the delivery of enough arms and ball cartridge to equip five thousand men. You might be wondering how they got to us. Now that they are in the hands of those who will use them it can be told. You know the great convoys of strike breakers and free tenants that Radcliffe and Plimmon organised from the North and East to replace those they hounded from their work and homes. The sight of those long processions of obedient folk with their carts must have been very pleasing to Radcliffe. He would not have been so delighted had he known that in dozens of those carts were concealed guns and ammunition that will make him smart before he's very much older. Longridge and his men from the West, Blakemore and his men from the South, will march on Thursday. They will be linking up with country labourers from the fields between. They will strike at all the towns, trying to get control of as many of them as they can. In the first few days they have agreed to avoid any pitched battle like the plague.'

'Why?' asked a voice from a corner. 'What goes on in the towns doesn't matter so much. Striking at several places is bound to mean splitting the total force. I'm against it. We've got plenty of followers but our number of armed drilled men is small and we've got to keep them together. There are not as many soldiers now as there were when the trouble began. Let Longridge find a place where he thinks he can meet the soldiers on something like equal terms and let him deal with them as soon as he can. Let the soldiers be told too that we

352

have no quarrel with them but that there can be no peace between us and the ironmasters as long as they remain here to terrorise our women and children and keep our best leaders in gaol or hiding or death.'

'There's a lot of sense in that,' said Eddie Parr. 'And many's the long night Longridge and his friends have been splitting their pates about it. Longridge made his final plan on these grounds. First, we've got some guns, plenty of zeal and a knowledge of the land in which we are to move. But we're not an army. Not if Longridge were God could he inspire a proper unity of action and aim in all who'll want to strike a blow against the ironmasters. Second, whatever we might think about the slowness of the Crown and Parliament of this land when it comes to providing redress for those who happen to be hungry and ill-paid, they would break their necks with speed when it came to flinging another ten regiments in here to beat us black and blue and stuff us dumb with cautions. So, even if we could lure the soldiers of Plimmon into some cosy little ravine where we could pour in detachments concealed in the clefts we still would not achieve anything like a victory which would give us much more than a breathing space for a few days. All we can hope to do is to make a tremendous gesture of which the news will travel to every corner of the land. The towns we take we won't be able to hold for long. But for as long as we do hold them we'll show how much better we are at ironworking than we are at soldiering and every foundry will be turning out pikes for those who have no guns and our friends in London will be putting it to the gentlemen in Parliament that since matters have come to such a pass it would be just as well if they took over part of the job at which we have already failed, that is, to knock some sense into the

353

landlords and ironmasters. Even they will pay some attention to working men if it's going to take a military campaign
to shut them up whenever they howl loud enough. Wars are
expensive even to folk who own a whole country.'

'Smash the foundries, I say. They are a dirty pox among
our hills. And such halls as Plimmon's too. If they want to
drag us down to everlasting poverty let's do as much for
them.'

'If we ever do that they'll have to drive us beyond reason
first. Let's hope they won't do that, for all our sakes. Reason
is something no body of men can be without for long without
going around in circles after their own tails. Leave the
foundries alone. Men will always make and want iron long
after they have ceased to make and want men like Radcliffe.
As for Plimmon's hall, let it stand. It's a good rough sketch
of what we'd all like when our present hovels get too small
for our bodies and too laughable for our minds.'

'And John Simon? What are we doing for him?'

'What we always said we'd do. Get him out of Tudbury
Castle, safe and unharmed. As you know, the harpist here
came out of Tudbury this morning on a free pardon. The
judges discovered something that we had always known,
that he had no hand in the killing of Bledgely, and that he
was in no way active as a Radical. We know his heart is with
us. No friend of John Simon Adams could be indifferent to
the plight of our people or hostile to their desires. But he has
always stood aloof in practice. But he's here and can help
us. First I'll outline the plan. Longridge sets great store on it
because he says freeing John Simon, who is not only a leader
we love but absolutely blameless of the crime for which they
propose hanging him, is as important a task as keeping our
wages on a level where they can keep us breathing and

354

human. He is going to concentrate his major force near the village of Mortle, the village standing at the head of that narrow valley with the great black rocks jutting out of the hillsides about five miles north of Tudbury. There are two or three large landlords there, men of might and substance, skilled hands at such manoeuvres as enclosing and evicting who need to be reminded that there should be a difference of status between the earth and the worker who tills it. Longridge will send out reports exaggerating his numbers and giving the impression that he is going to stake all on one immediate decisive battle. The soldiers will rush up, draining Tudbury of its forces. Then a detachment of Longridge's men will storm Tudbury Castle and free John Simon. Is that right, Katherine?'

'Right. According to the County Sheriff he's to die next Monday. This is Tuesday. If we fail to bring him out of that castle on Thursday night everything fails. What do you say, harpist?'

I shot my head up startled. I had been listening to what had been said, but remotely and never dreaming that by the tug of a single abrupt phrase I would be pulled into the crazy heart of the astonishing deliberations that were going on around me. I was tongue-tied, pecking around in my mind for some words of friendly entreaty which would tell them that I was with them with all my soul in all they wished to do, for all the wretched of the earth, for John Simon, but that I was not involved in their struggles, that I had already had enough, that they should let me stay just where I was, my head cosily pressed against the hot, sweet-smelling woodwork of the chimney place, until tyranny and revolt had placed their last nought and their last cross in their everlasting game. Then they could wake me and tell me I was free to go my way. But I said nothing of the kind. When I spoke my voice was calm, carrying, its tone as replete with brutal assumptions as any I had heard.

'There are not many soldiers in the castle,' I said. 'And they look a pretty lazy lot of kites. But you can be sure of one thing. A frontal attack on the place will be hard and costly. The castle is on a neat bare hill and as the soldiers squint out at you they will probably show themselves good at killing.'

'John Simon Adams strikes us as being more important than any of those considerations,' said Katherine. 'Were he engaged in this venture he would not count the cost to himself or to others. Say something that will help us and don't go arguing the case for sleep and self-defeat. Did that free pardon from the ironmaster break your spirit, harpist?'

'It broke nothing. I have never been enough among men to make the spirit breakable. I shall learn, but slowly, so slowly you will leave me far behind, or gladly choke me with the dust you raise with your racing feet. But I know something about that castle, something that might help you and John Simon. And about John Simon, there is more than one mind here that is black with pity for him.'

'Granted, harpist, granted. You are a stranger among us, and your ways are such we must be patient with you. But about the castle...'

'I don't know how reliable this is going to be. But there was an old man, a drunken old clown called Bartholomew Clark, a gaoler in the wing where they kept John Simon and me. It was a free and easy sort of place and this Bartholomew treated us well. I remember his telling us something about a door, a small door, ivy-covered, about forty yards to the west of the main entrance. It leads into a

356

tunnel, now nearly blocked up with stones, at the end of which is a door, long disused, which leads one into the corridor where we were lodged. Old Bartholomew was a hell of a boy for the flesh and now and again he used to nip out of this door for a drink or a woman without notifying the guards.'

'Isn't that section of the gaol patrolled by the troops?'

'Sometimes I heard soldiers, but not often. Off and on they got frightened that Bartholomew was getting lax and a detachment of foot soldiers came marching around. They did a lot of fussing and shouting, but they did not seem to take the matter very seriously. You know that the castle hadn't been used as a prison at all for a year before Plimmon decided to show off as a hammer unto traitors and put us in there. Bartholomew was a caretaker and they didn't think we'd be there long enough to merit any change in the arrangements. Old Bartholomew took kindly to me. He set the tone. He was a clown, as I said, a clown full of feelings that had grown mouldy with age and drink.'

'You talk of clowns as if there were some kind of comedy in this for John Simon Adams,' said Katherine. 'You seem at times to forget him.'

'At no time do I forget him.'

'Will this Bartholomew be of any assistance? Does he sympathise?'

'Only in ways that no one else can follow. In any case, Bartholomew is pretty well near death's door. He might recover. He's a drunken and delirious man, and God knows what he might take death's door for. I hope he will get well. A new head gaoler would be less easy to deal with if we did manage to get in.'

'What about that outer door? How is that to be tackled?'

'If I know anything about that castle, that door, covered with ivy, should not be strong. A few men would not find it hard to get through. Once in, John Simon's cell wouldn't be much more than twenty yards away and a thick wall and Bartholomew's room between you and the nearest soldier, unless you decide to break down the door into the corridor at the very moment when they are organising a patrol towards it. It may work. At least it's worth trying, and even if it fails it'll cost you a lot less men than putting in an attack against the main entrance.'

'If it does fail,' said Lewis Andrews, 'Longridge's men can still be ready to go up the hill before Monday. The harpist's plan sounds mad to me, but he's the only one of us who knows anything about the castle so you might as well consider what he says.'

'Right,' said Eddie Parr. 'How many men do you think will be needed, Alan?'

'Six or eight.'

'You'll be with us, of course?'

I gave no immediate answer. The fire in the chimney place collapsed and the burst of flame made Katherine's face clear to me.

'It's his plan,' said the rumbling voice of the man in the far corner. 'Without him we couldn't move an inch. And whether he says so or not, he'd like the chance of saving John Simon. Are you sure of the position of that door?'

'I think I could take you to it. Twice Bartholomew told me that when he came through the door out of the castle he could see right across to Slaney's gin shop. I'll be in Tudbury before Thursday. I'll make sure.'

'Thursday night then.'

'How will the moon be?'

358

'Utterly absent.'

'Good enough.'

'And there's another thing,' I said, 'you talk of attracting the soldiers away from Tudbury when you make the attempt on the castle. That's a good move. Even I see the point of it. But I think two good diversions would do even better than one. What about a raid on Moonlea?'

'That's been thought of, harpist, and arranged. There's Benny Cornish in the cells under the court and Mr Jarvis's long list of debt records. We should do something about those things.'

'The man I'm mainly thinking of,' I said, 'is Radcliffe. Since that trial I've had his face in my mind a lot, and it's not a good face to have lodged in such a tender part of one for days on end. Most of that jury looked a deaf lot of sods but none deafer than Mr Radcliffe. He sniffed impatiently every time a new witness or a new point cropped up to delay the moment of judgement for which he had been waiting. I wouldn't like Moonlea and Mr Radcliffe unscathed. He's a great teacher of men, Mr Radcliffe. The lessons he wishes to apply are hard and precise. He would benefit from having the rod laid as hard across his own fingers.'

'You're learning a few lessons yourself, harpist.'

'A man pinned under a rock will show bruises, if not understanding.'

'Agreed, Katherine?' asked Eddie Parr. 'The final decision in this should rest with you.'

'I'm not agreed,' said Katherine, and I could feel all the men in the room turn their heads in her direction. 'What is there in the face and voice of this harpist that beguiles people and softens their wits? For a few moments here he had us all nodding agreement with his simple antics. I don't fully trust him. I don't think there's any evil in him, any will to betray. Nothing like that. But most of the time he's out in a playful pasture of his own, and this is no time for play. He doesn't yet understand the nature of the men we are facing. He must be a complete fool to think that we would suspend our own plans in favour of this crack-brained scheme of his. That talk of unguarded doors in castle walls and father-like gaolers sounded fantastic and suspicious to me. The harpist is as much a citizen of fairyland as of this earth. That Bartholomew is just such a silly sot as he described him as being, but he took a long time becoming father-like with me when I went down on my knees for weeks on end trying to get a permit to see John Simon.'

'There is a door,' I said as coolly as I could, 'and it isn't used by fairies.'

'All right. Let the harpist's plan proceed. But I insist on one thing: that while he's groping among the ivy and getting in fraternal touch with Bartholomew our men shall carry out their original plan of storming the main gate and reaching John Simon that way.'

'At the same time?'

'At exactly the same time. In addition to giving us some slight chance of success it will also distract attention from the harpist's capers on the flank.'

'Shall I send word to Longridge of this?'

'There's no need. All he needs to do is act precisely as has been arranged.' She stirred up the dying fire restlessly with her shoe. 'The harpist's suggestion is a private one. I wouldn't like to ask anyone to risk his life supporting it. He might only have dreamed of that magic doorway.'

'I'm with him,' said Eddie. 'Five of us will go with the harpist. Lewis, Mathew, Ellitt, Wilkins, are you willing too?'

360

'Certainly,' came the voice of Mathew Humphries answering for the rest.

'Right. We'll meet at various points along the road from Moonlea to Tudbury. I'll let you know definitely about places and times tomorrow.' Some of the men stood up from their stools and chairs. 'We'll have to be careful. When the ironmasters and the soldiers learn that Longridge is on the move they'll have a lynx watching out in every bush.'

The men made ready to disperse. Katherine opened the door slightly, then shut it hastily again.

'The horsemen are coming down. Stay here until they are well past. Patrolling so late must mean that the gentlemen are getting nervous again.'

We waited several minutes, listening to the jingle and clatter of the passing troop. Two of the cavalrymen were singing softly, some air of lovers that I found pleasing to my ears. Then, in the fresh silence, in ones and twos, the men who had been sitting in the kitchen made their way from the cottage, starting out in different directions along the hillside. Only Katherine, Eddie Parr and I remained.

'You two can stay here,' said Katherine. 'John Simon's old bed will do for you.'

'Thank you, Katherine,' said Eddie. 'But I don't feel much like sleeping. I'd like to stay here and look at the fire for a bit.'

'You'll find some logs in that box you're sitting on, harpist. Build the fire up. These days, looking into fires is as wise a thing to do as any. Anything that persuades the hours to pass is good.'

I stood up, lifted three or four of the larger logs from the box and replenished the fire.

'And, Alan,' said Katherine as she turned to enter her

361

bedroom, 'I want to thank you.'

'For what?'

'For coming back here, for wanting to help. You could easily have slipped away and known no further danger.'

'You knew I'd come back. I didn't. I tried not to. I went up to Penbury's. I talked to the old man. He looks as if his wick is more than burned down to half. He said he goes nearly mad when he wakes up from dreams of John Simon being hung. He said things about tenderness that filled me with a weeping wind. So you see how the bits of mercy in their dark corners are shaking off the cramp and preparing to come together into one majestic whole. He's sensitive, this Penbury, and can't stand these crude things. His daughter entertained me too in a small and lovely room the like of which I had never seen before, save in frenzies of longing when the winter rains have made me more than usually comfortless and sick of the earth. She gave me a ticket to America.'

'America? The question I asked before I ask again. What kind of spell do you exercise over people, harpist? Why should they want you as far away as that?'

'She talked of my root and of how it might improve with a change of pot. She doesn't think much of the soil I'm likely to find in this land from now on. It was funny at first to hear myself treated as if I were a kind of shrub. But I got used to it. I drank some coffee and took the ticket. Listening to you tonight I got an idea about it. On Thursday, if the gods and the stars have a scrap of mercy and gumption we shall see John Simon free. At freedom he will be full of hatred and the need to be avenged. Even vengeance will be a dangerous and terrible thing for him. If he comes out of Tudbury castle erect and breathing that's the nearest he'll come to not being

362

utterly defeated. He's done enough. Let the world rent itself another chopping block. He owes something to himself and to you. What if you and he should make tracks for that ship to America, Katherine?'

She said nothing for a while. I could hear her fingers tapping lightly nervously on the woodwork of the door against which she leaned.

'What do you think of that, Eddie?' I asked.

'I think it's a notion of great beauty and one that brings me as near to tears as Penbury's talk of tenderness brought you. We won't win for a long time to come. It's as Connor always said whenever some of us wanted to go out and start breaking things up right and left. We are still shovelling the things we have known and which will one day make us wise into a single heap. The blade and handle of our sword are still not one. That Connor would have persuaded a wounded lion to be hopelessly serene. This is a small land and Plimmon will not be content until he has John Simon under a part of it. Let others rise and take some of the blows for a change. Not that I think anyone can ever decide these things for himself, but bear the thought of America in mind, Katherine.'

'The yes or no will be John Simon's. He'll know. I've always heeded his thoughts.'

'Good night, then.'

23

On the Thursday night I met Eddie Parr in the shadow of the oak clump at the crossways three miles out of Moonlea. As I had left Moonlea a clock in the town's centre had been striking nine and it was past the half hour when I heard him give the agreed signal of two low whistles from the darkness.

'I expected a much longer wait,' said Eddie.

'I got tired of kicking my heels. I had thought of going into The Leaves After the Rain for some ale and a talk with Abel about the great martyrs of the past. But those two chaps who looked like crows, the two who helped truss up John Simon and myself, were there, watching Abel as if he were going to blow up under their very noses. So I took one look through the window and went back into Moonlea to kill the time before meeting you. I saw no soldiers.'

'There isn't a single one left in Moonlea. They left at noon today, the whole lot of them. They're frightened, harpist. They obviously think Longridge will have his men in one spot nice and compact where they can be pummelled numb. I hope they've spread the alarm to Tudbury and emptied that place too. I've heard that Jeremy won't be able to detach as large a force for the attack on the castle as he thought he could. And I heard too this morning that the Yeomanry and the army are patrolling in force on those roads leading north from Tudbury along which those boys for the castle will be coming.'

We had left the main road. We were walking through trees that were moved by only the faintest stir of a teasing wind. I could see no path where we were walking, but Eddie seemed to tread surely and the way was familiar to his feet. I was conscious of stars but did not observe them with the passionate acuteness that filled my eyes when the stars were large and clear. They shone at us through the thin stripped branches.

We were climbing the leftward slope at the top of which we would have our first view of Tudbury.

'When are they attacking Moonlea?'

'An hour from now. Pray as you walk.'

At the hilltop we met another of our companions who said we would be joined by other members of the group at various points between there and the town. He added that during his period of waiting he had heard heavy volleys of musket fire from afar off.

'Wouldn't it be better if we went in singly?' I asked.

'I don't think so. From now on we can expect to be challenged and searched. Singly we would be easy game. Together we could put up some kind of a fight for it.'

'What weapons have you?'

'Pistols, daggers. Have you got anything?'

'Nothing.'

'There's a spare pistol for the harpist if he wants one.'

'I know nothing about such things,' I said. 'You are all safer with me unarmed.'

Within half an hour we were walking into Tudbury. At the entrance to the town we were joined by the last and sixth of our number, Lewis Andrews. He looked very grave.

'I got some news an hour ago. They say there's been some bad fighting between here and Mortle. Our lads coming down into Tudbury were worsted by the Yeomanry. Some got through. Whether enough to make any sort of attempt on the castle, I don't know.'

'We'll see,' said Eddie. 'We'll go on in the hope that they will be there.'

Even though the hour was late, groups of citizens were standing and walking about the streets, talking excitedly and exchanging news and opinions. I asked an old woman who had a black shawl over her head the reason for all this ado. She said in a voice that would not have been more muffled if she had been talking through the shawl that the ironworkers and miners had taken to arms through the length and breadth of the land.

'They'll make trouble, but they'll make not a penny of profit,' she said disgustedly and put her shawled head right under my face. She smelled of sage and onions.

'Have the soldiers left the castle to fight them?' asked Eddie.

'Not yet. We haven't seen them go out as yet. But we've heard rumours that they'll be on the road before morning.'

A man ran around the corner at the end of the street.

'Here they come now,' he shouted. He stood there facing away from us, his arm extended.

We hurried to where he stood. The castle on its hill stood clear before us. The great gates had been flung open. A small detachment of horse came cantering down, followed by a column of about twenty foot.

'That must be the whole garrison,' I said.

'Hardly likely. There may be forces who only moved in today.'

We waited until the cavalcade had passed from view along the road to the west, the Moonlea road. We heard the castle gates pulled to. The old woman with the shawl had come up with us again. Her eyes were aglow and her breath coming in gasps at the sight of the soldiers.

'Fine boys,' she said, putting her elbow into my side. 'Wonderful boys. Have a bite, love.' She offered me a pig's trotter from a bag which she had fished up from inside her dress. I thanked her and took one, wanting something to grip. I felt part of my disquietude pass into the cold, greasy handful. The people moved away. The old woman had drawn the shawl around her and was chuckling away as if the whole town had turned into a solid layer of joyful jest.

'They'll settle with them,' she said. 'Those boys will settle with them.'

'A bitch, full of rancid desires and pig's trotters. There are some for whom crushed skulls, pulped hearts and all the damned scenery of death are really toys, things that bring refreshment and delight.'

'This Tudbury has a dark middle,' said Eddie. 'It's centuries old, they tell me, and some of the founders still seem to be about. What now, harpist?'

'You see the main gate?'

'It's right ahead.'

'See the thick ivy patch well over to the left?'

'Yes.'

'The door should be in there somewhere. Here's what I suggest. We've got to avoid that hill in front of the castle. There's bound to be somebody watching, townsfolk, runners, soldiers. On that smooth turf and on a night so clear with stars they'd see a fly. Let's get well around the castle, then come back towards the place we want in the shadow of the castle wall. About a furlong to the left here I seem to remember seeing the moat filled in and a path made.

We can cross over there.'

'What about Longridge's men. Shall we wait for them?'

'They may come, they may not. We've come too far to turn back.'

We made our way through the narrow streets of Tudbury's old quarters. There were still small knots of revellers taking advantage of any opportunity to stay out of bed. They were young people in the main, and time and again we heard old wrathful voices barking at them from upper windows, bidding them to be gone and have done with all their noisy frolics.

'No one,' said Eddie thoughtfully, 'is easy about the real ownership of this globe. Except Plimmon.'

We reached the spot at which the moat had been filled. We had followed the curving line of the castle wall, out of sight of the nearest streets. We ran swiftly, one at a time, up the short slope and waited in the dark shadow of the wall. I felt no doubt now, no qualms, no itch of strangeness. I was playing some kind of melody that pleased me. I cast my eye around the group now dourly silent and tense. The sight of them made me think of Mayhew, possibly sleeping within or perhaps praying actively for those who had just left the castle to restore social calm, intent on his mission of hope and wholesomeness. As I thought of him and of us, I was glad of the rawly, fiercely stimulating contrasts that churned up the earth of our living, excitedly glad that one day the bitter blades of difference might lead us to the furrow which would end in an untorpid and undisgraced tranquillity.

We moved forward, my hand and Eddie's feeling into the ivy to familiarise ourselves with the details of the wall's surface so that we would recognise any irregularity that might indicate a door.

We were approaching the front wall of the castle again. The night had darkened. We stopped. I had the feeling of the shadows waiting to bring something forth that would be momentous. I saw groups of figures scrambling up the castle hill. The men at my side saw them too, and I heard them catch their breath. Some sentries on the castle walls had seen them now. There was ragged uncertain firing and one great elaborate scream from one of the men coming up the hill. We crouched further back into the wall's shadow. I saw a brief flame near the castle gate. Some seconds elapsed and there was a roar of powder exploding. The hole made could not have been large for I could see some of Longridge's men waiting by the gate for their turn to enter, firing without much aim at the walls to answer the sentries' volleys.

'The battle will be fought in the yard and in that entrance hall,' I said. 'It'll give us time to see what we can do.'

'I've felt nothing yet,' said Eddie. 'I hope to God that Bartholomew didn't just see that door in his drink fumes.'

'He might have. He was soaked the whole day long. He worked up enough fumes to see the whole future of... Sshh... I've got it. Careful now.'

It was a tiny opening, barely four feet high. One could tell by the touch how the ivy at that spot had been torn and left to hang deceptively over the space through which Bartholomew in his nightly rambles had come and gone. I pressed against the door with my foot. It did not yield.

'Let's all go at it together,' said Eddie. 'With that noise going on they won't hear us. And we can't stay here too long, either. If those boys of Longridge's get driven back, and don't forget that they've just come fresh from another bit of bloodiness, the garrison will be combing every inch of these walls for accomplices and survivors. So let's go at it. The

369

woodwork must be as rotten as can be by now.'

Three of the men took up their positions before the door. At a word from Eddie, they kicked with all their might. With a kind of puffing gasp the door fell inward. Eddie went in and we followed.

'There's a deathly stink in this tunnel,' said Eddie. 'And watch your heads. I can't see anything. I'll keep my arm out and when I come to something I'll shout.'

He called out. He had reached one of the large falls of stone which Bartholomew had mentioned. We crawled over them painfully. The roof heightened as we went forward and by the time we heard Eddie say that we were at the tunnel's end the tallest of us could stand upright with ease.

'Show a light,' said Eddie.

One of the men produced a small lantern and another a short but thick crowbar with a chiselled end. A door faced us, a strong, brass-nailed door, wrought as if by one who liked cutting people off from where they would mostly like to be.

'Work it loose from the hinges. Then a few shoves will do the rest.'

The men worked methodically, as if all the manoeuvres were known and easy to them. They made no comment. They hardly seemed to be breathing. After about five minutes they laid down their tools and told Eddie that they thought the door would now yield. We drew back and then went forward in a violent concerted rush. I went headlong over a stone and found myself ramming Lewis Andrews from behind. He laughed and the sound of it eased the sense of absurdity. The door gave with a squeal on the second try and we found ourselves in the long dark fetid corridor where John Simon had been lodged. The sound of fighting was much nearer now, more intense, more frightening. We stood still at my command, listening with every stitch of hearing.

'We might have been heard,' I said. 'If we can do this without any fighting, so much the better.'

'All right,' whispered Eddie. 'Quietly now, lads. Not a sound.'

We crept along the corridor. One of the men in the rear had got his mouth full of dust and he kept scraping his throat while the rest of us hushed him to silence, but glad all the same that the stillness was not total. I had reached the cell which had been mine. I felt the thick dampish woodwork of the door and looked quickly through its small grille. Then we came to the door of John Simon's cell. I tapped on the wood, peering, with my excitement pressing up through my head like two fists, into the interior. It was too dark for me to make anything out of the shadow within.

'He may be sleeping,' said Eddie.

'Yes, sleeping,' I said, and in both our voices there was the darkening underside of doubt and unbelief, for no one could have slept through the tumult that was now raging in the castle courtyard.

'John Simon, John Simon,' said Eddie. 'Wake up!' His voice was rising now with an excitement that he could not control. 'It's Eddie, Eddie Parr. We've come for you. Wake up and get ready when we open the door.'

'We're going into Bartholomew's room for the key,' I said, pushing my lips alongside Eddie's at the grille. 'If he's not there, we have guns. We can blow the door open.'

There was no sound from the cell. The shadows appeared to loom ironically thicker around their substance of smells, but there was no movement of a body, no sound of a voice.

'He's not there,' said Eddie in a voice that was flat,

stepped on. 'They've moved him. What game are you playing at, harpist?'

'We'll find out.' I ran along the corridor, my friends at my heels. I flung myself upon the door of Bartholomew's door. In the few seconds since I had discovered that John Simon was no longer in his cell I had been thinking of Bartholomew, of how he would appear to me when I opened the door of his room. In the forefront of my mind was a picture of him lying clay-coloured on his trestle, possibly dead, with his chin strapped up in the way I once saw practised with a dead man. But as I charged through the unlocked door Bartholomew was neither stretched out nor dead. He was sitting on a chair facing me, his face mottled, red, merry in a mad peculiar way, his eyes not to be seen under their falling and ascending hoods of puffed flesh, his hands lifting his bottle over a glass. With every fresh volley and cry from beyond the door he threw back his head in a roar of laughter and shouted: 'Death's best day, death's best day.' Then he became aware of me.

'Who's there?' he asked, lifting his broad filthy face. He acted like a man willing his own blindness.

'The harpist,' I said. 'You remember me, Bartholomew. The harpist who was here with you in the cell down the corridor.'

His face became grey and still with concentration. Then he smashed his glass down on his knee, spilling the red wine down his breeches. Then he began to laugh, the loudest, craziest laugh I had ever heard, a clumsy, bedlam chime of breath. I stared right into his face. The little eyeholes were filling with cloudy tears. I laid my hands on his shoulders and shook him, I as mad as he, I crying like he, my mind and body on the back of a climbing torment.

372

'Where is he, man? Where is John Simon Adams?'

Eddie stepped forward and brought his open hand across Bartholomew's forehead. Bartholomew's laughter slipped down into a gentle hiccupping whine. A smile remained around his lips and when he spoke his voice was distinct, his words, as if by some miracle unveiled, quite deliberately clear.

'Harpist,' he said, 'I always knew that at the bottom of one of these bottles a jest mocking the whole of truth would one day be uncovered. This is the bottle, this the jest, this the scarlet bloody night that has lain in watch for me like a dog at the end of my dreams. They hung John Simon this morning, with all the men of law and the men of God attending.'

'You're a drunken filthy liar, Bartholomew. But you're cunning. You're playing for time until those red-coated crows have finished with our lads out there and are ready for us. They've changed John Simon's cell. They're hiding him somewhere. Tell us or I'll kill you with my own hand.'

'That would be a pleasure, harpist, to be killed by you. Don't be daft. In all the silly clod of me there isn't a place where even a lie would want to rest. Mr Radcliffe with a tail of other gentlemen came here two days ago. They were summoned into conference by the Deputy High Sheriff. They said that trouble was brewing all around, that an attempt would surely be made to free Adams and make him the spearhead of a movement to trample our liberties underfoot. I also heard Radcliffe say that Mr Penbury was getting the most terrible nightmares and that his mind was likely to collapse under the strain of waiting for Adams to be decently choked. So, for Christ's sake, they said, hurry the business up. I was taking some wine into them when they were

373

laughing at the thought of all the inconvenience that Mr Penbury was being put to and the laughter had such an effect on me I could have taken that wine off the tray and helped myself. It was done this morning. It will be my last job. I'm sorry, harpist. Little Jacob and Mr Mayhew are sorry too. Little Jacob was sick at the sight of it and you could have heard Mr Mayhew crying a mile off, and they left the castle as soon as it was done. Oh, I'm sorry, very sorry. They buried him by that birch tree outside the chapel gate. A good grave as graves go. I didn't think this last bit of defilement would come my way. You and Adams threw a lot of light on my days. The look he gave us all! God, none of us should ever be clean again after that. And you came to fetch him.... Oh Christ, merciful Christ...' And his laughter began again. We watched him in sickened terror. His body swayed and slumped off his stool on to the floor. We watched its writhing, fascinated and, to the last nerve, sickened. We were turning away when we heard shouts and running steps from beyond the door on the courtyard side. The door flung open. I saw the red of a soldier's tunic and the soldier and Eddie fell at the same instant. I saw the wound in Eddie's head. I watched his face, for a second, facing Bartholomew's on the floor. The whole room was flooded with a tide of men all wishing to kill us. The soldiers were roaring with a murderous joy as if the victory they had just won outside had been full of brandy to them. I caught a glimpse of the man in pursuit of whom the soldiers had stormed into Bartholomew's room. He was young and lay dying by the door near which he had fallen. He had his head swathed with some bandage from a wound he had probably sustained earlier in the day. I shouted as a knife or bayonet took a length of skin from my shoulder. Then I ran down the

374

corridor followed by two of my friends, which two I could not see. We hurled ourselves through the tunnel, tearing our skin as we shot over the piled obstacles of stone. The third man hit his head with a killing force against a low-hanging obstruction of rock and dropped. I and my second companion reached the open and dived down the embankment. He kept straight on. I bore to the right towards the crossing place across the moat. I heard the cries of the soldiers as they appeared at the opening we had discovered in the wall. They fired their muskets. I heard my friend scream. I looked over my shoulder as I ran. I saw him lift his arms and fall. His body vanished into the moat.

I stopped running only when I reached the shelter of a street. The street in which I found myself was narrow, filled with a reek of vegetables that was familiar to me. I looked carefully around me to see if I could get my bearings. I heard the voices of running men, eager men, come nearer on the other side of the building. I clearly heard the voice of a man who was giving orders, telling his companions to take different directions. I crouched in a doorway, too dazed and winded to wish to run any longer. I looked up at the sky, glad to see that the darkness which had come upon the face of it as we had waited to enter the castle had not thinned. As my eyes lowered they became fixed on a signpost that hung above the doorway in which I stood. Even in that shadow I could recognise upon it the vividly coloured, familiar bands of the national flag. I looked more closely at the windows of the building. I recognised the blue-and-white curtains that covered the glass. It was the very tavern into which I had gone for a meal on the morning of my release from Tudbury, the inn which had been mentioned by Katherine as being a meeting place of men who sympathised with John Simon. At the end of the streets came a rattle of footsteps and the thud of metal on wood as a pair of soldiers prodded their bayonets into the dark recesses of houses and shops.

'If he's anywhere about here,' said one of the searchers, 'we'll split him from tip to toe for the trouble he's given us. I got a couple of teeth loose in that damned tunnel.'

They came towards where I was standing. I knocked softly on the tavern door. Within half a minute it was opened, just as if the answerer had been stationed near the window watching out for me. He pulled me in and closed the door again noiselessly.

'This way,' he said.

He led me across the main room of the inn. I heard him lift part of the counter and as we walked forward I could feel my foot kick against pots and slop buckets. I heard a barrel being drawn to one side and a door lifted.

'Feel your way carefully down there,' he whispered. 'The steps are steep as a cliff face. It's not cosy down there, but you'll be safe. Hurry. Those noisy sons of hell will be around the premises any second now.'

At the very moment of his dragging the barrel back into position over the trap door through which I had descended there was a sharp rap of gun butts on the front door and the grunt of voices demanding entrance. The door was opened and I heard the landlord ask, yawning and astonished, what it was they wanted.

'Don't play the innocent, Jameson. You know you've been harbouring as ripe a crew of traitors in this tavern for months past as ever saw a gaol. There was a raid on the castle tonight. Apparently they were after the chap we hanged this morning. We think one of them got away. He

376

was wearing a long, dark coloured coat and lighter trousers.'

'I don't know what you're talking about.'

'You'll feel it on your skin if we have to come in there and explain.'

'Oh, leave me in peace. I'm watching out for my trade. If any rebels make use of my seats or drink my ale that's because I keep a public house. I've seen nothing of your fugitive.'

'You'd better not either, Jameson. We're having this place watched. If the man does turn up here, save yourself and us a lot of trouble and turn him over.'

'I'll do that. A quiet life suits me. Longridge and his kind are only kicking at a fire that'll make ashes of them in no time at all. A raid on Tudbury Castle! Good God, what could they have been thinking of? They must have been mad.'

'We lost fifteen of ours to forty of theirs. You remember that free-preacher, Eddie Parr?'

'Parr? Let me see. Oh yes, I recall him. Dark, pleasant-looking chap, nice voice. He was the one who used to keep on seeing visions of heaven. What about him?'

'He's not seeing anything now. He's up there in the castle. Dead, with old Bartholomew Clark at his side, dying. It's a hell of a night for death up at the castle. So long, Jameson, don't forget what I told you.'

I heard the soldier give a command that the streets of the town be kept absolutely clear to let patrols pass through quickly, then the door closed. Several minutes had gone by before Jameson, having carefully tested the shot bolts of the front door, moved back the barrel behind the counter and came down the steps to join me. He searched in a corner and lit a candle. It was a small cellar with wet green walls. Jameson was a man of fifty with a small grey moustache and eyes kindly bright.

'This is a second cellar that we don't use any more. I hate to have to keep you down here, but I dare not let you upstairs even into my own private part of the house. The great industry in these parts now is spying. I never did think much of this place Tudbury, but since the High Sheriff made his appeal to all patriotic citizens to keep their eyes open for treasonous activity I've had to keep a button on my guts. Every idiot in the place has developed a nose a foot long for traitors. I'll bring you down some food, a dressing for that cut and a change of clothes. They spotted that long contraption you're wearing. I'll bring you down a set of garments my brother used to wear. He was about your build and is now dead. Do you hear what I'm saying?'

'I hear. Why do you ask?'

'You were sitting there with your mouth gaping, looking as if you were daft or deaf.'

'This has been a bad night. More than that, this has been a bad year.'

'You'll get over it.'

'I'm telling myself that.'

'It was a bold stroke, getting into the castle. But if I were you I'd have weighed the chances.'

'Never thought we'd fail. We saw nothing to weigh.'

'I'll get you something to eat and drink. Sure you won't mind staying down here? I'll give you something to sleep on.'

'I'll do anything you say. You are very kind.'

'In the next few days a lot of the boys are going to be needing my hospitality. That's why I can't be too careful with those soldiers. I've only got to give them half a chance and they'd burn the place down with pleasure.'

'I'm sorry I didn't speak to you when I was in here last.

378

Do you remember seeing me?'

'Yes. You are the harpist, John Simon's friend.'

'John Simon's dead.'

'I heard that.'

'I should have spoken to you. But that day I wanted to run and that was all I wanted. I started out for the north but I came back.'

'You were just out of the castle. A man's got the right to stand aloof for a bit when he's been through what you went through.'

I took off my coat and laid it down on a ledge of the wall while Jameson went to fetch me food and drink. He brought me some cold meat and a glass of rum. I drank half the rum, and after it I did not mind the sound of rats which was loud in the walls around.

'Those men,' I said, as Jameson stood over me washing and covering the cut in my shoulder, 'those men who sat by your fire that day, I could see they wished to speak to me. I bet they thought I was a funny one, a weak one.'

'They wanted a word with you. They are good lads, miners, from Lagley way. They wanted to welcome you out and be of help if they could.'

'Thank them. Where are they now?'

'With Longridge.'

'I hope they'll fare well, better than we.... I should never have meddled in all this. I have no touch for handling lives other than my own. John Simon's dead.'

'You told me.'

'Bartholomew said they buried him outside some chapel, near a birch tree.'

Jameson said nothing. I chewed mechanically, without hunger or taste, at one of the smaller bits of meat. It had the quality of cloth between my teeth.

I finished off the rum. My head was filling with horribly lucid and freezing thoughts about John Simon.

'I still have no great hatred in me, no sense of knowing my way towards those great impersonal loves and rejections that seem to sustain most of us. But I'm growing and the appetite for them is edging in.' I waved my hand in the direction in which I thought the castle lay. 'That's a bad place, a bad place for the whole earth. I hope they'll burn it down.'

'He was a good lad, John Simon. When we find the things that really signify to say about such things, leaving no more to be said, great things will happen in the following silence. Now I'll get the palliasse and blankets for you. And when I lay them down try to sleep, harpist. You're shaking.'

24

I hid in Jameson's cellar for two days. Each time the landlord came down he gave me news of the brief whirling campaign that was fought between the light ill-equipped guerrillas under Longridge and the reinforced columns of horse and foot under Wilson, the soldier whom I had first seen at the Penbury house. The detachment of workers which had fallen on Moonlea had done some damage, but in withdrawing had run into a force moving quickly from the east to support Wilson. They had been routed. But it was at the end of the second day that Jameson brought me the heaviest news. A troop of dragoons had split and broken up the body of labourers who had taken arms and were moving from the west to join Longridge. Longridge had been forced to concentrate his men in a spot favourable in all ways to the enemy and had been defeated. He himself was reputed killed and his men either captured or in flight. A silence as dark and green as the cellar walls fell upon Jameson and myself when he told me this news.

'I know but little of these things,' I told him when he began picking up the dishes and scraps left over from my last meal. 'Longridge I saw but once. John Simon I could rarely see except as something projecting from my own self. But no men should ever have so little chance as these. They bit at something that was unripe, bitter. They should have waited. They were in too much of a hurry. Has death some special call that lures these lads its way? They should have waited. They had too little cunning. Cunning is a slimy thing; it might have rusted away some of the fetters they've smashed their lives on.'

'We state the facts,' said Jameson. 'We state them now softly, now loudly. The next time it will be softly for our best voices will have ceased to speak. The silence and the softness will ripen. The lost blood will be made again. The chorus will shuffle out of its filthy aching corners and return. The world is full of voices, harpist, practising for the great anthem but hardly ever heard. We've been privileged. We've had our ears full of the singing. Silence will never be absolute for us again.'

'That's so,' I said, looking up at him, my head less heavy now. 'That's so. The silence will never again be absolute. The back of our dumbness will have been broken and it must have been a granite sort of spine while it lasted. But the ears of John Simon, that once could hear music in every voice, on every wind, are stopped. Will that fact ever cease to make me sick, a stranger to myself and the whole of life, in those moments when it takes me by the thumbs and strings me up?'

'The fact will grow into you. Finally it will be all of you, your new root.'

'I hear much talk of roots.... I'd better go. You've been kind, Mr Jameson. Is it safe for me to go now?'

'There's not much danger. Tudbury's letting itself go. This is a day of feast for Tudbury. Slavishness goes deeper than the sewers in this little town. The High Sheriff and his friends have declared a state of chronic holiday to celebrate the overthrow of the disloyal and the disaffected. I'll be selling ale and wine far into the night. This place will have a special appeal for the revellers. The Flag. The flag is waving proudly over the castle. The thoughtless and the replete will have three or four days in which to swill and vomit over their vows of allegiance. On Sunday they will foregather and the vicar, the dean, the bishop will explicitly identify John Simon Adams with the devil and the pious will moan with joy at having been relieved from the peril that overhung them.'

I transferred the envelope which Helen Penbury had given me from my own coat to the shorter thinner one that Jameson was lending me. He climbed up the stairs and looked about.

'No one here. Come on.'

I followed him up the steps, shook hands with him and walked out into the street. I found myself walking without plan in the direction that would take me to Moonlea. Towards me came a great throng of men and women, shouting, singing, tripping, wearing bright ribbons and the bright mindless look of people who are engaged on a festival rite of mass obeisance. I could see timid folk hanging back pensively on the side of the road swept into the procession and borne along. The unanimity of the mob frightened me and when its first waves began to lap my legs, I conformed and became one with them. At the end of the street a dozen musicians, wearing rosettes and blue cockades, were waiting, and with them at our head we marched out into the vacant square that lay between the streets of Tudbury and the castle hill. Then we danced, the rhythm, the shouting, the joy curving upward. The dancing ceased when a fat man, a butcher I should have said by his clothes, and, judging by the roar of approbation that rose when he mounted the barrel that was brought forward, a popular orator. The music, the shouting, died as he began to speak. He had a vast trumpeting voice and he had learned to use it in a way profoundly enjoyable to himself. His theme was the wickedness of those who cannot put themselves at peace in a world which, for all its temporary impurities and flaws, is generally habitable at bottom. The man's ideas were thick, fleshy, meat to be flipped neatly over the oaken counter of his solid convictions. He spoke of the merriment which on the great feast days of Yuletide and Whitsun united the high and the low of Tudbury, and indeed the whole land in a bond of heaven-sent glee. Those who with the sombre swords of envy, ambition and discontent tried to maim that merriment should always meet the same fate as those who had recently tried to disturb the realm's happiness and the King's Peace. The crowd applauded madly. He mentioned John Simon. The crowd groaned with a loud resentment as if each of them had lost a leg. Adams, he said, had paid the price. The crowd, glad to be done with that groan which had caused a cold uneasiness to fall upon some of them, cried 'Hurrah, hurrah.' Adams was dead in the castle graveyard, a crushed pest. The people turned their faces towards the grey huge walls and seemed to caress with their eyes and feelings the idiot, assuring thickness of its bastions. I elbowed my way out of the throng and made my way towards Moonlea. I still did not know why I wished to do so. I felt that there was something there that I should see and know and that was all.

I took the same road back as I had travelled on the way in with Eddie Parr. As I walked through the late autumn wood the sound of my footsteps in the leaves had an eloquent clarity. I heard Eddie's voice, faithfully echoed to the last whimsical syllable in the hollow vessel of my grieving. I heard the voice of John Simon, like the doomed and lovely leaves I

384

trod in its rich remembered rise and fall. I stopped abruptly, leaned against the bark of a larch and wept with a soft obscene abandon into its wise grey roughness.

When I came within sight of Moonlea a thick smoke hung over the whole south side of the town, where most of the public buildings were concentrated. It was a pall thicker by many fathoms than any which would have been caused by the furnaces. Longridge's men had started a bonfire. I quickened my step, then slackened it again for there was nothing ahead of me that I did not really know.

A half mile out of Moonlea a solitary man sat upon the roadside bank, his head between his knees and as still as the dead. There was something familiar in the cut and colour of his clothes. I was quite close to him before he raised his head. It was Lemuel Stevens. At the first sight of me his face showed terror of the least answerable kind and the wish to flee. Then the terror itself fled as if convinced that there could be no more flight for its victim that could lead to anywhere but the very same spot on the circle's edge. His features, after the last ripple of recognition had passed his ear on its quick journey outward, arranged themselves again in a stupid hurtless calm and in the chinks of my loathing there stirred a bowelful of compassion for the man and his intensely wasted patch of goodness and delight. I stood by him. His hands grasped my legs and his whole body shook with sobs. I lifted him to his feet, uncurious about the cause of his condition, impressed only by the spectacle of such a complete, perfectly laboured grief, so similar in texture to that which had overtaken me in the wood. I led him forward, gently and without a word.

The door of The Leaves After the Rain stood open as we came abreast of it. We made our way through the groups of soldiers who stood in the front yard. They laughed at the bent shattered mien of Lemuel and he turned his head neither to left nor right, gone beyond any need to acknowledge or refute their ridicule.

I sat him down on the very bench where we had sat on the night when I had gone to Plimmon Hall. I nodded gravely to Abel as I bought my drinks and waited for him to speak to me.

'The clouds are pretty dark, harpist.'

'They shouldn't be. The storm's been spent. What's up with Lemuel?'

'You shouldn't have brought him in here, harpist. He's lucky to be alive. Why bother with him?'

'I'm lucky to be alive too. We're in the same guild. What's up with him?'

'You see the smoke. They burned a quarter of the town when Longridge's men came in. The people who weren't cowed by Radcliffe went mad. They beat the new immigrants to a pulp, fired the Council buildings and law-offices and made a special job of making embers of Lemuel's shop. He and Isabella got out, but she went out of her mind at the sight of their property going to the devil and she rushed back into the flames to save what she could. That was the last seen of her. The crowd got hold of Lemuel. They were going to part him from his limbs, just when the soldiers came up. They did to the crowd what the crowd had thought to do to Lemuel. Katherine was there. She was like the flames, at the head of it all, everywhere, so bright and hot with hating she could not be missed. She screamed at the soldiers and dared them to kill her.'

'Is she dead?'

'No. She walked slowly through them and no one lifted a

386

finger. It was a queer sight.'

'And Lemuel?'

'He's been wandering about around this tavern ever since, looking bludgeoned, lucky to be alive.'

'Nobody's lucky to be alive.'

I sat opposite Lemuel, sipping at my drink, waiting for him to begin. He drank a good deal but the ale seemed to affect him hardly at all. It was as if the grief that had bitten him had been incisive enough to open in him a gulf that would take an eternity to fill either with resignation or liquor. But after a while he began to hang a smile on to his silent mouth, not the smile of one who has taken the measure of and made a formal truce with his burden but the hopeful grimace of one who has got at least one arm free from beneath the fall that pins him down.

I went to the counter for a refill. Abel was looking dejectedly across at Lemuel.

'If I were you,' he said, 'and that man had done to me what he's done to you, I wouldn't let him live. Not for a minute I wouldn't.'

'We're both learning, Lemuel and I. Bigger or littler, we're all growing. One of us will end shrunken all to hell because in this particular fall of pain he will have found the full stop, the rock that blocks the tunnel. I don't think it'll be me.'

When I returned Lemuel put his hand on mine as I laid his drink before him.

'I worked very hard,' he said. His eyes were fixed on the woodwork just behind my head. His tone was simple and clear, without any of the cautious whine that had been part of it before. 'And now I have nothing. I'm sorry, harpist, for what I did to you and to John Simon. Isn't it daft to say that, though? It's like the fire that took my shop and

387

Isabella too, licking its way towards me and saying "I'm sorry, Lemuel, for what I did to you and Isabella." It seemed all right at the time. The fire enjoyed itself. That day in the court, harpist, I saw in the face of John Simon Adams that he knew I would pay the full price. Prices are the only things on earth that are really full. I had never felt big or secure, and I wished to do so. Often, in myself, I would have liked to live without labour or struggle, to listen to John Simon telling me of the wonderful happiness that will come to men one day when men will have laid aside the need to be betraying themselves and others. I've done a lot of betraying, harpist.'

'I know that. We all have our skills. Drink up, boy. Your thoughts are ploughing deep. Water the furrows. God knows what'll be growing there next.'

'For myself, I could have sat down. I could have wept to hear those tunes you played upon the harp because there was a clean peacefulness about them that told me of all the many ill-tasting jokes that have been played upon me, that I have played upon myself. But Isabella drove me on. Isabella was a fine woman.' As he said that his face became crucially pensive. 'Now I have nothing.'

'Penbury and Radcliffe will help you. They'll be grateful to you, Lemuel. You've helped them a lot in all this profitable butchery that they've just completed.'

'I don't want their help. That isn't what I want at all. I was never much at home with them, harpist, honest to God. Often I felt sick, grasped in their warm strong hands, used, used, used, sick as I often felt with Isabella in the night, cold, cold, getting kicked and slapped for them to line their bit of dark with gold.'

'That pub you told me of in Tudbury, Lemuel, you should

have stayed there.'

'I was happy there, in the stables at the back of The Mitre. Oh, the girls were kind to me. And it was all so simple. The days locked together and made a kind of daisy chain. Or am I dreaming all this? Did I just imagine all those things to keep myself breathing when Isabella was freezing me to death with work and purity?'

'She's dead now. You can find out. There's nothing for you here. Go to Tudbury. Every beetle has his dung ball; perhaps yours is there. Perhaps there will be somebody called May or Violet who will never wish tomorrow to be richer or safer than today, who will be blazing for you constantly. You've earned the right to be cosy, Lemuel.'

He stood up and shook my hand solemnly.

'I've never had much luck, harpist. I'd like to think that the things you mentioned, the dung ball and all that, May and Violet and all that, were waiting for me. I'm going back to Tudbury much as I came from it. But I bet there's still somebody who thinks we've not had enough of killing, who'll make an end of me on the way. You, perhaps. I feel a terrible hatred for me in you, harpist, but it's new to you. You haven't found the handle to your hate, you can't make it plain, draw it like a sword. I never really get much luck.'

I took him out of the inn. I set him towards Tudbury and watched him stumble his way slowly along the road. I returned to have a last word with Abel.

'The Penbury home will be blazing with lights tonight,' he said.

'Why? What have they got against the dark?'

'Plimmon wishes to celebrate the coming of peace, and to show how little he's dismayed by the few marks of charring which were all we managed to convey of our feelings about the ironmasters. Plimmon's own hall got a few hard knocks when Longridge's men fell on it, so the revel will be at Penbury's, with Plimmon grinning over his wine at his lady love.'

'That will be a good sight to watch.'

'Good luck, harpist.'

'Goodbye, Abel.'

As dusk came down I climbed the hillpath to Katherine's cottage. The lamp was already lit as I stepped inside. Davy was working in a corner, nearly sleeping, his big handsome mindless head sunk over whatever task it was that he was doing. Mrs Brier and Katherine were both busy in front of the fire. They both looked up as I entered. Davy did not heed me. I could see Katherine's face plain, and her thoughts too, poised assuredly and for ever, on the very brink of the unbearable. She said nothing, had nothing to say; nor had I. Without a word I stepped out of the cottage and closed the door behind me.

Night had fallen completely when I began the climb of Arthur's Crown, walking up the same path as I had descended on my way into Moonlea. On its summit I looked down. There below me was the house of Penbury, big, smiling and living with light. I turned, walking away from Moonlea, yet eternally towards Moonlea, full of a strong, ripening, unanswerable bitterness, feeling in my fingers the promise of a new enormous music.

RAYMOND WILLIAMS

Raymond Williams was born in the Welsh border village of Pandy in 1921. He was educated at Abergavenny Grammar School and at Trinity College, Cambridge and he served in the Second World War as a Captain in the 21st Anti-Tank Regiment, Royal Artillery. After the war he began an influential career in education with the Extra Mural Department at Oxford University. His life-long concern with the interface between social development and cultural process marked him out as one of the most perceptive and influential intellectual figures of his generation.

He returned to Cambridge as a Lecturer in 1961 and was appointed its first Professor of Drama in 1974. His best-known publications include *Culture and Society* (1958), *The Long Revolution* (1961), *The Country and the City* (1973), *Keywords* (1976) and *Marxism and Literature* (1977).

Raymond Williams was an acclaimed cultural critic and commentator but he considered all of his writing, including fiction, to be connected. *Border Country* (1960) was the first of a trilogy of novels with a predominantly Welsh theme or setting, and his engagement with Wales continued in the political thriller The *Volunteers* (1978), *Loyalties* (1985) and the massive two-volume *People of the Black Mountains* (1988-90). He died in 1988.

PENRY WILLIAMS

Penry Williams was born in Ynysfach, Merthyr Tydfil in 1798. He was the son of a stonemason and house-painter and began his working life as an apprentice to a local printer. At the age of 16, his pictures of Ynysfach, the Cyrfarthfa Works and of the Merthyr riots, attracted the attention of William Crawshay, owner of the Cyfarthfa Works, who then supported his artistic training. He studied at the Royal Academy School of Art in London before moving to Rome in 1826, where he remained for the rest of his life. His masterpiece is considered to be the representation of a religious procession that he saw near Naples, *The Festa of the Madonna del Arco*. He died in 1885.

PARTHIAN

A Carnival of Voices

www.parthianbooks.com

LIBRARY OF WALES

The Library of Wales is a Welsh Government project designed to ensure that all of the rich and extensive literature of Wales which has been written in English will now be made available to readers in and beyond Wales. Sustaining this wider literary heritage is understood by the Welsh Government to be a key component in creating and disseminating an ongoing sense of modern Welsh culture and history for the future Wales which is now emerging from contemporary society. Through these texts, until now unavailable, out-of-print or merely forgotten, the Library of Wales brings back into play the voices and actions of the human experience that has made us, in all our complexity, a Welsh people.

The Library of Wales includes prose as well as poetry, essays as well as fiction, anthologies as well as memoirs, drama as well as journalism. It complements the names and texts that are already in the public domain and seeks to include the best of Welsh writing in English, as well as to showcase what has been unjustly neglected. No boundaries limit the ambition of the Library of Wales to open up the borders that have denied some of our best writers a presence in a future Wales. The Library of Wales has been created with that Wales in mind: a young country not afraid to remember what it might yet become.

Dai Smith
Raymond Williams Chair in the Cultural History of Wales,
University of Wales, Swansea

LIBRARY OF WALES
FUNDED BY

Noddir gan
Lywodraeth Cymru
Sponsored by
Welsh Government

CYNGOR LLYFRAU CYMRU
WELSH BOOKS COUNCIL

SERIES EDITOR: DAI SMITH

LIBRARY OF WALES

WWW.THELIBRARYOFWALES.COM